"HOW DARE YOU ENTER MY BEDCHAMBER WHEN I AM IN MY SHIFT!" she demanded hotly.

"Let me help you with your wedding gown," he said silkily.

"No!" she spat out.

Rodger gave her a level look. "Put on your wedding gown, or I shall put it on for you."

"Don't you dare touch me!"

"I will touch you, by God, anytime and anyplace I choose!" With a foul curse, Rodger picked her up and tossed her onto the bed, then threw himself on top of her to prevent her escape. In her struggle to free herself, Rosamond's breasts spilled from the low-cut linen shift. She lay panting beneath him, knowing that both his anger and his lust had been fiercely aroused.

"I will make you obey me if it's the last thing I do." He snatched up the wedding gown from the bed and began to put it on her. Rodger was so determined that her struggles to elude him were all in vain.

When Rosamond finally stood before him dressed in her wedding gown, she was panting with fury. "You devil, de Leyburn! You have made it plain the marriage is inevitable, but it shall be in name only. I shall never yield myself to you!"

Sir Rodger threw open the door and spoke softly to Nan. "Please see to her hair." He turned to Rosamond. "I'll wait right outside. If you give us any more trouble, I shall take you across my knee and tan your arse. . . ."

Also by Virginia Henley

A WOMAN OF PASSION
A YEAR AND A DAY
DREAM LOVER
ENSLAVED
SEDUCED
DESIRED
ENTICED
TEMPTED
THE DRAGON AND THE JEWEL
THE FALCON AND THE FLOWER
THE HAWK AND THE DOVE
THE PIRATE AND THE PAGAN
THE RAVEN AND THE ROSE

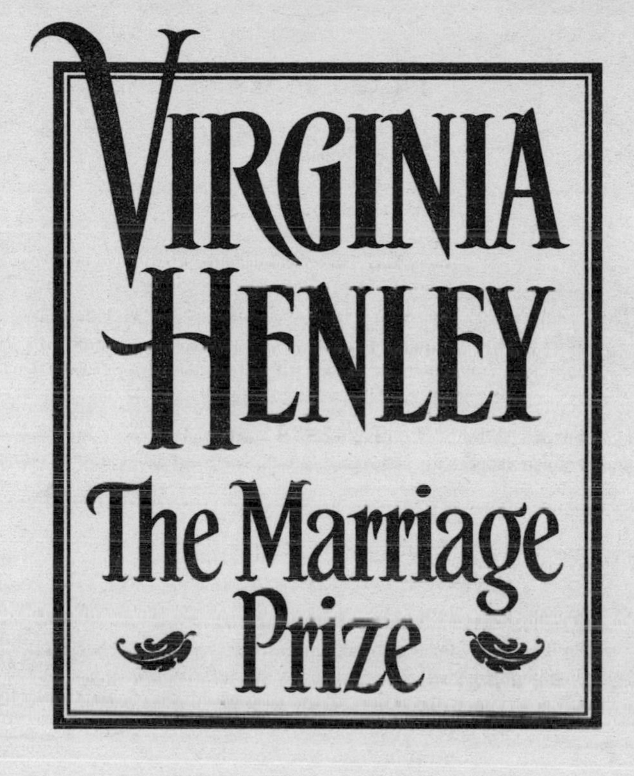

ISLAND BOOKS

ISLAND BOOKS

Published by
Dell Publishing
a division of
Random House, Inc.
1540 Broadway
New York, New York 10036

Library of Congress Catalog Card Number: 99-059897
ISBN: 0-440-22209-5

Reprinted by arrangement with Delacorte Press

Printed in the United States of America

Published simultaneously in Canada

July 2001

10 9 8 7 6 5 4 3 2 1

OPM

For my eldest grandson
Daryl Jason Henley

Principal Characters

Rosamond Marshal (fictional)
Niece of the late William Marshal, first husband of Princess Eleanor Plantagenet

Sir Rodger de Leyburn
Royal Steward to Prince Edward Plantagenet

Prince Edward Plantagenet
Known as Lord Edward; heir of King Henry III

Princess Eleanora of Castile
Wife of Prince Edward Plantagenet

Simon de Montfort
Earl of Leicester
Known as the Great Warlord; second husband of Princess Eleanor; chosen leader of England's barons

Eleanor de Montfort
Countess of Leicester
Born Princess Eleanor Plantagenet; sister of King Henry III and Richard of Cornwall

Demoiselle de Montfort
Daughter of Eleanor and Simon de Montfort

King Henry III
Plantagenet King of England

Queen Eleanor of Provence
Queen of England (wife of Henry III)

Richard of Cornwall

Brother of King Henry III and Princess Eleanor (de Montfort)

Harry of Almaine

Son of Richard of Cornwall and the late Isabella Marshal; half-brother of Richard de Clare

Richard de Clare

Earl of Gloucester; England's leading peer; half-brother of Harry of Almaine

Gilbert de Clare

Known as Gilbert the Red; son of Richard de Clare

Alyce de Clare

Wife of Gilbert de Clare; daughter of Guy de Lusignan, half-brother of King Henry

Roger Bigod

Earl of Norfolk, Marshal of England

Humphrey de Bohun

Chief Justiciar of England

PROLOGUE

Kenilworth Castle, Warwickshire
May 1253

Twelve-year-old Rosamond Marshal clung to Eleanor de Montfort's hand as her guardian led her into Kenilworth's library. The young girl was dressed in a plain gray mourning gown, and her face was as pale as the linen head-cloth that covered her fair hair. Her eyes appeared to be too large for her small face, and she looked at the people in the room as if she did not really see them. Rosamond was in shock. Three days ago, her brother Giles, who had been all of fourteen years of age, had been killed in a jousting accident.

When Rosamond felt Lady Eleanor squeeze her hand, she sank into a curtsy before King Henry, who was her royal guardian's brother. Lady Eleanor's husband, Simon de Montfort, was standing beside the king, and Prince Edward, the fifteen-year-old heir to the throne, waited to one side with his friend Rodger de Leyburn.

The official document that would betroth Lady Rosamond Marshal to Sir Rodger de Leyburn lay on the oak table awaiting only the signatures of those present in Kenilworth's library. Lady Eleanor picked up the quill pen, dipped it into the inkwell, and handed it to Rosamond. "Sign here, my dear."

Without even glancing at the youth to whom they were betrothing her, the royal ward took the pen and signed the document as if she were in a trance. She had withdrawn to a place deep inside of herself in order to escape the unbearable pain caused by her brother's death. Because the young heiress was now alone in the world, everyone had thought it best to betroth her to a suitable husband. Rosamond went through the motions of the betrothal, accepting her guardians' decision without question.

Prince Edward nudged his friend's shoulder, and Rodger de Leyburn stepped up to the oak table and added his bold signature to the betrothal document. He was darkly attractive and his green eyes held a serious look that befitted the solemn occasion. De Leyburn's manner showed that he was perfectly willing to betroth Rosamond Marshal, yet he did not appear to be eager. Then the king, the prince, and the de Montforts affixed their signatures to make it official. Lady Eleanor and Rosamond were the first to leave, and when the library door closed behind them, Edward turned to his friend and said, "Rodger, you won't regret this; Rosamond Marshal is a great marriage prize."

The young heiress most certainly was a sought-after prize. King Henry had wanted Rosamond for his foreign half-brother's son, Geoffrey of Valence. But Simon de Montfort had told the king bluntly that the barons would be up in arms if one more English heiress was given to a foreigner. Simon had made it plain that the barons were sick and tired of their king squandering money, land, and castles on his foreign relatives. So Henry had grudgingly allowed his son Edward to choose Rosamond Marshal's future husband.

For the next five years, King Henry willfully ignored the growing anger of the barons. He appointed foreigners to high office and called Parliament only when he was in dire straits for money, making promises he had no intention of keeping. Finally, the barons had had enough. Choosing Simon de Montfort as their leader, they issued King Henry an ultimatum: Either he transferred the authority to govern to a council of leading English peers, or there would be civil war.

King Henry immediately turned submissive and signed the Provisions of Oxford, which laid out the barons' demands. The king's half-brothers, who had been living in luxury, fled back to the Continent, and the barons believed they had saved England from ruin. Flush with their victory at Oxford, the Marcher barons left to subdue an uprising in Wales. Prince Edward, now twenty and newly returned from Gascony, joined the campaign, and Henry of England took himself across the Channel to sign a treaty with Louis of France over disputed provinces. But at the first opportunity, Henry intended to take a major step toward reasserting his authority at home—he would ask the Pope to absolve him from his oath to uphold the Provisions of Oxford. He would show the barons who ruled England. The king, and the king alone!

One

Kenilworth Castle
November 1258

A wave of stark terror swept over Rosamond Marshal, snatching her breath away. She began to run the moment she saw the dark horse and rider, knowing instinctively they would pursue her. Relentlessly! The rider was faceless. All she knew was that he was dark, but it was the horse she feared most. It was huge, black, and terrifying.

An icy shiver slithered down her spine. Her pale golden hair tumbled wildly about her shoulders as she pulled her skirts high, baring long, slim legs, in a desperate attempt to escape being trampled by the cruel hooves. Her lungs felt as if they would burst as she gasped for just one more breath that would carry her to safety. Her pulse hammered inside her eardrums, deafening her as she turned to look over her shoulder. Rosamond's eyes widened in horror and a scream was torn from her throat as she saw the black forelegs rise above her, then helplessly she tumbled beneath the murderous hooves.

Rosamond's eyes flew open. Slowly, she became aware of her surroundings. She was lying in her bed, her hair a wild tangle, her night rail twisted about her body so that her long legs were bared. Heaving a ragged sigh of relief, she sat up.

"Whatever is amiss, Rosamond?" Demoiselle de Montfort asked, throwing back her covers and padding barefoot across the spacious bedchamber they shared at Kenilworth Castle.

Rosamond tossed back her hair in a gesture of dismissal to reassure her young friend. "It was nothing, Demi."

"But you screamed," the young, dark-haired girl insisted. "Was it the old nightmare come back to haunt you?"

"No, of course not," Rosamond said. She was seventeen, almost three years older than the Demoiselle, as everyone affectionately called young Eleanor de Montfort. The unusual nickname had been given to her by a French nursemaid because mother and daughter had the same name. Rosamond was determined not to alarm her friend. She laughed with bravado. "It would take more than a bad dream to frighten me."

"Could we have a light?" The Demoiselle had always been afraid of total darkness, which was why Rosamond shared her chamber, high in the Lady Tower.

"I'm so sorry I disturbed you, Demi." She lit the square, scented candle in its metal stand and tucked the Demoiselle back into bed. Back in her own bed, Rosamond offered a silent prayer of thanks that she was safe and secure at Kenilworth. Located in the midland county of Warwickshire, eighty miles from London, the castle was her haven, her refuge, where she felt protected from the harsh world. Rosamond watched the shadows flicker upon the wall. She hadn't had the trampling dream in a long time and had hoped she was free of it, but apparently she was not completely free. Though Rosamond knew what caused it, she never spoke of it anymore.

Because her parents had both died while she and her brother Giles were children, they had become royal wards. Since Giles was the same age as Prince Edward Plantagenet, he had joined the prince's household, becoming one of a dozen noble youths who were Edward's companions. Rosamond, however, had joined the household of the king's sister, Eleanor de Montfort, Countess of Leicester, because Rosamond was the niece of the late William Marshal, who had been Princess Eleanor's first husband.

The brother and sister had seen each other often because Simon de Montfort, Earl of Leicester, was Prince Edward's godfather, and the young noblemen received their military training from the great warlord, reputed to be the ablest warrior in Christendom. By the time he was fifteen, Lord Edward, as the heir to the throne was called, had towered head and shoulders over the other men of the court. His companions were all high-spirited youths, guilty of excesses. Some of them were his cousins from Provence and Lusignan, who thought themselves above curbs and restraints.

Though King Henry had forbidden them to joust, Lord Edward and his companions had ridden over to Ware to take part in a tournament. That was the fateful day that Giles Marshal had lost his life in a jousting accident. Because Rosamond was only twelve at the time, the gory details had been kept from her, but she had heard whispers of the half-wild charger that had trampled his body. At first the nightmares had come every night, but with time, they had become less frequent, and she had been free of them for almost two years.

Rosamond remembered the months following the accident, how everyone had been kind to her. Giles's companions, led by Lord Edward, had been soberly contrite and extremely solicitous. Because she was all alone in the world, several had sought her hand in marriage, and at Lord Edward's insistence she had been betrothed to his dearest friend, Rodger de Leyburn, who held the coveted post of royal steward in the prince's household. Yet Rosamond could not help feeling a secret resentment toward Edward and his high-spirited companions.

Rosamond sighed. It had happened five years ago, yet still she thought of the prince and his friends as arrogant, lawless, spoiled young devils! And it was true. They had all been wild and courted trouble with a vengeance. She thought of the Demoiselle's older brothers, Henry and Simon de Montfort, who had been Lord Edward's first companions. They were no different. All they thought of were weapons and horses and tumbling the maidservants.

Her thoughts inevitably drifted to a more worthy knight, Sir Rickard de Burgh. He was the son of the wealthy and noble Falcon de Burgh, Lord of Connaught. Sir Rickard was a twin, and reputed to possess the mystic gift of seeing into the future. He was a mature man of middle years, not a dissolute youth, but maturity only enhanced his rugged good looks. His thick black hair had a distinguished touch of gray at the temples, and his brilliant green eyes had attractive laugh-lines at their corners. His voice, so low and melodious with its Irish lilt, had insinuated itself into Rosamond's heart the first time she heard it, and it made her sigh whenever he spoke.

To Rosamond, Sir Rickard de Burgh was everything that was honorable and chivalrous, for he had pledged himself to serve and guard Princess Eleanor Plantagenet when she was tragically widowed by William Marshal's untimely death. It was rumored that he remained unwed because no lady had yet touched his heart. Rosamond secretly daydreamed that perhaps she would be the one he would honor with his favor. Her pulse fluttered at the mere thought of Lady de Montfort's knight-errant. Her maiden's heart overflowed with awe and admiration for the handsome Irish warrior.

In the morning, Rosamond forgot about the dream as she and Demi dressed and learned from their tiring-women that Earl Simon had returned from Wales with a large group of knights. As she saw the joy transform her friend's face, banishing the worry Demi experienced whenever her father went on campaign, Rosamond was thankful she no longer had to live with such paralyzing fear. To love someone and lose them was the worst thing that could happen in this world.

The Demoiselle was eager to see her father, and Rosamond blushed, hoping that Sir Rickard de Burgh also had returned and not tarried in Wales at one of his castles. The girls spurned the head veils held out by their tiring-women, and like two hoydens, picked up their skirts and raced from the ladies' quarters of the castle down to the Great Hall.

Kenilworth was like a royal court in its size and importance. The household was a hive of activity, with Eleanor de Montfort, Countess of Leicester, presiding over it like a queen bee. She was the sister of King Henry of England, but she took as much pride in the title her husband had given her as she did in the title of princess. Though Eleanor now had grown children, she was still a beautiful woman. She was vividly dark, and far too vain to allow her hair to turn gray. These days, however, she wore her hair up, fastening the curls with jeweled pins or braiding it into a regal coronet to enhance her small, five-foot stature. She wore cosmetics, painting her mouth with lip rouge, and using kohl to outline her startling amethyst-colored eyes and to darken her lashes.

Eleanor prided herself on her slim figure. Her waist was almost as tiny as it had been before she had given birth to her children, and the necklines of her gowns were always cut to show off her beautiful breasts. Pride of blood showed in her every gesture. Eleanor was a vibrant woman who loved to laugh almost as much as she loved clothes and jewels. She was both a princess and a countess down to her fingertips. Her husband not only adored her, but also trusted her implicitly.

When Simon spied his daughter, he swooped her up in his massive arms and swung her about. "Can this young lady possibly be my little girl? Demoiselle, you have grown into a woman in the months I've been gone. You rival your mother in beauty; I just hope and pray you are neither as willful nor as wicked as she." Simon's dark eyes found Eleanor's and gazed into them for a moment, deliberately reminding her of the passion they had shared when he'd arrived home in the middle of the night. Though he was in his fifties, Simon was still an extremely virile man, with a commanding presence. He had a soldier's body; the muscles on his six-foot, four-inch frame were well honed from the rigors of the Welsh campaign. Simon de Montfort also had a supreme air of confidence that drew younger men like a lodestone.

His daughter dimpled with delight and gave him an affectionate kiss of greeting. "The castle felt empty without you, Father."

"It is filling up by the hour as the men return from Wales. No doubt it will burst at the seams when your cousin Edward arrives."

"Lord Edward is coming?" Countess Eleanor raised a perfectly plucked eyebrow at her husband. Her brother King Henry and Simon de Montfort were almost enemies.

"I *am* Edward's godfather, Eleanor. Just because his father and I disagree on every conceivable matter doesn't mean that Edward and I cannot be friends."

"I agree, darling. You have been a wonderful influence on him. My nephew Edward will make a magnificent king. I warrant he will put both his father and grandfather in the shade when it is his turn to rule."

"In spite of their reputations as hell-raisers and carousers, he and his young nobles acquitted themselves well in the Welsh campaign."

"Such wild boys!" Eleanor said indulgently.

"Boys no longer . . . they are men, make no mistake."

Rosamond rolled her eyes ceilingward and Demi giggled as they imagined the spoiled boys parading about like men. In truth, Rosamond found it hard to picture them at all, for a month after her betrothal, the royal family had traveled to Spain, where Prince Edward, heir to the throne, was married to ten-year-old Eleanora of Castile. The political marriage had taken place to ensure peace between England and Spain, and immediately after the ceremony, Lord Edward and his nobles had ridden to Gascony, where he had been installed as ruler. When he returned to England at twenty, Lord Edward had his own household at Windsor, which had been especially built for him. Rumor had it that the young nobles, influenced by continental ideas, were wilder than ever. Edward now commanded a large troop of young Gascons and was so eager for military action, it had been impossible to keep him from the campaign in Wales.

As the two friends broke their fast, Demi confided, "I don't remember much about Edward except that his hair was flaxen and everyone called him Longshanks because he was so tall."

Rosamond's glance, which had been searching the hall for a glimpse of one particular knight, came to rest on Demi's pretty face. "That's because it has been five years since we've seen him . . . thank the Lord!"

Demi laughed at her friend's irreverence. "I can't remember any of the young men in his household."

"How very fortunate for you," Rosamond teased. "They were a pack of uncivilized beasts, forever fighting and trading blows with each other. The only one I could tolerate was Harry of Almaine, and that's because his mother was Isabella Marshal and he's my second cousin."

"What about Rodger de Leyburn?" Demi asked avidly.

"What about him?" Rosamond shrugged a pretty shoulder to show her complete indifference.

"He's your betrothed!"

"Not for long! I'll soon rid myself of the ugly devil," Rosamond said lightly, licking honey from her fingers.

"Is he truly ugly?" Demi asked with compassion.

Rosamond's throaty laugh bubbled forth. "He left such an indelible impression upon me, I don't remember."

The girls finished their breakfast and hurried off to their first lesson of the day. Eleanor de Montfort was a stickler for learning and would not excuse the Demoiselle from her lessons simply because her father had returned. They studied languages with Brother Adam, a learned Franciscan who had helped compile the library at Kenilworth. Both young ladies were fluent in French, and Rosamond had recently developed a flair for Spanish, while Demi preferred to learn the Welsh tongue. They also studied history and government, as well as music and art.

Along with this liberal education, each was preparing to become the proficient chatelaine of her own castle. They learned how to run a kitchen, a laundry, a stillroom, and a household of servants. They learned how to make herbal cures from the nuns of St. Bride's and were taught to stitch, cauterize, and dress the wounds of men-at-arms in case bloody action became necessary in times of emergency.

On top of all this knowledge, Rosamond had acquired something far more valuable. She had acquired a measure of self-confidence and was no longer the vulnerable, insecure child she had once been. Because she revered Princess Eleanor, Lady de Montfort had become her role model. She imitated the magnificent woman's sparkling wit, her full-bodied laugh, her exquisite clothes, and her regal demeanor. Eleanor could swear a blue streak with the stable boys or freeze the Queen of England with a haughty stare, and Rosamond Marshal was fast becoming the same sort of vibrant woman as the Countess of Leicester.

The next morning, Rosamond chose a lavender gown whose shade matched the color of her eyes. It was richly embroidered with delicate seed pearls on its sleeves and square-cut neckline. Her beautiful clothes not only gave her pleasure, they also lent her a great deal of confidence. She picked up the journal she was compiling on the medicinal properties of herbs and plants, and hurried to the stillroom, where she had been secretly experimenting with bayberries versus bay leaves to ease the pain and length of labor in childbirth.

The nuns had been outraged when they discovered Rosamond reading a medical journal from Cordoba, Spain, the world's undisputed center of medicine. It not only contained information on the painkilling properties of plants, but listed herbs that prevented conception, such as dragonwort. The nuns lectured that herbal remedies to ease pain should be reserved for men who received wounds in battle. Rosamond vigorously argued that from what she had seen, the pain of childbirth was so great, it was quite reasonable to use herbs to relieve it. The nuns, however, insisted it was *natural* pain, which should, indeed *must*, be endured, and Rosamond lost the argument. Undaunted, she continued to distill her syrups surreptitiously, providing the women of Kenilworth with the soothing concoctions that were much in demand.

Rosamond set down her herbal book to examine the bayberries she had gathered and hung in bunches to preserve them. She was pleased that they were not rotting, but drying nicely as she had hoped. She made a note in her journal and moved on to a new perfume she was creating. She had blended rose petals and apricot blossoms and mixed in a little almond oil. The fragrance pleased her, so she dabbed a little between her breasts and then on a sudden impulse decided to climb to the castle ramparts to view the men-at-arms still streaming into Kenilworth.

Water had been dammed from the River Avon to create a mere around the outer walls of the castle, and the only entrance was over an earthen causeway and through the portcullis. The morning sun glistened on the water, and Rosamond thought it the most beautiful place on earth. Her heart sang with happiness that the fighting was finished. She shaded her eyes, trying to identify the devices on the fluttering pennons, but from this distance the flags and the men all looked alike, so she left the ramparts, curbing her impatience to catch a glimpse of Sir Rickard de Burgh.

She had made herself late for her lesson with Brother Adam, so she hurried along an upper passageway that led to a stone staircase descending to the library. Suddenly, about thirty feet ahead of her, she spied Sir Rickard de Burgh. Delighted to find him right in front of her, walking down the same passageway, Rosamond quickened her steps and breathlessly called, "Sir Rickard."

When he did not turn around, she realized he hadn't heard her. She hesitated for a second, wondering if she was doing the right thing. What harm is there in welcoming him back to Kenilworth? she asked herself as she closed the distance between them. "Sir Rickard?" she repeated.

He turned and Rosamond's heart hammered as she saw the wide mail-clad shoulders, the jet black hair, and the green eyes. But these green eyes were not the ones she had expected to see. The expression in them was so bold, she gasped in protest, "You are not Sir Rickard!"

"Alas, I am not." The man openly assessed her, his green gaze sweeping over her, lingering on hair that flowed about her like pale golden honey. Her eyes were neither blue nor purple, but some unique shade in between, and her generously shaped mouth looked equally capable of laughter or a sensual pout. Her breasts were high and thrust impudently from the neckline of her expensive gown, and beneath that gown he imagined legs as long as a colt's. He couldn't help but smile at her. "Will I do in his stead, chérie?"

Rosamond stiffened and froze him with a haughty stare. "Indeed you will not!" Inexplicably, she was furious at the resemblance between this insolent devil and the honorable knight of whom she daydreamed. "How dare you look at me in such a bold fashion?"

His eyes filled with amusement. "I was but paying homage to your beauty, chérie."

"Indeed you were not! You looked at me as if—"

"As if I'd like to bed you? Such conceit. You are obviously an ice maiden in need of a thawing. I'm on my way to the baths, if you'd care to join me. A plunge in hot water might be just the cure."

Rosamond drew back her hand with every intent to slap the dark insolent expression off his face, but quick as mercury he captured her fingers and drew them to his lips. "Mmm, apricots and almonds . . . good enough to eat." His white teeth flashed as if he would bite her.

"Unhand me, you uncouth knave, or I shall scream!"

"In hope that the worthy Sir Rickard will come running to your rescue?" he asked mockingly.

Rosamond's temper exploded. "You bastard, I need no man to rescue me." Swiftly she brought her knee up between his legs and made contact with the codpiece that protected his genitals.

Just the thought of the damage she could have done him lit a fierce green flame in his eyes.

Rosamond gave him her sweetest smile, then her eyes slid down his body to the apex of his legs. "A plunge in hot water might be just the cure."

Stormy green eyes watched her descend the stone steps. "Just wait, my beautiful little witch, we have a score to settle." He shook his head, both angered and impressed by the girl's fighting spirit, then suddenly he laughed, his good nature restored.

In the late afternoon it was the custom at Kenilworth for the females to gather in the solar. The countess had a wardrobe mistress and a dozen sewing women, but all of the tiring-women were proficient with a needle and could embroider a sleeve or repair a tapestry, and many of the younger maids were given lessons. It was an enjoyable part of their day, where the women of the castle could socialize and exchange gossip.

When Rosamond arrived, the women's excitement was palpable in the air. She soon learned that the heir to the throne had arrived, and by their description Lord Edward was nothing less than a golden god. His companions were so overwhelmingly handsome and charming that a squabble had broken out among the bathhouse women over who would attend them.

All eyes swung to Bertha, a strapping young matron in

charge of the bathhouse, for confirmation. Bertha couldn't wait to embellish the tale. "Lord Edward called one of the men Dick and the other Rod—never have names been more fitting!"

The corners of Rosamond's mouth rose in a smile. "Surely the measure of a man should be his intellect?" she said.

Her tiring-woman, Nan, winked. "I prefer brawn over brains any night of the week. Come, my lamb, it is time for you to dress. You must look your best tonight in the hall."

When Rosamond entered her chamber, the Demoiselle was already dressed in her new deep red gown. The sleeves of her white silk underdress were embroidered with garnets to complement the gown and set off her dark coloring. She pirouetted before Rosamond. "Mother wants me at her side tonight; I must hurry."

"That's because she wants to show you off! You look absolutely lovely; don't forget to make a grand entrance." At fourteen, the Demoiselle was quickly learning her female power.

Rosamond knew that every woman at Kenilworth would be adorned in her finest attire tonight, and she decided to wear her peacock blue velvet, which had a small train in the very latest fashion. Nan brushed Rosamond's long golden hair until it crackled, then held back the curling tendrils with a silver circlet studded with aquamarines.

The sound of voices from the Great Hall could be heard the moment Rosamond left the ladies' quarters. At the entrance, Nan left her to join the other servants, who sat below the salt. Even in that crowd, it didn't take Rosamond more than a moment to pick out the royal heir to the throne. Conversing with Lady Eleanor, who was dressed in royal purple, and the Demoiselle, Lord Edward dwarfed the two beautiful dark-haired females.

Rosamond was astonished at the prince's appearance.

He was resplendent in a crimson tabard embroidered with three golden lions, while soft leather boots encased his long shanks, but it was not his stylish clothes that astonished her; it was the man he had become. No longer a lanky youth, he had a man's muscular torso and wide shoulders. Above a close-cropped golden beard were brilliant blue eyes, burning with zeal and a passion for life.

When Eleanor spied her ward, she beckoned to her, and as Rosamond approached Lord Edward, she sensed his immense energy. Lady de Montfort reintroduced them. "Believe it or not, this is Rosamond Marshal."

As she went down in a curtsy, Edward stared at her in amazement. "Splendor of God, the rose has bloomed!" He reached down, took possession of her hands, and lifted her to her feet. "What happened to the grubby urchin who cursed the stableboys?"

"I still curse when the occasion demands it, my lord Edward, and may I say your own transformation is nothing short of miraculous."

Eleanor threw back her head and laughed. "Indeed, he is splendid enough to revive the belief in the godlike origin of kings."

"No wonder Simon adores you, it is your silver tongue." Edward slipped his arm about Rosamond's waist. "May I steal her for a moment?"

As he led her down the long hall, all eyes were upon them. "I cannot wait to see the look on his face when he first lays eyes on you."

"Who?"

"Rod."

An unbidden picture of the man the bathhouse matron had described brought a blush to her cheek. A small knot of people who were gathered about Simon de Montfort stepped aside as Lord Edward approached. Rosamond stiffened when she saw the man deep in conversation with Earl Simon; she might have known the green-eyed devil she'd encountered earlier in the day was the Rod who had set the maids atwitter.

"Rosamond Marshal, it gives me the greatest pleasure in the world to reacquaint you with your betrothed, Sir Rodger de Leyburn."

They stared at each other in stunned disbelief. Rosamond saw him recover from the shock before she did. The look on his face told her the news pleased him greatly. He looked like a man who had just discovered a pearl inside an oyster shell. She knew her behavior was gauche, but she couldn't stop staring at him. He was almost as tall as Lord Edward and Earl Simon. He too was elegantly garbed in continental fashion. He wore an emerald green tabard emblazoned with a golden eagle. Below it his long, muscular legs were encased in soft leather thigh-high boots.

Rosamond stood mutely as he bowed, then reached for her hand and drew it to his lips. His green eyes shot her a look of triumph and once again his white teeth flashed as if he would bite her. "My lady, I am enchanted."

The bold devil was mocking her, and she felt an urge to wipe the smug look from his dark face. "Betrothed? No, no, I wouldn't dream of holding Sir Rodger to a chivalrous gesture he made five years ago to comfort a distraught child."

His green eyes narrowed; his powerful fingers tightened possessively on her hand. "My lady, I am honor-bound."

"My lord, I release you!" Rosamond snatched back her hand and kicked her train behind her in a gesture that lent finality to her words.

Lord Edward's laughter rolled over her. "The wench is toying with us, Rod. She knows this match pleases me."

Rosamond felt thwarted and cast a desperate look at Earl Simon, who remained silent, much to her annoyance. Knowing she could not stand and argue with the royal prince, she did the next best thing. "My lords, will you kindly excuse me? I must find my cousin Harry; I have neglected him shamefully."

"We will excuse you for the moment, Rosamond, but later you will join us on the dais for supper." It was a royal order.

She did her best to decline. "I should dine with Harry."

"You forget, our cousin Harry of Almaine is royal too. He'll be up on the dais with me."

Rosamond knew better than to pit her will against Edward's; he always got what he wanted. Seething inside, she sank into a curtsy and murmured, "Until later, then."

Two

At the first opportunity, Simon de Montfort took Rodger de Leyburn aside. Rod had hero-worshipped Earl Simon since he was a boy. The earl was a magnetic figure who had earned the reputation of being the greatest warrior in Europe. He appealed to young men's idealism with his unswerving devotion to a cause. Compared with the weak and feckless King Henry, Earl Simon was a knight in shining armor. The barons had chosen him for their leader, and even nobles who had been royalist, such as Richard de Clare, Earl of Gloucester, had recently switched their allegiance to Simon de Montfort.

"Thank you, Rod, for persuading Edward to visit Kenilworth."

"He seeks your guidance, my lord earl. He has a natural military instinct and more energy than any man I've ever known. You have taught him to be a great soldier, and if he will but listen, you will teach him to be a great king."

"If he commits to the right course and is steadfast, Edward has it in him to be England's *greatest* king."

Rod smiled. "He allows nothing to stand in his way; he is fanatical about achieving whatever goal he sets himself."

"Which is, of course, the only way to succeed." Simon's black eyes examined de Leyburn's face. "I suspect you are much alike."

Rod glanced at Simon warily. "Does my determination to wed Rosamond Marshal offend you, my lord?"

"Good God, no, I find no fault with a man ambitious enough to wed an heiress; I did it myself. Rosamond Marshal is a great marriage prize. She will bring you two estates, whose income should increase steadily. I heartily congratulate you."

"Thank you, my lord earl."

"Are you and Rosamond planning to wed soon?"

"I would marry her tomorrow, if she were willing, but I believe Rosamond needs a little more persuading. Certainly I should like to make her my wife before we return to London."

"With King Henry away in France, it is wise that Lord Edward return to the capital. As heir to the throne, it would be politic for Edward to get to know the Council of Fifteen appointed by the Provisions of Oxford, before Parliament opens."

Rod knew a political struggle loomed between de Montfort and King Henry, and it was obvious to him that Simon wanted Lord Edward on his side in the coming conflict. "Lord Edward is a shrewd man; he can always be counted upon to act wisely."

"Your intense loyalty to Edward is to be commended."

"Thank you, my lord earl."

Rosamond found her cousin Harry paying his respects to his aunt Eleanor de Montfort. She felt relieved that he looked much the same as she remembered. Compared with his cousin Edward, who was so physically mature, Harry's rosy cheeks and chestnut curls made him look youthful in the extreme. Rosamond knew he resembled his mother, Isabella, but she was careful not to stir painful memories by telling him so, for lovely Isabella Marshal was dead. His father, Richard of Cornwall, the brother of King Henry, was now remarried to a foreign princess.

"Harry! Thank heavens the fighting is over and you are safe."

"What rubbish! I am a soldier; I enjoy fighting. I now lead my own troop of men from Cornwall. There is nothing like a Welsh campaign to turn adolescents into men. Have you seen Edward?"

"Yes, he is greatly changed, but not nearly so much as Rodger de Leyburn . . . I did not know him!"

"Rod is two years older than Edward. He came to manhood before the rest of us. The ladies are mad for him, cannot resist that dark, dangerous face."

"*I* can resist him! He is paying unwanted attention to me, and I need you beside me at supper to make him keep his distance."

"You must be daft in the head, Rosamond. Everyone loves Rod; he makes friends easier than any man I've ever met. He has qualities that make others genuinely like him. He's Edward's favorite and the undisputed leader of the bachelor knights. You should consider yourself lucky to receive his attentions."

"Well, I do not. In fact I wish to end the betrothal."

"Has a maggot eaten your brain? He can have any woman he desires; he doesn't have to settle for you, Rosamond."

"*Settle* for me?" She lifted her chin and kicked at her train. "Harry, you still have a very blunt tongue. I should box your bloody ears."

He grinned boyishly. "Ah, but you need me at supper."

Richard de Clare, Earl of Gloucester, clapped Harry on the shoulder. "Behave yourself, little brother, I've got my eye on you!" Richard was Isabella Marshal's eldest son from her first marriage, to Gilbert de Clare. Harry was her son by her second husband, the king's brother, Richard of Cornwall. Richard de Clare was twelve years older than Harry, and though both had inherited their mother's fair complexion, Richard had florid cheeks that quickly turned even redder whenever his famous temper flared out of control.

"Richard!" Rosamond gave him a kiss of welcome. "I had no idea you were here; I expected you would ride straight to Gloucester."

"I am here to demonstrate my support for Simon. More nobles will ride in every day, and the names of those gathered at Kenilworth will be reported to the king. If he sees that we are solidly united against him, he will not dare make trouble."

Rosamond's sparkling eyes clouded. Why couldn't everyone live in peace? One fight was barely settled before they were discussing the next. Her brows drew together. If Earl Simon and the king were again drawing up sides, what the devil was the king's son doing at Kenilworth? It was inconceivable that Edward would turn against his father. It occurred to Rosamond that Lord Edward and his men could be spying. Then it came to her that perhaps that was exactly what Earl Simon wanted them to do. He was far too clever and seasoned to allow a pack of arrogant young wolves to outwit him.

Suddenly, Rosamond's hopes soared. If lines were being drawn between the earl and King Henry, then surely Simon and Eleanor de Montfort would not allow their ward to marry Rodger de Leyburn, who would be in the enemy camp.

With a sense of relief and a renewed confidence that her betrothal would be broken, Rosamond placed her hand on her cousin Harry's arm and allowed him to lead her up onto the dais. When de Leyburn greeted her with a bow and held a chair for her, Rosamond walked past him as if he were invisible.

Harry led her to Lord Edward's side, intending to seat Rosamond between the prince and himself, when suddenly he caught an unmistakable look of royal disapproval. Harry did an immediate about-face. "Rod, would you take my seat next to Rosamond? I see my brother Gloucester summoning me."

"Be damned to you, Harry," she hissed, chagrined that he put loyalty to his friends before her.

Edward's blue eyes glittered with amusement. "You may have the airs of a lady, but you still have that blunt Marshal tongue." He winked at his friend. "Rod, it seems you will have your work cut out for you, trying to curb her. I don't envy you."

"I wager every other man in the hall envies me, my lord." His words were gallant, but the devilish gleam in his green eyes told her plainly he would relish the challenge of bringing her to heel.

"A spirited young filly needs a strong hand and a touch of the spurs," Edward teased unmercifully.

"And unruly young stallions are in need of the horse whip," Rosamond retorted.

"Touché! My lord, the lady has wit." Rod's mouth curved with appreciation. He gestured to his squire, Griffin, to pour them wine, then he lifted his goblet to salute her.

Rosamond sipped her own wine, then ran the tip of her tongue over her lips. "Nay, it simply passes for wit when I banter with those who are witless."

"She must mean you, Rod; to call a prince of the realm witless would be tantamount to treason." Clearly, Edward was enjoying himself.

Rodger smiled into her eyes. "Very likely I *was* witless when last we met. I was only seventeen."

She was seventeen! Was the damned fellow insulting her? "I don't recall anything about you. What do you remember about me?" she asked pointedly.

His mouth curved. "You trailed about with the dogs, wading in the mere, looking very bedraggled. When Harry called you a drowned rat, you pelted all of us with stones."

"Cursing like a demon," Edward added.

Rosamond blushed at the picture they painted of her.

"If my manners were so appalling, then it must have been my manors that you found so appealing." She had the satisfaction of seeing Rodger de Leyburn stiffen at her insinuation.

The smile also left Edward's face. "What the devil are you getting at?"

She continued heedlessly. "Why did he offer for me? There is only one answer: because I am an heiress," she said bluntly.

"No, Rosamond, you are quite mistaken," the prince retorted, his voice sharp with annoyance. "He offered for you because I asked him to. It was an arrangement that pleased everyone. The barons were forever screaming about our heiresses being given to foreigners, so I made sure you went to an Englishman."

Her lashes fluttered to her cheeks in dismay at Edward's annoyance. She had brought this humiliation upon herself. It was her cursed insecurity raising its ugly head. A sense of inadequacy had dogged her since childhood. Losing her parents and brother had made her feel unworthy of a family and somehow undeserving of love. Suddenly, Rosamond felt her hand being covered by another. Its comforting warmth seeped into her.

"You were a prize beyond belief. It was my great honor to betroth a lady from the noble Marshal family."

Was Rodger de Leyburn sincere or was he mocking her? she wondered wildly. At least his words had restored the prince's good humor; Rosamond saw that Edward was once more grinning.

"I am the only married man among my bachelor knights; it is time that I had company," the prince said.

"But you are married in name only," Rosamond pointed out bluntly. She felt de Leyburn squeeze her fingers in warning.

"Not for much longer. Eleanora of Castile will soon be sixteen. Elegant quarters have been especially designed for her at Windsor."

"Do you even remember her, my lord?" Rosamond challenged.

"I certainly remember the splendid entertainments at the wedding in Castile—the vivid colors of the costumes. The tournaments they held were spectacular. I was knighted by King Alphonso and gifted with a magnificent Spanish charger. It served me well in the jousting; I unseated every challenger."

At the mention of jousting, Rosamond snatched back her hand. "Well, the horse made a lasting impression, if the bride did not," she said with exquisite sarcasm.

Lord Edward was distracted from the conversation by the presentation of the dessert, which Lady Eleanor had arranged in his honor. A dozen huge plum puddings, floating in syllabub, were brought in on silver salvers. A lit torch was touched to each, setting them ablaze, then they were carried around the hall as the flames turned to blue fire. Musicians followed, playing the beautiful, haunting melodies of Wales to celebrate the success of the recent campaign.

Rodger de Leyburn was acutely aware of the young female who sat beside him. He studied her lovely profile in the flickering blue light and could only guess at her thoughts. The gods must surely have been smiling upon him the day he betrothed the unremarkable twelve-year-old. Edward had arranged the match for him as a reward because the Marshal girl was an heiress. Who could have known she would turn into a cool beauty with a hot temper—an utterly tantalizing woman? He knew she wanted nothing to do with him and would do her utmost to end the betrothal. But what she wanted made not the slightest difference to him. Now that he had seen her, he intended to have her. And sooner rather than later.

His glance moved over to the prince's profile. What Earl Simon said was true: he and Edward *were* much alike. They were both cursed with insatiable ambition. That was the reason for their deep friendship, that and the fact that they knew each other's secrets, and would keep them at any cost.

At any cost . . . the words echoed in his mind as he glanced about the hall, counting the men who would let nothing stand in their way to achieve a goal. How many were prepared to do *anything* or sacrifice *anyone*? There were only two. Simon de Montfort and Edward Plantagenet. What of himself? he wondered. In the dark depths of his soul he suspected that his own name would raise the count to three. He had already committed most of the seven deadly sins in his twenty-two years. He was guilty of all but sloth. That had been his father's sin, and because of it his family had been reduced to grinding poverty. Thank God his uncle had ambition. Through his influence at court, he had secured his nephew an appointment as page and told Rodger his future was in his own hands. Rod looked down at those hands now and he smiled. There was no way he was going to let Rosamond Marshal slip through his fingers.

The talk of marriage unsettled Rosamond, and the moment the servitors began to clear the tables, she made her escape. The Demoiselle joined her, filled with breathless curiosity. "Oh, Rosamond, he is so handsome! What did he say to you?"

"Lord Edward?" Rosamond teased.

"No, silly, Rodger de Leyburn."

"You think him handsome?"

"Oh yes. Tall, dark men are so compelling. When I looked up into those green eyes, I went weak at the knees and felt my heart turn over. What about you?"

"Yes, he had a similar effect on me . . . I felt my stomach turn over."

Demi laughed. "Oh, Rosamond, you are so bad."

"I know. I deliberately accused him of betrothing me because I am an heiress."

"But that is the only reason any of us receive offers of marriage. The daughters of noble families are not married for love. Is that what you secretly long for, Rosamond?"

"Love?" Rosamond scoffed. "That's the last thing I want!" She had lost everyone she had ever loved. She would never let herself care so deeply about anyone ever again. "I shan't sit with him tomorrow night," she vowed fiercely. "I shall find some way to break off this accursed betrothal. He is obviously a determined devil, but if he thinks I will wed him and hand over my dowry, he is doomed to disappointment!"

Simon and Eleanor's apartments were high in Kenilworth's great Caesar Tower. After the banquet, when he climbed the stairs and opened the door to their private sanctuary, he saw that his wife had lit scented candles and placed them on the hearth before the crackling fire.

Simon's blood began to throb with anticipation. He knew that Eleanor liked the warmth of a fire in their bedchamber so that she could walk about nude. He felt his pulse beating heavily in his throat, and in his groin, as Eleanor came through the adjoining door. She had removed her jewels and gown, but still wore her shift and stockings, so that he could finish undressing her. He opened his arms and she ran to him eagerly.

"Welcome home, Sim." She used the diminutive of his name, as she always did when they made love.

He enfolded her against his heart and murmured, "You make my life complete." Then he held her at arm's length to gaze down at her. He dipped his head and kissed her closed eyelids, amazed after all these years that his need for her was as great as it had been when he had persuaded her to wed him secretly. "Have you any idea how much I missed you?"

"Of course! You showed me when you arrived home in the middle of the night. Now it's my turn to show you." Her tone was deliberately teasing to mask the intensity of her emotions. Whenever Simon rode off to war, she was afraid she would never see him again. Over the years, she had schooled herself never to show him her fear. How could he believe in his own invincibility if she doubted him?

She clung to her beloved fiercely, knowing deep in her soul that one day he would not ride home in victory. She pushed the thought away and laughed up at him. "I always forget how big you are."

"Let me refresh your memory," he said with a suggestive smile, pressing his arousal against her soft belly.

"Not just there," she said, laughing, "everywhere."

His hands were impatient as they removed her shift and then, one by one, her hose. "Walk about for me," he urged.

Eleanor took the pins from her hair and let it fall about her, cloaking her body. Then, prideful as a cat, she walked across the chamber to the far corner. Though she was over forty, she knew that in Simon's eyes, she would remain forever young, forever beautiful.

He undressed and followed her, unable to resist the tempting invitation of her body.

"Carry me to bed," she whispered, and when he swept her up in his powerful arms, she exulted in his strength and his passion. When he was away on campaign, she had to be strong, but now that he was here with her in the big bed, she could be soft, and clinging, and feminine. The things he did to her made her deliciously weak. His hands sought out all of her body's sensitive places and touched them intimately; he knew exactly how to arouse her with his fingers and his mouth, and she reveled in the sensuality and desire his hard, powerful body evoked when he pulled her beneath him. Then with total male assurance, he filled her with his great passion.

Eleanor knew exactly what he wanted. She wound her arms about his neck and yielded everything, crying, "Sim, Sim!"

When he heard her use his Gaelic name in the throes of passion, it raised gooseflesh on his dark skin. "I love you so much, my precious jewel."

She touched her lips to his. She had never loved him more than she did tonight.

The next day was marked by more arrivals. Two brothers, Lincoln and John de Warenne, Earl of Surrey, rode in with a large train of knights. Then, two hours later, Richard de Clare's son, Gilbert, arrived with his wife. His father had not allowed him to go on the Welsh campaign because he was only fifteen. Instead, he had been put in charge at Gloucester in his father's absence.

Rosamond and Demi were delighted to see the red-haired Gilbert, whom they'd known since they were children, but they stared in disbelief at the dark-eyed beauty who accompanied him. Because of the great de Clare fortune, King Henry had married Gilbert to his foreign niece five years ago, but this was the first time they had seen her. They watched Gilbert greet his hostess, then make a quick escape to seek out his friend, Harry of Almaine. If Eleanor de Montfort was surprised to see the young woman at Kenilworth, she did not show it. "This is Alyce de Clare, Gilbert's wife. May I present my daughter Demoiselle, and Rosamond Marshal?"

"Welcome, Lady Alyce," Demi said dutifully.

Alyce's glance passed over the younger girl without interest and came to rest on Rosamond. "Not another Marshal . . . there is no end to them." Alyce spoke with a provocative French accent.

Rosamond's eyes flashed with indignation and she opened her mouth to protest.

"No, no, please do not try to explain your relationship to my husband, it is too, too confusing. His cousins are as numerous as Gloucester sheep!" Alyce turned back to the countess. "Lady Eleanor, you are aware that Gilbert and I keep separate bedchambers, separate quarters?"

Eleanor de Montfort looked her straight in the eye. "I am aware of *everything*."

Gilbert's squire struggled in with a large trunk. Alyce

said, "Ah, here is part of my luggage. First, I will need a bath, no?"

With a straight face, Eleanor replied, "You need a bath, yes. Come upstairs with me now."

"To wash off the smell of all those bloody Gloucester sheep!" Rosamond declared before the elegant female was out of earshot.

The king had married his half-brother's daughter, Alyce of Angoulême, into the wealthiest family of England. No matter that Gilbert de Clare had been a boy of ten at the time of the marriage, while Alyce had been a sexually ripe young woman of sixteen.

"Poor Gilbert," Demi murmured, "it must be awful to be married to an older woman who is waiting for you to grow up."

"She doesn't think him old enough to share her bed, but she's quite willing to share his wealth," Rosamond remarked.

"Yes, I saw that her riding cloak was trimmed with ermine."

"That's to proclaim to the world that she has royal connections. Is it any wonder that the barons hate the king's foreign relatives? They are like a plague of locusts, which outnumber sheep any day!"

Demi giggled. "Mother was decidedly frosty with her. I warrant she will wear something spectacular tonight, to outshine her."

Lord Edward spent the first of what would be many days with Simon de Montfort. They talked for hours, as they walked shoulder to shoulder, exchanging ideas and sharing knowledge of warfare, in which Edward had an intense interest. But they talked also about the best ways to govern a country like England.

Earl Simon was a persuasive man, determined to win the heir to the throne over to the side of the barons. He hoped Lord Edward would see the popularity of the cause, as evidenced by the number of earls and nobles who were present at Kenilworth. This time they were determined to force the king to abide by the promises he'd made at Oxford. Englishmen must hold the highest administrative offices, rather than Henry's foreign relatives and favorites.

Simon made sure to compliment Edward on his role in the Welsh campaign. "I believe Llewelyn of Wales was persuaded to sign the two-year truce because we stood together. When a Plantagenet unites with his barons, it is an unbeatable force."

As the two men talked, Edward realized the wisdom of Simon's words and he became more aware of the gravity and responsibilities of the inheritance he would come into. Simon believed that the king had a duty to his subjects as well as vice versa, and explained in detail how he felt. Though he knew the prince loved his father dearly, he hoped he was not blind to his deficiencies as a king.

Simon de Montfort discussed the Provisions of Oxford, which the barons had forced King Henry to sign, and pointed out that they were not drastic but reasonable, designed to provide a system of fair government that would benefit noble and commoner alike and make England stronger and far more prosperous.

Edward and Simon argued different points, but their discourse was affable and they found themselves in accord on many political and military matters. They were joined by Richard de Clare, Earl of Gloucester, who was the leading peer in England. His name appeared first on the Provisions of Oxford, though it was clear that Simon de Montfort was the driving force behind the barons' cause.

When it was time for the evening meal, Eleanor de Montfort quickly rearranged the seating on the dais at Lord Edward's request, so that he was flanked by her husband and Richard of Gloucester. Soon, the trio were engrossed in conversation, oblivious to those about them. Simon and Gloucester were arguing a political point. Richard thought the advantages gained by the Provisions of Oxford should apply only to the nobility, while de Montfort insisted even the common men who were dependent on the barons should benefit and have a voice in Parliament. Lord Edward listened to their different opinions intently.

Lady Eleanor wore a gown of deepest blue, with her famous sapphires clasped about her throat. She had sent Bette, her own tiring woman, to the Demoiselle's chamber with instructions that tonight her daughter was to wear pristine white.

"Bette, it makes me look too young," Demi protested. "I want to wear red. Alyce de Clare will be sure to wear something dramatic to make herself the center of attention!"

"Take your mother's advice, she is very clever," Rosamond urged. "White will make you look virginal, something Alyce de Clare should be, but obviously is not."

"Rosamond is right, my lamb," Bette coaxed. "Let me thread some pearls into your pretty hair."

The Demoiselle capitulated and sat before the mirror as Bette took up the hairbrush. "What will you wear, Rosamond?"

"Something drab and colorless," her friend declared. "I don't want to draw the unwanted attention of you-know-who, and I will come to the hall late, after everyone is seated."

Thirty minutes later, Rosamond stood before the polished silver mirror while Nan fastened the back of the dun-colored tunic. "Perfect," she declared as she covered her hair with a cloth.

"Perfectly hideous!" Nan contradicted. She knew Rosamond's beautiful clothes lent her confidence, something the young woman did not always feel, though she hid it well. "You have just enough time to change; I'll get the vivid jade green gown that makes your hair look glorious."

"No thank you, Nan," she said stubbornly, "please go

down to eat, or all the seats will be taken." After her woman left, Rosamond tarried another quarter hour, then made her unhurried way down to the Great Hall. Her mind was busy thinking of ways she could avoid sitting on the dais if a place had been saved for her. *If Lord Edward insists, I suppose I have no choice, but at least I will have kept them waiting, and this ugly, drab tunic will show Rodger de Leyburn I have no interest in attracting his attention or pleasing him!*

Rosamond had never seen the hall as crowded as it was tonight. All the tables and benches were filled from one end to the other. As she looked about for an empty place, the servitors rushed past her with food-laden trays, as if she were invisible. No squire or page stepped forward to aid her. Rosamond's gaze was drawn to the raised dais, where she had dined last night. It was brilliantly lit, with torches and wax candles showing off the splendid garments and jewels of Kenilworth's guests of honor.

Lord Edward had certainly not saved her a seat. He was so engrossed in his conversation with Earl Simon and Richard de Clare, he wasn't even aware of Rosamond Marshal's existence at this moment. Lady Eleanor sat regally beside her husband, her throat ablaze with sapphires. At her side the Demoiselle looked like a fairy-tale princess, and redheaded Gilbert de Clare sat staring at her with worshipful eyes.

Rosamond's gaze moved down the table and came to rest on her cousin Harry of Almaine. Not even Harry had saved her a place. Curse the rogue! There he sat, stuffing his face, swilling his wine, and laughing like a lunatic at something the lady beside him said. Suddenly Rosamond's eyes widened in disbelief. It was no lady at all, it was Alyce de Clare. And the attentive dinner partner on her other side was Sir Rodger de Leyburn! Alyce was flirting openly with the dark devil beside her, smiling up into his eyes, slapping him playfully, then lifting her hand to whisper something intimate.

Harry's words came flooding back to her: *He can have any woman he desires; he doesn't have to settle for you, Rosamond.* Splendor of God, the woman was sitting in *her* seat, flirting with *her* betrothed, and to add insult to injury, the bitch was wearing a vivid green gown! Rosamond looked down at her own dun tunic in dismay and slowly backed out of the hall. Never had she felt so unattractive, never had she felt so insignificant, never had she felt so utterly sorry for herself! No one seemed to be missing her at all!

THREE

Alyce de Clare had smooth, jet black hair that fell to her shoulders. In contrast, her skin was pale as parchment and her dark eyes were made to look even darker by the artful application of kohl, imported at great expense from Egypt. She had mastered the art of flirtation and behaved in a provocative manner to all men save her husband.

Alyce was now a sensual and sophisticated woman of twenty-one, but even at sixteen, when she had first come from Angoulême, she had been able to wrap her uncle, King Henry, about her finger and easily manipulate him. In a magnanimous gesture, the king had married her into the wealthy de Clare family. Wisely, Alyce had made no protest that Gilbert the Red was only ten years old, for one day he would inherit the powerful earldom of Gloucester. Gilbert's father, Richard de Clare, the Earl of Gloucester, had been flattered at the alliance with the royal family, but the marriage had raised many eyebrows and the barons had been angry that another foreign favorite had been allowed to dip her fingers into English coffers.

At this moment, Alyce dipped her finger into a wine goblet, then sucked it provocatively. "Mmm, delicious."

Rodger de Leyburn lifted a dark brow. "You do know that's my wine, Alyce?"

"Of course I know. Where's the pleasure in dipping my finger into my own . . . chalice?"

"You are a born tease, and greedy too," Rod murmured.

"And I am impatient!" She stuck out the tip of her tongue.

He eyed her with amused tolerance. "Keep that in your mouth."

"Oooh, I bet you say that to every female you bed!"

"I don't need to persuade them." He grinned.

"Rod, Rod . . . there is something about your name I adore. It is so very wicked and suggestive."

"You are the one who is being wicked and suggestive, Alyce."

"Yes, we 'ave so much in common."

"We do, chérie." He raised his goblet and winked at her over its rim. "You must behave yourself for just a little while longer."

She gestured for Sir Rodger's squire, Griffin, to clear the table, then tapped long nails in an impatient staccato. "Anticipation is said to harden the pleasure, no?"

"Heighten the pleasure," Rod corrected, "though there is likely more truth in the way you say it."

Alyce dragged her attention from Rodger's handsome face to eye Harry. She slapped his wrist and hissed, "Stop eating, or we'll never be able to leave."

Rod winked at him. "Some of us have other appetites to slake."

Rosamond had no appetite at all, so it mattered little that she would get no dinner tonight. She snatched off the ugly head-cloth and paced her chamber, venting the anger she felt toward those who had ruined her tranquility. Her mind was filled with the picture of Alyce de Clare up on the dais, with her beautiful black hair, her exquisite clothes, and her potent allure. Rosamond spoke to the empty room. "Why does she have to be so bloody attractive? And why did she have to come to Kenilworth?" Rosamond answered her own questions. "Because all the *men* are here, and it is disgustingly obvious that Alyce loves men!" Well, she could have them. Rosamond had been content enough at Kenilworth until Lord Edward and his lecherous steward had arrived to swagger about, remind her of her betrothal, and destroy her peace of mind.

The image of Rodger de Leyburn rose up, darkly compelling and undeniably attractive, and suddenly it was crystal clear why the maddening Alyce de Clare had come rushing to Kenilworth. "Oh my God," she whispered, "the green-eyed devil is dallying with a married woman while he is pledged to me!"

Slowly, Rosamond realized that here was her opportunity to rid herself of the odious de Leyburn. She would go to him and ask him straight out to release her. Under the circumstances, he could hardly refuse, especially if she caught him and Alyce together!

Rosamond wasn't even sure which chambers had been assigned to Lord Edward and his companions, but unquestionably they would be staying in one of Kenilworth's five great towers. The impregnable Caesar Tower was the private domain of Eleanor and Simon, while the chamber she shared with Demi was in the Lady Tower. Most likely the young nobles had been accommodated in the Warwick Tower, which was larger than the others and close to the bathhouse.

Rosamond opened the wardrobe to find a cloak with a hood that would cover her pale hair. The passageways of the castle late at night were dim, some even unlit, but she didn't want to be recognized prowling about the knights' quarters, and her golden hair would identify her immediately.

Rosamond slipped on a dark purple cloak and took great pains to tuck every last strand of her long hair inside the hood. When she opened the chamber door, she could hear music from the Great Hall and knew she would have time to climb to the castle ramparts before the evening's entertainment ended. By avoiding the gatehouse that looked out over the causeway, and by keeping to the shadows,

Rosamond evaded the soldiers on night patrol. When she came to the Warwick Tower, she stationed herself on the parapet, where she could keep watch through an arrow slit. Then she wrapped her cloak tightly about her and leaned against a stone merlon to wait.

It was a long time before Lord Edward climbed the tower stairs, but within a few minutes, she watched the rest of his gentlemen arrive, including Rodger de Leyburn. She noted that he occupied the chamber next to Edward's, and schooled herself to patience while their own squires and a few of Kenilworth's servants took care of the young nobles' needs. When the tower fell silent, Rosamond began to doubt her vigil would bear fruit. Surely no lady would venture forth to this all-male bastion at this ungodly hour? Rosamond gauged that it was close to midnight, and she certainly had never before been abroad so late.

Then she saw her. The lady was cloaked, but hadn't bothered to cover her hair, so there was no mistaking Alyce de Clare. Rosamond heard her rap twice on Rodger de Leyburn's door. It swung open immediately and the black-haired vixen disappeared inside.

Rod smiled down at the slim beauty and removed her cloak. "Alyce, I thought you had changed your mind."

She stood on tiptoe to kiss him. "You know me better than that, darling. In fact, I warrant you know everything about me. I am more eager tonight than I was five years ago."

Rod grinned. "Anticipation hardens the pleasure." He snuffed the candles, and heard the tempting rustle of her garments in the darkness. As he moved toward the bed, his memory winged back to that unforgettable night five long years ago.

The wedding of Alyce of Angoulême and Gilbert de Clare was solemnized at Westminster Palace, where the bride's father lived in luxury. The marriage of the king's niece was a glittering occasion, with celebrations lasting for an entire week, all at the expense of Henry, who was eager to impress and earn the admiration of his half-brothers from the Continent.

The dark-eyed bride received the name of de Clare, the noblest in the land, which brought her untold riches and wealth, not only in money, but in land and castles. Gilbert, the ten-year-old bridegroom, received only a hunting dog as his reward. Yet Rod clearly remembered thinking that they had both been shortchanged. All week, Alyce had flirted outrageously with him. She was sixteen and overripe for her first sexual encounter. It was obvious that she could not be expected to wait for Gilbert to grow up and satisfy her, so Rod took it upon himself to solve her dilemma and, at the same time, reap his own reward.

He fondly recalled the details of that first encounter. Alyce wore a cream-colored gown of rich lace. They fed each other wine and sweetmeats and wedding cake, laughing together as the guests became more and more intoxicated. When Alyce could no longer keep her hands off him, he pulled her to her feet and led her through the labyrinth of Westminster until they reached his bedchamber.

Rod could still remember unfastening the lace gown—exactly twenty-four buttons—then opening the adjoining door to fifteen-year-old Prince Edward's suite of rooms. "My lord, here is a bride who has been sorely neglected. She is desperately in need of royal succor. As a prince and a gentleman, I know you will not ignore her plight." Rod kissed her hand with gallantry. "Alyce, I promise you a *knight* you will never forget."

Now, as he lay on the bed with his arms folded behind his head, Rod smiled into the darkness with satisfaction. The day after the two half-cousins had spent the night together, Lord Edward had appointed Rod steward of his royal household.

Rosamond waited outside the door, giving the couple inside enough time to compromise themselves. She would not knock; there was nothing polite about her intent. She would simply throw open the door and surprise them in each other's arms. She gathered her courage for what she was about to do and took a deep breath. Her fingers closed about the iron ring, and she firmly turned it until the bar lifted. To her complete chagrin, the heavy oak door swung open to reveal nothing but total darkness and complete silence.

She let out her breath and took a tentative step inside the chamber. As her eyes adjusted to the darkness, she saw light coming from beneath another door across the room. Realizing the couple were in the adjoining chamber, she moved silently across the floor, then paused to listen. Rosamond heard a woman's sensual laugh, and there was no mistaking to whom it belonged.

Without warning, she felt a powerful hand cover her mouth. Rosamond almost came out of her skin and would certainly have screamed if the hand had not prevented her. Her breath caught in her throat and her heart hammered with fright.

"Do not open it, Rosamond."

The fierce whisper was so low, she wondered if she had imagined it, until she felt his mouth touching her ear. She knew who it was immediately, and struggled to remove his hand. Then his arm came around her like a steel band to hold her motionless.

"Hush!"

It was a command she could not disobey, and as she stilled, Rosamond heard a rustle and a laugh that told her Alyce was directly on the other side of the closed door.

"Edward, you really do have the longest shank in the realm!"

"Shank? It is a royal scepter, my little wanton."

"It is a formidable weapon; sheath it before I faint."

"I'll make you faint, by God," he growled fiercely, thrusting himself inside her.

Rosamond heard Alyce cry out, then she heard a steady, rhythmic thumping against the door. It seemed to go on forever, accompanied by the couple's moans and gasps. *"Oooh I love to be taken against the door, it shows your towering impatience for me."*

Even in the darkness, Rosamond knew she was blushing. She felt the warmth from her cheeks spread to the tips of her breasts. She had always been sheltered from carnal knowledge, but the pair's amorous coupling against the door was so graphic, it left little to the imagination. Rosamond felt hot threads spiral inside her belly, and she became acutely aware of her undergarments brushing against her skin, arousing sensations that were new and strange.

"Now, now, oh please, Edward, now!"

"You beg so prettily, Alyce, how can I resist?"

The thumping came faster and louder until a half-scream began and was quickly muffled. A long silence was followed by a heartfelt sigh. *"Your mouth ravages me like no other—carry me to bed."* The laughter of the playful couple gradually faded as they moved away from the door, until all was quiet. Rosamond could hear her own pulse beating against her eardrums. She closed her eyes and felt the blood drain from her face. She had just heard Alyce de Clare commit adultery with Prince Edward.

Rodger de Leyburn removed his hand from Rosamond's mouth and led her silently to the far side of his chamber. He lit a torch in the wall bracket, then pushed back her hood until her golden hair spilled about her. One glance at her pale face and trembling lips told its own story. Without a word, he poured her some wine and lifted it to her lips.

"How did you know it was me?" she whispered.

"Your fragrance is unique. Drink," he ordered softly, pushing her down into a chair.

She obeyed him and felt a blood-red rose bloom in her breast.

"Rosamond, you are privy to a secret that none save you and I knows about."

"I . . . I thought she was with you."

"That is the whole idea. Everyone has thought that for five years. All are willing to look the other way at a little dalliance. It is another matter entirely for Lord Edward to be bedding the wife of Gilbert de Clare. You must not breathe a word of this dangerous secret to anyone."

Rodger de Leyburn could see how shaken she was, and it dawned on him just how innocent Rosamond Marshal must have been until tonight. She had intended to catch him alone with Alyce, but the sexual act she overheard had shocked her badly. "Come, I will see you safely back to the Lady Tower." He reached out to pull her hood forward, but she drew back from him to avoid his touch. A muscle ticked in his jaw as he opened the chamber door and led the way up onto the moonlit ramparts.

When they passed a guard, Rosamond pulled her hood close, but Rod exchanged a quiet greeting with the man, as if it were a natural occurrence for him to be on the castle roof with a woman. When they reached the Lady Tower, Rod paused and leaned a powerful, muscled arm across the door, effectively blocking her escape.

She whirled to face him and found him towering above her, their bodies almost touching.

"Will you keep the secret, Rosamond?"

Silence stretched between them.

He reached out with firm fingers and raised her chin, forcing her to meet his eyes. "Will you keep silent?" he demanded.

"Will you end our betrothal?"

He stared at her with disbelief. "You dare to bargain with me?"

"You want to prevent a horrendous scandal—"

"I want to prevent murder! You know Richard of Gloucester's temper and towering pride. He would take it as a personal insult from the crown. His quarrel with the prince could end in death for one of them."

"If I swear I will be silent . . . will you release me from the betrothal agreement?"

He took hold of her shoulders with powerful hands. "No, Rosamond, I will never let you go. I will have you at any cost!"

The appalled look on her face scorched his pride. His knighthood and high royal office seemed to mean nothing to her. "Why do you not wish to marry me?" he demanded.

"Why must I be forced to honor a promise I gave when I was twelve?" she countered defiantly. Rosamond knew she did not want to be uprooted from her serene life at Kenilworth. The dark man who towered above her both frightened and fascinated her, though she would not openly admit it. If she placed her fortune and her future in this man's hands, she would lose control over her own destiny.

"Spend time with me . . . allow me to court you . . . I will soon change your mind, chérie," he promised persuasively.

She felt the heavy oaken door against her back and was forcibly reminded of the sexual encounter she had overheard. For one blinding moment, she thought Rodger de Leyburn would sweep her into his arms, take possession of her mouth, and dare her to defy him then! All her senses were heightened as she became aware of his strength, his masculine scent, and his ruthless determination. Her heartbeat accelerated and she began to pant in anticipation of what was to come. When he removed his hands from her shoulders, she swayed toward him, then steadied herself with a hand against his chest. Her thoughts and her emotions were in total disarray. What the devil was the matter with her? She prayed it was the wine on an empty stomach that made her thoughts so fanciful. When he opened the tower door for her, Rosamond fled through it.

Hoping not to awaken Demi, she entered her bedchamber quietly, although her heart was pounding. She undressed in the dark, laying the cloak and her tunic across the bottom of the bed, and slipped beneath the covers. As the events of the evening replayed themselves in her mind, Rosamond trembled with humiliation and anger, most of it directed at herself. Why was she so headstrong, so impulsive? Why had she gone to Rodger's chambers? Her tranquility was shattered, her peace of mind destroyed. If only she could turn back time and start the evening all over again, she would put on her prettiest gown and gladly go down to the Great Hall for dinner. Rosamond didn't want to know anyone's secrets, least of all the prince's. Resolving to put Rodger, Alyce, and Edward out of her mind, she escaped into blissful sleep.

Slowly she became aware of his masculine scent. "No!" she breathed. He swept her into his arms and took possession of the mouth that dared to deny him. When she struggled, he pressed her back, imprisoning her against the hard oaken door. Then he slid a hard, muscular thigh between her legs and deepened the kiss until she stopped struggling and clung to him. It was forcibly brought home to her that she had no defense against his powerful strength. Only when he had mastered her resistance did he lift his mouth from hers.

As she looked up into his intense green gaze, she realized how pleasurable it was to feel the hard door pressing against her bottom, and to feel his hard length pressing against her belly.

"Say it again," she whispered.

"I will never let you go, Rosamond. I will have you at any cost." He gazed deeply into her eyes.

Excitement rose within her. He wanted her not just for tonight, but forever. He wanted to marry her, not for just her castles, but for herself! How delicious it was to keep him waiting, keep him begging, keep him aching for the consummation. Her fingers traced across the pulse beating in his throat, then up across his lips. He had the most beautiful, demanding mouth she had ever seen. Surely it could not lie to her? He had pledged that he wanted her for herself alone, not her Marshal inheritance, and more than anything in the world she longed to believe him, longed to have someone love her.

Rosamond caught her breath on a shiver. She was intoxicated with the nearness of him and swept her lashes to her cheeks lest he see the wild desire she was feeling. His hands moved up her body, then his fingers slid into her hair to hold her captive for his mouth's ravishing. His lips claimed hers with such ferocity, Rosamond was lost, lost. She opened her mouth, welcoming his thrusting sleek tongue deep inside. Then she rubbed her woman's center against his hard body until she could feel the heat of him. "I am no longer an ice maiden in need of a thawing . . . love me, Rod, love me!"

When Rosamond opened her eyes in the morning, her dream still lingered. As she recalled all the sensual details, she was shocked by her wanton feelings for Rodger de Leyburn. How could she have allowed him to kiss her and touch her intimately, even in a dream? Rosamond denied that she found him attractive and put the blame on last night's actual events, as the memory came flooding back to her. She blushed deeply, covered with shame for the sexual encounter she had overheard. That the lovers were Lord Edward and Alyce de Clare made it a thousand times worse, shocking her beyond belief. She took refuge in anger; it was all that devil de Leyburn's fault that she had accidentally learned of the scandalous affair!

Rosamond did not want to share this shameful secret with him, nor share anything else, despite the fact that she had found him attractive in her dream. Blood of God, if he had his way, she would soon be sharing his bed, sharing his life! As her eyes fell on the purple garment at the foot of her bed, her blush deepened. Whatever had possessed her to conceal herself with the cloak and go to his chamber at midnight? It was time she stopped behaving recklessly and acted with reason and resolve. She would go to the one person who would help her, the lady who had been both mother and guardian angel to her since she was a child. Rodger de Leyburn was no match for Countess Eleanor de Montfort!

"Lady Eleanor, may I speak with you about something that has been deeply troubling me?" Rosamond dipped a curtsy, and the chatelaine of Kenilworth, who had just finished breaking her fast and was about to leave the hall, sat back down at the table.

Eleanor patted the seat beside her. "It's about your betrothal, isn't it, Rosamond?"

"Yes! How did you guess?"

"You wish to end the betrothal and marry."

"Yes . . . no! I want to end the betrothal, Lady Eleanor, but I do not wish to marry!"

"Rosamond, dearest, you are seventeen, quite old enough to be a wife. You have learned your lessons well and will make not only a beautiful bride but a most efficient chatelaine."

"I don't want to wed Rodger de Leyburn; I don't want to leave Kenilworth."

"Oh dear, I'm afraid we've sheltered you too much from the world. I should have encouraged you to visit your own properties more often, so you could take a hand in running them. I fully understand that Kenilworth became your refuge when you were a young girl, but now you are a grown woman. I want to see you spread your wings and take your rightful place in the world."

"Rodger de Leyburn wants only my Marshal inheritance!"

"Rosamond, that is not true. As Lord Edward's steward, Sir Rodger is a wealthy man in his own right. If the thought of becoming part of the royal household intimidates you, put your worries aside. Ancient Westminster Palace allows you to live right in the city of London, and Windsor Castle is a wondrous place with many newly built towers right on the River Thames."

"It is *Sir Rodger* who intimidates me," Rosamond blurted.

"Rosamond dearest, Sir Rodger took breakfast with me this morning. He sang your praises to the high heavens and is obviously besotted with you. Take my advice and don't hold out against marriage as I did with Earl Simon. It will do you no good; a man as determined as he will have his way at any cost."

"Goddamn the man!" Rosamond cursed. "The devious devil got to you before I did. He is not in the least besotted."

"Rosamond, you haven't the faintest idea how lovely you are. Your hair is the most glorious shade of gold, and your eyes are like violets. You remind me of a long-legged gazelle I once saw in the Arabian desert. Your explosive reaction to Rod tells me you are not indifferent to him, by any means. A clever woman like you should be able to wrap him around your little finger. Learn your feminine power, Rosamond, then don't be afraid to use it!"

FOUR

During the next week, Simon de Montfort and Edward Plantagenet spent every waking moment in each other's company. Clearly, Earl Simon was trying to woo the prince to side with the barons. He was a persuasive man who focused on his goal single-mindedly, and as the days passed, the two powerful men, one dark, the other fair, found they had a great deal in common. Both were big men with abundant energy and driving ambition. They could hunt all day, then stay up all night discussing weapons, warfare, and military maneuvers. With great enthusiasm they organized training exercises for their men-at-arms and personally demonstrated the best way to wield a broadsword, mace, or battle-ax.

Simon pointed out that the leadership qualities required to direct men in battle were similar to those needed to lead a country. It took courage, foresight, strategy, determination, tenacity, generalship, and an unswerving belief in your own destiny. Lord Edward had these qualities in abundance, and Simon recognized, too, that the prince was developing a shrewdness as keen as his own. De Montfort was an ambitious man who knew Edward had the qualities of leadership. How long would it be before Lord Edward exercised his shining magnetism and royal aura to draw men to do his bidding and transfer their loyalty from Simon to himself? Before

Edward recognized his full power, de Montfort wanted him to sign a solemn oath that he would abide by the Provisions of Oxford.

To this end, Earl Simon sought out Rodger de Leyburn, another shrewd young man, but one who was passionate about the baronial cause. "Rod, you are closer to Edward than any other of his captains. Am I right in thinking him persuaded to our cause?"

"He would like to heal the rift between the barons and the royalists, because he knows it would be best for the country. Continual hostility leads to the people's discontent and enmity. He has no objection to Parliament meeting on a regular basis to enforce the laws of the land and discuss state problems. He hopes a stronger government will solve problems, not create them. He now agrees with you that the king's advisers should be Englishmen of vision who will follow wise policies, encourage trade alliances, and veto expensive foreign wars that drain the treasury."

"I too think he will not oppose the Provisions, but I need more," Simon said. "Before Parliament convenes at Candlemas, I would like his signature swearing that he will *abide* by the Provisions."

"I will use whatever influence I have, Earl Simon."

"You are a good man, Rod. Have you set that wedding date yet?"

Rodger laughed ruefully. "There is a problem; my betrothed has no interest in marrying me. Lady Eleanor advises me not to take no for an answer, but it seems to be the only word Rosamond wants to say to me."

Simon threw back his head and laughed. "You think that a problem? Have you any idea of the obstacles I had to overcome? Eleanor had taken a vow of chastity, so we wed in secret. When the marriage was discovered, the church declared it invalid. I had no choice but to go to Rome and bribe the Pope! All you need do is persuade one small female!" Simon clapped Rod on the back. "If all else fails, surely you know the tried-and-true method of changing a lady's answer from no to yes? Get her with child!"

Rosamond found the Demoiselle in the stillroom, where she was crushing some red berries to add to the wax of the Yuletide candles she intended to mold. The air was redolent with the piquant fragrance as Rosamond took a deep breath and announced, "I have decided to journey to my property of Pershore." She wanted to get away from Rodger de Leyburn, and her conversation with Lady Eleanor about her own properties had provided her with the perfect solution. It was obvious that her guardian welcomed and approved of her imminent marriage to Sir Rodger de Leyburn, which greatly disappointed her. But Rosamond stubbornly refused to resign herself to the arranged marriage. A visit to Pershore would delay the nuptials and give her time to find a way to put an end to the betrothal.

Demi lifted the pestle from the mortar and stared at her friend. "Has Mother given her permission?"

"It was she who suggested it," Rosamond said airily, assuring herself it was only a tiny lie. "She reminded me that I am a grown woman and should take a hand in running my own properties."

"I suppose that is so. How exciting for you! Pershore must be close to twenty miles away. Will you also visit your castle of Deerhurst?"

Rosamond lowered her lashes to hide the stab of pain she felt. Deerhurst Castle had belonged to Giles, and she hadn't been there since her brother's death. It was now hers, of course, but she didn't think she could face going there. "I doubt there will be time if I am to return to Kenilworth in time for the holy days of Christmastide."

"Oh, you must be back in time for the feasting and celebrations, because I heard a whisper that we might be going to London after the Yuletide!"

"Of course," Rosamond said thoughtfully as her mind darted about like quicksilver, "there is to be a Parliament at Candlemas." Lord Edward and his knights would soon depart for London; perhaps they would be gone before she returned from Pershore . . . if she lingered there.

That night Rosamond wore a fetching gown of carnation red velvet and sought out her cousin Richard de Clare in the Great Hall. She had learned that when a woman wanted a favor from a man, she was far more likely to get it if she looked her prettiest. She spotted him quickly and made her way to his table. "May I sit with you tonight, my lord?"

"It would be my pleasure, sweeting. You have grown unearthly fair, Rosamond; what is it you want from me? No, no, don't protest, when a woman seeks out a man, she always wants *something.*"

She gifted him with a dazzling smile. Though he was in his mid-thirties and a good twelve years older than his half-brother Harry, Richard had inherited the Marshal looks of his mother, Isabella, and was still a handsome man. "I am traveling to my property of Pershore and need an escort," she said.

"Well, that's an easy enough favor to grant. I have knights and men-at-arms returning to Gloucester every day, who pass close by Pershore."

"Thank you, Richard, I knew I could count on you. Please don't tell Harry, he will blab it to that devil de Leyburn."

"Oho, a lover's quarrel, eh?"

"Yes," Rosamond said faintly, "something like that."

At that particular moment, the devil's green eyes were upon her. Though the Great Hall of Kenilworth held over two hundred tonight, Sir Rodger had seen her the moment she arrived. Not only was she the tallest female present, she was the only one with a glorious mass of golden hair. When she walked a direct path to Richard of Gloucester, Rod held his breath. *She wouldn't dare be so reckless*, he told himself fiercely. He leaned over to Lord Edward and spoke briefly. Edward summoned the squire standing behind his carved chair and sent the youth hot-foot with a message for Gloucester.

"Lord Edward begs the pleasure of the lady's company, my lord."

Rosamond overheard and hissed, "Edward never begs, he commands."

Richard grinned. "And a command from a prince cannot be ignored; royalty has its privileges, you know."

Rosamond closed her eyes and felt the color drain from her cheeks. *Blood of God, Richard, you have no idea!*

When she arrived at the head table, a place had been set for her between Edward and his steward. As Rod gallantly rose and held her chair, Lord Edward's blue eyes glittered with amusement. "Sir Rodger craves the pleasure of your company."

"The pleasure is all *his*." Rosamond darted a swift glance of annoyance at the dark face beside her, and suddenly she realized why she had been summoned away from Gloucester. "Give me credit for some intelligence, my lord."

"Beauty, intelligence, and a temper of fire are a combustible combination."

"Aye, come too close and you'll get burned!"

Rod immediately took up her challenge by covering her hand with his. Rosamond wanted to jab the point of her dinner knife into his hand, but controlled the impulse and instead pinched him hard, drawing blood with her fingernails. He didn't even wince at the pain, but his green eyes narrowed dangerously. "You are too impulsive for your own good. It is time you were tamed." Desire flared in his eyes and his groin, and he made no effort to conceal it.

"Would you like the job?" she taunted, tossing back her hair.

Lord Edward dipped his head to murmur in her ear. "Rosamond, I can hear every word of your byplay."

She flashed him a defiant look. "*We* have no secrets to hide." The moment it was out of her mouth, she could have bitten off her tongue. She felt Rod squeeze her fingers until they hurt, but knew she deserved the warning to watch her impulsive tongue.

He smoothly changed the subject to save her. "Tomorrow should prove entertaining if you watch from the castle ramparts. Earl Simon has proposed our men-at-arms swim the mere in full armor."

"Will you be joining them?"

"Of course."

"Good! A plunge in freezing water might be just the cure for that swelling." She laughed wickedly, then added, "On your hand."

Rodger de Leyburn was damned if he'd let her have the last word. He had made inquiries about a knight called Rickard and learned it could be none other than Sir Rickard de Burgh, whose wealthy Irish family owned everything west of the River Shannon. When his squire, Griffin, had brought him the information, a burning streak of envy had ripped through him. Envy for such a father and such vast estates. Rosamond Marshal had been breathless just speaking the man's name, and he burned with jealousy.

"Your knight-errant, Sir Rickard de Burgh, has returned to Ireland, I understand."

She drew in a swift breath. "Ireland?"

As he watched her his eyes burned with green fire. "Something about a wedding. The bride is Irish, of course. I suppose it's only natural to marry in one's homeland."

No, no, it cannot be! It cannot be! Rosamond felt as if a cruel hand were squeezing her heart, and she feared it would not stop until it burst. She sat there drowning in misery, oblivious to everything about her, aware only of the pain within. Her throat closed tightly so that she could not speak, could not even breathe. Tears scalded the back of her eyelids, and the roar inside her ears was deafening.

Rodger watched Rosamond closely and saw her emotional turmoil. He had relished giving her the news, but now felt a prick of guilt for upsetting her. He contemplated offering a word of comfort, then crushed down the impulse. He'd be damned if he would encourage his future bride to harbor feelings for another man, especially the redoubtable Rickard de Burgh.

Rosamond did not know how long she sat there before she regained her senses, but she saw with relief that the tables were being cleared. She fought the compulsion to flee as long as she could, but she knew she must get away or go mad. As if she were in a trance, she arose from the table, curtsied to Lord Edward, and glided from the Great Hall.

Even when she was safely back in her bedchamber, the compulsion to flee remained. Rosamond decided on the spot that she would leave for Pershore at dawn. Tomorrow would be a perfect time to escape Kenilworth, because everyone's attention would be riveted on the mere. She finally told Nan about the visit to Pershore, and they stayed up late packing. She would put off asking Lady Eleanor's permission until dawn, for Rosamond knew she could face no one else tonight. When at last the packing was done, she crawled into bed, emotionally spent, and fell into a dreamless sleep.

Rosamond's agony was still full blown at first light, when she sought out the countess to reveal her plans. She knew that Eleanor was pleased at her initiative. She also seemed secretly amused. *She knows I'm running away,* Rosamond thought. *She thinks I'm running away from Rodger de Leyburn, and she's right . . . but I'm also running away from myself and the anguish I feel! I cannot bear the fact that Sir Rickard is to marry, yet I cannot stay at Kenilworth, drowning in self-pity. I must get away! If only I could be someone else for a while, until the pain in my heart stops.*

"Be sure to take a groom, dearest, and any other servants you need. I'm sure your bedding and a supply of fresh linen will not come amiss."

Because the men returning to Gloucester set off at an early hour, the travelers expected to reach Pershore just before noon. During the entire ride, Rosamond was lost in deep, pensive thought. How could she have been foolish enough to fall in love with Sir Rickard de Burgh? Granted, he was the ideal knight, one any maiden would sigh over, but how ridiculous she had been to form more than a passing infatuation for the handsome Irish warrior.

To love someone was to lose them; it had ever been thus! When would she learn her lesson? She had guarded her heart so well, whatever had possessed her to let down her defenses? Had Demi been right? Did she secretly long for love? If so, she must put an end to such fancy immediately, for love's only reward was heartbreak! And Rosamond knew well that a woman could die from heartbreak. It had happened to her mother, when her father was killed in battle. As she rode along, Rosamond resolved to build an iron carapace around her heart, but it did not lessen the pain she felt over Sir Rickard de Burgh's marriage. She knew only time could do that.

The travelers arrived at their destination at the hour of noon. Rosamond offered the knight in charge of the men-at-arms Pershore's hospitality, but he declined, explaining that they wanted to reach Gloucester before dark. She thanked the knight warmly for his escort, then she and Nan, along with a young groom leading a pair of pack-horses, rode through the gates of Pershore.

In the bailey, hens and geese flapped and squawked as two mangy-looking dogs chased them. Four men sat about a cask of ale with tankards in their hands. They stared at Rosamond openmouthed, but none rose to his feet to aid the travelers, nor showed the least respect for the mistress of Pershore. Rosamond was furious. "Who is in charge here?"

After a moment, one of the men got to his feet, but when he staggered, Rosamond realized with horror that he was drunk . . . they were all drunk! "You filthy, idle sots, I am Rosamond Marshal! Where is my steward?" When there was no reply, she dismounted and handed the reins of her beloved white palfrey, Nimbus, to the groom. "Ned, take the horses to the stables and feed and water them while I rout out my bloody steward!"

She found him gorging himself in the dining hall along with the entire household of inside servants. Both the quality and the quantity of the food and wine on the tables astounded her. These people had as many dishes before them at noon as the people of Kenilworth and their noble guests had at an evening banquet. The steward arose, obviously annoyed to have his dinner interrupted. He was a thickset man, whose face looked like lumpy porridge, but his tunic was made of the finest velvet, and he wore a gold chain. He eyed Rosamond and Nan insolently. "State your business."

Rosamond drew herself up to her full height and lifted her chin. "I am Rosamond Marshal, come to inspect my property, sir, and what I find displeases me!"

"That's too bad. I am in full authority here."

"I am the mistress of Pershore!"

"I am Dymock, master of Pershore. You are nothing more than a young girl with her middle-aged nurse in tow. You don't seriously think you can come in here and start tossing out orders?"

"Just watch me, Master Dymock . . . I dismiss you from my service for your insolence!"

He laughed derisively. "Well, Lady Muck of Turd Hall, you can't dismiss me. I was appointed by the Earl of Gloucester to manage Pershore as I see fit. I've had no complaints from that quarter in the three years I've been in charge here."

At that moment, Rosamond's groom came seeking her in the hall. "My lady, the stables are filthy; the stalls cannot have been cleaned out in months. The stableman refused me fodder, and it is no fit place to shelter our horses."

She gasped in outrage at his blackening eye. "Did the bastard strike you, Ned?" She slashed her riding crop against her boot. "I shall come and see the conditions for myself. In the meantime, Master Dymock, you will see that this lady is served lunch. Sit down, Nan; this might take me a little while."

As Rosamond entered the stables, the acrid stench of manure and urine-soaked straw hit her full force. She hesitated for only a moment, then, pinching her nostrils closed, she strode inside. She found the place as filthy as Ned had described it. There were only a half-dozen horses stabled, but it appeared that when their six stalls had been fouled to a depth of two feet, the animals had been moved to other stalls, where the cycle was repeated. Rosamond was furious at the condition of the stables, and cursed herself for bringing only one groom, when Lady Eleanor had offered her as many servants as she wanted.

Summoning her authority, she spoke to the only stableman present, a burly lout with a red face. "I am Rosamond Marshal, and Pershore belongs to me. First, I want you to understand that I will not tolerate you abusing my groom. I have five horses, including my two pack animals, that need food, water, and shelter."

"Dymock would have my balls if I gave your animals fodder." He stood before the oat bins with arms folded across his barrel chest. Rosamond was so angry, she raised her riding crop, but he snatched it away from her with a beefy hand. "You'll find yourself on your arse in the horseshit, and he'll have another black eye, unless you get the hell out of my stable."

"You filthy swine, I hope you suffocate in this stench! Come, Ned, I'll help you draw water from the well for our animals."

"I'll do it, my lady . . . I'm sorry I was no match for him."

"I shall help you, Ned; I must work off my anger

before it chokes me. I am beginning to realize a female has no authority whatever. Even though I own every inch of land, and every stick and stone upon it, the men will not take orders from me. In the name of God, how does Lady Eleanor manage to run Kenilworth?"

"Begging your pardon, my lady, she doesn't do it in the name of God, she does it in the name of Simon de Montfort. If a lady has a man of strength and power behind her, all run to do her bidding."

Digesting the truth of his words, Rosamond carried a wooden bucket of water to Nimbus. "We'll have to tether the horses in the meadow behind the stable, Ned. The night will be cold, but at least they'll be able to forage the stubble from the hay crop. We shall leave tomorrow!"

When they had done all they could for their horses, Rosamond helped Ned carry in their own luggage. Then she bade him follow her into the dining hall so they could eat. Dymock was nowhere in sight, but the rest of the servants were still at the table. Nan was sitting exactly where she had left her, but Rosamond could clearly see she had been served no food. It was the last straw. Her temper exploded.

She strode over to the head table with the light of battle in her eyes. "I have taken all the abuse I am going to take." She raised her arm and swept everything from the table to the floor. Molded jellies were awash with gravy, and giblets floated about in a river of spilled wine, while pewter plates and goblets rolled across the flagstone floor. "If *we* don't eat, *you* don't eat!"

Rosamond headed toward Pershore's kitchen, summoning Nan and Ned to follow her. The cook had three chins and her red face branded her the twin of the brute in the stables. "This is my kitchen. Get out!" the cook ordered insolently. Rosamond grabbed a long-handled ladle made of heavy copper and brandished it with intent to maim. "Stand back, you fat bitch, or I will spit you over your own fire and render you down to a tub of lard. We will feed ourselves, which certainly won't be hard with the amount of food lying about this kitchen. I have never seen such willful waste in my life! Nan, prepare three plates for us. Ned, fill that basket with cheese, fruit, and wine; we'll take it upstairs for later." Rosamond picked up a meat skewer and prodded the cook's belly. "Your days of ruling the roost in my kitchen are numbered. Now, get out of my sight, you're ruining my appetite."

When they ventured into the rest of Pershore, they found neglect of every kind. The chambers were filthy and damp, the furnishings rotted and dilapidated, except for the cozy rooms occupied by the servants. The rest of the dwelling had been left without fires, and the dampness had mildewed the hangings and even the stone walls.

It took the three of them all afternoon to make a bedchamber with an alcove habitable. Ned chopped and hauled up wood for the fire. Nan helped Rosamond lift a couple of mattresses before the flames, then she scrubbed the wooden floor, while her mistress washed the mildew from the walls and cleaned the windows. "Thank the saints in heaven that Lady Eleanor suggested I bring my own linen; I vow I shall never travel without it from this day forth. Ned, you will have to sleep in the alcove; I'm afraid we won't be safe unless we all stay together."

They ate supper in the chamber, before the fire, then Rosamond lit a couple of scented candles she'd brought. "We have no choice but to return to Kenilworth tomorrow. When I report the dreadful conditions at Pershore to my cousin Richard, I'm sure he will look into it for me. He can have little idea what's been going on here." She looked at her companions. "Thank you both so much for helping me. I feel wretched about this."

"It's not your fault, my lamb. I think I packed warm

quilted bed-gowns for us, and we'll need them in this place. You look tired to death. Let's all get some rest; we've a long ride tomorrow."

As Rosamond lay watching the shadows flicker on the wall, she was angry with herself. Though Nan had been kind enough to declare it wasn't her fault, Rosamond knew she must take the blame for what she had found here at Pershore. She was the one who had neglected her lovely property, content to allow others to administer her Marshal lands and holdings, while she stayed safe, happy, and oblivious at her haven of Kenilworth.

Rosamond did not dare let go of her anger, for once she did, she would sink into despair. Never in her life had she felt so helpless, useless, and insignificant. A young, unwed female had less authority than one of the mangy dogs in the bailey. Even they had a measure of control over the geese they chased. The last thing she wanted to do was run back to Kenilworth in defeat, crying for help, but she knew she had no choice but to swallow her pride.

Rosamond furiously told herself to hang on for just a few more hours, that things always looked better in the light of day. The lump in her throat almost choked her. Last night, thoughts of Sir Rickard de Burgh had left her heartbroken. Tonight, Pershore made her feel as if her spirit was close to breaking.

FIVE

At Kenilworth, most of the day was taken up by military exercises in and around the mere. It was discovered that some soldiers could not even swim, so that was the first lesson that had to be taught. Lord Edward and Sir Rodger noticed that the men from Wales had little trouble after long hours in the water, and questioned their Welsh squires.

Griffin, who was not short and dark like most Welshmen, but tall and fair, grinned at Rod. "There are so many wild rivers in Wales that if you didn't learn to swim across raging waters, you'd drown. It's as simple as that!"

"I admire their skill with the longbow too," Lord Edward said, shrugging off his hauberk. "I intend to become expert at it, and I've ordered that some of these six-foot bows be made for my Gascons; I believe them superior weapons to their crossbows."

Rod laughed. "They are only superior if they are shot by expert longbowmen."

Both Griffin and Owen, Lord Edward's squire, agreed. "It takes years of experience, my lord."

"Then we'd best get started," Edward said, grinning. "Get some hay bales set up as targets in yon field beyond the mere, and I'll ask Simon to loan us a troop of his Welsh archers to teach us how it's done."

"Edward, because it seldom happens to you, you

forget that men tire," Rod protested. "Our men have struggled through freezing water for hours today. Cannot the archery lesson wait until the morrow?" He removed his heavy hauberk and handed it to Griffin.

Edward roared with laughter. "Soft, the lot of you!" He peeled off his wet linen shirt, and Rod followed suit. Suddenly a great female cheer went up from the ramparts of Kenilworth, and the two bare-chested males lifted their eyes to observe their admirers. "Well, I'll be damned," Lord Edward said, "do you suppose I could have my pick, Rod?"

"I have no doubt of that whatsoever, my lord." Rod frowned. Where the devil was his beautiful ice maiden? Surely she could have let her guard down long enough to come and watch him traverse the cold mere, if only to rejoice in his discomfort. What would it take to chip through her frozen exterior? Her interior would be hot enough, if her temper was any indication. Suddenly, in spite of his clinging wet chausses, his cock began to swell and harden.

Edward glanced down with wry amusement at his friend's erection. "Show-off! I'm shriveled to the size of a worm."

Rod chuckled. "A one-eyed snake perhaps, never a worm, Edward."

A few hours later as Rod entered the hall, he was looking forward to supping with Rosamond. He was starting to suspect she enjoyed exchanging barbs with him, if only to sharpen her claws. He held out hope all through the first course, knowing she was quite capable of being late purposely, just to keep him waiting. When Alyce de Clare noticed his inattention to her, she began to pout prettily and thought up ways to plague him. Alyce usually amused Rod, but tonight she simply annoyed him.

When the meal was over and the tables were being cleared, Rod sought out Lady Eleanor and her daughter Demoiselle. "The fair Rosamond is avoiding me, I fear. Could you not persuade her to dine in the hall tonight, ladies?"

Eleanor gave him a sideways glance. "Ah, that would prove rather difficult, I'm afraid, Sir Rodger. Rosamond will be dining at Pershore tonight."

"Mother! She didn't want anyone to know," Demi protested.

"Nonsense. A lady runs for the sheer pleasure of being pursued . . . at least I always did."

Rod thanked Lady Eleanor. She was more than hinting; she was giving her tacit approval for him to join her ward at Pershore and look over the property that would soon be his. It would also give them a chance to be alone together. He could not leave tonight, because he knew Edward needed him to be there until long past midnight, but come dawn, Rod knew nothing would hold him at Kenilworth.

Sir Rodger told Griffin to be ready to ride at first light, then retired to his chamber to pack. When Edward arrived in the Warwick Tower, Rod explained his plan.

"Ha, the fiery wench has decided to lead you a merry chase. This is somewhat of a departure from your usual easy conquests, my friend. Perhaps you've met your match!"

"I think perhaps it is Rosamond who has met her match, my lord."

"Splendor of God, you are looking forward to this battle of the sexes, unless I miss my mark."

"I am," Rod conceded with a wolfish grin. "I know who the victor will be!"

"You ruthless devil, you desert me without a thought, caring little if I die of night starvation."

"You'll survive, my lord. I'm not leaving until dawn, which will give you ample time for one or two jousts."

Close on midnight, when Rod opened his chamber door to admit Alyce, he was in a playful mood. "What makes you think Edward is up to it tonight after spending most of the day in freezing water?"

"You are teasing me, chéri. I too can play games." She stood on tiptoe to kiss him, then deliberately cupped his cock with her hand and felt it harden. Her lips caressed his ear as she whispered, "Anytime Edward is not up to it, I know you can give me satisfaction. Never forget I chose you first, my beautiful Rod."

He playfully slapped her bottom and ushered her toward the inner door. If he had resisted her charms when she was an overripe virgin of sixteen, he surely had no difficulty resisting her now. Rod stripped and lay down on his bed in the darkness, glad of the cold night air that blew through the arrow slits of the Warwick Tower to cool his flesh. In spite of his exhausting day, sleep did not come. He could dimly hear the love play coming from the adjoining chamber, and he tossed restlessly as he tried to mentally block the arousing sounds. At first, it seemed impossible, until he began to think about Rosamond Marshal.

Her image came to him full blown, exactly as he had last seen her in the carnation red velvet. Her eyes were dark violet, fringed with long golden lashes, her cheeks were sun-kissed, and her mouth was the same luscious, bright red as her gown. He watched the tip of her tongue lick her top lip, then the full bottom lip, and he felt a surge of blood rush into his cock. Her glorious hair caressed her shoulders, then fell down her back, brushing her waist and curling about her hips. She knew the silky, waving mass attracted him, for she deliberately tossed it behind a saucy shoulder, then bent forward so that it spilled over her breasts, possessively touching and taunting.

Her full-throated laughter was like music to his ears. It was provocative and sensual and whenever he heard it, he wanted her in bed beneath him, laughing up at him, no matter what he did to her. A tempting laugh was one of the most arousing gifts a woman could bring to a man's bed. He could hear her wicked laughter now. *A plunge in freezing water might be just the cure for that swelling.*

His phallus jerked. *A plunge is definitely the cure for my swelling, but I prefer your honey pot.* Her scent of roses and almonds floated in the air about him, and he suddenly had a wild desire to taste her. He closed his eyes and his mouth was filled with the luscious juice of an apricot. He felt his balls tighten pleasurably, and he felt his pulse beating in his throat and in the soles of his feet.

He had tantalized himself long enough. He knew he must undress her and touch her all over or go mad. He wrapped his arms around her, unfastened the back of her gown, and watched the carnation velvet pool about her feet. Christ, he had no idea she would be this lovely. Her breasts were perfect, her high mons was covered by golden tendrils, and her legs were the longest he'd ever seen. Suddenly the ache in his groin became unbearable, and he was in agony. With a foul curse, he flung himself from the bed and snatched up a wine jug. He paced across the chamber floor, tipping back the jug, trying to quell the insatiable desire her image had aroused in him.

At Pershore, Rosamond and Nan awoke to Ned's snores. They didn't awaken him until they had dressed, packed up their quilted bed-gowns, and folded their bedding. The three of them broke their fast with the bread, fruit, and wine that was left in the basket. Rosamond knew she would have to face the insolent servants once again before she left, because there was no way her pride would let her leave without speaking her mind and giving them fair warning of the dire consequences they could expect in the very near future.

She went directly to the kitchen and was appalled at the conditions she found. Dirty cooking utensils from yesterday were stacked waiting to be washed, and food had been left uncovered to spoil and attract vermin. The cook was nowhere in sight, but a pale young scullery maid was trying to light the kitchen fire. "Where is the cook?" Rosamond demanded.

"She's in bed, ma'am," the girl answered in a frightened voice.

"But it's almost nine," Rosamond protested.

"She never rises afore ten, ma'am," the girl whispered.

"What is your name?" Rosamond realized the girl was terrified of authority, even hers.

"Edna," she murmured, wiping her hands nervously on her dirty smock.

"Well, Edna, this kitchen needs a thorough cleaning. Is that your job?" she asked, not unkindly.

"Yes, ma'am. That's why I'm lightin' the fire, so I can boil the water."

"When you knew things were left undone from last night, you should have started earlier."

"I did, ma'am," she said faintly. "I had to gather wood from the forest, then get water from the well."

"You shouldn't have to get firewood or haul water, Edna, there should be kitchen boys for that. Are you the only scullery maid at Pershore?"

Edna nodded warily. "I'm not complainin', please, ma'am."

"I can clearly see you are terrified of the fat bitch, but I promise you, Edna, that things are going to change around here."

Rosamond went into the larder to get food for their journey. She wrapped up a few capon legs and a loaf of bread, and directed Nan to bring some apples and two bottles of red wine. As they entered the hall, the steward was descending the stairs.

Though she feared him, she did not dare show it. "We are leaving, Master Dymock, but let me warn you that your days of authority here at Pershore are numbered. I intend to report you to my cousin, the Earl of Gloucester; I have a full catalog of your deficiencies as steward, and your insolence to me!"

Dymock threw her such an amused, mocking glance that Rosamond suddenly felt uneasy. What did he know that she did not? She swept past him with the hauteur of a countess, though inside she felt more unsure of herself than the little scullery maid.

When Rosamond stepped outside, the cold air in the bailey took her breath away. The temperature had plummeted in the night, and her heart suddenly went out to their horses, tethered in the meadow. She pulled her cloak more tightly about her and said, "We'll give the poor animals those apples, Nan."

They crossed the bailey and skirted the stables, but when they came in view of the field, their horses were nowhere in sight. Rosamond swung round to see the stableman watching them, his beefy arms folded in satisfaction.

"Where are our horses?" Rosamond demanded, abject fear waging a battle with anger inside her breast.

The brute shrugged. "Stolen maybe."

For one moment, anger won out. "Stolen by you and that swine Dymock, I warrant!" The next moment, ice-cold fear wiped out her anger. Without horses, they were trapped here, at the mercy of these ruthless men. They had disposed of her and her servants' mounts, what was to stop them from disposing of them?

"Oh, my lamb, whatever are we to do?" Nan cried.

"I'll check inside the stable, my lady." Ned set down the bags he carried and pushed past the ruddy-faced stableman, courageously risking another black eye. When he emerged, the droop of his shoulders told its own story.

Rosamond felt weak at the knees, but she knew they must get away by any means possible. Though she was racked with worry for Nimbus, she had to deal with the pressing problem of their own safety. "We will have to walk, we are not staying here. We must leave the luggage and find the main road. I'm sure I remember our passing a village a few miles from here." Rosamond spoke with as much confidence as she could muster, hoping it masked the despair that was threatening to overwhelm her.

After they'd walked about a mile, Rosamond's heels had blistered and her feet hurt, but at least she could still feel them, which was not the case with her fingers. They seemed as cold and numb as her heart. Suddenly a horse and rider appeared on the road some distance away. Rosamond feared she was hallucinating, then seeing double, as one horse became two. Only when Ned pointed them out did she finally believe they were real. As the lead horse galloped closer, her heart filled with hope. Could it be Sir Rickard de Burgh, her knight in shining armor, come to rescue her?

As the dark horse and rider drew closer, a wave of stark terror swept over Rosamond, snatching her breath away. She turned and began to run, knowing instinctively they would pursue her. Relentlessly! The rider was faceless, all she knew was that he was dark, but it was the horse she feared most. It was huge, black, and terrifying.

An icy shiver slithered down her spine. Her pale golden hair tumbled wildly about her shoulders as she pulled her skirts high, baring long, slim legs in a desperate attempt to escape the cruel hooves. Her lungs felt as if they would burst as she gasped for just one more breath that would carry her to safety. Her pulse hammered inside her eardrums, deafening her as she turned to look over her shoulder. Rosamond's eyes widened in horror and a scream was torn from her throat as she saw the black forelegs rise above her, then helplessly she tumbled beneath the murderous hooves.

Rodger de Leyburn leaned down from his saddle and swept up Rosamond Marshal in his powerful arms. He realized that for some reason she was fleeing in terror. He lifted off his helm so she could recognize him, but to his dismay felt her become limp as she lay in his arms in a dead faint. "Bones of God, what are you doing trudging down the road like vagabonds?"

Ned told him about their horses and the stableman at Pershore, then Nan described in graphic detail the condition of Rosamond's property and the vile reception she had received at the hands of Dymock the steward. As he listened in disbelief, his rage soared higher with every word they uttered. Rod looked down at the woman cradled in his arms and watched her lashes flutter, then rise.

"Sir Rodger," she whispered with relief.

His green eyes blazed with anger. "Why did you flee from me?"

"I . . . I did not realize it was you. I feared your huge black stallion, I was terrified that it would trample me. I felt so utterly powerless, just as I did at Pershore, where they showed me how completely vulnerable and insignificant I am."

Rod stared down at her. He had no idea she had a fear of horses, no notion that she feared anything. She had always managed to give the impression of cool courage, which he admired. Now he admired her even more, for it was obviously a carefully constructed facade she used for self-protection. It came to him in a flash that she had revealed her weakness and he now held the key that would unlock the guarded door behind which she hid her thoughts and her emotions.

Rodger de Leyburn was a brilliant student of human nature. His lessons had begun of necessity, while he was still a pageboy. It had allowed him to survive, and then thrive. He now possessed the ability to affect, persuade, control, or even dominate those about him without alienating them in any way. He was such a master of manipulation that those about him had a deep and genuine affection for him. Sir Rodger now had a mission to make Rosamond Marshal respond to him, and the task would be amazingly simple. All he had to do was make her feel as if she were the most important woman in the world.

"Are you feeling ill, Rosamond?"

"No, no, I am fine, my lord. If you will take me back to Kenilworth so that I can report this dire situation to my cousin Richard of Gloucester, I will be forever grateful."

"Griffin, take Nan up behind you. Ned, you'll have to return on foot," Rod directed, setting the spurs to his mount.

"My lord, you are going the wrong way!" Rosamond cried in alarm. "I need my cousin Richard."

"Why in the name of God do you need Gloucester? Pershore is yours, not Gloucester's. I'll take care of this matter." As he rode through the gates into Pershore's bailey, he immediately noted that no guards patrolled the property and that the bailey was in disorder, filled with flocks of fowl, unchained dogs, and rows of beer kegs. Autumn weeds grew up around every building, giving the place an unkempt look and showing willful neglect.

Sir Rodger swung down from his saddle, awaiting his squire's arrival. When Griffin rode in with Nan behind him, Rod handed him the reins of his stallion, Stygian. "Look after the ladies for me." He took a gauntlet from his saddlebag and strode into the stables. Rod's nostrils flared at the stench of the place. A barrel-chested stableman set down a horn of ale and lumbered to his feet. De Leyburn's eyes narrowed as he took the man's measure, then he pulled on his gauntlet and closed the distance between them. He stopped thirty inches in front of the brute and, without uttering one word, smashed his fist into the man's red face. The stableman dropped like a dead horse, and Leyburn placed a spurred and booted foot on his gut. "I trust you're the man who likes black eyes, since you'll have two by nightfall . . . and by nightfall I will have a clean stable." Rod picked up a shovel and thrust it into the beefy fist. "Use this to muck out every stall, or use it to dig your own grave . . . the choice is yours."

Sir Rodger strode from the stables to find Rosamond and Nan sitting atop their luggage while Griffin watered the horses. "Help yourself to the fodder in the stable, but tether them here in the bailey for now," he instructed his squire. "The stableman begs our patience until he can make the place spotless."

Young Ned, who had just arrived on foot, eagerly asked what he could do to help.

"Just follow me and bring the baggage. Come, ladies, I think you will benefit from the warmth of a good fire." He removed the bloody gauntlet and held out his hand to Rosamond. When she lifted her eyes to meet his, Rod made her a silent promise that she need have no fear. Rosamond took his hand and arose from her perch, then walked at his side as he led her back into Pershore.

Dymock stepped forward officiously, eyeing the swarthy knight. Sir Rodger walked past him into the hall without any acknowledgment. He led Rosamond to a padded bench beside the roaring fire, then waited until she sat down. He nodded permission for Nan to sit beside her mistress, then he turned his full attention upon the steward. "State your name."

"I am Dymock, master of Pershore. Who are you?"

Rod placed his bloody gauntlet on the table before him, then he withdrew his broadsword from its sheath and laid it beside the steel glove. "There is only one master of Pershore—Sir Rodger de Leyburn. I am he." He watched Dymock's eyelids hood his eyes, a protective gesture that showed fear. Rod knew that in any encounter between two people, one dominated, the other submitted.

"I was appointed steward by the Earl of Gloucester three years ago. He has had no reason to complain."

Leyburn pierced him with an icy green glare. "Sir Rodger," he prompted.

"Gloucester has had no reason to complain, Sir Rodger."

"Then Gloucester is an imbecile. Fortunately, he has no official authority here at Pershore. The lady who now graces this hall with her presence is betrothed to me. She will very shortly be Lady Rosamond Marshal de Leyburn. I suggest you go now and bid her welcome."

Dymock immediately acted upon the suggestion. He

approached the lady and with the greatest show of respect, bowed and welcomed her to Pershore.

Rosamond nodded once in acknowledgment of his words.

Reluctantly Dymock returned to stand before the mail-clad knight, whose squire was now beside him.

"My lady's horses will be restored to Pershore today," Sir Rodger stated. Silence stretched between them until the steward nodded his understanding; only then did Sir Rodger continue. "Summon the household servants, then bring me Pershore's account books."

Fear flickered in the steward's eyes as he licked lips gone bone dry. "Will that be all, my lord?"

Sir Rodger raised incredulous black brows. "All? That is only the start. I am not in the habit of explaining my intentions to underlings, but in your case I will make an exception. With all possible speed, you will do your utmost to restore Pershore from the pigsty it has become." Again he waited until the steward nodded his understanding.

"And then, my lord?"

"And then I shall hang you," Sir Rodger said quietly.

Six

My lord, may I speak with you?" Rosamond got to her feet, alarmed at Sir Rodger's threat. Dymock had been insufferably insolent to her, but that was not reason enough to forfeit his life. She did not wish to be responsible for his death.

"We will speak later in private," Sir Rodger said firmly.

He had rescued her and her servants, and Rosamond was profoundly grateful. Moreover, he was putting the steward in his place and forcing him to obey, so she knew she must not interrupt and undermine his authority. Wisely, Rosamond remained silent.

Rod spoke to his squire in a soft voice so that he could not be overheard. "Griffin, Dymock is your prisoner. Don't allow him to get farther than pissing distance from you. Once he has made arrangements to get the horses back and turned over Pershore's account books, make sure you lock him up securely."

The household servants gathered uncertainly in the hall. The tall, dark knight clad in chain mail was an authority figure they dared not disobey. When he beckoned to her, Rosamond traversed the room to stand beside him as he addressed the people of Pershore. "I am Sir Rodger de Leyburn, royal steward to Lord Edward, heir to the throne. It is an honor and a privilege to present Rosamond

Marshal, the lady who owns Pershore, and who is soon to be Lady de Leyburn. You will obey her in all things. Her wish must be your command. You will strive to please her every moment of every day, in every way. Together we will not only restore Pershore to its former glory, we shall make it the envy of the whole county."

Though she smiled, Rosamond clenched her teeth when he announced so cavalierly that she was soon to become Lady de Leyburn. She wanted to kick his shins for such barefaced arrogance, but restrained her impulse to attack him until they could be alone.

As her eyes traveled over the servants, Rosamond thought them a sorry lot compared with Kenilworth's clean, industrious staff. When her glance fell upon the red-faced cook, she raised her chin. "I am so pleased to see you up and about, madam," she said. "I shall come to inspect Pershore's kitchen in an hour's time, and trust you will have the evening meal well under way by then. Until I choose a replacement for you, I am afraid you'll have to manage without Edna. She will be assisting my tiring-woman with my personal things." Rosamond's glance dismissed the cook and she raised her eyes to the others. "The rest of you can start cleaning. Pershore needs stripping and scouring, chamber by chamber. If your work pleases me, I may retain your services; otherwise you will be turned out." She looked pointedly at two male servants. "I want a fire lit in every room. Thank you, that will be all for now."

After they all filed out, Nan picked up a bag and indicated that Edna do the same. "We'll return these to the chamber you chose last night."

When Rosamond and Sir Rodger were completely alone, Rosamond tossed her hair back over her shoulder in a gesture of defiance, though she spoke with exaggerated meekness. "I beg your permission to speak, my lord."

Rod's eyes filled with laughter. "I might intimidate the

rest of them, but not you, my Rosebud. I warrant now that we are alone, you will speak your mind whether I give you permission or not."

"Well, since I am so soon to become Lady de Leyburn, I might as well start out as I mean to carry on." Her sarcasm was tart.

"If I am to have full authority and have them obey my orders, and ultimately yours, you know full well I had to inform them I would be the new master here."

Rosamond said with mock solemnity, "If your work pleases me, I may retain your services; otherwise you will be turned off."

"You were magnificent," he said with a grin.

She suddenly wished he had seen her yesterday when she had swept the dishes from the table and threatened to maim the cook with the copper ladle. "I realize now that you had to threaten the steward with hanging to make him obey."

The amusement left his eyes. "No, Rosamond, that was no threat. I do intend to hang Dymock."

"I won't have his death on my conscience, not for insolence!"

He led her back to the padded settle before the fire, then leaned against the mantelpiece. "My orders are on *my* conscience, not yours. But perhaps it is best that you hold your own court and try him legally. That way the verdict will be the same, but your conscience will be clear."

She searched his face. "I don't understand."

Rod hesitated for a fraction of a second, loathing to strip away her innocence, then decided he had little choice but to begin her education. "Rosamond, the management of Pershore and its lands has been left in the hands of a corrupt steward whose sole purpose has been to enrich himself at the expense of not only you, but your tenants. You know the despair you felt at his hands, but can you imagine the horror he has imposed upon those who work your land?"

"Oh, no! How negligent I have been."

"You were not to know; it is Gloucester who has been negligent. Lord Edward and I were guilty of the same sort of laxity. When we returned from the Continent and began visiting his royal castles, we discovered a number of the stewards had been enriching themselves by making slaves of the tenants. Not only were they being worked to death, they also were being starved, beaten, raped, and even hanged at the whim of the men in charge. It is no wonder that so many people in England hate their king and his family and are turning to Simon de Montfort for their salvation."

"Were you able to right the wrongs of these corrupt stewards?"

"Yes. Before we embarked on the Welsh campaign, I spent an entire year traveling to Edward's royal holdings, appointing trustworthy men to positions of authority, and meting out just punishment to those who had committed unconscionable crimes."

"Sir Rodger, will you do that here at Pershore?"

"My lady, I am honor-bound."

Rosamond remembered the last time he had said those words to her, and how coldly she had rejected him. She knew it would be ungracious of her if she did not thank him. "Sir Rodger, I appreciate your help in bringing the Pershore staff under control." She doubted that he was helping her because he cared for her. Most likely he wanted to improve the value of the property he would gain through marriage to her. Clearly, he had become an authority figure to the servants, but Rosamond did not want him to try to assume authority over her, for she was certainly not willing to submit to his wishes. She lifted her chin, determined to show him they were equals. "There is no reason why we cannot be friends, my lord," she said loftily.

Rod smiled at her, but he was careful not to touch her. Before he was done, she would crave his touch. He silently vowed they would be far more than friends, more even than husband and wife; they would be lovers. "Later today, once your horses have been recovered and Dymock is safely locked up, I will ride to Worcester Castle, which is only seven or eight miles from Pershore, and bring back a staff who will soon have your household restored and running efficiently. I will also bring men-at-arms who will guard your property and hold it secure in your name."

"Sir Rodger, are you sure Worcester will lend us their people?"

Rod laughed. "Worcester is a royal castle, and I am a royal steward. I have the authority to use Worcester's resources as I see fit."

"Forgive my ignorance, my lord." The tone of her voice deliberately held an edge. "Will it be possible for you to return today?" Rosamond did not wish to reveal the anxiety she felt at the thought of staying at Pershore without him.

"I will leave Griffin with you—you may entrust him with your life, and I promise to return today, no matter how late the hour."

Relief washed over her, but determined to hide it, Rosamond said coolly, "Thank you, my lord. I sincerely appreciate your aid in this matter."

At Kenilworth, Simon de Montfort was experiencing some anxiety of his own. Rumors were beginning to reach him that King Henry had no intention of returning to England in time for the February Parliament, and without the king's presence there could be no Parliament. Earl Simon had many informants who traveled with the king's court in Europe, and it took only four days for merchant vessels to sail from the Continent and bring messages to England.

The institution of regular sessions of Parliament was the first and foremost of the Provisions of Oxford, but obviously it was the provision that stung Henry's colossal pride the most. Until now, calling a session of Parliament had been solely the king's prerogative. He had had time to recover from the panic that had made him sign the Provisions, and now he wanted to rule personally once again, without a council dictating to him.

Simon was furious. He knew Henry would use the French treaty as a last-minute pretext for not returning in time for Parliament. So before the king wrote to the justiciar, the marshal, and his other nobles, asking for a postponement, Earl Simon decided to forestall him and write to the nobles himself, summoning them to London for the Candlemas Parliament in February. He assured them that Lord Edward Plantagenet, heir to the throne, would be at his side.

Simon hoped Rodger de Leyburn would return to Kenilworth soon. That persuasive young man would be indispensable in helping him to convince Lord Edward to replace the king in Parliament, if Henry did indeed refuse to return in time.

Alyce de Clare was furious that de Leyburn had taken himself off without so much as a by-your-leave. With Rod absent, it was impossible for her to spend the night with Edward, so it was pointless for her to remain at Kenilworth under Eleanor de Montfort's contemptuous gaze.

Alyce scribbled a note for her lover and gave it to his squire, Owen, since he was the only one she dared to trust.

Mon Amour,

I shall persuade Richard to return to Gloucester, but shall proceed to London and stay at Westminster in my father's apartments. I wish you would return to Windsor before Christmas, so we could spend it together, but if not, I will come to you whenever you send word.

It was an arrangement they had used before. As well as access to Westminster, Alyce often enjoyed carte blanche at the numerous de Clare castles close to London, without the presence of her odious young husband. She and Gilbert hated the sight of each other and were happiest when they were separated by a goodly distance. Alyce was alarmed that Edward was allying himself with Simon de Montfort, though she was far too wise to voice her objection to her lover. Instead, she would voice it to her father-in-law, Richard de Clare, when the opportunity presented itself.

The following day, Edward hid his amusement when Richard de Clare bade him farewell. "I've absented myself from Gloucester for far too long. Gilbert has decided to stay on awhile—he hero-worships Simon, you know—but duty calls me. You must come and stay with us at Gloucester and sample our hospitality."

"Thank you for your generous offer, Richard; I have every intention of sampling it one day soon."

At Pershore, Rosamond tasted each of the dishes set before her. The food was good, and she was able to enjoy it because she had inspected the kitchen and found it clean and tidy. Rosamond and Nan sat alone at the head table, while the household servants sat much farther down the hall. "I give credit where it is due, they have earned their dinner today."

Nan replied, "The change in attitude is amazing. It is difficult to believe it was only yesterday we were treated like dirt beneath their feet. We owe it all to Sir Rodger."

"Yes, a royal steward has a great deal of power and authority."

"My lady, even if he had no such office, the result would be the same, I warrant. It is the *man* they are obeying, not the office."

"Yes, it is a man's world—I will never doubt that again. All the power is in their hands."

"If a woman is fortunate enough to marry a powerful man, and clever enough to hold that man in the palm of her hand, she gains all his power for herself," Nan pointed out.

"That is certainly what Lady Eleanor de Montfort has done, and I know what you are trying to tell me, Nan; I'm not oblivious to the fact that I am betrothed to Sir Rodger de Leyburn."

Nan smiled knowingly. "He reminds you of it every time he looks at you with those devilish green eyes. Surely he sets your pulses racing and heats your blood, my lamb?"

"He does not!" Rosamond declared, yet an inner voice called her a liar.

"Have you ever noticed the marked resemblance between Sir Rodger and Sir Rickard de Burgh?" Nan asked innocently.

"Yes . . . no . . . I don't know what you're talking about."

"I'm talking about their bodies—shoulders so wide and powerful, they make a female feel faint, hair blacker than midnight, eyes like green pools of temptation a woman would willingly drown in, and the same rich, dark laugh that makes your very spine tingle. Both are wickedly handsome warriors who could lure any lady to wantonness."

Rosamond tried to picture Rickard de Burgh, but it was Rodger de Leyburn who rose up vividly in her mind, completely obliterating her ability to conjure the older knight, who until recently had filled all of her daydreams and fantasies. She shivered, for Rod de Leyburn was real flesh and blood, not some ephemeral fancy.

Just as she drained her wine goblet, Griffin, accompanied by Ned, came into the hall with news. "My lady, your horses have been safely returned. Ned has just fed and watered them."

"Oh, how wonderful! My palfrey means so much to me; I would dearly love to see her. Has darkness yet fallen?"

"Yes, my lady, it is dark outside, but I will light your way, you need have no fear," Griffin assured her. "But you will need a warm cloak, for the night is bitter cold."

"I will fetch your cloak, my lady," Ned said. "You will be so pleased at the condition of the stables." He almost ran from the hall.

"Griffin, you and Ned must stay and eat; I can visit the stables tomorrow."

"We are both eager for you to see the vast improvements in Pershore's stable. We will both enjoy our food better after we have seen the pleasure in your eyes."

Such a concept startled Rosamond. The very notion that her happiness could bring them pleasure made her feel quite special.

When she arrived at the stable, flanked by Griffin and Ned, her heart overflowed with affection for her little palfrey, and Nimbus greeted her with a soft nicker and a nuzzle. As Rosamond stroked the filly, she breathed in the clean smell of soap and fresh hay. "I can hardly believe what has been accomplished."

"Sir Rodger has been known to move *mountains*, my lady."

Rosamond laughed. Griffin had an earthy sense of humor, for indeed Sir Rodger had moved mountains of horse dung. As she crossed the bailey, she lifted her eyes to the brilliant stars. There was no cloud cover tonight and it was cold enough for frost. She pulled her purple cloak closer about her and thought of de Leyburn. Surely he would not rout people from the warmth of Worcester Castle tonight. Nay, he had told her he would return today to keep her from being afraid. Likely it was done in kindness, yet she didn't appreciate being treated like a child.

She glanced about nervously. Where was the brutish stableman this night, or the men of Pershore who had been drunk in the bailey? The pockmarked face of Dymock rose up in the dark and she felt her fingers tremble as they clutched her cloak. She liked Griffin very much, and Sir Rodger had told her she could trust him with her life, but Rosamond knew she would not feel secure tonight without de Leyburn's protective presence.

The entire wing of Pershore where Rosamond had her bed-chamber had been scoured and cleaned, and each room had been aired by its own fire, so tonight Rosamond had her own private quarters. Nan took an adjoining room, while Ned would sleep in the knight's quarters with Griffin.

As Rosamond readied herself for bed, she imagined her chamber as it would be once improvements had been made. She visualized a plush carpet on the floor and rich, artistic tapestries upon the walls. A rug and cushions before the fireplace would lend a cozy atmosphere, and deep-red hangings about the high window would make the room feel both warmer and safer. Rosamond loved vivid colors. Her hand caressed her crimson bed curtains and goosedown quilt, their familiarity bringing a measure of comfort, as she silently thanked Lady Eleanor for suggesting that she bring her own bedding.

She went to the window searching for some sign of de Leyburn, but other than the stars, she could see only blackness outside. She climbed into bed and the incredible events of the day replayed themselves in her mind. Rosamond didn't believe she had ever fainted before in her life, and could not explain how her trampling dream had overtaken her senses while she was fully awake. She told herself that the events leading up to it must have taken an emotional toll on her. The terrifying black horse must be a symbol of her fears threatening to overwhelm her. If she conquered her fears, she wondered if the trampling dream would stop.

Eventually her eyelids became heavy and she began to drift down into sleep. In the distance there was a low rumble. Thunder? No, it was far too cold for thunder. It was more like the drumming of hoofbeats on the frozen ground, coming ever closer. A wave of stark terror swept over Rosamond, snatching her breath away. . . .

At Worcester, Sir Rodger de Leyburn received a warm welcome. The castle had always been a royal stronghold, where he and Edward had entertained the young Marcher barons of Hay, Clifford, Wigmore, and Ludlow. During the previous year, most of the old barons had died off, leaving their castles and titles to sons who were approximately the same age as Lord Edward.

From Worcester Castle's vast staff, Sir Rodger selected a dozen household servants he intended to put in charge at Pershore. He also picked land stewards to oversee the tenant farms, and chose guards for its walls and grooms for its stables. To replace Dymock, he picked a man called Hutton, who was Worcester's under-steward. Rod promised that his wife, Lizzy Hutton, could be head housekeeper in charge of the other maids. She was so flattered that she helped him cull some of Worcester Castle's royal furnishings to help replenish Pershore.

By the time the wagons were loaded, it was time for the evening meal at Worcester. Rod put Hutton in complete charge and told him that tomorrow would be a better time for the eight-mile journey to Pershore. Though the night was bitter cold, Rod had assured Rosamond that he would return, no matter how late the hour, and it never occurred to him to do otherwise. He had left Griffin in charge, but the responsibility for Rosamond's safety was far too heavy for one lone squire. Pershore harbored more than a few disgruntled servants who had been allowed to rule the roost.

When he arrived at Pershore's stables, it was after ten. He gave Stygian a thorough rubdown, then led him to a stall that had been made ready with clean straw. As Rod offered his horse a handful of fresh hay, his eyes traveled about the dimly lit stable with approval. His nose told him better than his eyes that his orders had been followed to the letter.

Griffin awaited him and showed him to a chamber with a fire, a clean bed, and a supply of wine, the three things he was most in need of. Rodger learned that the missing horses had been returned, that all had remained amazingly quiet at Pershore, and that Dymock was securely locked up in a cell beneath the stillroom. Griffin indicated the account books stacked on the table and withdrew for the night.

Rod removed his boots and heavy leather doublet, then warmed himself at the fire. When he felt that he was beginning to thaw, he poured himself a goblet of wine. His eyes fell on the account books, and he picked one up and carried it to an easy chair before the fire. Rod finished his wine before he opened the book, knowing from experience what he would find in the ledgers.

Suddenly, from an adjoining chamber came a blood-curdling scream that made the hair on the nape of his neck stand on end. He knew it was Rosamond before the chilling sound died away, and in a flash he was on his feet and running, his palm clasped about the hilt of his dagger.

Rod found no one in the chamber except Rosamond. She was lying in her bed, her hair a wild tangle, her night rail twisted about her body so that her long legs were bared. He sat down on the edge of the bed and gripped her shoulders. "Rosamond, wake up, sweetheart, you're having a nightmare!"

When the girl on the bed opened her eyes, they widened in horror and another scream was torn from her throat. The dark form towering above her blotted out the light from the candles that burned in their iron stand in the corner of the room, and she fought him desperately.

Rod took possession of her hands as they clawed at his

face, and gripped them tightly. "Rosamond, it's me, it's Rod!"

His voice was so compelling, it penetrated her consciousness. "De Leyburn?" she gasped.

A light flared behind them as Nan rushed into the chamber. She stopped dead in her tracks at the scene before her. "Bones of God, Sir Rodger, are you ravishing her?"

"She is screaming from a nightmare, not me. I'll take care of this, Nan, go back to bed."

Nan hesitated. "Rosamond . . . ?"

"I'm . . . all right." The quaver in her lady's voice did little to assure Nan, but Sir Rodger de Leyburn was such a dominant male presence, the tiring-woman had little choice but to withdraw and allow them their privacy.

"Tell me what terrified you."

She shook her head, unable to speak, unable to do aught but cling to him. When he felt her body trembling, he slipped his arms around her protectively and held her. Some inner instinct told him not to press her to talk; he somehow knew that at the moment, all she needed was his strength. He could feel her heart pounding, feel the tremor of her lush breasts as they lay against the hard muscles of his chest, and hear her shuddering breaths as her lungs fought for air. The scent of her, the feel of her soft body, and the feminine way she clung to him were aphrodisiacs that aroused his lust, but he crushed it down with an iron determination. Gradually, in the warm haven of his arms, her breathing eased and her trembling stilled.

As Rosamond clung to him she realized she had never felt as totally safe and secure in her entire life as she did at this moment. His powerful protection was all-encompassing, and so seductive she longed to stay in his arms, pressed against his heart forever. As his warmth seeped into her, she felt a need to reveal her nightmare, hoping his strength could erase it forever. She had not spoken of it for years; she had suppressed it for so long, it had become a terrible secret, almost shameful; but now she felt an overwhelming compulsion to share it. "I . . . I have a recurring dream . . ." she whispered.

"Tell me," he murmured, stroking her disheveled hair, with his strong, soothing hand.

Rosamond could feel the steady, comforting beat of his heart beneath her cheek, and she was no longer afraid to speak of it. "It is a . . . trampling dream. Always the same. The rider is faceless . . . though I know he is dark. It is the horse I fear most. . . . It is huge, black, terrifying." She shuddered. "My blood turns icy with fear, for I know his pursuit will be relentless!" She took a deep breath before she could continue. "I desperately attempt to escape the cruel hooves. . . . I run faster and faster, until my lungs are ready to burst, but I cannot escape. As I look back over my shoulder, the black forelegs rise above me. . . . I scream and tumble beneath the horse's hooves. . . ."

Rod was a good listener, which was why so many people confided in him. Listening was an art; he neither offered advice nor tried to solve the problem unless he was asked. He simply listened. He understood that if he did for Rosamond what she must do for herself, he would only end up heightening her fear and diminishing her confidence in herself. His arms tightened about her and he drew her closer.

In the haven of his arms, Rosamond's thoughts began to disentangle themselves and she saw things with a clarity that had evaded her up until now. "Of course," she whispered, "the black horse symbolizes death! I am running away from death . . . my parents' death . . . my brother's. . . . I've never fully accepted Giles's death. Whenever I am threatened, I have the trampling dream!"

Rodger began to rock her gently. He cradled the back of her head with his hand and pressed her face into the hollow of his shoulder. His lips brushed the curling tendrils at her temple.

"The nightmares began when I heard whispers that Giles had been trampled to death by his maddened horse in the jousting."

At that moment, Rodger de Leyburn thanked heaven and hell that Rosamond Marshal could not see the grim expression on his face. Giles Marshal had not been killed by his horse. He had met his death by a human hand. Rod closed his eyes and knew he must wed her quickly, before she learned who had killed her beloved brother. The marriage must be soon, or the dark rider of her dream might no longer be faceless.

Seven

When Nan waited an extra hour in the morning before she attended Rosamond, her mistress realized Nan was giving Sir Rodger time to withdraw from her chamber discreetly, if he had spent the night with his betrothed.

"I'm sorry I disturbed you last night, Nan. When I went to bed, I didn't feel safe with Sir Rodger away at Worcester, and I had a nightmare. But when I saw that de Leyburn had returned after all, it put my fears to rest."

"I wanted to stay, my lamb, but he dismissed me, and he can be very intimidating."

"Yes, I know, but strangely enough he doesn't greatly intimidate me any longer. I have been guilty of saying the most dreadful, cutting things to him, but instead of being fierce with me, he is amused."

"Perhaps he is tolerant because you are not yet wed. Perhaps he wouldn't be quite as amused if his *wife* was insolent to him."

"You are not very consistent, Nan. Yesterday you were pushing me into matrimony; today you are warning me against it." Rosamond hid a smile. "Help me choose something suitable to wear—the new staff from Worcester Castle will be here this morning."

When she went down to the hall, Rosamond was

wearing a dark green tunic over a white lawn underdress. A gold chain decorated with jade beads was artfully criss-crossed once beneath her breasts, once about her hips in Grecian style, and her long golden hair had been drawn up in a knot at the back of her head, then allowed to flow to her hips in a long fall.

When she saw Rodger de Leyburn, her cheeks turned pink and her eyes went directly to his, to gauge his reaction.

"Good morning, my lady." His smile was friendly but not intimate, and Rosamond heaved an inner sigh of relief. He signaled to a woman at the other end of the hall, who came immediately. "This is Lizzy Hutton. I think she will make a good head housekeeper in charge of Pershore's female servants, but only if she meets with your approval, my lady. Lizzy, this is Rosamond Marshal, the mistress of Pershore."

Lizzy bobbed a respectful curtsy. "I will do my very best to earn your approval, ma'am. What would you like for breakfast?"

Rosamond liked her immediately, not only because she had a motherly look, but because she was immaculate, with a starched white smock and cap, and clean fingernails.

Lizzy curtsied to Nan also and asked what she would like to eat. When she went happily off to the kitchen, Rosamond smiled at Sir Rodger. "I think she's lovely. I hadn't expected them to be here this early."

His green eyes smiled into hers. "I swear I didn't threaten them, I just think they want to impress you and show they are eager to serve you and Pershore. I recommend that you make Lizzy's husband steward in Dymock's place, but of course the decision is yours. If you don't agree once you have talked with him, we'll get another man."

"If you recommend Hutton, Sir Rodger, that's good enough for me; you have far more experience than I."

Lord in heaven, she thought, *why did I speak of his experience? He could think it a double entendre!*

But Rodger nodded seriously. "I know them to be a capable couple, both decent and trustworthy. They brought some furnishings from Worcester Castle to make Pershore more comfortable."

"Oh, are you sure that is permissible?"

Rod smiled. "Yes, I gave them permission to bring the stuff and now I give you permission to enjoy it."

The corners of her mouth turned up in a smile. "Then how can I refuse?"

"Oh, you are quite capable of refusing what I offer, Rosamond," he teased.

She remembered how his arms had felt in the night, and lowered her lashes to her cheeks. *I didn't refuse your strength*, she thought. *It's the only thing you have that I need . . . the only thing I want!* Another voice spoke to her. *If you agreed to marry him, you would gain that strength.* Rosamond silently answered the voice. *Yes, but he would want more from me than I am prepared to give.*

"I hesitate to ask, Rosamond, for it could be harrowing, but would you consider riding out with me to visit the tenant farms this morning? I will go alone if you prefer."

She liked the way he included her in all he undertook, whether it was choosing a steward or visiting the tenants. When she'd arrived at Pershore, she'd felt completely insignificant, but Sir Rodger was changing that. "Of course I will visit my tenants." She gave him back his own words. "I am honor-bound."

"Thank you. I'll saddle your palfrey while you break your fast, and await you in the bailey."

De Leyburn never failed to surprise her. Would he really saddle her palfrey himself, rather than have a groom do it? Everything he did had a way of making her feel special. After breakfast, when she went up to her bedchamber for her cloak and gloves, her jaw almost dropped with amazement. The room had been transformed. Not only was there a lady's slipper bath and a lovely polished mirror, but the floor had a plush red carpet and the walls were hung with rich tapestries. Roger de Leyburn had surprised her again, and it began to dawn on her that he was a man who enjoyed surprising a lady and gifting her with life's luxuries.

As they rode to the first tenant farm, with Hutton, the new head steward, in tow, Rosamond thanked Sir Rodger for his thoughtfulness.

"It is my pleasure. Most beautiful, highborn ladies take these things for granted."

She touched the dark brown marten fur that edged the hood of her green velvet riding cape and wondered if he really did think she was beautiful, or was he merely being gallant? Compared with his swarthy handsomeness, she was extremely fair, and she wondered if he was truly attracted to her. Then she blushed, for she knew of a certainty that when she tossed her long honey-blond tresses about her shoulders, he became aroused. She found his eyes upon her as she tucked a windblown strand of hair back inside her hood, and her blush deepened. Lord, she hadn't felt this feminine in her entire life!

As they rode through a copse of beech trees, they startled a family of roe deer, who in turn disturbed myriad game birds as the deer bounded off through the woods. When they arrived at the first farm, Rod dismounted immediately and went to Rosamond's stirrup to aid her. Unused to such male attention, she found how pleasurable it was to be lifted down from the saddle.

At every farm, six in all, the scene was basically the same. Her tenant farmers were afraid of their visitors. It stabbed Rosamond to the heart when the children screamed and went into hiding. The men were gaunt, the women thin and timid, and all were in rags, overworked and underfed.

As Hutton assessed what needed to be done in the way of repairs to the dwellings and outbuildings, de Leyburn drew out the farmers and got them to talk. To Rosamond it was clear that he had dealt with situations like this before, and she was profoundly grateful for his experience. She listened to their painful stories and was devastated by what she heard. Their sheep had produced more wool this year than ever before, yet the people who were responsible were almost starved. They learned that Dymock had hanged a farmer who cut up a dead lamb to feed his family and neighbors, and a twelve-year-old youth had been beaten to death for hunting Pershore's game.

After they heard the first horror story, Rodger de Leyburn turned to Rosamond and asked her if she would hold a court to try Dymock for his crimes. When she agreed, he told her to ask the tenants to bring their grievances to the hall later that day.

"My lord, I want you to ask them. They will not listen to me regarding Dymock; they'll be too afraid to trust the authority of a woman, even though I am the mistress of Pershore."

When de Leyburn encouraged them to come and bring their grievances, and promised they would be addressed, most looked as if they might be willing to attend the court at Pershore. Rosamond then spoke to the women. "Please come and bring the children. When court is over, I want you to dine in the hall tonight."

On the ride back, Rod did not try to hide his admiration for her. "That was most thoughtful of you, Rosamond."

"Judas, I have been thoughtless overlong, never giving these people a moment's attention for years; please do not praise me."

"No guilt, Rosamond. It serves no useful purpose; it neither restores the dead nor fills bellies, but it *can* kill happiness."

* * *

Alyce de Clare had never experienced a pang of guilt in her life. She snuggled down into her sable fur cape, lined with red velvet, as she rode beside her ever indulgent father-in-law, Richard of Gloucester. Actually, she quite liked him; he was the sort of man she could cozen with her feline femininity. He was neither quick-witted nor shrewd. He did have a volatile temper, but she was careful never to rub him the wrong way, and she knew it added to his towering pride and prestige to have such a highborn, attractive lady for a daughter-in-law.

"I always get the impression that Simon de Montfort resents you for being England's leading peer, my lord."

"Really?" Gloucester sounded surprised.

"His ambition is legend. He wishes to control the barons, but now it seems he wants to control you and Prince Edward too."

"You shouldn't concern your pretty head with politics, my dear."

"Oh, I don't, my lord. I simply don't want you to provoke the king's displeasure." Now that she had sown the seeds, she was happy to leave the subject alone.

"Would you like to stop at Pershore for the night? It belongs to my young cousin, Rosamond Marshal, and since I appointed the steward there, we are guaranteed a warm welcome."

"I'd prefer we go on to Gloucester, my lord. Your little Marshal cousin took an instant dislike to me."

Richard nodded his approval at her willingness to remain in the saddle. "Perhaps the reason Rosamond acted coolly toward you was Rodger de Leyburn. He always flirts outrageously with you, Alyce."

She gave him a provocative glance. "Most men flirt with me, my lord. There is something about a French female that men cannot resist, *n'est-ce pas?*"

"You are a delectable morsel, Alyce; I swear even the king himself is half in love with you. I know it has been a sore trial to you to be married to a boy all these years, but Gilbert is fifteen, almost sixteen, and I warrant he's now old enough to consummate your union." Richard grinned. "Gilbert needs an heir, Alyce. You won't make me wait too much longer for a grandson, will you, sweetheart?"

Alyce suppressed a shudder. The redheaded Gilbert with the flaming temper was anathema to her. There was only one man on earth whose son she'd be willing to bear, and that man was her half-cousin, Prince Edward Plantagenet. The trouble was, Edward was far too clever to impregnate her. Though he adored the bedsport she provided, he never allowed his seed to spend until he had withdrawn from her. Next time they were intimate, perhaps during the celebration of the New Year, she would have to lure him into forgetting himself.

"It is my fervent desire to give you and Gilbert an heir for Gloucester, very, very shortly, my dearest lord." She pulled her sables more closely about her and thought of the emeralds and diamonds she would demand as her reward for risking her figure to provide the de Clares with an heir. She hadn't much thought about it before, but now that she considered the matter, Alyce realized that if she provided Richard of Gloucester with a grandson and heir, it could make Gilbert the Red quite redundant.

Alyce gave her father-in-law a brilliant smile. "I wish to spend Christmas at Westminster, in my father's beautiful apartments, my lord. When I become *enceinte*, I will need a complete new wardrobe, and the only place in the kingdom where the French fashions are available is London. You will not mind too much if I run off and indulge myself before I settle down to motherhood, will you, Richard?" Her lips made a pouty little moue she knew he would not be able to resist.

In midafternoon the tenant farmers of Pershore and their families came to the castle as a group, no doubt feeling there was strength in numbers. The court was held in the dining hall, and Rodger advised Rosamond that the entire household should attend. It would be a strong deterrent to the servants who had aided and abetted Dymock in his tyranny. When all were assembled, de Leyburn asked Griffin to bring the prisoner from his cell. Sir Rodger and Rosamond, sitting in judgment together, listened intently as the tenants aired their grievances.

As the grave complaints and injuries were piled one on top of another, Rosamond's heart hardened against Dymock. When she listened to the man accuse the steward of ordering his son's death for snaring a rabbit in the woods, Rosamond's eyes searched out the boy's mother. That was the moment she knew she would hang Dymock, and she would try to do it without guilt. Now she understood why most women left the decisions to men. With power and authority came responsibilities and hard decisions, but she resolved to do her duty without flinching. Rosamond did not wait for Sir Rodger to take the lead. She stood and spoke directly to Dymock. "You are to be taken from this place and hanged by the neck until you are dead. If you need a confessor to unburden your soul before my sentence is carried out, you may have one."

She looked directly into the faces of the men and women before her. "If there are other charges against any who are employed at Pershore, I am ready to hear them." Without looking at Sir Rodger, she knew his eyes were upon her with approval and respect for what she had just done. But she also acknowledged to herself that it was his strength that had given her the courage to do it.

There were two men, who were ostensibly Pershore's guards, who had sexually forced women against their will. Rosamond dismissed them from her service immediately, with a dire warning to the other males employed at Pershore. "If this ever occurs again, I shall not hesitate to pass a sentence of death upon you." Rosamond's gaze traveled about the hall seeking the girl, Edna. "Do you wish to lay a complaint against the cook, Edna?"

The girl's eyes went as round as saucers, but she shook her head decisively. Rosamond's icy gaze pierced the cook's for long, drawn-out minutes as she pondered how to deal with the obese woman. "I do not want you in my kitchen; your standards of cleanliness will never match mine. I believe your bulk is more suited to being a laundress. It takes a good deal of strength to lift and scrub wet sheets, and at least I can be certain your hands will be clean henceforth."

A ripple of laughter went around the hall and Rosamond blushed slightly, knowing she had delivered that last cutting remark with the hauteur of a countess. She held up her hands for silence and became humble. Looking around the hall, she said, "I deeply regret all the horror and hardship you have suffered. Until I came to Pershore, I was in complete ignorance of your circumstances. I pledge to do all I can to improve both your working and living conditions. You are free to take wood from the forest for your fires, and I give you my permission to hunt Pershore's game. Should there come a time when the forests are depleted, I may suspend hunting rights until the deer and game birds thrive again, but please rest assured there will always be meat on your tables. I have appointed a new head steward by the name of Hutton from the royal castle of Worcester. He will begin making improvements to your farms right away, so please do not hesitate to discuss your needs with him.

"One of your needs is quite evident. Before winter sets in with a vengeance, you will all need warm clothing and footwear, and the material for these shall be provided." Rosamond smiled her encouragement. "Please stay and partake of our hospitality tonight. The fires are warm and the food and ale is plentiful. Enjoy!"

Sir Rodger took both her hands, squeezed them, then lifted first one, then the other to his lips. "You are flushed with success, chérie. Today you made the journey from girlhood to womanhood, and it becomes you."

"How will I pay for all the things I've promised?" she whispered, experiencing sudden anxiety.

"Pershore's coffers overflow and fortunately Griffin and I have unearthed them from where they were hidden. I'll show you later. Go and receive your people's homage, Rosamond, you deserve it."

Rosamond watched him as he crossed the hall. He singled out a thin, dark boy for his attention. Out of curiosity, she followed him. De Leyburn was offering the boy a chance to become a page on the household staff of Pershore and was explaining to the boy the opportunities that this would open for him, perhaps even leading to the position of steward one day.

Looking at the sullen, ragged child, she thought Sir Rodger was not being kind to dangle such an unobtainable prize before his nose, for he looked like a most unlikely candidate in her eyes. She murmured, "He cannot read or write, nor has he been taught even rudimentary manners, my lord."

"He can learn," Rod said firmly. "I would like him to have a chance to be more than a shepherd; after that it will be up to him. He reminds me of someone I once knew. I should have asked you first. I will take him into my service if you deem him unsuitable for Pershore."

Rosamond smiled at the boy, whose eyes looked as if they had seen things no child should witness. "Go and find Lizzy Hutton and tell her you are to be my personal page. She'll find you a new suit of clothes, but I warn you, she will likely insist you take a bath and cut your hair short." The dark boy hesitated for only a brief moment, then he flashed her a cheeky grin and darted off. Rosamond realized instantly that the boy reminded de Leyburn of himself.

Before the feasting was finished, darkness had fallen and the chatelaine of Pershore gave her tenants permission to stay the night in the hall of the castle, if they so wished. When Rosamond and Nan climbed the stairs to retire for the night, Rod followed them and invited Rosamond into his chamber so that she could see for herself the coffers he had found.

She lifted her eyes from the boxes of coins. "How did you learn the steward had hidden gold?"

Rod avoided answering her directly, knowing she would not wish to know how he had persuaded Dymock to confess. "The records he kept for Gloucester were falsified, showing no profits for Pershore. The books show that the income from wool and mutton equaled expenses, which is ridiculous when he spent nothing on the upkeep of either Pershore or its tenant farms."

"Will there be enough to do everything I have promised?"

"Yes, there's plenty of wood in the forests to make necessary repairs, and the tenants can do the work themselves now that the crops are in, the shearing finished, and many of the animals sold for slaughter. I'll organize a hunt tomorrow, and the venison and game can be salted down to last through the winter. Hutton suggested we buy some swine. They'd almost feed themselves in the oak and beech woods. Also, many of the women know how to weave cloth, if we provide them with looms." He grinned at her. "I've told the farmers to help themselves to the mountain of horse manure piled behind the stables. It will give them bumper crops next year."

"You are full of surprises, my lord."

His green eyes held hers. "Do you like surprises, Rosamond?"

She searched his face, knowing it was an intimate question. "Up until now, I have not liked surprises; they have always been unpleasant. But I must admit I am woman enough to like the bathing tub and the mirror."

He walked with her to the door, then he bent close. Rosamond thought for one wild moment that he was about to kiss her. She had never been kissed by a man and wondered what it would feel like. But instead of kissing her, Rod simply opened the door, and Rosamond realized she was the only one who was thinking of kisses.

"I believe you are woman enough for anything," he said softly.

A frisson of pleasure curled inside her. *Perhaps I am*, she thought.

As she began to undress, her glance fell upon her pillow. There lay a sprig of mistletoe and Rosamond wondered how in the world it had gotten there. Had Nan put it there? No, of course not. Rosamond knew very well who had put it there, and it proved to her beyond a shadow of a doubt, she was *not* the only one thinking of kisses.

Leaving only one scented candle burning, Rosamond climbed into bed and went over the events of the incredible day. The decisions she had been forced to make had made her stronger. She realized that those decisions had been easier for her because de Leyburn had been at her side. She lifted the mistletoe to her nose and sniffed. It had little scent, yet it brought her a great deal of pleasure. Her thoughts drifted back to last night when Rodger had come to her in the darkness and held her securely for hours.

Her brows drew together in apprehension. Surely, the nightmare wouldn't come again tonight to terrify her? If it did, she took comfort in the fact that Rodger de Leyburn was in the adjoining chamber and would not hesitate to come if she needed him. The corners of her mouth went up. What if she merely pretended she was having a nightmare? All she need do was cry out, and she would be in his arms once more. Rosamond blushed. Why in the world was she having such wicked, wanton thoughts?

EIGHT

The following day, Rosamond decided she would not hunt, but she did join Sir Rodger and the other hunters on the first leg of their ride, happy to exercise herself and her palfrey in the crisp, cold sunshine. She wore an amber-colored cape that flew open as she rode to reveal an apricot-colored riding dress. She knew both shades complemented her honey-gold tresses. This morning she wanted to look attractive in her companion's eyes, and by the way his green gaze devoured her, Rosamond knew she had succeeded.

Pershore was on the banks of the River Avon, which had frozen solid a couple of days before, and it was a novelty for Rosamond to ride Nimbus across the ice to the bank on the other side. As they cantered beneath the tall trees, powdered snow that had fallen in the night came drifting down from the heavily laden branches, and she lifted her face skyward to catch the flakes on her eyelashes. To Rosamond the day seemed perfect. When the hunters caught sight of their first roe deer, they thundered off after them, and Rosamond waved farewell, then cantered slowly back across the frozen river to Pershore.

She found the household servants decorating the hall with holly, ivy, and evergreen boughs in honor of the December Holy Days of Saint Nicholas, and she and Nan joined them, fastening red-berried holly across the mantel of the massive fireplace. The spicy smell of mincemeat pies baking in the kitchen filled the air with their piquant aroma, and Rosamond took a handful of cloves from the larder to the stillroom to mold some clove-scented candles.

Later in the day, when the wax had set, she decided to take a scented candle to de Leyburn's chamber. She recalled that when she had been there to see the coin-filled coffers, the room had looked extremely austere. As she looked about the chamber she was mildly surprised that he had not softened the Spartan effect with some of the furnishings from Worcester. From the cut of his clothes, he seemed the sort of man who enjoyed the luxuries of life. She stripped off his bed and remade it with some of her own fine sheets, since she imagined he was fastidious about his body linen. She considered putting a sprig of mistletoe on his pillow, then decided against it. Instead, she fastened the sprig of white berries at the neckline of her apricot velvet gown.

The hunting party did not return until the last light had gone from the afternoon sky. They had bagged dozens of deer and scores of hares, as well as a few wild boar. Nothing on the animals would be wasted. The skins would be cured, and the boar tusks and deer horns used to fashion handles for tools and utensils. Even the hooves would be boiled down for soap, mucilage, and gelatin.

Bathed and changed from his bloody attire, Sir Rodger joined Rosamond in the hall for dinner. "It looks like Yuletide tonight, and if I am not mistaken I smell mince pie and roast goose."

"With chestnut dressing, I might add," Rosamond announced with sparkling eyes. "Doesn't the hall look inviting?"

Sir Rodger eyed the mistletoe at her breast. "Inviting, yes. A man appreciates a warm welcome, whether he is returning from the hunt or from battle. If there is a lady who awaits him with a smile, and praise for his efforts, life is much sweeter."

Rosamond's pulse quickened as it occurred to her that

Rodger de Leyburn was courting her. The meal turned out to be a total success, and she enjoyed every delicious mouthful of her food. She admitted that his company added to her pleasure. When the meal was over and Rosamond told the servers to refill all the wine cups, everyone in the hall spontaneously broke into the old Welsh air:

Deck the halls with boughs of holly,
Fa la la la la la la la la.
'Tis the season to be jolly,
Fa la la la la la la la la.
Don we now our gay apparel,
Fa la la la la la la la la.
Troll the ancient Yuletide carol,
Fa la la la la la la la la.
See the blazing Yule before us,
Fa la la la la la la la la.
Strike the harp and join the chorus,
Fa la la la la la la la la.
Follow me in merry measure,
Fa la la la la la la la la.
While I tell of Yuletide treasure,
Fa la la la la la la la la.

As the tables were being cleared, Rosamond took her wine and sat on the padded settle next to the fireplace. Rod joined her, stretching out his long legs to the warm blaze.

"You look so content here, I hesitate to broach the subject of Deerhurst," he said.

"I . . . I haven't been there since Giles's . . . accident. Dear God in heaven, I hope it isn't being run as Pershore was."

"It's much closer to Gloucester, so perhaps Deerhurst's steward dare not be an out-and-out thief right under Richard de Clare's nose, but conditions could certainly be less than ideal." Rod searched her face. "There's only one way to find out." When Rosamond looked apprehensive, he offered, "I will go to Deerhurst without you if you cannot face going there alone. Was it where you lived as a child?"

"Yes, Deerhurst was my father's castle," she said wistfully.

"Childhood memories can be almost unbearable." Tenderly, he covered her hand with his, then threaded his fingers through hers.

"No, I had a happy childhood, until my father was killed in battle." Then Rosamond realized it was de Leyburn's own childhood that prompted his words. "How far is Deerhurst from here?"

"Possibly eight, certainly no more than nine miles south. We would just follow the river."

Rosamond shook her head. "'Tis unfair to ask Nan to ride farther, especially if the place is filthy and dilapidated."

Rod squeezed her fingers. "We could go alone."

His tempting suggestion hung in the air between them for long minutes as she debated its positive and negative points. It was certainly her duty to inspect Deerhurst, not only for the sake of the tenant farmers, but for the memory of Giles and her parents. On the other hand, traveling alone with Sir Rodger could bring them one step closer to matrimony. She decided that time alone with him would not be a bad thing. Being wooed was pleasurable, like an exciting game. Rosamond now admitted to herself that she found Rodger highly attractive, but he would have to be persuasive indeed to make her change her mind about marrying him. "When?" she asked impulsively.

"Tomorrow."

She watched his gaze linger on the mistletoe (or was it her breasts?), then rise to her mouth. She caught her breath, knowing that her assent had been reckless. Now he imagined it was permissible to kiss her! When he lifted her hand to his lips and kissed her fingers, a feeling akin to disappointment washed over her. *I swear he's doing it apurpose,* she thought, *making love to me with his eyes so I will anticipate his wicked mouth! Well, perhaps two can play that game.*

Rosamond raised her wine cup slowly and sipped. Then she lifted her lashes so that she looked directly into his green eyes, and allowed the tip of her tongue to brush across first her top lip, then her full bottom lip. Her gaze dropped deliberately to his mouth, where it lingered for an indecent length of time. Then she sighed, allowing her lush breasts to rise and then to fall. She watched as the expression in his eyes grew hotter and she saw his jaw harden with desire. The moment he dipped his head to take possession of her lips, she jumped to her feet.

"I must pack if we are to leave at dawn. Good night, my lord."

Rod's dark brows drew together and he swore beneath his breath as he watched her depart. He cautioned himself that Rosamond was a wise little wench; he must not underestimate her intelligence. Then he laughed; at least she had joined the game!

Rosamond dressed in the warmest gown she had brought from Kenilworth and then wrapped herself in her emerald velvet cloak with the marten fur hood. She had packed only a few clothes, opting instead to take her own bed linen rather than fancy gowns.

As Rod helped her into the saddle, she smiled as she remembered Nan's knowing glances that she was being left behind. Rosamond had not been able to convince her that it was out of consideration for her comfort.

"I know what you're up to," Nan had said, "but you're an innocent, remember, and he's five years older and lived at the licentious royal court in *Gascony*! You'll be like a lamb going to slaughter."

"It was Gascony, not Gomorrah, Nan."

"Same thing, from what I've heard," Nan had sniffed.

"You and the rest of the world expect me to marry him, yet you cavil at our being alone together. Nan, in spite of the fact that I find Sir Rodger attractive and admit that my feelings are thawing toward him, I'm not going to fall into his hands like a ripe plum." Rosamond had smiled reassuringly. "Nan, Sir Rodger may be worldly, but I assure you that I am more than a match for him!"

Now, as Rosamond trotted her palfrey from the bailey, she heard the tinkle of silver bells and saw that de Leyburn had fastened some to Nimbus's bridle. It was a lovely gesture on his part. She realized that he paid attention to the details, and to a woman that meant a great deal. Her next thought was that he knew far too much about pleasing a woman. She asked herself if she cared, and the answer came back *Yes!*

"Your palfrey is bred from the famous milk-white steeds of Wales. The stallions make good war horses. My black horse is French, bred for swiftness. He doesn't make you nervous, does he?"

"Not so long as you are there to control him. I'd be afraid to ride him," she admitted, but not without a blush. Their horses seemed to be an extension of themselves, his so powerful and dark, hers so long-legged and blond. Why did the stallion and mare make her think of mating? Rosamond's blush deepened, and she feared he would read her thoughts. Quickly she changed the subject. "If the household servants at Deerhurst are found wanting, where can we get others?"

"That's an easy one. Tewkesbury Castle is only two miles from Deerhurst."

"I assume Tewkesbury is a royal castle?"

"It used to be, but Tewkesbury now belongs to me."

"You?" She could not keep the surprise from her voice.

"It was given to me by the crown for services rendered."

Rosamond was embarrassed. She had had no idea he owned such an impressive property when she'd accused him of wanting to marry her for her landholdings. "I apologize for accusing you of acquisitive ambition, my lord."

Rod grinned at her. "It's completely true. If an ambitious man has one castle, he wants two. If he has two, he lusts for four!"

Rosamond gasped at the audacity of the man. "How very flattering! You openly admit you want me because I'm an heiress?"

"I'd be a bloody hypocrite if I didn't, but you have much more to offer than castles, chérie."

"Such as?" As soon as she asked, she knew the question revealed her vulnerability.

"You have an ancient noble name; you are educated, intelligent, and trained to be a competent chatelaine. You are witty, proud, innocent, and breathtakingly beautiful. A rare prize indeed."

Her violet eyes widened. She had never received such compliments before and didn't know how to respond. "May I remind you I am a prize you haven't yet succeeded in claiming?" Rosamond's reply was as challenging as the cold wind.

When they had ridden five or six miles, he raised his voice above the wind to inquire, "Are you warm enough, Rosamond?"

If she said no, would he take her before him to protect her from the harsh elements? She shivered at the thought of their bodies touching. Which would serve her better, to cling, or be provocative? She chose the latter, and threw back her head to laugh at the weather. "I love the wind, it exhilarates me!" Her fur hood fell back and her hair streamed out like a golden banner.

"You know you are more tempting when you are disheveled, and you are too damned proud to admit that you are freezing cold!" he said. "I think we should stop at Tewkesbury for the night."

So that was his game! Nan's warning came rushing

back to her. If she agreed to spend the night at his castle of Tewkesbury, it would be tantamount to inviting him to take whatever liberties he desired. "I think not, my lord." Her reply was as icy as the wind. She urged Nimbus forward to take the lead. She was uncertain of the way, but hadn't he said they just had to follow the river?

Tewkesbury Castle loomed before them at the juncture of the River Avon and the River Severn. Suddenly, Nimbus stepped on a wolf trap hidden beneath the snow, and it snapped closed on her hoof. The palfrey screamed in fear and took off across the ice of the river. Nimbus managed to shake off the iron snare, but kept on galloping at a frantic pace.

De Leyburn knew the ice on the wider, deeper, fast-flowing Severn would not bear the weight of a horse and rider. "Rosamond! No!" he bellowed. "Halt, halt!" With his heart in his mouth, he watched Nimbus flounder as she went through the ice, disappear below the surface of the water, then resurface and plunge toward the riverbank. To Rod's horror, he saw that the saddle was empty.

"Help! Help me!" Rosamond screamed, then the icy water closed over her mouth, cutting off her cries. She knew the water was deep as she sank down, down. The weight of her velvet cloak and boots was making her sink like a boulder. Her boots touched the riverbed, telling her she could sink no farther, and she began an exhausting struggle to the surface.

The current had carried her beneath the ice, away from the hole her horse had made, but when the top of her head hit the frozen surface, it cracked the thin ice. Rosamond had no time to pray, nor even think coherently; sheer panic took over. The more she tried to grab on to something, the more ice broke from the edges of the hole until it gaped wide.

Rosamond had never experienced cold like this in her entire life. It penetrated her skin, seeped into her blood, chilled her flesh and froze her very bones to the marrow.

Her lungs felt so waterlogged, she couldn't breathe, yet somehow she was screaming.

"Rosamond! Don't panic!" Rod thundered, pulling a rope from his saddlebag.

"I'm sinking!" she screamed.

"Remove your cloak!" he ordered.

Rod's mind flashed about like mercury. He knew the ice would not support him, even if he flattened himself on its surface and crawled. He knew he had no time to waste; she could drown or die from the cold. Rod fastened one end of the rope to a tree and tied the other about his waist. Then he went into the river after her. The icy waters of Kenilworth's mere were like a bathing pond compared with the Severn. Before he could reach her, Rosamond disappeared beneath the surface and he had no choice but to dive for her.

As he swam about beneath the ice, Rod felt panic rise because he could not locate her. Ruthlessly he forced the panic to subside and came up for air. He knew the rope would let him go no farther, and was about to plunge down again, when he saw her head bob above the surface. "Rosamond! I'm here! Come to me!" His deep voice held total confidence, though Rod felt no such thing.

He knew he needed more rope, so he untied it from about his waist and wrapped the end about his thick wrist. With ferocious effort, he stretched out through the icy current and fastened his fingers in the cloth of her gown. He heard a whimper. "Sweetheart, hold on! You're so brave!" Rod stopped shouting to conserve his energy. He would need it to get them both back to the riverbank.

At that point, Rosamond was incapable of speech or even thought. The feeling in her arms and legs was long gone, and now the rest of her body had grown numb from the icy-cold river. She was on the brink of total exhaustion. She kept her mouth above water to gasp an occasional breath by sheer instinct alone, but she was dangerously close to the edge of unconsciousness.

Rod willed his arms to have the strength to hold on to her and at the same time swim toward the bank that seemed so very far away. He was totally focused—there was no room in his mind for failure. He would get her out, no matter what. The difficult part would be to get her out before she froze to death in the icy water. Suddenly he realized that her horse was beside them, floundering wildly in the water, and the turbulence it created pulled them beneath the churning eddy.

He knew he could not let go of either Rosamond or the rope, so he clung to both doggedly. As he and Rosamond resurfaced he felt the cloth of her gown rip and knew he must anchor her body to his, or he would lose her. With one brutal pull that tore the garment in two, he managed to bring her close enough to grab her leg, then he wrapped his arm tightly about her waist.

When Rod reached the riverbank, he hauled her up out of the water first, then clawed his own way out of the freezing river. As he knelt over her, gasping to refill his lungs with air, he saw that she was unconscious and had stopped breathing. Refusing to panic, Rod turned her body face-down, straddled her, and splayed his large hands across her rib cage. He pressed and released in a rhythm that simulated natural breathing, and immediately Rosamond began to cough and gag up water. She didn't open her eyes, but he knew she was at least breathing on her own.

Rod picked her up and held her pressed against his chest. She needed warmth and she needed it now. He whistled for his horse and felt weak with relief when Stygian obeyed. "Good boy . . . hold still," he murmured as he pulled himself into the saddle, clasping Rosamond to his side. He dug his heels into the stallion's flank, and it galloped forward toward the castle. As he shouted to the watchman in the barbican and thundered across the drawbridge, he was vaguely aware of hoofbeats behind him.

Before he reached Tewkesbury's bailey, grooms were

running from the stables to aid him. He slid from the saddle with Rosamond clutched to his breast and turned the horse over to a groom. From the corner of his eye, he caught a glimpse of Nimbus's cream coat and was grateful he would not have to tell Rosamond her palfrey was missing. As he ran with her across the bailey toward the castle, he called over his shoulder, "Check the palfrey's leg—she stepped in a wolf trap!"

Shouting orders, Rod strode through the studded oak portal, then headed for the stairs as his castellan and household servants stood gaping openmouthed. *There had better be a blazing fire in my chamber, or somebody will be flogged,* he thought grimly. He took the stone steps two at a time, strode down the hall, and booted open his chamber door. He laid Rosamond before the fireplace, then dragged a fur cover from his bed and knelt beside her to strip off what was left of her sodden garments. Rod wrapped her naked body in the lynx fur, and only then did he notice his legs were trembling from muscle fatigue.

Burke, his castellan, entered the room, bringing towels and a flagon of brandywine. "You'd best get out of your own clothes, my lord." He went to the wardrobe and brought forth a bedrobe. "I'll fetch you some hot soup from the kitchen. Is there aught else I can do, Sir Rodger?"

Rod shook his head. "Thank you, Burke. I'll manage."

"You always do, my lord."

As Rod gently wiped Rosamond's face with a towel, she opened her eyes, but closed them again without the least flicker of recognition. He was thankful she was starting to regain consciousness, and gathered her long, wet hair into the towel, wrapping it about her head as if it were a turban. Her skin was tinged blue with cold, and he knew he would have to restore her circulation or she would expire from her lowered body temperature.

Impatiently he tore off his own wet, cold garments and flung them to the side of the hearth. Then, naked, he knelt over Rosamond and lifted the lynx fur from her body. She was so slim, so fragile, it caught at his heart. A rush of protectiveness washed over him, and he realized cynically it was the first time he had ever felt any emotion for a woman other than lust or contempt.

He poured warm brandy into his hands, then began to massage her body, starting at the shoulders. With firm, circular strokes, he moved down over her breasts, across her belly, to her hips. His fingers moved in firm circles, rubbing, massaging, kneading the brandy into her flesh so that her blood's circulation would improve. Rod poured more liquor into his cupped palm, then, lifting one of her thighs, he rubbed her leg with long, firm strokes. Her legs were even longer than he had imagined in his sexual fantasies, and suddenly he became highly aroused at the sight and feel of her bare flesh beneath his powerful hands. He had never done this to a woman before, but now it was brought home to him how pleasurably erotic a body massage could be. He promised himself to indulge in this pleasure in the future, once Rosamond was safely recovered.

His cock went rigid as blood flooded quickly into his groin, and it began to throb as his hands lifted Rosamond's other thigh and started to briskly massage it. Rod did not lose his erection, even when Burke arrived with the soup, but his castellan didn't blink an eye as he set down the tray and laced the chicken broth with cream. Rod pulled the fur cover across Rosamond's nakedness to preserve her modesty. "I won't try to feed it to her until she fully regains her senses," he said.

"The soup is for you, my lord, but perhaps you're hot enough."

Rod flashed his castellan a warning glance, but Burke had learned that de Leyburn's bark was worse than his bite. "You've never lost a woman yet, my lord. Who is she?"

"She is Rosamond Marshal."

"Judas Iscariot, why didn't you say so! Get on with reviving her, and I'll get a maid up here to attend her."

"I want no bloody maid; I'll tend her myself. Get the hell out of here so we can have some privacy, man."

After Burke withdrew and closed the chamber door, Rod lifted Rosamond into his lap. He pulled the towel from her hair and cupped her cheek in his powerful hand. "Rosamond, Rosebud, open your eyes!" After he had ordered her three times, her lashes fluttered, then her lids lifted. As she gazed up into the green eyes, her own eyes widened with recognition as she became aware of the man, then memories of the ordeal they had been through came rushing back to her. "I'm . . . so . . . cold. . . ."

With one arm wrapped tightly around her, Rodger poured some brandy into the broth and lifted the bowl to her lips. "Slowly," he cautioned. As she raised her hand to steady the bowl, it trembled like an aspen leaf, and he quickly covered it with his own hand to warm her frozen fingers. Rosamond took a few sips, which seemed to exhaust her. "Rest for a minute." Patiently he held the bowl steady until she caught her breath, then once more he urged the bowl toward her lips. Again she managed a few sips, then turned her face away.

Rodger laid her gently down on the bed, propped up the pillows to support her head, then tucked the lynx fur about her. He noticed that her color had improved only slightly; she still had a bluish tinge about her mouth. "You are going to be all right, sweetheart. Are you warmer now?"

Rosamond stared up at him; her hands and arms, her feet and legs were like ice. "Colder . . ."

De Leyburn made his decision instantly. He turned back the covers and climbed into bed beside her. Then he reached out and pulled her into his arms. He knew only one sure way to warm her. He began to rub her back with long strokes from her shoulder blades to her round bottom cheeks. His hands were large and calloused, and he knew they would feel rough upon her silken skin.

When Rosamond began to make small mewling sounds, he knew the feeling was returning to her frozen flesh.

His erection lay marble-hard against her soft belly as his hands moved firmly up and down her back. Rod tried to ignore it, hoping it would diminish, but of course, the more he massaged her bare flesh, the harder he became. The continuous rubbing of his cock against her silky skin brought heat to his body, if not to hers. Rosamond whimpered as if she were afraid. "No, no, don't be afraid. Trust me, Rosamond. If you can feel what I'm doing, that's good. Give yourself up to me, feel it, feel it."

"Hurting . . ." she gasped.

Rod realized she had not cried out from fear, but from pain because his rigid phallus was like a sword thrusting against her softness. Quickly he turned her around in his arms, so that her back lay against his chest, and he nestled his stiff manhood in the cleft between her buttocks to cushion its hard length. Then his hands stroked over and between her soft breasts, brushing across her heart, then sliding to her belly, rubbing in circles.

Without asking, Rod knew Rosamond was getting warmer. As her body heated up it gave off the scent of brandywine and woman, and he knew it was the most intoxicating aroma he had ever smelled. With her head tucked beneath his chin, he held her spoon-fashion to allow his body's scalding heat to seep into hers.

Rosamond had neither the energy nor the desire to protest what he did. It was as if she had no will of her own, wanting only to yield her body into his possessive hands. As she lay curled against him she gradually became euphoric, drifting in a warm sea of delicious sensation. His hands were magnificent; she wanted him to go on stroking her forever. Her eyelids finally lowered and she gave herself up to sleep and the warm haven of Rodger de Leyburn's body.

He felt her body totally relax against his, and finally knew that Rosamond slept. Rod lay as still as he could so that he wouldn't disturb her slumber, though he himself was highly disturbed. Gradually the light faded from the day, and dusk descended. Though he closed his eyes, he could not sleep, for his body raged with unspent passion and desire for the woman he held in his arms.

Nine

Rod knew the moment Rosamond awoke, for she immediately withdrew her body from his and half turned so that her back lay upon the bed, rather than upon him. Silence stretched between them as she recalled what had led to this shocking intimacy. In order to warm her, de Leyburn was sharing her bed, and what's more, they were both stark naked! Though her modesty had been assailed, strangely, Rosamond wasn't angry; rather, she was thankful for his common sense. He had shared his body's heat with her, which had likely prevented her from becoming gravely ill.

Though Rosamond wasn't angry, she *was* feeling uncomfortable, shy, and rather strange. She had no idea how long they'd been abed, but it was now fully dark, and they lay bathed in moonlight. Finally she found her voice and murmured, "My lord, I find myself in the most peculiar circumstances. . . . I am sharing a bed with a man; indeed, I believe I have actually slept with you! The world would call me a wanton, yet I swear I have never even been kissed."

Rod sat up and bent over her. "That is easily remedied."

As his mouth sought hers, Rosamond drew in a swift breath, then yielded her lips to him. His kiss was hungry, but not ravenous, at least not at first. The firm pressure of his mouth made her part her lips slightly, which encouraged Rod to deepen the kiss. Rosamond found the experience pleasurable and responded softly, warmly. That's when his mouth turned ravenous. Desire ran along his veins, turning his blood hot and demanding. His arms slid about her fiercely, and she felt her breasts crush against the dark hair on his heavily muscled chest. The sensation was arousing and Rosamond lifted her arms, sliding them about his neck. The kiss went on and on, neither of them withdrawing from the hot, melting gratification of their senses.

Their mouths parted at the same moment. "You may consider yourself kissed, Rosebud." Rod searched her lovely face. "How are you feeling after your ordeal?"

"The ordeal of the river or the ordeal of the kiss?" she asked breathlessly.

"The kiss was an ordeal?" he asked, amused, raising an eyebrow.

She smiled dreamily. "It was as cataclysmic as falling into the river."

"I doubt that, chérie; when I pulled you from the water you were unconscious. The kiss didn't even make you swoon."

"Perhaps you should try again, I felt very close to fainting." He responded to her invitation immediately, cutting off further words. He was rampant with need, kissing her savagely, allowing the wildness in his blood free rein, until he cautioned himself that Rosamond was still a virgin. He knew he could seduce her at this moment, but if he took her maidenhead, she might deeply regret it and accuse him of taking advantage of her when she was completely vulnerable. Which would be completely true, he freely admitted.

Gradually, Rod managed to curb some of his passion, though not all. He was still hard and throbbing and knew he would be so as long as they lay naked together. Being with her this way was a divine torment, one he was not willing to relinquish quite yet. With purposeful intent, he drew down the fur cover until it lay across her hips. "I want to look at you." Rosamond blushed in the moonlight as his eyes roamed over her face and her body.

Her violet eyes were fringed by long, golden lashes that cast shadows on her lovely cheekbones. Her lips were swollen from his kisses, which made her mouth look even more sensual and seductive. Her long hair was wildly disheveled from being wet, then dried in bed, without having its tangles brushed out. Her throat was a long column of shadowed alabaster, merging into soft shoulders and delicate collarbone. Her breasts, so lush and round, were far too tempting for Rod to leave untouched, untasted.

His palm cupped one of the firm, upthrust globes, weighing it, caressing it, stroking it with tender reverence, then his thumb brushed across its pink tip, turning it jewel hard. His hand brushed across her heart, then took possession of her other breast, giving it even more attention than the first. Unable to resist longer, he dipped his head to kiss them and lick them and taste them as if they were ripe fruit. It took her breath away, and her beautiful breasts rose and fell rapidly beneath his hungry mouth.

When his hand brushed across her belly, sliding down to where the lynx fur mingled with her golden curls, Rosamond murmured a protest, as Rod fully expected she would. He stayed his hand while he persuaded her to his will. "There is no harm in what we do, Rosebud. I only want to show you a little love play. I promise you will still be a maiden—it will not compromise you in any way."

She wondered if she could trust him to keep his word. She had put her life in his hands, and his great strength and determination had saved her, but could she trust him with her virtue? More to the point, could she trust herself? Lying with him in the bed brought her more pleasure than she had ever known. Perhaps it was heightened because it was forbidden pleasure, or perhaps she was so grateful that he had rescued her, she wished to reward him. Perhaps she was merely curious about the male-female mystery about which she had heard so much but had never experienced herself. Whatever the reason, she purposely remained silent, giving tacit permission.

Rod pulled down the fur cover and tossed it aside, then he stared at her as if mesmerized by the female loveliness spread before him. "You are exquisite to look upon, Rosamond. You are like a lily from the Song of Solomon." He bent over her to drop a kiss into her navel, then continued gazing at every delicious inch of her. "You have the longest legs I've ever seen; they set my imagination aflame. I can feel them wrapped about me when we make love . . . if we make love, but not tonight, my sweet, I promise."

With his intense green gaze upon her, Rosamond felt beautiful. She was unused to a man's undivided attention and found it highly flattering. His dark face and midnight-black hair set her pulses racing, and the contoured muscles of his chest, covered by black hair, tempted her fingers to touch him, trace him, tease him. But she knew she must not arouse him further; he was already on the verge of losing control.

When Rod threaded his fingers through the golden curls on her high mons, Rosamond gasped and, arching her body, cried, "No!" He withdrew his fingers immediately and instead took hold of her hand and drew her fingertips to her woman's center. "Enjoy the sensation, feel the pleasure, sweetheart." He brushed their joined fingers across the sensitive place, allowing her to get used to the intimacy. He knew the moment she thrilled to the touch, and pressed the pads of their fingertips against the sensitive spot hidden inside her scented flesh.

The tiny moan in her throat told Rod that she was experiencing her female sensuality for the first time. He dipped his head and took possession of her lips with his mouth, then set up a rhythm with the tip of his tongue, that matched the pulsations their fingers produced. Almost immediately, he felt her become dewy, and knew she was becoming sexually aroused. Moving in delicate circles around her bud, he enticed her to feel passion. He circled slowly, firmly, never increasing the tempo, knowing a woman craved a faster cadence, but knowing also the slower the pace, the longer the pleasure and the harder the climax.

Rosamond felt a hot ache start in her woman's core, then threads of flame raced up into her belly and fanned outward and upward into her breasts, making them hard and tingling. The scalding threads spiraled higher and higher and ever higher, until she peaked and shattered into a million delicious shards of ecstasy.

Rod immediately stopped the movement of his hand and cupped her mons instead, pressing firmly as she pulsated and quivered, until her last tiny spasm was spent. Then he enfolded her in his arms and held her securely so she could savor the enchantment of what had just happened to her. Rod knew he had held himself in check too long and realized his lust was ravenous and savage. He wanted to mount her and bury himself in her silken sheath, thrusting until he had mastered this woman and made her his forever.

His need made him shudder convulsively, and he knew if he did not find release, he would ravish her. As gently as he could, he drew her fingers down his body, and, holding them within his, wrapped them about his marble-hard shaft. It took only a few manipulations and suddenly he was crying out his release. He covered himself with the soft linen sheet, knowing he could not yet impregnate her with his seed. That was a pleasure he would have to postpone until she was his lawfully wedded wife.

Rosamond buried her face against his shoulder, feeling shy yet strangely empowered from the intimate experience they had shared.

"I'm sorry, Rosamond," he said, the frustration in his body only partially relieved, "please believe I did that for your sake, as much as my own."

When she awoke in the morning, Sir Rodger was nowhere in sight. At the sound of a polite knock upon the door, Rosamond looked around and saw his gray velvet bedrobe lying on the floor. She slipped from the bed, covered her nakedness with the robe, and cracked open the door. Two servants wheeled in the most amazing bathing tub she had ever beheld. It was carved from wood in the shape of a Viking ship, painted bright red, with a dragon masthead.

Behind the servants came Master Burke, Tewkesbury's castellan, carrying a silver basket filled with sponges, exotic bath oils and soaps. "If there is aught else you need, my lady, please let me know. This is a well-run household, with sufficient maids to attend you, but Sir Rodger has rebuffed my suggestion to provide you with a lady's maid."

"You are very kind, Master Burke. I wish you were my castellan." She gave him a brilliant smile. "I can certainly manage without a maid, but if you are thinking of propriety, I'm afraid it's a little late."

"Never, my lady." He bowed with polite dignity and backed from the room.

Rosamond knew whatever secrets she had, or secrets de Leyburn had for that matter, would be inviolate with Master Burke.

Sunshine splashed through the tall windows, saturating the spacious chamber, and for the first time she was able to appreciate the room. She knew instinctively it was Rodger de Leyburn's bedchamber and his carved bed they had shared. It was furnished luxuriously and dramatically. The fireplace and hearth were made of gray slate probably imported from Wales. The window drapes and bed curtains were crimson velvet; the plush carpet was charcoal gray and crimson in an exotic Persian pattern. The walls were covered with Flemish tapestries, whose colors were predominantly crimson and gray. A massive wardrobe took up an entire wall, and beneath the windows there were ebony tables inlaid with red Spanish leather. One of the tables held a chess set whose pieces were Grecian gods and goddesses, carved from black marble. Rosamond decided the chamber revealed much about Sir Rodger de Leyburn. He had flamboyant, yet expensive, taste. He was clearly a man who appreciated the finer things of life and had been collecting them for some time.

As Rosamond removed the bedrobe to climb into the bathing tub, an unusual scent stole to her. She sniffed with appreciation—what was the tantalizing fragrance? A silver urn stood in the corner filled with crimson chrysanthemums, but that was not the source. She lifted her arm to her nose and breathed in the perfume of her skin. Had it come from the robe, or had it come from de Leyburn? Whichever, it was extremely exotic, even erotic, Rosamond realized with a blush.

When the door swung open and de Leyburn walked in, Rosamond slid down in the water and reprimanded him. "You didn't knock!"

"I am unused to knocking on my own chamber door." Amusement danced in his eyes. "Since you haven't a stitch of clothing to put on, I thought I would solve your dilemma, or were you planning to walk about naked for me?"

He was in a teasing mood and she felt a great relief that he had taken a figurative step back from their amorous intimacy of the night before. "You are a devil, de Leyburn." Amusement lurked in the depths of her own eyes as she admitted, "In truth, I had forgotten that I had no clothes."

He opened the box he was carrying. "I have a couple of ells of amethyst velvet that will be enough for a gown and a cloak, if you like it. I have a woman sewing a shift for you as we speak."

She gasped with pleasure when she saw the material. "Oh, is it French-cut velvet? Wherever did you get such beautiful cloth?"

"From France, I believe," he said with a straight face.

"This chamber is magnificent; you have a taste for luxury."

"Whenever I see something beautiful, I have an overwhelming urge to possess it." His gaze lowered from her eyes to her mouth, then dipped even lower.

When Rosamond glanced down, she saw that her breasts were bobbing in the water. Pink suffused her cheeks, yet secretly she was proud of her lush breasts and not displeased that they had been accidentally displayed for him. There was no doubt that Sir Rodger found her physically attractive, and Rosamond realized that there was no point in lying to herself—she found him more than attractive; she found him as magnetic as a lodestone. He was a far more complex man than she had first suspected, and she was intrigued by him. If she could be certain that he wanted her for herself as well as her rich dowry, if she could fully trust him, she would welcome marriage to this compelling man.

A knock upon the door interrupted her thoughts. It was a maid-servant with a breakfast tray. "Oh dear, I wanted to wash my hair, but I don't want the food to get cold—"

Rod picked up a small table and moved it beside the Viking bathing tub. He took the tray from the maid and set it close to Rosamond. "I would feed you, but that would lure me into the water with you and I would soon find myself out of my depth." He winked to show he was teasing. "The sewing woman will bring you that shift and take your measurements for the gown. Enjoy your food; there is a compote of pears and honey from my own orchards."

Three hours later, when Rosamond emerged from Rodger de Leyburn's bedchamber wearing a classic-cut tunic gown made from the amethyst velvet, she knew she looked pretty. The mirror on his wardrobe door had shown her that the color of the French-cut velvet made her freshly washed hair shimmer like fine-spun gold. She had used a golden chain she had found to cinch in the waist of the tunic and suspected it was real gold. When Rosamond had opened the wardrobe, overflowing with his fashionable garments, she had finally identified the scent that clung to them as exotic sandalwood.

As Rosamond walked along passageways that opened into castle chambers, she saw that Tewkesbury was filled with treasures. There were marble figures that must have come from Italy, refectory tables and settles covered with Cordovan leather from Spain, carpets from Egypt that must have been brought back from the Crusades, and vases that must have originated in the Orient. The chrysanthemums in the vases must have been grown in a greenhouse.

She found de Leyburn consulting with his castellan, and when Master Burke excused himself to give them privacy, she liked him even more.

"No one seeing you would believe you almost drowned yesterday." Rod lifted her fingers to his lips, then pressed a kiss into her palm.

The scent of sandalwood stole to her as she fingered the chain belt self-consciously. "I borrowed this."

"Keep it; it adds elegance to the tunic."

"But it's real gold!"

"Anything less would be unworthy of you."

Rosamond laughed. "That is a very flowery speech, my lord. I like you better when you are less glib."

"*Do* you like me, Rosamond?" His green eyes searched her face.

Her heart skipped a beat. She had begun to trust him. "Yes. I didn't want to like you, but I do in spite of myself."

"Then I am content—for the moment."

"Tewkesbury is as filled with surprises as you are, my

lord. You are a collector of beautiful things from around the world."

"It is a passion with me. Lord Edward calls it a compulsion. I collect many things: swords from Scotland and Toledo, pottery from Greece and Phoenicia, art from France, glass from Venice. Wherever I go, without exception, I find something I want."

"I am sure you found nothing at Pershore," she challenged.

"On the contrary, I wanted everything at Pershore, its land, its castle, its chatelaine."

"You *are* a compulsive collector," she said lightly.

"I once told you I would never let you go. I meant it, Rosamond."

Sir Rodger de Leyburn made her feel as if she were the most important woman in the entire world. When they were together, he focused his whole attention upon her, and she could not help but respond to such flattering and complimentary behavior. Yet she cautioned herself to be wary, for she knew he was a practiced courtier, who could have, and likely had had, any woman he wanted.

"Do you feel up to visiting Deerhurst today? It is a scant two miles away."

There is no doubt you will want it too, once you have seen it, Rosamond thought. "Yes, our time grows short. Christmas is less than a fortnight away; at Kenilworth they will be wondering what has happened to delay us."

"You are a lady who is free to make her own choices, her own rules. Eleanor de Montfort has always done that; she will expect no less of you, Rosamond."

"Lady Eleanor is a princess and a countess," she pointed out.

"Eleanor is first and foremost a woman, as are you, chérie."

Rosamond laughed. Rodger's words always imbued her with self-confidence. "I must go and see Nimbus; she was very frightened yesterday. Thank heavens the wolf trap did not lame her."

"We'll leave in an hour. I have asked Master Burke to ride with us to Deerhurst, if you have no objection."

"Master Burke is your one possession that I covet."

Rod slanted a teasing eyebrow. "Not the Viking bathing tub?"

"That too," Rosamond conceded with a smile.

As Deerhurst Castle came into view Rosamond wondered how she could have stayed away so long. It immediately insinuated itself into her heart and firmly embedded itself there. But a deep sadness washed over her as she thought of her brother, Giles, cruelly plucked from life before his prime. Would the sharpness of the pain ever dull, ever be blunted? Rosamond sighed heavily to disperse the scalding pain in her heart and forced herself to think of happy childhood memories.

She saw that de Leyburn's eyes were upon her, probably gauging her mood, guessing at her thoughts, yet he said nothing intrusive, allowing silence to prevail between them. Rosamond noticed that the bailey had no weeds, the dogs were penned, and all looked to be in order. A groom came to tend their horses, and Deerhurst's steward, Master Gore, greeted them and showed the proper respect when he learned their identity.

Servants were dispatched to plenish chambers, and the cook was sent word that the evening meal must be special for the lady of Deerhurst and her betrothed. As they warmed themselves before the fire in the Great Hall, they were served spiced cider. Master Burke set an iron poker into the coals, and when its end glowed red, he plunged it into Rosamond's goblet, then he mulled de Leyburn's cider in the same way.

While Sir Rodger and Burke examined the account books, Rosamond spent the afternoon exploring Deerhurst

Castle's many chambers. She spent a poignant hour in the room her parents used to share, and finally braced herself to enter Giles's bedchamber. Drawings of his favorite dog still lay upon his desk, the paper now brown and withered. Rosamond trailed loving fingers across the charcoal sketches. The inkwell was dried up, the quills stubbed and broken; Giles had had little patience for letter writing.

When she opened the wardrobe and found some of his garments from when he was a boy, a lump came into her throat. When she gathered the sleeve of a doublet against her cheek, her eyes filled with tears. He was a true Marshal male, preferring the somber colors of dark green, mole, and ecru. She decided to take the doublet and a pair of his chausses; until now she had had nothing that belonged to him. She folded the garments and put them on the end of the bed, then she touched the articles on the bedside table. There was a silver dagger, and a pewter casket that likely held a youth's treasures. When Rosamond lifted the lid and found a collection of ladies' ribbons, she was momentarily disconcerted. Then the corners of her mouth rose, and she smiled through her tears, realizing the wild rumors concerning Lord Edward's companions were not unwarranted. She picked up the dagger and placed it alongside the garments she intended to keep.

She and de Leyburn dined in the Great Hall, where she insisted that Master Burke join them. The meal was not up to Tewkesbury's standards, but it was good, and after dinner Rosamond paid a visit to the kitchen to thank the cook and her assistants. An elderly woman bobbed her a curtsy. "I made gingerbread for you, my lady; it was Sir Giles's favorite."

A wedge of anger in her throat made it difficult for Rosamond to speak. Giles should have dined with her tonight, enjoying his gingerbread. *Goddamn the Fates!* she thought bitterly. *Why wasn't he allowed to live out his life?*

She took a piece of the gingerbread and smiled at the woman. "I shall eat it for him."

Rosamond was in no mood for company tonight; she preferred Deerhurst's ghosts. She bade the two men good night and retired to her chamber. She sat gazing into the fire for over an hour, then suddenly the floodgates opened and she sobbed out her heart. When at last she quietened, Rosamond removed the amethyst gown, deciding to sleep in her shift. She dreaded the coming night, fearing the trampling dream.

A soft knock came at the door and Rosamond stiffened. She had been half expecting him, for once a man had shared a bed with a woman, especially one as bold as de Leyburn, he likely assumed he would be welcome there anytime.

"Rosamond, unbolt the door."

"Please, leave me be, my lord."

"Have you been crying?"

"Yes . . . no . . . I want to be alone."

"You *have* been crying. There is no way I am going to let you sleep alone tonight. Open the door!"

His demands were so loud, Rosamond feared everyone at Deerhurst would hear. With fire in her eyes, she drew back the bolt and flung the door wide. "I will not sleep with you again!" Her anger melted immediately, for he held a pup in his arms. She saw the amusement in his green eyes and knew he was laughing at her.

"Nor will *I* sleep with *you*, chérie; the torment is unendurable."

"Come in, you noisy devil."

"I brought you a little bitch. Giles had a Welsh terrier; this is likely one of her whelps. They are prized for ridding the stables of vermin, but they make faithful companions."

She took the dog from his arms. "Thank you, Sir Rodger, that was most thoughtful of you."

"Can you not call me Rod?"

Rosamond blushed hotly. Indeed she could not call him Rod—the sexual connotation was too blatant for her tongue.

His gaze licked over her hair and her shift with the searing heat of a candle flame, then came to rest on her mouth, lingering there with a look of longing. "We'll ride out to the tenant farms in the morning. Good night, Rosebud." He had her and the dog in his arms in a flash, kissing her swiftly, hungrily, then he was gone.

The kiss left her dizzy. She put the dog down and spoke to her. "What shall we call you? Something Welsh, I think. How about Chirk?" The dog barked her agreement and it was settled. When Rosamond romped with the pup, her melancholy mood lifted, and she reflected on how wise de Leyburn was. She was suddenly glad that she had at last found the courage to come to Deerhurst. When she climbed into bed, Chirk jumped up beside her, proceeded to prepare a spot for herself in her bedcovers, then curled up in it. "Your ancestors were wolves," Rosamond told the pup, "and instinct makes you dig a hole in your cave before you can sleep."

Rosamond stayed awake a long time, apprehensive about the trampling dream, but when she did finally fall into a deep sleep, she dreamed of her cousin Harry of Almaine. In the dream, their conversation repeated itself:

"Sir Rodger de Leyburn is paying unwanted attention to me, and I need you to make him keep his distance."

"You must be daft in the head, Rosamond," Harry replied. "Everyone loves Rod; he makes friends easier than any man I've ever met. He has qualities that make others genuinely like him. You should consider yourself lucky to receive his attentions."

Suddenly she found herself alone with de Leyburn. He was wearing a skull helmet and a wolf pelt and carrying her to his Viking ship. Magically the ship turned into a bed, and indeed she did feel lucky to be receiving his attention. "I wanted you to come," she whispered. She lifted her eyes to his and saw that his need was even greater than hers. "Will you ravish me?"

"If that's the only way I can have you."

He stripped off her shift and set his hot, hungry lips to her flesh, then slowly, thoroughly, he began to make love to her with his beautiful mouth.

TEN

When Rosamond and Rodger rode out to the tenant farms, they heard no complaints. Though the children they encountered seemed shy and quiet, at least they did not appear to be afraid of them. Burke asked questions of every tenant about their stock and about Gore, the head steward. The farmhouses and outbuildings were not in disrepair, and when she compared Deerhurst with the conditions she had found at Pershore, Rosamond felt a measure of relief that nothing was gravely amiss.

It was almost dark by the time they returned to the castle. As Rosamond warmed her hands at the fire in the Great Hall, the air was filled with the aroma of roasting meat. Rod handed her a cup of mulled cider. "Would you take dinner with me privately, Rosamond? There are a couple of things I'd like to discuss with you."

She suddenly felt apprehensive. "Will we need to hold a court?"

"No, I don't believe that will be necessary. I heard no real grievances."

"Oh, that's good, I was worried for a moment. Is there aught amiss?"

"Not really. We'll talk when we can be private."

Though his words did little to dispel her disquiet, Rosamond nodded and went upstairs to bathe her hands and face. She had no other gown into which she could change, but at least she could freshen up and brush the tangles from her windblown hair. When de Leyburn arrived at her chamber, two servants carrying trays laden with food accompanied him.

"We'll serve ourselves, thank you," Rod said, dismissing them.

When they were alone, Rosamond smiled at him warmly. Not only was she starting to enjoy their time together, she was beginning to put her trust in him. Her pulse quickened as she anticipated his touch. She knew it would come sooner or later this evening, and in her heart hoped it would be sooner. He was wearing a deep purple doublet and chausses that complemented her amethyst gown, reminding her of two lovers she had once seen in a play, who were costumed in varying shades of the same color.

When Rodger lifted the silver covers from the food, she looked at his powerful hands and shivered, then wondered if he had seen. De Leyburn missed very little with those devilish green eyes of his. Rosamond tried to focus on the food. The soup made from leeks was thick with cream. It was accompanied by a small rack of lamb and vegetables. Rod set the food on a small table before the fire and held her chair. Did she only imagine that he lightly touched her shoulders before he took his own seat opposite her?

As the sexual tension mounted between them, they ate in silence until he poured them wine and offered a toast. "I think we should drink to Deerhurst, or rather to its future."

Rosamond lifted her goblet, then paused. "Its future?"

"The Deerhurst Castle and landholdings are run adequately, but they don't prosper as they should. I would like to see the tenants' children laughing, its pastures filled with milky herds, its castle chambers replenished more luxuriously. Rosamond, we can make Deerhurst *thrive*!"

"We?" Rosamond's pulse began to throb.

"My castle of Tewkesbury is so close, both would benefit from joint management. If Burke was made castellan in charge of both, Deerhurst would soon rival Tewkesbury. It would be a great union . . . as would ours."

Rosamond could not mistake his meaning. Her thoughts beat about rapidly like the wings of a caged bird trying to escape. She sipped her wine to gain time. He made no bones about the fact that he wanted her landholdings, and he had almost convinced her that he wanted her too. Perversely, she decided to test him. "I have no objections to Master Burke becoming my castellan, but you and I, my lord, can we not become secret lovers, rather than husband and wife?" If Rodger truly wanted her, he would be unable to resist her offer. If he wanted only her wealth, he would refuse such an arrangement.

His gaze lingered on her mouth, then moved up to her eyes. Rodger was far too wise to ask her why she did not wish to marry him. Her bold suggestion showed him just how much Rosamond did want him. He knew marriage would take a little more sensual persuasion. "We can indeed become lovers, my beauty." He immediately rose from the table and held out his hand in invitation.

Rosamond drew in a swift breath and quickly set down the goblet, silently cursing her impulsive tongue. After a slight hesitation, she placed her hand in his, and in the next heartbeat he swept her into his powerful arms.

"Open your mouth to me, darling, I want you to enjoy the feel of me inside you." His lips persuaded hers to yield to his desire, and instantly her own desire blazed up to match his. She felt the thrill of his kiss spiral through her body. A curl of fire began in the pit of her stomach and stretched its fingers upward into her breasts and down to her most sensitive female place. She could no longer deny the need she felt for Rodger de Leyburn. His sensual masculine appeal made her weak with yearning.

Rod slowly pulled his mouth from hers and ran the tip of his tongue up and down the curve of her throat. When he heard Rosamond moan with desire, he knew he had her where he wanted her. He pressed his advantage, licking her ear and whispering, "What if there is a child, my love?"

Rosamond drew in a swift breath, pulling away from him. She stared up at him aghast. Splendor of God, she had never thought about a child. Babies were vulnerable little beings. She knew it was not uncommon for them to die during infancy. She could never risk having a child, loving a child, losing a child! She took a deep, steadying breath. Was this the reason she had sought to end the betrothal? Was she afraid of marriage and motherhood? She had never thought of herself as a coward before, but now she did. Was she so terrified of death that she was afraid to live, afraid to love?

Rodger took both her hands in his, lifting first one and then the other to his lips. Then, with his back to the fire, he went down on his knees before her. "Rosamond, my love, will you marry me when we return to Kenilworth?"

The proposal caught her completely off guard. Rodger had never asked her to marry him before! He had arrogantly taken it for granted that the marriage prize was his for the taking. His tender words melted her resistance. She felt his powerful strength through his hands. She wanted that strength, lusted for it. It would mayhap hold her safe against the Fates. "Yes, yes, I will!" she heard herself say quickly, making the commitment before doubts and concerns could stay her tongue.

Without rising, he pulled her down to him before the fire. He could not hide his exultance. He had besieged the castle and it had yielded to him. Could the victor now enjoy the spoils? Not completely, he warned himself. Rosamond Marshal could change her mind right up until the moment they exchanged vows. Rod decided he would give her a loving that left her craving more.

He kissed her hungrily, possessively, mastering her with his tongue until she clung to him sweetly. As their food lay forgotten, his bold hand slipped beneath the folds of the amethyst tunic and made its slow, purposeful journey up her calf, across her knee to the soft flesh of her inner thigh. His fingers trailed up past her garter to her bare skin, going ever higher seeking the precious object of his desire.

She gasped beneath his lips as his fingertips circled her woman's center. He toyed and teased and played there until he felt that she was thoroughly aroused, then he withdrew his hand from beneath her gown. The tiny moan of protest was music to his ears, telling him he was free to undress her completely. He unfastened the gold chain, lifted off the tunic and then the shift.

She lay before him on the lynx fur in silken splendor with the fireshine playing over her luscious breasts and golden mons. Her black hose were such a contrast to her pale flesh, they added to the erotic picture she made. Rod knew she must be feeling deliciously wicked wearing only the hose, far more wanton than being completely naked.

"You are so unearthly fair, perhaps I'll just look and not touch." He heard the swift intake of her breath and watched her breasts rise and fall. "I want to imprint this picture on my mind so that I can conjure you when we are apart." He opened her knees, and his gaze smoldered as he saw the pink rosebud nestled between her legs. Then he dipped his dark head and kissed the honey-gold tendrils.

"No!" she cried out, but he knew she was not forbidding him; rather she was shocked that a man would do such an intimate thing to a woman, and he felt exultant that she was so innocent.

"Yes, Rosamond," he murmured, blowing softly on the golden curls to tease and arouse her. "I'm going to taste you."

Rosamond thought she must be dreaming; surely this could not really be happening. The moment his mouth touched her, she shivered with pleasure and knew it was very real. She opened her thighs wantonly and arched herself into his hungry mouth. When she felt his tongue curl about her, licking and tasting, she wanted to scream with excitement. She could feel the heat from the fire on her naked flesh, but his tongue was hotter than any flame.

For the first time, she realized she could give her body to him without yielding her heart, and it was like a revelation. She could feel passion without feeling love. She could lose herself in the sensations he aroused in her and allow him to teach her the sensual secrets that would pleasure them both. They would be united in marriage, in name, in lands and castles, and in the flesh, but Rosamond would be able to keep her inner self separate.

Rod was extremely careful when he thrust his tongue inside her. He would keep her virgin; her maidenhead must not be breached until their marriage was consummated. Beddings were an ancient custom, and if no blood was found on the sheets the next morning, the bride would be shamed. He never wanted Rosamond to feel shame; he wanted her to feel pride, in her marriage and in her husband.

He felt her first tiny fluttering pulsations, then heard her cry out in her passion. Quickly he moved up over her, to cover her lips with his own, then cradle her in his arms.

"I can taste myself on your mouth," she whispered, shocked.

Her words inflamed him. He wanted her in the bed, beneath him; craved her long legs wrapped about his body while he buried himself in her honeyed sheath. His erection was so pronounced, he could feel his blood pounding and pulsing in his shaft. Forgetting his resolve, Rod lifted her high against his heart and carried her to the bed. As her hands came up to divest him of his doublet, incredibly, he heard a soft knock upon the chamber door.

"Peste!" Who would dare disturb him? He padded to the door and listened. He heard a scratching sound on the wood, instinctively palmed his dagger, and cautiously cracked open the door. Chirk was through the opening in a flash, while Burke stood at the threshold.

"Griffin has just arrived with messages, Sir Rodger. As soon as you repair to your own chamber, I will send him up."

De Leyburn nodded and closed the door. Chirk was wagging her tail, eager to jump up on the bed, but waiting for permission from the dominant male presence. Rod sat upon the bed and took Rosamond's hand to his lips. "My squire has tracked us down. Can you be ready to return to Kenilworth on the morrow?"

Rosamond laughed tremulously, knowing she would be married upon her return. "Since I have nothing to pack, I am ready, my lord."

On the ride back to Kenilworth, Rosamond, Rodger, and Griffin broke their journey at Pershore, and the following day, joined by Nan and Ned, they arrived at their destination. Rodger de Leyburn had received two messages summoning him back to Kenilworth; one from Lord Edward, the other from Simon de Montfort.

Lord Edward greeted his steward and friend with great warmth. Rod knew the prince so well, he could tell he was bursting with impatient energy to confide something. "Rod, I've heard rumors that my father has no intention of returning for the Candlemas Parliament."

Rodger de Leyburn knew if King Henry returned and tried to repudiate the Provisions of Oxford, it could lead to civil war. So the king would stay out of England and whittle away at the Provisions one by one. "Simon de Montfort is adamant about holding a Parliament. If the king reneges after signing the Provisions of Oxford, we could find ourselves at war," Rod cautioned.

"Earl Simon *will* hold Parliament. If my father doesn't return, he will hold Parliament with *me* in charge."

Rod knew Simon de Montfort would do it without hesitation.

Edward drew close and searched his friend's face intently for a full minute. Though they were completely alone,

Edward lowered his voice to speak confidentially. "I feel it in my bones that Simon wants to put me on the throne in my father's place and make me King of England."

Rodger de Leyburn recoiled sharply, but it was on the inside. His dark face registered none of the shock Lord Edward's words evoked. *Christ's Blood, I thought I was shock-proof. I thought I was the most cynical bastard who ever drew breath, but I was wrong! I know Edward to the core, know his driving ambition, so why am I shocked?* Rod drew in a deep breath. He had committed himself to Edward years ago, and his loyalty was rock solid, come what may. "Never say it out loud again, Edward," Rod advised. "Walls have ears." He deliberately changed the subject. "I too have news. Rosamond Marshal has agreed to marry me."

Edward grinned. "Good man! Mayhap we'll both achieve our goals."

Simon de Montfort took Rodger de Leyburn to his private chambers in the Caesar Tower. With his cynicism restored, Rod was prepared to hear any proposal without being shocked.

"I have information that leads me to believe King Henry will not return for the Parliament."

Rod did not reveal that he had already heard this. "The king cannot swallow his pride; it chokes him."

"Henry's pride will be his downfall. Anticipating that the king would use delays over the French treaty as an excuse, I wrote to the justiciar, the marshal, and the other nobles, summoning them to the February Parliament. I assured them that Lord Edward would be at my side." He looked de Leyburn directly in the eye. "Can I count on Edward's presence?"

"Edward will be there, Earl Simon."

"I want the prince to add his signature to the Provisions of Oxford and speak for the barons' cause at that Parliament. Can you persuade him?"

Rod's green eyes did not waver as he stared back at de

Montfort. Did Simon really have it in his mind to set Prince Edward Plantagenet on the throne, supplanting Henry as king? Or was de Montfort ambitious enough to want to rule himself? Rod was far too wise to voice such treasonous and perfidious questions. The earl might want Edward to *assume* de Montfort would set him up as king. It was a deep game, and the players, Edward and Simon, with their shrewd minds and ruthless ambitions, were certainly well matched in shrewd calculation. "Together, I believe we can persuade him, my lord earl."

"Splendid! Is there aught I can do for you in return, Sir Rodger?"

"Rosamond Marshal and I are to be wed. Could we impose upon you to have the nuptial ceremony at Kenilworth?"

"That is no imposition. Eleanor would have my balls if I allowed Rosamond to be wed from anywhere but Kenilworth! I'll even give the bride away. She's a ward of the crown and that duty should be performed by a royal, but I assume Edward will be your groomsman. Congratulations!" Simon winked. "Pershore and Deerhurst are well worth the trouble of a wife."

"Oh, my dear, I am utterly delighted that you and Sir Rodger are to be wed!" Eleanor de Montfort exclaimed. "What made you change your mind, Rosamond?"

"I have discovered how useful a man can be in helping me manage my estates." Rosamond blushed, then added, "And I have actually come to find Sir Rodger compellingly attractive, in spite of the fact that I don't completely trust the handsome devil."

Eleanor gathered Rosamond into her arms, then released her so that she could appraise the change in her. "You look absolutely radiant! Mark my words, marriage will be the making of you, Rosamond. We must waste no time; the nuptials can be celebrated just before Christmas, say the twenty-third; that gives us only a week to prepare.

The moment the Yule celebrations are over, we shall all be off to London. We go to Durham House, and I imagine Sir Rodger will take you to Windsor or Westminster."

"Thank you, Lady Eleanor, you are very generous to have the wedding at Kenilworth."

"Kenilworth has long been your home, and I want you to remember that you may come back anytime. We love you very much, Rosamond."

"I love you too . . . you have been like a mother to me, my lady."

"Since you and Rod have been off on your own for some time, I assume he has taken it upon himself to teach you the mysteries of becoming a woman?"

Rosamond blushed. "Yes . . . no . . . I am still a virgin. On the wedding night . . . when the bridegroom broaches the hymen . . . I have heard gossip that there is much pain and blood. . . ."

"Oh my darling, I am the one woman in the world you shouldn't be asking about this. My experience was so devastating—" Eleanor stopped midsentence when she saw Rosamond's eyes widen with apprehension. "Come and sit while I tell you. You will feel only relief that your wedding night will not be like mine."

Rosamond sat down on the padded settle before the fire beside Eleanor de Montfort, wildly curious about her first marriage.

"My father, King John, died when I was one, and I never knew him. The important man in my life when I was a child was William Marshal, your uncle. I didn't just love him, I worshipped him. He was my heart's desire and they married me to him when I was nine years old. Poor William! He was a great soldier, the marshal of England, and a mature man of thirty years.

"He did not take me to live with him until I was fifteen. Those were the six longest years of my life. I lived at Windsor and worked like a fiend at my lessons so that I would become a perfect wife. But even when we lived under the same roof, William's sense of honor would not allow him to make me a woman until he thought I was old enough to bear a child."

Eleanor sighed, remembering. "When I was sixteen, William's sister Isabella married my brother, Richard of Cornwall. At long last William decided that their wedding night would be our wedding night as well. I was so excited, I wanted to scream. I was extremely obsessive when I was young. I loved William with all my heart and soul, and he had become my obsession, I'm afraid.

"The wedding was at Westminster, and William and I were given one of the towers, which consisted of two rooms, one above the other. That night I went up to the sleeping chamber first, and readied myself for bed. William remained below so long, I simply couldn't wait! I went down to him and he carried me back up to bed. I remember he had a man's body, a soldier's body—hard, well muscled, strong. Splendor of God, I still recall every minute detail." Eleanor's sapphire eyes became liquid with unshed tears.

"At last we were abed together. It was so intimate, so private, so secret . . . it was like Paradise. William was so gentle with me. When he joined his body to mine, I felt the pain and the fullness, but I exulted in it. It spread inside me like a glorious, burning sunburst, and I loved the closeness, the heat, the weight of his body. I think I screamed, but I heard him cry out too. Slowly, I realized that his weight was too much for me . . . he was hurting me. When he didn't speak and didn't move, I thought he had fallen asleep. When I couldn't awaken him, I knew something was wrong. In my ignorance, I thought he had fainted from the hymenal rite."

Eleanor swallowed hard and whispered, "William was dead. . . . He had been poisoned by an enemy. I don't know how long I lay there in terror before I began to scream. It was Rickard de Burgh who came in and lifted William's body off me. Sir Rickard was ever the perfect knight. I don't know what I would have done without him."

Rosamond touched her hand. "Lady Eleanor, I had no idea."

Eleanor swiped at her eyes and laughed. "So you see, if I could face all that on my first wedding night, you can face an ardent Rodger de Leyburn."

"I didn't want to marry Sir Rodger because I fancied myself in love with Rickard de Burgh," Rosamond confessed.

"Sir Rickard is a most chivalrous knight, and devastatingly attractive, but far too old for you, darling. You lost your heart to him because he was like a father to you, much as William Marshal was to me. I didn't realize it, of course, until after I fell passionately in love with Simon de Montfort. And it will be so with you and Rod."

No, Rosamond thought, *I will marry Sir Rodger, but I will never allow myself to love him. What you have just told me proves that to love someone deeply is to lose them. I will try to never love anyone again.*

When Rosamond was alone with Demi, she told her friend that she had finally agreed to marry Sir Rodger de Leyburn. Demi was thrilled and asked her what had happened to make her change her mind. Rosamond told Demi about falling through the ice, and how de Leyburn's strength had saved her life. She did not tell her any intimate details of what had followed the rescue, because she felt Demoiselle de Montfort was too young to learn about sexuality.

Chirk, however, provided plenty of innocent entertainment. She made the young women laugh, and Demi had no objection to the Welsh terrier sharing their chamber. The feisty little dog was clean, well trained, and independent, never leaving little turds in the rushes, but going outside the castle, then miraculously finding her way back to Rosamond and Demi's bedchamber.

Rosamond did not have a minute to waste. A wedding

gown and new garments were being made by Lady Eleanor's sewing women, and she spent much time in the solar helping with the preparations for both the wedding and the Yule. Nan helped her into her peacock velvet gown with the small train. Tonight she and Sir Rodger would sit on the dais with Lord Edward, Lady Eleanor, and Earl Simon, to be feted for their upcoming marriage by all of Kenilworth.

"Rickard de Burgh is back from Ireland; have you seen him yet?" Demi asked, as her maid threaded pearls through her dark curls.

"Rickard de Burgh . . . did he bring his bride back with him?" Rosamond asked breathlessly, crushing down her emotions at the mere mention of his name.

"Sir Rickard isn't married, Rosamond."

"But . . . but I thought he returned to Ireland to wed—"

"No, no, you have it mixed up. It was his twin brother, Michael. It was *Mick de Burgh* who took a wife."

Rosamond sank down on the edge of her bed in shock as the blood slowly drained from her face. Then shock gradually turned to anger. Rodger de Leyburn had deceived her. Her temper simmered and then sizzled as she realized he had done it deliberately. He had no doubt figured that if she believed that Sir Rickard de Burgh had pledged his troth to another, she would stop mooning over Sir Rickard and be more receptive to his own seduction of her. When her fury reached the point of explosion, she acted upon it.

ELEVEN

You bastard!" Rosamond stood on the threshold of Rodger de Leyburn's chamber in the Warwick Tower. With her hands on her hips and her chin held high, she added more invective. "You manipulating swine! You deliberately *misled* me to believe that Sir Rickard de Burgh had returned to Ireland to be married. Well, sir, he is back at Kenilworth with no *bride* in evidence!"

"Rosamond, I do not appreciate foul language and insolence in a lady, and certainly not a wife." His face was grim, his words forbidding, but she heeded not the warning.

"Rot in hell!" Rosamond turned on her heel and kicked the train of her peacock gown with the hauteur of a countess.

He clamped a powerful hand on her arm and whirled her to face him. "Never turn your back on me again, lady. If you want a knockdown fight with me, be woman enough to stand your ground. What possible difference does it make to you whether Sir Rickard de Burgh is wed or not?"

Rosamond's cheeks tinted pink. He was trying to goad an admission from her. "Remove your hand from me, sir. Such possessive gestures are inappropriate from you, for you will never own one small part of me."

Rather than removing his hand, Rod clamped the

other one to her, cupping both shoulders. "I shall, Rosamond," he vowed. "I shall!"

De Leyburn was far stronger than she, and the only way Rosamond could hurt him was with words. She laughed in his face. "You will never have my heart; I lost it long ago to Sir Rickard, as you well know, or you would not have found it necessary to lie about him!"

Rod's green eyes narrowed, masking his jealousy. "He can keep your heart. I'll settle for your body . . . and your castles."

"You devil, de Leyburn! You are mad if you think I would marry you now; the wedding is off!"

"Do not delude yourself, Rosamond, you *will* be my wife!"

In Kenilworth's map room, Simon de Montfort unrolled the parchment of the Provisions of Oxford on the black oak table and held it steady for the prince. Lord Edward dipped the quill and with a bold flourish signed *Edward Plantagenet.*

Rodger de Leyburn's speculative gaze traveled from Lord Edward to Earl Simon. Which of the two would emerge as top dog? Each would use the other to achieve his goal. But in any encounter between two men, one dominated, the other acquiesced; one led, the other followed. In the short term, Earl Simon would be the leader, but de Leyburn knew Edward Plantagenet better than any man breathing, and he had no doubt who the ultimate victor would be. But for the present, the spirited warhorse and the young stallion, in harness together, would make a formidable team. Rod knew that neither of them acted for personal glory alone, but for a better government, a better England. Both men believed that the end justified the means, and to a point, so did he.

"If it suits your plans, Edward, I would like to depart for London the day after Christmas," Simon declared.

"We would have celebrated Christmas at Windsor if

Sir Rodger's wedding were not imminent. We will hold the New Year's celebrations there instead. I will billet my Gascons at the Tower of London."

"It is good strategy to keep your fighting men close by you," the earl said. "In London, trouble can flare up at any time."

Rod did not mention that Rosamond Marshal was again refusing to marry him. He still had two days to change her mind. As he and Edward left the earl's private quarters in the Caesar Tower, the prince said, "I am more convinced than ever that de Montfort intends to make me king. I would like to do something to reward him. Not merely a costly gift for Christmas, but rather something that would honor him. Any suggestions?"

Rod's mind worked quickly. "Why don't you knight one of his sons? It would honor him above all things."

"Splendor of God, you always know exactly the right thing to do. Which son? Simon is his namesake, but it had best be Henry, his heir. I will knight him at your wedding celebration!"

Rod knew there might be no wedding celebration if he did not act decisively. He excused himself from Lord Edward and with firm resolve sought out Sir Rickard de Burgh. The Irish warrior was the barrier that stood between himself and Rosamond, and Rod was determined to remove that barrier. He already felt envy for the Irish knight, and now he had to add jealousy, if he was being honest.

"Hilda tells me you refuse to be fitted for your wedding gown. You are to be wed on the morrow—what on earth is going on, Rosamond?" Lady Eleanor could not hide her annoyance. She had a hundred things to see to for the Yule celebration and another hundred for her household's removal to Durham House at Charing Cross, just outside the city of London.

"I have called off the wedding, Lady Eleanor. I cannot marry Rodger de Leyburn."

"What nonsense, you cannot call it off—the plans are set. You are just having the jitters; all brides suffer such misgivings."

"Sir Rodger lied to me—he manipulated me so that I would agree to the marriage."

"Rosamond, all men manipulate to get their way, aye and women too for that matter. 'Tis human nature. The betrothal has stood for years. You cannot play fast and loose with the man, saying yea one minute, nay the next. The two of you have traveled together—in the eyes of the world you are lovers. If you create a scandal now, no other man will have you."

Rosamond flushed rosily. How could she deny they were lovers when they had slept in the same bed? "He wants only my castles," she protested lamely.

"That shows he is ambitious, a quality to be admired. Rosamond, you are thinking only of yourself. Earl Simon wants this marriage; Lord Edward wants this marriage. The nuptials will help cement the bond that grows between them, and that bond is of paramount importance to the future of England. I want you to go up to the solar and let Hilda give you the final fitting for your gown."

Rosamond lowered her lashes to mask the defiance she felt. *I am just a pawn in their political power struggle!* she told herself. She curtsied and headed for the stairs. Rosamond did not go to the solar, however. She went up to Kenilworth's battlements, into the cold fresh air where she could think. She filled her lungs with the invigorating winter air and gazed out over the sere landscape that showed pockets of snow lying beneath leafless trees.

Rodger de Leyburn dominated her thoughts. Why had he lied to her? Could it possibly have been because he was jealous of her feelings for Sir Rickard de Burgh? Her heart skipped a beat. If Rodger was jealous, did it mean his feelings for her ran deep? Nay, he had lied to get his own way!

"Rosamond . . . my lady." The beautiful voice with its Irish lilt brought her from her reverie.

She turned from the crenellated wall, and her eyes widened when she saw who spoke to her. "Sir Rickard," she breathed, unable to finish her sentence or even her thought. Had she conjured him? Rumor had it that he was a warlock with special powers. His resemblance to de Leyburn was quite strong. They had the same green eyes and jet black hair, the same lithe and powerful build. Rosamond shivered.

"Permit me, lady." Sir Rickard drew off his cloak and gently laid it across her shoulders. Rosamond saw the weathered lines about his eyes and mouth, the silver threads in his ebony hair. "Would you walk with me, Rosamond?"

His manner was so chivalrous, she felt almost mesmerized. She placed her fingers on his outstretched arm and walked beside him. "You . . . you are newly returned from Ireland, Sir Rickard?"

"Yes, I carried messages to my father from Earl Simon."

"Is it true that your brother was married while you were there?" she asked in a rush.

"Yes, Mick was married," he said reflectively. "I understand *you* are to be wed tomorrow?"

"No! That is, I *was* to be married, but I have changed my mind."

"Sadly, that seems to be a lady's prerogative. I hope you have good reason, Rosamond. I hope it has naught to do with me."

Rosamond was aghast. Who had told him she fancied herself in love with him? Demi? Lady Eleanor? "I . . . I did have a tendresse for you, Sir Rickard . . . you are such a chivalrous knight . . . it was only a girlish fancy," she confessed. "Then my betrothed deliberately lied to me, telling me you had returned to Ireland to be wed." She laughed nervously. "I imagined myself to be heartbroken."

He placed a comforting hand over her fingers. "Sir Rodger did not lie to you, my dear. I did return to Ireland to be wed."

Rosamond stopped walking and searched his dark face.

"When I returned to Connaught, the lady told me she could not live with the special powers I have, and that in my absence she had fallen in love with my twin brother. Mick is far less complicated than I am."

"Oh, my lord, I am so very sorry! I know what it is to lose someone you love," she said passionately.

"Nay, Rosamond, 'twas no great tragedy. I lost my heart years ago to another. One I could never have."

She gazed up into his eyes and suddenly she knew. "It was Lady Eleanor, wasn't it?"

He smiled, remembering. "Princess Eleanor, already wed to the marshal of England. When he died, she swore a vow of chastity and almost became a nun."

"Earl Simon married the woman you loved," she said wistfully.

"I rejoiced that he did so. She needed a man strong enough to stand up to the king, and the bishops, even the Pope."

"But you *loved* her, Sir Rickard!"

His lips curved into a smile. His mouth was beautiful. "When you truly love someone, you want what is best for them. Earl Simon was *best* for Eleanor." He lifted her fingers to his lips. "Rodger de Leyburn is best for you, Rosamond."

She took in a swift breath. It seemed she was the only one in the world unsure of this marriage. "How do you know that?" she demanded. "Is it your gift of second sight?"

Rickard de Burgh laughed softly. "Some consider it a curse, not a gift. I don't want to frighten you, my dear, but the future brings a great conflict. Rodger de Leyburn's strength and position will give you the protection you need. It will be a rough road for all, but in the end you will not just survive, you will flourish."

As she looked up into his eyes, she saw that they were not really like de Leyburn's at all. Though Rickard de Burgh looked at her, he did not really see her—he saw some vision. When de Leyburn's bold green gaze was upon her, he not only saw her, he undressed her! Lady Eleanor's words came back to her: *Sir Rickard is a most chivalrous knight, and devastatingly attractive, but far too old for you, darling. You lost your heart to him because he was like a father to you, much as William Marshal was to me. I didn't realize it, of course, until after I fell passionately in love with Simon de Montfort. And it will be so with you and Rod.*

"Thank you for sharing this confidence with me, Sir Rickard. I will think hard on what you have told me." Rosamond handed his cloak back to him and descended from Kenilworth's battlements.

When she entered her chamber, she found her wedding dress lying upon her bed. Apparently, Hilda had finished it, without a final fitting. It was a costly gown, designed to serve her at Windsor's court functions. Rosamond touched the forget-me-not blue silk with her fingertips, wishing it away, wishing Sir Rodger de Leyburn had never come to Kenilworth. Because of him, her thoughts were in disarray, her temper in chaos, her poise shattered, and her tranquility vanished. De Leyburn was a devil who had insinuated himself into her life and was determined to bend her to his will.

The things Lady Eleanor had said about this marriage cementing the bonds between Lord Edward and Earl Simon made her feel like a marionette. And she suspected that someone had asked Sir Rickard de Burgh to seek her out and persuade her to their cause. Rosamond decided that she would not go to the hall to dine tonight, but remain in her chamber. She would remain here all day tomorrow as well, avoiding everyone. When she did not show up at the chapel at the appointed time, all Kenilworth would know that the wedding was off! Rosamond had a mind of her own; she would show them that they could not pull her strings to make her obey!

That evening both Demi and Nan left her to herself. Both believed that Rosamond was pensive because she was nervous and because very soon she would be leaving Kenilworth, which had been her home for so many years. They did not wish to intrude on Rosamond's last night as an unmarried lady. Before leaving Rosamond's bedchamber, Nan, who had already packed most of her mistress's clothes, linen, and other belongings for her move to London, glanced over at her fondly. Chirk lay curled on Rosamond's lap, her eyes closing in ecstasy as her ears were gently rubbed. *I hope this marriage is right for her,* Nan thought silently as she softly closed the door.

By first light on December 23, Kenilworth Castle was a hive of activity. The chapel was decorated for the nuptials and for the Holy Days of Christmas. The kitchens were filled with tantalizing aromas; the loaves of bread had gone into the ovens before dawn and then dark fruitcakes took their place. Outside, a great pile of oysters was being shucked, traditional fare for weddings, while stags and boar were spitted over fire pits. Barrels of October ale were being brought from the brewhouse, and red wine, imported from Gascony, was hauled up from Kenilworth's cellars.

In the Warwick Tower, the door was ajar between the adjoining chambers of Edward Plantagenet and Rodger de Leyburn. Their squires, Owen and Griffin, scurried back and forth as the two nobles dressed for the wedding. Lord Edward was in high good humor, shouting bawdy advice to his friend about the best way to rid a virgin of her hymen. Rod gave as good as he got, reminding Edward that soon his own virgin bride would be brought to Windsor.

"You are a lucky devil, Rod. Not only do you gain a

wealthy heiress, you avoid saddling yourself with a mother-in-law. What on earth she sees in an ugly fellow like you, I have no notion. She should leave you standing at the altar!"

Rod suddenly went cold with premonition. Since Rosamond had told him to "rot in hell," she had purposely avoided him. Rod assured himself that she would come to the chapel, she would not dare do otherwise. But an inner voice warned him that Rosamond was not like other women. She had a reckless will of her own, and a flaming temper when she chose to display it. A good deal of her appeal was the challenge she represented. To avoid the risk of public humiliation, Rod decided he had better make sure of her.

He walked into Lord Edward's chamber. "Here is the ring, try not to lose it." It was a wide band of twenty-two-carat gold inscribed with their names: **Rosamond*Rodger**, the letters forming an infinite circle. "Excuse me, there is something I must do."

"Enjoy your last hour of freedom, your leg shackles await!" Edward taunted as he slipped the ring into his doublet emblazoned with the Plantagenet lions.

To avoid running into other people, Rod climbed to Kenilworth's ramparts, then crossed to the Lady Tower. He descended the stone steps that led to Rosamond's door.

From the moment she awoke, Rosamond had had a dilemma on her hands. Nan brought her breakfast and urged her to hurry. "I'm not going through with it," Rosamond said quietly.

Knowing how stubborn her charge could be, Nan resorted to a little manipulation of her own. "You willful girl, I am going to be sick!" Nan clapped her hand over her mouth and fled to the garderobe.

The Demoiselle awoke, hugged her friend, and urged her to hurry. This time Rosamond wisely remained silent. Before the bathwater was cleared away, the visiting began. It seemed every female at Kenilworth wished to visit the bride this morning. They exclaimed over the elegant wedding dress and gave Rosamond whispered advice regarding marriage, and the wedding night in particular.

Rosamond knew pandemonium would ensue if she breathed a word about her decision, so she said nothing. They would know soon enough, when she did not show up at Kenilworth's chapel. Her first pang of guilt came when Demi put on her lovely gown of silver tissue. She was to be Rosamond's maid of honor, and she was bubbling with excitement. The next pang of guilt came when Lady Eleanor arrived, bringing Bette, her own tiring-woman, to style Rosamond's honey gold tresses.

Nan returned with compressed lips and Rosamond suspected that it was she who had summoned the countess.

"Since you are a royal ward, darling, Simon and I will *both* give the bride away," Lady Eleanor declared with regal pride.

Sacrifice the pawn, you mean! Rosamond tried to summon anger, but all she felt was guilt. She sat obediently in her linen shift while Bette brushed her hair, then fastened on the circlet of silk snowdrops. The females in the chamber chatted endlessly, completely oblivious to Rosamond's inner turmoil. It was only when Eleanor, Demi, Nan, and Bette collectively reached for the wedding gown that Rosamond broke her silence. "Oh, please, no! Could I be alone?" she pleaded.

Everyone in the room except Nan put it down to bridal nerves. Lady Eleanor ushered them all out. "Rosamond, rub some rose petals on your cheeks, you are far too pale. Nan, be sure she isn't late." When the chamber door closed, leaving Rosamond and Nan alone, an uncomfortable silence stretched between them. Filled with guilt, Rosamond felt bad about her decision to remain in her room. She would have changed her mind if the alternative had not been worse.

Rosamond watched Nan busy herself, gathering together her mistress's toilet articles, her new night rail and bedgown to take to the bridal chamber that had been especially prepared in the Clinton Tower, so named for Geoffrey de Clinton, who had built Kenilworth in the twelfth century. When another tap came at the door, Rosamond's patience flew out the window. "Please go away!" she admonished.

The door was opened with such force, it crashed against the wall. Sir Rodger de Leyburn, clad in midnight blue, stepped across the threshold. Rosamond gasped. "You cannot be in the ladies' quarters, it is forbidden!"

"I revel in the forbidden." He gave Nan a telling look, then nodded toward the door. The tiring-woman, relieved to turn the problem over to him, quickly departed.

De Leyburn's dominant male presence sparked Rosamond's temper and doused her guilt. "How dare you enter my bedchamber when I am in my shift?" she demanded hotly.

"Let me help you into your wedding gown," he said silkily.

"No!" she spat.

He gave her a level look. "Put on your wedding gown, or I shall put it on for you."

"Don't you dare touch me!"

"I will touch you, by God, any time and any place I choose!" Rod grabbed her by the shoulders and pulled her to her feet most ungently. She reached for his face to scratch it, but Rodger saw her intent and quickly imprisoned her wrists and lifted them above her head, forcing her struggling body closer to his. He dipped his head, intending to master her with a possessive kiss, but Rosamond deliberately bit his lip. With a foul curse, he picked her up and tossed her onto Demi's empty bed, then threw himself on top of her to prevent her escape.

In her struggle to free herself from the dark devil, Rosamond's breasts spilled from the low-cut linen shift. She lay panting beneath him, shocked beyond belief that she was becoming aroused. She gasped as his warm breath swept over her naked breasts, then moaned as his hot mouth covered her nipple, sucking greedily. Rosamond knew both his anger and his lust had been fiercely aroused. He whispered hot words, dark words against the sensitive peak of her breast.

"Stop, stop!" she begged breathlessly, fearing that soon it would be too late for either of them to stop.

He lifted his dark head and raked her with his fiery green gaze. "Will you put on your wedding gown?" he demanded. She stared at him a moment, taken aback by the fierce expression in his eyes. When she nodded her assent, he slid from the bed and offered her his hand.

"Rot in hell!" she cried, rolling from the bed and pulling her shift up to cover her naked breasts. Rosamond tossed back her wildly disheveled hair and lifted her chin defiantly.

Rodger's eyes narrowed. "Either you put on the gown or I carry you to the chapel in your shift; the choice is yours."

An icy shiver ran down her spine. Rosamond knew he meant it. "If the choice were mine, sir, I would remain a spinster! But the choice is not mine. I am being forced into this marriage by the de Montforts, by the prince, and by you!"

Rod decided to reason with her. "Rosamond, you are a beautiful, aristocratic woman, just like Eleanor de Montfort. You need a powerful man beside you, in order to take your rightful place in society. Did I not put Pershore back in good running order? This marriage is exactly right for you." Rod looked directly into her eyes and said quietly, "What you feel is not anger, Rosamond, it is fear."

She glared at him fiercely, but could not deny his accusation. He reached for her hand and held it tightly. "Tell me what you fear, my sweet."

"Nothing!" She felt his warmth seep into her fingers. It was a barefaced lie, of course. "Least of all, *you*!"

His green eyes lit with amusement. "Then prove it, Rosamond. Put on your wedding dress and come down to the chapel."

She knew she really had no choice in the matter. She told herself that she had only agreed to marry him because he had saved her life, and now the powers that be would not allow her to change her mind. She was being forced to marry against her will. Rosamond didn't trust herself to speak as she stood before him in angry defiance.

"You willful, stubborn little witch! I will make you obey me if it's the last thing I do." He snatched up the wedding gown from the bed and began to put it on her. Rodger was so determined that her struggles to elude him were all in vain.

When she finally stood before him dressed in her wedding gown, she was panting with fury. "You devil, de Leyburn! I will give you more trouble than you have ever dreamed of! You have made it plain the marriage is inevitable, but it shall be a marriage in name only. You may take my castles, but I shall never yield myself to you!"

Sir Rodger threw open the door and spoke softly to Nan. "Please see to her hair." He turned to Rosamond. "I'll wait right outside. If you give us any more trouble, I shall take you across my knee and tan your arse!"

In a remarkably short time, the door opened and the bride joined him. Rosamond had never looked more beautiful. The blue silk gown with flowing sleeves and train was a perfect foil for her golden hair that fell to her hips. She offered him her hand and he took it to his lips before he placed it on his sleeve. Behind them Nan gathered up the bridal train, and they set off for the chapel. Rosamond's eyes glittered like amethyst ice. "It is bad luck for the groom to see the bride before the wedding."

Rod glanced down at her, amused. "I make my own luck."

TWELVE

Nearly mesmerized by the flames of the tall candles on the altar, Rosamond suddenly heard the priest solemnly intone, "Wilt thou obey him, and serve him, at bed and at board; love, honor, and keep him, in sickness and in health; and, forsaking all others, keep thee only unto him, so long as ye both shall live?"

Rosamond hesitated. *Obey? Love?* She wanted to pledge neither, but finally yielded to the pressure. "I will," she murmured.

"Who giveth this woman to be married to this man?"

Eleanor and Simon de Montfort stepped forward. "We do."

She watched, fascinated, as Lord Edward laid the heavy gold wedding band on the book that the priest held open. Then Sir Rodger took her left hand and slipped the ring on her finger. "With this ring I thee wed, with my body I thee honor, and with all my worldly goods I thee endow."

Rosamond pictured the Viking bathing tub with which she had just been endowed and felt an urge to laugh.

"Those whom God hath joined together let no man put asunder," the priest warned. "I pronounce that they be man and wife together, In the name of the Father, and of the Son, and of the Holy Ghost. Amen."

The moment it was done, Rosamond felt panic rise up

inside her. *They have made me commit the mistake of a lifetime!* Her eyes widened as Sir Rodger dipped his dark head and brushed her lips with his. *It is done and cannot be undone. He is my husband for better or for worse, but he will be my husband in name only!* she vowed stubbornly.

The voices of Welsh squires soared like a choir of angels. Rosamond twisted the heavy ring on her finger. The scent of burning candles and incense was overwhelming. She watched Demi bend and gather up her bridal train, then felt de Leyburn's powerful arm steady her and lead her down the aisle.

The moment they stepped outside the chapel, Rosamond heard the bells begin to peal in celebration. A flock of doves, suddenly startled, rose up in the sky. She lifted her eyes and fervently wished she too could fly free. Then the newlyweds were being showered with rice, and amid shouting and laughter, they made a dash for the shelter and warmth of Kenilworth's Great Hall.

The gaily decorated hall, which could seat four hundred, was bursting with celebrants. As well as the men and women, ladies and knights, servants and squires who resided at Kenilworth, there were Earl Simon's Welsh bowmen, Lord Edward's Gascons, and Harry of Almaine's fighting men from Cornwall. Young Gilbert de Clare was still there with his knights, as were the de Warenne brothers from Surrey with their own train of fighting men.

As Rosamond looked down from the dais at the sea of faces, she decided to smile. Any resentment she had would be put aside and kept strictly private until she was alone with Sir Rodger. She had far too much pride to allow anyone to suspect she was anything but blissfully happy. When Griffin stepped forward to fill their goblets, Rosamond gave him a radiant smile that reached to her eyes. She genuinely liked de Leyburn's squire and had no misgivings about the fair-haired young Welshman.

Lord Edward raised his hands for silence. "Join me in a toast to the happy couple. I'm sure I speak for everyone at Kenilworth today. We wish you great joy—now go forth and multiply!"

Raucous laughter and foot stomping ensued, until the groom got to his feet and raised his goblet. "Today I am the luckiest of men, for I have at last achieved my heart's desire. My wife is a prize beyond belief; I am honored to be united in wedlock with the noble Marshal family. Ladies and gentlemen, join me in a toast to my beautiful bride, Lady Rosamond de Leyburn."

Lady de Leyburn, it is even awkward to say, Rosamond thought silently as everyone in the hall raised a goblet. She thanked them with a dazzling smile and raised her own goblet. But instead of acknowledging the groom's chivalrous toast, she offered one of her own. "I would like to propose a toast to Lady Eleanor and Earl Simon de Montfort, who have always loved me like a daughter."

Rod suddenly realized that Rosamond had capitulated because of her deep feelings for the de Montforts. It had little to do with her feelings for him. His towering pride was pricked. So, the prize was not yet his after all, he conceded. He would have to siege the castle and mayhap scale her walls before she yielded to him.

As the toasts progressed, the couple was presented with many wedding presents. Some were costly, like the magnificent set of monogrammed silver plate from Lord Edward Plantagenet; others were exquisite, like the brilliant tapestries from the de Montforts, and a pair of silver chalices mounted with rubies from the Demoiselle. Richard of Gloucester had sent them a silk Oriental carpet brought back from the last Crusade, and Harry of Almaine gifted them with a full set of Cornish pewter for their dining hall.

After the gifts came the banquet, with one course following another until even the staunchest trenchermen were replete. During the entire meal, Rosamond was aware of her husband's possessive eyes upon her. Today his face had a hungry look, as if he were ready to devour her, and it did nothing to quiet her inner turmoil. She did not know which she dreaded most, the bedding ceremony, or the inevitable conflict that would follow when they were alone. With resolution she put both out of her mind, recklessly drained her goblet of wine, and smiled.

The musicians arrived, but before the trestle tables were moved back for the dancing, Lord Edward strode to the front of the dais and summoned young Henry de Montfort. A hush fell over the celebrants as the tall, dark youth attended the prince. Edward Plantagenet drew his sword from its jeweled sheath. "Kneel." When Henry went down on one knee, Edward touched the blade to each shoulder. "Henry de Montfort, I hereby bestow knighthood upon you for loyal and brave service. Rise, Sir Henry." When Edward presented Henry with the golden spurs, the hall resounded with cheers.

Rosamond watched the ceremony, feeling admiration for Edward. When the prince returned to his seat beside the bride, she said, "How generous of you to honor the de Montforts in this way."

"It was Rod's suggestion," Edward murmured.

When she bestowed a look of surprise upon him, Rod felt a pang of guilt. The knighting had not been done from generosity; it was politic, done with calculation for a further fetch. His guilt vanished when he saw how happy and proud Eleanor and Simon were.

The day was a triumph for the de Montforts. Their firstborn son had been knighted by Prince Edward Plantagenet, and their lovely ward had made a good marriage with Sir Rodger de Leyburn, a royal steward who stood high in the prince's favor.

Simon took Eleanor's small hand in his and looked down at her tenderly. "Does this not bring back memories of our own wedding, my love?"

Eleanor glanced up at Simon with a teasing light in her eyes. "Indeed it does not. We were wed secretly, in the middle of the night, because you had pursued me relentlessly and seduced me shamefully!"

Simon took her hand and placed it on his muscular thigh. "And like a little wanton, you responded to every enticement."

"As I recall, my lord, we spent our wedding night apart."

Simon grinned down at her. "I shall make it up to you tonight."

Eleanor squeezed his thigh. "Arrogant Frenchman!"

He bent and whispered in her ear, "See? You cannot keep your hands from me."

Eleanor laughed up into his dark eyes. "'Tis the wine; you know it makes me insatiable."

Simon winked at her and summoned a page to refill her goblet.

It was late afternoon when the dancing finally got under way. The bride and groom did the honors of the first dance, but then Rosamond was claimed by Lord Edward, Earl Simon, Harry of Almaine, and Gilbert de Clare in such quick succession, it made her light-headed. Or was the wine to blame?

And then she found herself swept away by the powerful arms of a dark knight with green eyes. "Sir Rickard, I thought you were my husband!" she gasped.

"You flatter me, Lady Rosamond. I envy him both his youth and his lovely bride."

She blushed warmly and lowered her lashes, unaware that her husband's green eyes watched every gesture, every sigh, every shy smile she bestowed upon the Irish knight. She only became aware of de Leyburn when she found him beside her. As Sir Rickard surrendered her to her husband, Rosamond's pulse beat a rapid tattoo and her breath caught in her throat. The words she had thrown at him came rushing back to her: *You will never have my heart; I lost it long ago to Sir Rickard, as you well know!*

Rosamond expected a rebuke or at least a taunting remark, but Rodger made none. His eyes and his touch, however, were completely possessive. "Don't look at me like that," she whispered icily.

"As if I'd like to bed you? But I would, chérie."

The teasing words he'd said the first time they'd met heightened the sexual tension between them. Her eyes flashed. "You are a devil, de Leyburn!"

"'Tis said the new fashion of wearing trains attracts devils; they like to ride on ladies' tails."

Rosamond flung her hair back over her shoulders in a gesture of defiance, then picked up her train and gave it a sharp shake. "I am a match for any devil."

His mouth twitched with amusement, and he responded to her challenge. "As for these trailing sleeves—" Rod slipped his hands inside her wide sleeves, then, sliding his palms up her arms until he cupped her naked shoulders, he drew her close and kissed her.

Those about them who saw what the groom was up to laughed and applauded his boldness.

Rosamond shivered. His touch made her hot one moment, icy the next. She had told him that she feared nothing, least of all him, but now she admitted to herself that she *was* afraid of him. As Nan had once suggested, perhaps he had been tolerant with her because they were unwed, and he would treat a wife very differently. His friends thought him the best natured man of their acquaintance, yet beneath the polished surface, Rosamond had always sensed unplumbed depths that hid who-knew-what dark secrets.

As if the kiss were a signal, Rod's bachelor friends, led by Lord Edward, surrounded the newlywed couple and plucked the groom away from his bride. Rosamond, refusing to let panic sink its fangs into her, turned blindly toward the Demoiselle and Lady Eleanor. It was the first time that Demi had been allowed to attend a bedding, and Rosamond saw that she was flushed with excitement.

The ladies spirited the bride from the Great Hall with much laughter and whispering, and escorted her to the nuptial chamber in the Clinton Tower.

The raucous male laughter from the adjoining room prompted the ladies to divest Rosamond of her wedding finery as quickly as possible. Nan took charge of the elegant gown while the other ladies removed Rosamond's petticoat, shift, and hose. Swiftly, Lady Eleanor scooped up the white silk bedrobe, embroidered with golden lovers' knots, and managed to slide Rosamond's bare arms into its sleeves just as the group of rowdy young men burst into the room.

Singing a bawdy ditty, the groom's companions pushed him, stark naked, into the bridal chamber. The ladies screamed, pretending to be shocked, but proved they were not by looking their fill at the bridegroom's virile body. To preserve her modesty, and quell the rising panic she felt, Rosamond turned her back upon the men, and Lady Eleanor allowed the silk robe to slide down the bride's spine, then swept aside Rosamond's golden hair, revealing her creamy back and buttocks to show that she went to her husband unblemished.

Rod immediately stepped to Rosamond's side and lifted Lady Eleanor's hand from his bride's hair, and like a curtain it swung back to cloak her naked flesh. He flashed a smile at the countess, but it held an unmistakable message that Rosamond was inviolate.

As Demi picked up the silk bedrobe and helped Rosamond to slip it back on, Edward and Harry filched the bride's ribbons to wear on their sleeves. Rod made no protest, but jerked his head toward the door in an unsubtle suggestion. Amid grumbling that they hadn't seen the couple abed, Edward rounded up his gentlemen to usher them out. The prince knew it would soon be his turn for a bedding and decided not to allow matters to deteriorate from bawdiness to lewdness.

Eleanor turned down the covers on the bridal bed, then kissed Rosamond. Impulsively, Demi clasped her arms about her friend and anxiously whispered, "Will you be all right?"

Rosamond's throat was so tight, she could only murmur a brief "Yes," but she managed a dazzling smile to ease Demi's anxiety. When the last celebrant departed, Rod threw the bolt across the door and turned to face his bride.

Rosamond averted her eyes from his nakedness and turned away.

"I wish it could have been a happier day for you," Rod said.

"I don't know what you are talking about, it was a lovely day," she said with icy sarcasm. She turned to face him, the brilliant, false smile still in place.

"You married me for the wrong reasons, Rosamond. It was more to please Eleanor and Simon than to please you or me."

She did not deny it. "And you married me for the *right* reasons?" she challenged.

"I am convinced that I did," he said quietly.

Her lashes swept to her cheeks as she remembered the words she had flung at him: *You will never have my heart.* When she recalled his reply, it brought a wave of dismay: *I'll settle for your body . . . and your castles.* These were his reasons!

"Well, whatever the reasons, 'tis done, for better or for worse." She laughed to mask her hurt, and moved to the dressing table to busy her hands with the things Nan had brought. "That's odd." Rosamond picked up her brother's dagger that she had found at Deerhurst. "Why ever would Nan bring this?"

Rod approached her and lifted the silver dagger from her fingers. "Your woman thought you would have need of it."

Rosamond turned uncomprehending eyes upon him.

"Obviously Nan thinks you have already yielded your virginity to me." He moved to the bed and deliberately slit his thumb with the dagger; three drops of crimson blood fell onto the pristine sheets. "She doesn't realize you are willing to yield nothing to me."

"I have married you and yielded my property to you, but I won't yield my body to you. At least not willingly!" Rosamond tossed her hair back over her shoulder with a bravado she did not feel.

Rod pierced her with his green gaze. "I do not merely want you *willing*, as if it were a duty; I want you *eager*."

She avoided looking at his body. "I shall never be *eager*!"

Her insult mauled his male pride. "Oh, my love, you are quite mistaken." He padded toward her like a raptor stalking its prey. He could see she wanted to flee, but her pride kept her rooted to the spot. Rod did not pounce upon her, but slowly took her hand and lifted it to his lips. Into her open palm he placed a kiss and closed her fingers over it, then the tip of his tongue traced across the pulse point in her delicate wrist and trailed up the inside of her arm where the wide sleeve of her silken bedrobe had fallen back. He felt her shiver and knew it was from fear.

"If you ravish me, I vow I will hate you forever!"

"I have more pride than to ravish any woman, let alone my own bride. Rather, I intend to woo you to a giving mood, chérie."

"Perhaps other women cannot resist your seduction, but I am not other women, my lord!"

Recalling Edward's recent advice he rejoined, "No, you are an ice maiden in need of a thawing, and a stubborn little filly in need of a firm hand and a touch of the spurs!" Rod made a conscious decision *not* to tell her she had nothing to fear from him. He knew it would add to the titillation of his seduction. "Look at me, Rosamond."

When she kept her eyes on his, refusing to lower them to his naked body, he moved closer and allowed his erection to probe the silk bedrobe as if it were seeking an opening. He heard the swift intake of her breath and watched her glance down. Her eyes widened as she saw, for the first time, the long scar on the inside of his thigh, that ran from groin to knee.

"Did you receive that in battle?"

"It is an old wound; we will not speak of it."

His hands reached out to her, but did not remove her bedrobe. Rather they glided around her and began caressing her back through the slippery silk. Rod could feel how stiffly she held herself in her resolve to resist him, so his hands then slid to the front, cupping her breasts, stroking, weighing, circling until the friction of the sliding cloth heated her silken skin. All the while his swollen phallus probed against her belly, touching and teasing in an erotic mating dance. Rod knew she could feel the heat of his hands and his cock through the finespun silk, just as he could feel her warm flesh.

Rosamond splayed her hands against the naked muscles of his chest to push him away, but she might as well have been pushing against the stones of the castle walls. She drew in a swift breath to steady herself as his fingers reached out to caress her woman's center. The silk acted as a flimsy barrier, sliding over her mons, arousing her against her firm resolve. Her traitorous body seemed to have a will of its own, separate from hers. She silently cried out against it as she began to feel a wanton hunger. The silk covering her cleft became wet, then slick, and her woman's scent lingered in the warmth her body gave off, telling him the secret of her desire.

She prayed that he would not kiss her. Her mouth, which had not tasted his since Deerhurst, began to ache. She tried to banish all thought of his kisses, but once imprinted, never forgotten, she realized with yearning. Her husband was dark, dominant, and dangerous, and he excited her so much she wanted to scream. Desperate to hide her arousal, Rosamond took refuge in anger. She pressed her mouth against his muscular shoulder and bit him.

When she lifted her mouth from him, she saw his eyes

glitter with green fire, and when he raised his hand she thought he would strike her. Instead, Rod gazed down at her and traced her lips with his fingers. "That is the second love bite you have given me today. It tells me you have a passionate nature, *mon amour*," he said. Then he cupped her cheek and stroked his thumb across her cheekbone, seeing and touching every feature of her face as if it were both lovely and precious. His fingers threaded into her hair, stroking it, toying with its tendrils, lifting it to his face to inhale its fragrance, and even drawing a golden tress through his lips to taste its texture.

Rosamond both loved and hated the attention he paid her. It was like nothing she had known before, but it had a narcotic effect, melting her resistance and making her crave more. She dreaded yet longed for him to remove her bedrobe, yearning for him to lavish attention upon her body, yet silently screaming her denial. Of its own volition, her body arched against him, displaying her need, and his knowing hands plucked her strings like a harp, awakening, arousing, and exciting her female sexuality.

Slowly he unfastened her bedrobe and slipped his hands inside its silken folds. Then he proceeded to start the loving all over again, but this time directly upon her naked flesh. He dipped his dark head and took possession of her lips, luring her to open so he could plunder her mouth. Her stubborn resistance lasted for long, drawn-out minutes in a mating duel she tried valiantly to win, but finally, inevitably, Rod's insistent tongue delved deep, tasting her honeyed sweetness, then it plunged boldly in and out, in a rhythm that mimicked what he really wanted.

Rosamond's will was almost completely eroded by the magic of his wooing. Her ability to think was being drowned by her body's need to feel. Desperate, she blamed it on too much wine. She had drunk so much, her inhibitions had vanished. Her last coherent thought was that she could either fight his desire or fight her own, but she could no longer fight both. Her hands slid up his chest, and her arms went about his neck, so that she could press herself against the hard length of him. His male power excited her, making her feel soft and female and utterly fragile. She went up on her toes to arch against him, and his hands went beneath her bottom cheeks to lift her onto his jutting sex. His shaft lay along her cleft, and when he slowly walked toward the bed, the hot sliding friction made her gasp as her desire mounted.

Rod lay back on the bed and took Rosamond down with him. He held her in the dominant position above him and shuddered with pleasure as her long golden hair spilled down onto his chest and shoulders. She was truly a breathtaking prize, one he had rendered both willing and eager to experience the mystical hymenal rite. When Rod saw something beautiful, he always had an overwhelming urge to possess it, yet he knew that even if he did possess her tonight, he would not experience the deep satisfaction of ownership. For although Rosamond was now willing and eager to yield her body, she was nowhere near ready to yield her heart.

Her violet eyes gleaming with witchery, Rosamond slowly lowered her lips to his and felt a thrill as he responded passionately, unable to resist her feminine power. She quivered with little tremors as her breasts pressed against the muscles of his wide chest and her nipples were abraded by his crisp black hair. The fragrance of sandalwood mixed with his own primitive male scent was such an erotic combination, it acted as an aphrodisiac upon her. Inflamed by desire and needing to be filled with him, she rose up ready to impale herself upon his manroot.

In a flash, Rod had her beneath him. He suddenly felt a perverse desire to keep her a virgin. His towering pride wanted all or nothing. He wanted her to love him totally and completely when he made her his wife in the deepest sense of the word. He pressed a marble-hard thigh between her legs and felt her grip him and ride up and down on it, with a small whimpering sob. "Hush, sweetheart, I know what you need." His fingers unerringly found her woman's center, and allowing only his fingertips to penetrate her, he stroked with a slow, firm rhythm, taking her higher and higher until she erupted and dissolved into a thousand liquid tremors.

Rod cupped her entire mons possessively with his palm and held her until the last pulsation stilled. "Rosamond, you are beautiful in your passion. Say my name, I want to taste it on your lips."

His words shocked her, bringing her back to her senses. She had allowed him to take complete control over her. Her resistance had melted like snow beneath the blazing hot sun. Was she so starved for love and attention that he could seduce her against her will? Now he was even telling her what she must say.

He touched his mouth to hers. "Rod," he whispered, his lips against hers.

"Devil!" she hissed.

He laughed wickedly. Then his lips trailed along the curve of her throat, burning a path to her lush breasts, now firm and peaked from her arousal. His hot mouth sought her belly, and his tongue dipped playfully into her navel, before it inched ever lower toward its goal. He knew she would cry out when he ran the tip of his tongue between her legs, but when he curled it about her tiny bud he had not anticipated her scream.

"Stop, you devil!" she cried, writhing beneath his wickedly beautiful hot mouth.

Deliberately he began to lick and tease her, knowing her arousal had already begun again. He set up a delicious rhythm and smiled knowingly when she joined her body to the tempo. He was careful not to thrust too deeply, though he could feel the hot, wet pull of her on his tongue. Then he stopped the pleasuring and held still. "Rod," he prompted, his lips against her fiery core.

Rosamond remained silent for a full minute.

"Rod," he tempted, kissing a tiny pulse point.

Her silence stretched out for another minute, then on a shuddering sigh, she whispered, "Bastard!" and gave herself up to his beautiful mouth.

For hours he kept her at the peak of her arousal, making love to her with his hands and his mouth, then finally when he could bear the self-imposed sexual torture no longer, and his gut ached from the hours of love play that had not reached its natural conclusion, he knew he must seek release. Straddling her waist with his thighs, he slid his shaft into the valley between her upthrusting breasts, then he took the round globes into his hands and squeezed until his throbbing erection was sheathed.

She cried out in low protest, "My lord, what are you doing to me?"

Rod was too far gone for words. It took only a dozen thrusts for him to reach climax and scatter his seed across her silken skin.

Rosamond was stunned at how possessively he held her until he drifted to the edge of sleep. If he felt this way, why had he not consummated the marriage? Was it because she kept part of herself from him, so he had done likewise? She was amazed that she had been able to keep her vow and that they were still married in name only. Then her innate honesty asserted itself. It had absolutely nothing to do with her. He could have easily seduced her into yielding her virginity to him. But he had not, and somehow she felt as if she had lost the battle over sex. As she lay in his arms she realized that Sir Rodger de Leyburn was a complete mystery to her. He had taken all control away from her and made it plain that *he* would decide when to make her his wife.

THIRTEEN

Rosamond awoke when she heard a tapping on the chamber door. Nan entered carrying Rosamond's vivid green gown over one arm. She was followed by two maids who brought in a slipper bath and two more who filled it with hot water. Rosamond, surprised that it was morning, was vastly relieved that Rodger de Leyburn had departed.

"Good morning, my lamb." Nan wrapped her in her silk bedgown as two of the maids approached the bed and stripped off the sheets.

Rosamond blushed as she glimpsed the dark crimson drops. It was his blood, not hers; how cunning de Leyburn was!

"Hurry and bathe, my lamb. Lady Eleanor and Demi are coming with a special breakfast tray, and heaven knows who else will try to get a good look at you this morning. Brides are an irresistible curiosity. Those sheets will be the talk of the castle!"

"Good God, that's disgusting!" Rosamond said with a grimace. "Hold them off as long as you can. I want to be dressed before anyone sees me."

Rosamond was clad in the green gown, with her hair brushed into a smooth French knot, by the time her visitors arrived. While Bette carried in the huge tray, Lady

Eleanor pressed a kiss to her brow, and Demi hugged her close. "You look different!"

Eleanor laughed knowingly. "She will never be the same again. I warrant she feels both older and wiser. Marriage transforms a woman. Darling, you look absolutely radiant!"

Rodger de Leyburn filled the doorway, then stepped into the chamber. A richly embroidered surcoat covered his chain mail hauberk. While the ladies fawned over him he laughed good-naturedly. "I have come to give my beautiful bride her morning gift," he said gallantly. He placed a velvet pouch in Rosamond's hands, then dipped his dark head to reverently kiss those hands.

Forcing herself to remain outwardly unruffled, Rosamond opened the pouch and lifted out its treasure. It was a gold torque necklace carved in an exquisite Celtic design, with a huge cabochon emerald at its center. Every woman in the room gasped at its beauty and urged her before the mirror to put it on. When she clasped it about her throat, she saw that it matched her gown to perfection. With her hair drawn up to display the elegant curve of her neck, the torque made her look regal as a princess. Rosamond's glance met Sir Rodger's in the mirror, and his proprietary look of ownership stunned her. Suddenly she remembered reading somewhere that torques were slave collars to the ancient Celts. As her hand lifted to remove it, she saw that her husband looked hurt.

"Please, I want you to wear it while I'm gone," he said softly.

"Gone?"

A smile of regret curved his mouth. "I am a royal steward, chérie. I must go to London ahead of Lord Edward and our men to make preparations for their arrival. I want you to enjoy your last Christmas at Kenilworth, then travel in comfort with Lady Eleanor's household." Rod made it sound as if he wanted only her comfort and happiness, but the truth was he could not bear the torture of sharing a bed with her for one more night, without demanding his conjugal rights.

"Come, ladies," Eleanor said decisively, "the newly-weds need privacy to say their goodbyes."

When they were alone, Rosamond offered up a silent prayer of thanks that she had had the foresight to dress. Her beautiful gown gave her the confidence she needed, and she was ready for him, ready to snatch the offensive before he did. "You are a master of manipulation," she accused. "I drank too much wine last night and you took shameless advantage of me!"

Rodger saw that Rosamond held herself stiffly. She had withdrawn behind an invisible barrier, thinking to protect herself from him. Amusement filled his green eyes. "Rosamond, you are a beautiful little liar. Last night you deliberately challenged my manhood and pitted your will against mine. Although you swore you would not yield to me, I wooed you to a giving mood. You just don't want to admit that you lost."

She gasped in outrage. "I still have my virginity!"

He flashed a grin. "And therein lies the proof that you lost."

"You are a devil, de Leyburn!"

"A wicked devil," he agreed. She looked so vulnerable, it tugged at his heart. He wanted to take her in his arms, but the last thing he wanted was to have her recoil from him. "Lord Edward will bring you safely to Windsor. It's a journey of over eighty miles, which will take several days." When she looked relieved, he bit his lip. "Rosamond, when we meet again at Windsor, a brand new year will be nigh; I hope we can start afresh." When she did not reply, he went to the door and paused. "Bring Chirk with you, so you won't be lonely."

When he left, she suddenly felt abandoned. Damn him to hellfire, why hadn't he consummated the marriage? Why hadn't he told her he loved her? The answers were obvious. He did not love her. Now that he owned her castles, he was quite content that they remain married in name only!

King Henry was in a Plantagenet rage! News had reached him that Edward, his heir to the throne, was plotting with his archenemy Simon de Montfort. Terrified that they would overthrow him as king, Henry knew he must act swiftly. He asked his brother, Richard of Cornwall, to go immediately to London and win back the loyalty of Richard's stepson Richard de Clare, Earl of Gloucester. Once Richard was in London, Henry wanted him to set up an inner council consisting of himself, Gloucester, and the Chief Justiciar of England, Humphrey de Bohun, Earl of Hereford, in order to rally Plantagenet royalists. "Richard, you will give my traitorous son a message. Tell him I will make his brother Edmund heir to the throne if he does not immediately end this treasonous plotting with that whoreson de Montfort!"

Richard of Cornwall shook his head at the dire situation the king faced. "I advise you to get that Bull of Absolution from the Pope, even if you have to double the bribe, Henry. If the church nullifies the Provisions of Oxford, most of the barons will be ready to compromise and you will be able to resume royal power. Especially if you have a large troop of mercenary soldiers at your back."

Henry's queen made up her mind immediately to return to England and take Edward's sixteen-year-old wife, Eleanora, with her. Though the queen's figure had thickened and her golden hair had faded, she was still vain, and still extremely manipulative. She could think of no better bait than a beautiful young bride to lure Edward back into the royal fold. The queen decided to sail with the king's brother, Richard of Cornwall, since he had a swift vessel that would take them directly up the Thames to London.

When they arrived, the queen left her brother-in-law Richard at Westminster Palace and took Princess

Eleanora by barge to the elegant apartments that had been especially designed for the bride at Windsor Castle.

Sir Rodger de Leyburn and his squire arrived at Windsor to ready Lord Edward's apartments. As well, he intended to furbish his own suite of rooms to accommodate Rosamond. When the Queen of England arrived the following day, bringing Edward's bride, Rod forced himself to hide his total surprise.

When the queen found only her son's steward at Windsor, she confronted him immediately, demanding to know where Edward was.

De Leyburn bowed gallantly to the queen, as his facile tongue prepared to defuse her wrath. Rod knew she disapproved of him, along with all the "wild young men" of Edward's household, because she feared they had more influence over the heir than she did. "Lord Edward will be here in a few short days, Your Highness. He will be overjoyed to see you."

"I asked you where he was, Steward."

"He is returning from the successful campaign in Wales. We fought side by side with the Marcher lords from the Welsh borders and all extended their hospitality." De Leyburn knew better than to mention Kenilworth.

"You had best prepare Princess Eleanora's apartments. This will no longer be a household of bachelors," she warned.

"Indeed, Your Highness. I am now a married man myself and my wife will be honored to serve Princess Eleanora."

"Whom did you wed?"

"Lady Rosamond Marshal, may it please Your Highness."

The queen's eyes narrowed. It did not please her at all. If her name was Marshal, she was an heiress. De Leyburn was becoming too wealthy, and wealth meant power! She would find a way to rid her son of this upstart steward.

Sir Rodger immediately dispatched Griffin with a

message for the prince. Edward did not like surprises. Moreover, Rod knew that Edward and Alyce had plans to meet at Westminster and continue their liaison. Rodger also penned a note for Rosamond to let her know that Princess Eleanora was already in residence at Windsor. Rod knew that the last stop of the large cavalcade would be at Berkhamsted, and he bade Griffin await them there.

De Leyburn ordered the supplies Windsor would need, and alerted the servants that Lord Edward's household would be arriving shortly. The chambers must be cleaned, beds aired, wood chopped for the fires, and the stables plenished with oats and hay. When he was satisfied that no detail had been overlooked, Rod moved on to Westminster Palace, where he would undertake the same duties.

Another surprise awaited him at Westminster. When he learned that the king's brother, Richard of Cornwall, was in residence, he suspected that some plot was afoot. Deciding he would learn more if as few people as possible knew of his arrival, de Leyburn took a chamber in a wing opposite the spacious royal apartments and had a quiet word with the servants. All he learned was that the queen and Princess Eleanora had sailed with the king's brother, whose ship was anchored in the Thames. But late in the afternoon as he stood at his high window overlooking the stables, he saw Humphrey de Bohun, the Chief Justiciar of England, ride in with a troop of guards.

Sir Rodger was alarmed. The justiciar had obviously been summoned to London by royal order. Surmising that they were planning to prevent Simon de Montfort and Prince Edward from holding Parliament, Rod knew he must ride out to meet Edward and alert him.

During Christmas and the journey from Kenilworth, Rosamond had days to ponder her marriage and the changes it would bring to her life. Her husband's absence and distance allowed her to think rationally and be honest with herself. She could not forget how Rodger de Leyburn had come to her rescue at Pershore and, with his great authority, had single-handedly restored her property, righting the wrongs done to her people. And he had done it without being high-handed with her. In truth, he had treated her as an equal.

Then, with great strength and courage, he had saved her life, and afterwards she had allowed a certain degree of intimacy between them. Rosamond remembered how confident he had made her feel, and even if he had deliberately set out to make her feel special, she admitted how much she had enjoyed it. Something inside her wanted to recapture what they had shared.

A wistful shadow was cast over her thoughts, for she knew that tomorrow she would part from the familiar de Montfort household and go with Lord Edward to Windsor. Rosamond knew she had two choices: Either she could dread what lay before her, or she could think of it as a great challenge. She straightened her shoulders and spurred Nimbus forward to ride with Lady Eleanor. Rosamond needed advice. If she was to avoid loneliness and unhappiness, she knew that she and her husband must not become enemies.

"Lady Eleanor, how have you kept your husband's love all these years?"

"I think it is because we are well matched," Eleanor said, laughing. "I am not afraid to stand up to him and speak my mind. A clever woman has a great deal of power, which she must learn to use wisely. I like to have my own way, and Simon indulges me, but make no mistake, Rosamond, he is master in his own house. I have learned when to yield . . . and I wouldn't have it any other way!"

Rosamond knew that Eleanor had taken her husband's power and strength for her own, and she wanted to do the same. "I shall miss you sorely, my lady."

"Nonsense! Out from under my shadow, you will spread your wings like a butterfly and acquire your own power."

At that moment, Lord Edward galloped past them and bowed gallantly. With unflagging energy, he spent each day riding up and down the line, checking on the knights and men-at-arms, as well as conversing with Simon de Montfort for hours and also finding time to ride with the ladies.

Rosamond followed Eleanor's gaze as it fell upon Edward. With the sun touching his flaxen hair and glinting off his breastplate, he looked like a golden god. "I am astounded that my brother Henry produced such a magnificent son," the countess said. "Thank heaven he has decided to join forces with Simon. You played no small part in that, Rosamond. I thank you with all my heart for setting aside your reservations about Rodger de Leyburn and helping to cement the bond."

Suddenly, Rosamond felt proud that she had done her duty by the de Montforts. Someday the prince would be King Edward, and already he looked every inch a king. He had been gifted with an abundance of physical beauty, strength, energy, intelligence, and charm. If he used his gifts wisely, he would make a magnificent king.

When they arrived at Berkhamsted, Rosamond was delighted to see Griffin. She took the note from him and blushed, knowing it was from her husband. It was not a love letter, but his words were warm, informing her that Princess Eleanora was at Windsor, and assuring her that the chambers he had selected for her were quite lovely.

"What is the princess like?" she asked Griffin.

"I did not see her, my lady."

She realized Griffin had been sent with messages for Lord Edward, and that Sir Rodger's note to her was only a courtesy.

In Berkhamsted's dining hall, Edward shared the news with Simon. The message prompted more questions than answers. How long had the queen and Edward's bride been at Windsor? If the queen had returned from France, would King Henry follow? The spring

Parliament was uppermost in Simon's mind, while Edward's thoughts were filled with his Castilian wife.

The following morning, when the travelers departed Berkhamsted, the de Montforts would take the London road to Charing near London, while Rosamond, Lord Edward, Harry of Almaine, and their train of knights would head directly south to Windsor in Berkshire. Rosamond bade Eleanor and Demi goodbye. "I wish I could see Princess Eleanora," Demi said wistfully.

Lady Eleanor refrained from telling Rosamond what a bitch the queen was; she would learn for herself soon enough. Instead she kissed Rosamond and urged, "When you are at Westminster, you must visit us at Durham House, downriver."

Later in the day, Rosamond caught her breath when she realized that the rider galloping toward them was Rodger de Leyburn. She thought it a most gallant gesture for him to meet Lord Edward and herself and escort them to Windsor.

He greeted her first, seeming to have eyes for no other. She did not flinch as the big black destrier drew close, though she felt a moment's apprehension. Her husband lifted her gloved hand to his lips and held her gaze. "Welcome, Rosamond, you have never looked lovelier."

She was well pleased. "Thank you, my lord."

He wheeled his mount instantly and joined Lord Edward. Griffin followed him immediately. Rosamond knew he should have greeted the prince first and was flattered by her husband's chivalrous behavior. As she watched the two men become engrossed in their conversation, she was reminded of how darkly handsome Rodger de Leyburn was, and how at ease he was with the prince. He and Edward were truly bonded, and she felt a surge of pride at their close connection. She was blissfully unaware of the tense subject of the men's conversation or the rippling undercurrent of events that had already been set in motion.

"Thank you for sending Griffin to warn me that I have a mother and a wife awaiting me at Windsor. I shall gird my loins."

"I come with a very different warning, Lord Edward. Yesterday I went to ready your apartments at Westminster and found Richard of Cornwall in residence. I avoided him, but late in the afternoon the Justiciar Humphrey de Bohun rode in hell-for-leather with a large force."

"Splendor of God, there is some plot afoot. Too bad you didn't arrive in time to advise Earl Simon."

"I can ride to Durham House with your message."

Edward's brow furrowed. "De Montfort has spies; I warrant he'll know the moment he arrives." Edward sent his squire down the line to summon Harry of Almaine. When Harry reached the prince's side, Edward said, "Your father is at Westminster."

"My father?" Harry swallowed hard. "Mayhap you can persuade him to stand in Parliament with you and Simon and the barons."

"How would you like the job of persuading him?"

"Me? I shall avoid him at all costs. I would rather take the men-at-arms to the Tower, while you go to Westminster!"

"We will remain together at Windsor tonight. Tomorrow I shall see Richard, alone if you haven't the stomach for it. Rod can go to Durham House and learn de Montfort's thoughts on why the justiciar has been summoned hotfoot to London."

As Windsor Castle came into view, Rosamond caught her breath at how splendid it looked. The imposing Round Tower, built by King Henry II from beautiful Bedfordshire stone, was bathed in a golden glow by the setting sun. The cavalcade passed through the outer walls by way of the Curfew Tower and entered the Lower Ward. When grooms and servants rushed out to attend the travelers, they made obeisance to the prince, but it was de Leyburn, the royal steward, who gave them their orders.

Rosamond dismounted unaided and helped Nan from her saddle, then she lifted Chirk from her traveling basket and set the dog down on the cobblestones to pee. When both de Leyburn and Griffin came to attend her, she graciously demurred. "You have so many official duties; we will manage."

"I have no higher priority than your welfare. Nan, please direct Griffin to your baggage." Rod bowed to Rosamond, scooped up Chirk, and held out his arm. "Allow me to escort you to our apartments. Once you are safely in the hands of the servants, you will have ample time to bathe and rest while I attend to my official duties."

The new Henry III Tower, built with local heath stone, was the last word in luxury. Their chambers were bright, spacious, and richly furnished. The apartment consisted of two large rooms and two smaller ones, one of which was a dressing room with a carved wooden bathing tub. The bedchamber held a massive bed with green velvet curtains and mounting-steps because of its height. Rosamond averted her eyes from the bed and moved to the tall round-topped window that overlooked a walled garden.

Sir Rodger set Chirk down so that she could explore her new home, then followed Rosamond to the window. "We have a fine view of the Thames Valley and the Chiltern Hills beyond. When spring arrives, the colors of the entire landscape change. The royal apartments take up the entire two top stories of this new tower. The king and queen occupy the top floor when they are in residence. Directly above us are Lord Edward's apartments, and adjoining are those especially designed for Princess Eleanora."

Rosamond turned to look up at him. He had said that

he hoped they could start afresh at Windsor, and suddenly she wanted that too. She swayed toward him, but Rodger stepped back politely and she realized that an invisible barrier stood between them.

"If there is anything you need, Rosamond, you must *ask.*"

She stared after him as he departed. His words held a wealth of double meaning. She pulled off one of her riding boots and hurled it at the door he had just closed. "Ask? Ask? You devil, de Leyburn! You'll do the bloody asking!"

Edward Plantagenet had never failed to rise to a challenge in his life. After he turned his destrier over to his squire, he strode to the top of the Lower Ward, entered the new tower, and took the stairs to his apartments three at a time. Shrewdly, he anticipated a confrontation with his mother, and relished it. He dispatched the bowing servants for hot water, deciding to rid himself of travel stains before seeking audience with the queen. Edward poured himself a cup of ale to quench his thirst and wash the road dust from his throat. He drained it, and as he poured another he noticed that the door leading to the adjoining room stood ajar. A rustle of garments drew him to the doorway.

Edward stopped dead on the threshold and stared. Before him stood a female so lovely, his heart skipped a beat at the sight of her. Her rose pink gown showed her dusky beauty to perfection. Her dark brown hair fell in a profusion of natural curls that reached to her hips, while tiny tendrils framed her oval face. Her almond-shaped eyes were liquid brown, fringed by long, thick lashes. A soft flush touched her youthful rounded cheek as her red lips parted in a shy smile that revealed teeth as pretty as pearls. Her full breasts curved deliciously above the smallest waist he had ever seen.

Edward caught his breath at the sight of this girl on

the brink of womanhood who was so lovely, he couldn't believe his great good fortune. Was this dazzling vision his wife? All his senses were so involved, he knew he could not be dreaming. "Eleanora?"

Though her look was shy, her eyes shone with joy as she looked at him with adoration. "Eduward, I must use the English version of my name . . . Eleanor."

He laughed with delight at the way she pronounced his name. "Nay, Eleanora is beautiful, or Nora is sweet and pretty too, like its owner." He wrinkled his nose. "Eleanor is my mother's name."

She laughed shyly, and it was like music to his ears. He closed the distance between them, drawn to her like steel to a lodestone. His gaze drank in her sweetness, and as he raised his hand toward her, Eleanora did the same, and their fingertips touched. A current like lightning sparked between them, and he watched her breasts rise and fall with the excitement their touch begot. He took possession of her fingers and lifted them to his lips. "Eleanora, my sweet."

"Eduward," she said breathlessly, "I have waited six long years to come to you."

His lips brushed her wrist, and her rapid pulse told him how he affected her. "The waiting is over," he promised warmly.

"Not by a long chalk!" the queen interjected as she sailed into the chamber like a ship in full sail. "Eleanor, you will go upstairs immediately. What I have to say to my perfidious son is not for delicate ears."

Edward's fingers tightened their hold on the beautiful prize. "I am delighted to see you too, Mother," he said caustically, "but at the moment I wish to be alone with my wife."

"When the marriage has been consummated, she will be your wife, and not before. Until then, Eleanor is under *my* wardship, *my* authority."

Edward saw his bride's eyes flood with unshed tears.

Touched with compassion for her plight, he loosed his grip and watched her flee. "Is this how you exercise your wardship? Bullying the maiden because she is sweet and gentle?" Suddenly he realized his mother's true motives. "You used her as bait, making sure I would find her here unattended, then snatching her away to bring me to heel."

"You need bringing to heel! Plotting with that traitor de Montfort will have dire consequences for you. Your father's brother has come to Westminster to deal with you."

"The last I heard, Richard of Cornwall was not the King of England, nor are you, madam. If the king wishes to protest my political views, let him come and do so. I refuse to be ruled by a woman, be she mother or queen!"

FOURTEEN

Rosamond directed Griffin where to set the last of her trunks. "How long will my husband be about his official duties?"

"At least four hours, my lady; you must sup without him."

"Nay," Rosamond demurred, as a plan began to form in her head, "I shall wait and dine here with Sir Rodger, if you will be good enough to bring us a late supper, Griffin."

Rosamond decided to take Chirk for a run in the walled garden before dusk descended. There would be ample time to bathe later. Wrapped in her fur-lined cloak and carrying her Welsh terrier, she made her way down the stairs of the splendid new tower and wound her way along a path until she came to the garden. Inside the high walls, beneath the trees, there was hardly any light at all in the shadowed recesses. She set Chirk down and watched her scamper off, then decided she'd better follow.

"*Malo perro!* Bad dog!" a female voice scolded, then Rosamond saw a white ball of fur rush toward her through the shadows.

"Oh, I didn't see you in your dark cloak," Rosamond said. "I too have brought my dog to the garden." She scooped up the Maltese terrier and handed him to the young woman.

"*Gracias*, he is a bad dog running off like that. I find my new country so cold, but he loves this place."

Rosamond knew that a few of the words the young woman had spoken were Spanish, and she guessed her identity immediately. "You are Princess Eleanora, Lord Edward's bride! I am so honored to meet you. I am Rosamond de Leyburn, newly wed to your husband's friend and steward."

Just then Chirk returned to her mistress and showed great interest in the Maltese terrier.

"Oh, I am so happy you have a little dog, Rosamond. I do not think the queen likes my Bebe. I hope Edward likes dogs."

"He loves dogs! Your Highness, you are so cold, your teeth are chattering. You need a warmer cloak of fur. Here, take mine," she said, removing it and wrapping it about the shivering girl.

"Oh, I cannot, Rosamond!"

"Of course you can. You can give it back to me another time, when you get one of your own. Let's go back inside."

Lit torches illuminated the vaulted staircase, enabling the young women to see each other. Rosamond was delighted to find that the princess was beautiful. "You are still shivering," she observed.

"From excitement because at last I have seen Eduward!"

Love and adoration shone from Eleanora's big brown eyes, and suddenly Rosamond felt apprehension for her newfound friend. She wanted to warn her to guard her heart so that she would not risk being hurt, but she could not bring herself to spoil Eleanora's happiness. "Good night, no doubt tomorrow we shall meet formally."

Back in her own apartments, Rosamond told Nan that she would finish unpacking her own things and urged her to get some rest. Strangely, she felt energized as she hung her lovely garments in the dressing room wardrobe. She chose a white silk night rail, and in one of her trunks she found a rose-scented candle, and placed both beside the high bed. Then she called for water for her bath, and when the servants brought it, she asked them to bring hot water for de Leyburn when he retired for the night.

After her bath, she donned the white silk, covered it with a red velvet bedgown, and feeling satisfied that the scene was well set, built up the fire. She had decided to take matters into her own hands. It was time she became a woman, and Rosamond intended to set the time and the place, rather than allow her husband to control everything. Her only sexual knowledge came from de Leyburn, but she had learned her lessons well. He had seduced her by focusing his attention on her body and her pleasure, so tonight she would reverse their roles and do the same to him.

When de Leyburn arrived, Griffin accompanied him. "I will order your bath, my lord," he said, removing Sir Rodger's hauberk.

Rosamond lit the rose-scented candle. "There is no need, Griffin, I shall see to my husband's needs tonight. Bring our food in about an hour." She gave the squire a conspiratorial smile. She felt Rodger's speculative gaze upon her, knowing the red velvet bedgown did wondrous things for her pale golden hair, but before he could speak, the hot water for his bath arrived. "You have trained the servants so well, my lord."

They half filled the carved tub in the dressing room with steaming water, and Rosamond thanked them profusely as they left. Then she turned to her husband and said huskily, "Won't you join me in the . . . *undressing* room?"

Bemused, he followed her, his curiosity and his desire piqued. He sat on the edge of the tub and drew in his breath as she came close and reached out to lift off the linen chainse he wore beneath the chain mail hauberk. When her hands came into contact with his bare flesh, his arousal began. When her playful fingertips traced the dark hair covering his chest, his arousal lengthened, then as she deliberately stroked her palms over the slabs of muscle, his arousal thickened and hardened.

Amazed, he watched her kneel before him to remove his boots. When her head bent forward and her blond hair pooled over his groin, brushing across the swollen bulge inside his black chausses, he almost came out of his skin. He removed his remaining clothing quickly and exhaled with relief, glad to be free of the tight material. His pulse quickened as he watched Rosamond remove her red velvet bedgown, revealing the white silk night rail.

"It won't matter if I get this wet," she explained innocently.

Rodger stepped into the water, skeptical that Rosamond actually intended to bathe him, yet hope would not be denied. His eyes never left her as he lowered himself to a sitting position and his anticipation heightened as she knelt beside him. She picked up a long, hard sponge and rolled it between her palms as she contemplated where to begin. He found her gestures sexually provocative, and when he suspected she was well aware of it, his mouth went dry.

"You are a very big man," she said, gazing down into the water.

Rodger heard himself groan.

She soaped the sponge and, standing up, moved behind him, where he could no longer see her, but he could certainly feel her. She began to scrub his back with long, firm strokes, swirling, circular strokes, and short, swift strokes that scratched exactly where he itched. He closed his eyes and gave himself up to the pleasure, feeling the tension in his muscles loosen, while the sexual tension between his wife and him coiled tighter. It was Paradise; it was purgatory!

Rosamond came back into his view and again knelt beside the tub. She rinsed the sponge and allowed it to float, then she withdrew her hands from the water and wiped their wetness across the white silk. It immediately turned transparent, revealing the contours of her lush breasts tipped with thrusting pink nipples. Rodger caught his breath as she dipped her hand in the water to retrieve the sponge and just accidentally brushed the head of his phallus. He knew this was a game for her and he a willing playmate.

As she scrubbed his shoulders and chest, she had to reach across the wide expanse of his upper body, and in doing so her golden hair touched, tickled, teased, and tormented him. When her hands sought his armpits, it felt erotic, as if she were touching him in a forbidden place. She rinsed him thoroughly, then paused, holding the sponge in her hands tentatively. The silence stretched between them as Rodger willed her to proceed with washing the lower half of his body.

Rosamond licked her lips. "If there is anything you need, Rodger, you must *ask*."

He comprehended immediately. It was to be a game of wills, a dangerous game, and one he relished, but he felt reluctant to wash himself as he took the sponge from her and quickly finished his own ablutions. But when he stepped from the tub, she rejoined the game by taking up the towel and moving close. At first she rubbed him briskly, as he would have done if he had been drying himself, but then her hands, covered by the towel, began to linger in certain intimate places. When she dried his back, her fingers deliberately dipped into the cleft between his buttocks, eliciting a shudder he could not control. Then she moved before him and allowed her glance to roam over his glistening wet chest. She was tall enough that her head reached to his shoulder, which positioned her perfectly for what she did next. Before she touched him with the towel, her tongue darted out to lick the droplets of water that gathered and dripped from his nipples. He felt them harden immediately and his cock rose up between their bodies as if it too wanted to be licked. Molten fire ran through his veins as she slid down on her knees before him, but once more he experienced disappointment as all she did was dry his legs. When he glanced down, he saw that her eyes were examining the silvery scar that ran down his inner thigh. But she quickly raised her eyes until her glance caressed his full erection, then she licked her lips. "If there is anything you need, *Rod*, you must ask."

It was the first time she had called him Rod, and it played merry hell with his desire. More than anything in the world, he wanted her to fellate him, wanted to feel her beautiful lips kiss the pulsing head of his shaft, wanted her to take him into the hot, wet cave of her mouth, wanted to thrust until he was spent, but because of his pride, he found it impossible to ask.

Rosamond remained on her knees for a long, drawn-out moment, then she stood up and, with a wicked laugh, hung the towel on his upthrust cock and walked sensually toward their bedchamber. She tossed her honey-gold hair over her shoulder as she glanced back. "Come and warm yourself at the fire so you can remain naked." Her words were those of a practiced courtesan, and coming from a virgin, they had an unbelievably erotic effect on him.

He tossed aside the towel and followed her, mesmerized by the seductive spell she wove. She stood before the fire, the outline of her body visible through the finespun material of her night rail. His gaze licked over her like a candle flame, and the scent of roses made his nostrils flare. With her back to the fire, she began to draw up her night rail inch by inch, slowly exposing her limbs. Rod loved the lines of her long legs, and he wanted those legs encircling him, high about his back, while he plunged between them. He strode toward her and watched her raise her hand imperiously to stay him. "If there is anything you need, *Rod*, you must *ask*."

"What about your needs, Rosamond? Don't *you* need pleasuring?"

Her throaty laugh was accompanied by a toss of her glorious hair. "I can pleasure myself, if that's all you have in mind. Would you like to watch?" She inched up the white silk, then deliberately threaded her fingers through the curls on her mons.

It was too much for Rod. He swept her into his arms, determined to master her with his kisses. Rosamond did not remain passive; she returned kiss for kiss, touch for touch, arousing them both beyond the point of return. Suddenly she broke away and moved toward the bed. She ran up the mounting-steps, drew off her silk night rail, then slid to her knees. She dipped her fingertips into a goblet of wine beside the bed and anointed her nipples with the blood-red liquid. In a flash, he was after her, pulling her roughly against him, so that her breasts were crushed against his chest and his rock-hard phallus scalded her soft belly. His demanding mouth took possession of hers, and their tongues began a mating duel of hot, sliding friction that created a wild desire to touch and taste each other everywhere.

Dark erotic sensations inflamed his passion until all he could think of was the sound of her cries when he thrust inside her and felt the hot, wet pull of her around his throbbing sex. He took her down to the bed and rose above her. "Rosamond"—he brushed the backs of his fingers across her cheek—"I'm *asking*."

She gazed up into his green eyes. "Rod," she whispered, touching his beautiful mouth with her fingertips, "I'm *yielding*."

He gathered all her golden softness in his powerful arms, imprisoning her beneath the hard length of his body. Her thighs parted, inviting his thick male shaft to seek succor inside her. His hands slid down to cup her buttocks and he rubbed her against his hardness. When he heard her moan with need, he positioned the velvet tip against her cleft and, with one driving thrust, penetrated her hymen.

Rosamond screamed. She knew there would be pain, but it was sharp and short and was replaced almost instantly by a sensation of fullness that was almost too much to endure. A frisson of fear spiraled inside her that perhaps worse was to come. When Rod held still so that she could get used to his size, she became aware of his heartbeat deep inside her. Whispered love words poured over her. "My beauty, my golden treasure, wrap your legs around my back."

Rosamond resolutely pushed away her fear. She wanted his strength and his power, and she believed this was her way to get it. She slid her thighs around his hips and crossed her ankles, imprisoning him tightly. "Plunder me," she invited recklessly. Slowly at first, but very surely, unbelievable waves of pleasure began to sweep through her. She threaded her fingers through his black hair as her body began undulating to the rhythm of his thrusts, then her nails dug into his shoulders as she began to writhe and arch beneath his powerful torso. Her blood pulsed through her veins, her desire spiraling higher and higher, as his savage lovemaking demanded she meet and match his towering passion.

The sensations he aroused deep inside her finally became too exquisite to bear, and she surrendered everything with a sob. The next moment, she exploded with a scalding burst of fire that shattered into a million splinters of light. In the middle of her cry, she felt Rod erupt and his white-hot seed spurt up inside of her. Rosamond's cry turned into a scream of pleasure as her body pulsed with one climax after another.

They were deaf and blind to everything save each other; their entire world was the cocoon of the curtained bed. They did not hear Griffin knock on their chamber door when he brought food; they saw and heard only one another. Their game of wills paled into insignificance as they realized neither had lost, both had won. They held each other close as they drifted toward sleep. Rod's strength made Rosamond feel safe. She smiled as she lay curled against him; at last she was beginning to trust him.

Before the early light of dawn, Rod arose and dressed. When Rosamond's body was deprived of his warmth, she stirred. He came quickly to the bed and spoke softly. "Go back to sleep, my beauty. I accompany Edward to Westminster. I'll be back tonight," he pledged, brushing her disheveled hair from her brow. "Perhaps you'll meet Doña Eleanora today."

"We've already met. She is lovely, and sweet too, and madly in love with her husband, God help her!"

He felt the barb in her words. "If love is in the air, perhaps it's catching," he teased lightly, touching his lips to hers.

"Don't wish for the impossible, Rodger," Rosamond said, smiling softly. "God speed, my lord, I shall see you tonight."

Edward Plantagenet, flanked by Rodger de Leyburn and Harry of Almaine, led their cavalcade of knights and men-at-arms on the twenty-mile ride to London. Though Edward had not closed his eyes during the long night, his immense energy was not diminished. Lying abed, knowing that his beautiful bride was in a chamber directly above his, frustrated him beyond belief. A dozen times he had arisen to stride upstairs and assert his rights. A dozen times the thought of the royal row that would ensue with his mother made him hesitate. He was not afraid of losing the battle of wills, indeed the thought never entered his head, but he knew if he overruled the queen, her shattered pride would make her vindictive. If he exercised patience, of which he had little, perhaps he could accomplish his goal without a rancorous confrontation that would doubtlessly upset Eleanora.

"The men are expecting to be paid," Harry declared.

Edward and Rodger, each thinking of his wife, were jolted out of their reveries by Harry's practical statement. Edward nodded and said, "When they are settled in the Tower, I'll get their money."

"Will the crown pay my men of Cornwall?" Harry asked.

Edward winked at Rod. "Your father's nickname is Midas; his coffers overflow, while the king is in debt up to his crown."

Used to the ribbing about Richard of Cornwall's wealth, Harry grinned at his cousin. "Then you can ask my father for the money when you get to Westminster."

"You amaze me, Harry. You are fearless in battle, but gutless when it comes to your father."

At Richmond the river came into view, and the cavalcade followed it to Westminster. As agreed, Harry of Almaine proceeded with the troops to the Tower of London, and Rodger de Leyburn rode the short distance upriver to Durham House. Before they parted, Edward directed Rodger to meet him at Westminster Palace after his meeting with Simon de Montfort, so they could ride to the Tower together.

At Westminster, Edward greeted his uncle. The two men, both stamped from the Plantagenet mold, embraced each other. Edward was taller and broader, possessing the golden glow of youth, but Richard, now in his early fifties, was still a handsome man with a commanding presence.

"Does my father intend to return in time for Parliament?" Edward asked.

"There will be no Parliament, Edward. Simon de Montfort does not rule England."

Not yet, Edward thought. "De Montfort is adamant about convening Parliament at Candlemas, and he is the undisputed leader of the barons. The king signed the Provisions of Oxford, and I too have put my signature to it."

"You fool, Edward. Henry has asked the Pope to issue a Bull of Absolution from the Provisions!"

"Goddamn it, Richard, the Provisions of Oxford provide a system of fair government that will make England strong and prosperous."

Richard shook his head. "You are parroting Simon de

Montfort. Edward, you are a royal Plantagenet, for Christ's sake, how can you even think of breaking rank? Your father is threatening to make Edmund his heir if you take sides against us."

"I am parroting no one; I think for myself! England is my inheritance, my divine right, and neither my father the king nor Edmund will wrest it from me. I love England! Though my father is king, all his intimate friends and personal tastes are French. I will be an *English* king, and when it is time for me to rule, I want England united, not divided."

"If you think Simon de Montfort will put you on the throne, you are deluding yourself. His towering ambition is for himself."

Edward hotly denied that he had any such thought. But now he knew why his father had sent Richard to England, and why the justiciar had been summoned so urgently. Henry feared he would lose the throne. Edward immediately changed the subject. "My men need to be paid for the Welsh campaign."

"The crown's coffers are empty." Richard shrugged expressively. "However, I can always find coin for a loyal Plantagenet."

"Dangling another carrot," Edward accused bluntly, "like my mother, as if I were a bloody donkey!"

"Nay, we are well aware you are a lion, Edward," Richard said softly. Then he too changed the subject. "I hear Harry acquitted himself well in Wales. I am surprised he did not accompany you."

"Harry has taken our men to the Tower. I promised to join them there, but I shall be back to discuss this matter of Parliament further, Richard. And I shall bring your son with me; we stand together in this."

Edward decided to await Rodger de Leyburn at the stables. That way he could learn how many men Justiciar Bohun had brought with him. He counted seventy mounts, far more than he had expected.

Rodger rode in, and as he watered his horse his eyes followed Edward's thumb as he gestured toward the filled stalls. Rod nodded but did not speak until they were away from the palace stables. Once they were outside and he was certain that they could not be overheard, he said, "As you suspected, Simon knows Richard of Cornwall has come in your father's stead. He thinks it a clever move, for Richard is far more persuasive than Henry."

Edward nodded, adding cynically, "And Richard has coin to put where his mouth is! Did you tell him the justiciar brought troops?"

"Aye, but he already knew. The Earl of Norfolk sent him word."

"So, the marshal remains loyal, if the justiciar does not!"

Rodger nodded. "Simon knows the barons will be split if it comes down to civil war. He wishes to speak with you about this matter."

"It can wait a day; we have a more pressing problem. There is no payment for the men. Richard offered me a bribe, but I didn't bite."

"Then we'll have to provide the men with a diversion. We could throw a banquet at the Tower; more food and drink than they've seen in a year. As steward I still have a little left in the household accounts, and the merchants will supply on credit."

"See to it, and don't forget to order whores. A banquet is no good without whores; women are a better diversion than drink!"

Accompanied by half a dozen servants from the Tower kitchens, Rodger de Leyburn made the rounds of Billingsgate, then Leadenhall markets, buying everything from lampreys to lobsters, and plump pigeons to pickled pigs' feet. He bought barrels of ale from a warehouse on Thames Street and wine from a ship anchored at Tower Wharfe. In the East End of London, there was no shortage of brothels, and Sir Rodger hired all the bawds who plied their trade in the houses of Dog and Bitch Lane.

That night by ten o'clock, the banquet was well on its way to becoming a wild carousal. As Rodger watched the antics of the bare-breasted bawds, he thought wistfully of Rosamond awaiting him at Windsor. When he did not arrive, her trust in him would evaporate. It was not the twenty-mile ride that deterred him, it was his duty to Edward. Amusement filled his eyes as he watched two sisters having a cat fight over the prince. The buxom blondes were pulling each other's hair and trading vile curses.

"You fawning, fat-arsed strumpet! 'E saw me first!"

"You pox-marked, whey-faced harpy! You can kiss my fat arse!"

"And you can suck my duck till it quacks!"

Edward roared with laughter. "Fanny, Fancy, there is no need to fight. I have a solution that will keep peace in the family." He arose, forced them apart, then, taking the sisters by the hand, led them upstairs to a bedchamber.

Rod watched them disappear, then drained his wine cup, wondering if he could slip away. Then, like a miracle, Edward rejoined him. "This was an unqualified success, as are most of your ideas, Rod. But you and I have far lovelier damsels awaiting us at Windsor."

Rod flashed him an appreciative grin. "What the hell did you do with Fanny and Fancy?"

"Led them into Harry's chamber, of course!"

FIFTEEN

It was well past midnight when Edward and Rodger entered Windsor Castle's new tower. Both men had drunk enough wine to make them overbold, but luckily both had hard heads for drink and neither was completely intoxicated.

"Your task is a hell of a lot simpler than mine," Edward complained. "Your wife will be waiting in your bed. Mine will be surrounded by a fire-breathing dragon and a horde of dragonettes."

Rod flashed him a grin. "Your sword is stout; my money is on you, Saint George!" He watched Edward ascend the stairs before he opened the door to his own apartments. Chirk displayed frenzied delight by pawing at his leg and wagging her entire bottom.

"Sssh, I want to surprise her."

Rosamond, lying awake, was indeed surprised; she had given up on him long ago. Her trust in him slowly returned while she listened to the rustle of garments as he undressed in the dark, then felt the mattress dip as he joined her in the bed. He smelled of cheap perfume and expensive wine, and her trust evaporated instantly.

"Don't you dare touch me!"

Rod laughed. "Dare? Do you know how many miles I've ridden?"

"Don't you mean how many whores you've ridden?"

Her words mauled his pride. This was the thanks he got for being faithful. "I don't need to pay my women."

"Well, you'll have to pay this one a king's ransom to allow you to share even my chamber, let alone my bed!"

"Allow?" His voice held a dangerous note. "This is *my* chamber, *my* bed . . . *my* wife."

Chirk took heed of the danger, if Rosamond did not. A loud pounding on the outer door sent her scooting beneath the bed.

A foul oath fell from Rod's lips as he flung back the covers and strode naked to the door. "What the devil do you want?"

"I want to come in."

Rod recognized Edward's voice. It sounded as annoyed as he himself felt. He opened the door and lifted down a lit torch from its wall bracket to light the chamber.

"The bird has flown! The bloody royal apartments are deserted. There are times when I could cheerfully choke my mother; she is an infuriating bitch!"

"Name me a woman who is not!"

At the sound of Lord Edward's voice, Rosamond sat up, but she did not have time to put on her bedgown before he came striding into the bedchamber. She quickly drew up the sheet to cover her night rail.

"Rosamond, did you see the queen today? Did you see Eleanora? Do you know when they left or where they went?" The questions came one after another without pause.

"I was greatly looking forward to talking with Princess Eleanora. I walked in the walled garden for over an hour, hoping she would join me. I took my midday meal in the dining hall, expecting to see her, but she did not come. When I returned to my chambers, I found a note from her under the door. I ran to the window and was in time to see the royal barge going downriver toward London. That must have been about two o'clock."

"A note?" Edward asked eagerly.

Rosamond took it from the bedside table and handed it to him.

Alas, I must leave today. If I had a choice, I would not go. I am torn in half! One glimpse of him was not enough. I have waited too long and pray that Edward feels the same. Please tell him he fills my thoughts and my heart. Eleanora (Nora)

He looked up. "You have seen her, spoken with her?"

"We met the night before last, when we took our dogs to the garden. The princess was cold; I lent her my fur-lined cloak."

"Isn't she the most exquisite female you have ever seen?"

"Yes, she is exceptionally beautiful, Lord Edward."

"Beautiful and shy! Did you see her glorious hair and her skin? Her lips remind me of rose petals, and her skin is the color of dark honey. Such beauty must come from her mixed French and Spanish bloodlines. And she is so delightfully sweet and innocent."

Rodger listened in amazement as Edward extolled shyness and innocence as if they were virtues. They'd certainly never appealed to him before. Eleanora must indeed be a tempting morsel.

"She says I fill her thoughts and her heart."

"Please keep the note, Lord Edward."

"Thank you, Rosamond." He took her fingers to his lips to bestow a kiss of gratitude.

Rosamond noticed that he too smelled of cheap perfume and expensive wine. Wherever they'd been and whatever they'd done, they had done together. It was high time the prince had a wife to curb his wild, wicked ways.

"Don't mind me; I have all the patience in the world." A naked Rodger leaned against the bedpost.

"Go to the devil," Edward replied. "We want to talk of Eleanora. Tell me more, Rosamond."

She cast Rodger an amused glance, thoroughly

enjoying his frustration. Not without effort, she dragged her gaze from his lithe body and gave her attention to Edward. "She has a small dog, a Maltese terrier. She said the queen didn't like him, and asked me if you liked dogs; I assured her that you adored them, my lord."

"I told you my mother could be a bitch. She is using Eleanora as bait to bring me to heel."

"All women can be bitches," Rod commiserated.

Rosamond knew the barb was for her. "And by the smell of you both, you've had much recent experience with bitches!"

"Aha, I am interrupting something here." Perversely, Edward was glad his friend would also find his bed cold this night. As Rodger accompanied him to the door, Edward winked at him. "Never mind, it will soon be dawn."

Richard de Clare and his daughter-in-law Alyce traveled to London together. Though Alyce would have preferred to go alone, the Earl of Gloucester had received a summons from his stepfather, Richard of Cornwall, and Alyce had graciously accepted her father-in-law's escort. The earl left his son Gilbert the Red in charge at Gloucester and, with a small coterie of knights, rode to Westminster Palace.

When they arrived, Alyce took the luxuriously furnished apartments that her father, Guy de Lusignan, had occupied before the bloody barons had banished the king's half-brother from England. She was livid to learn, through servants' gossip, that the queen had brought Lord Edward's bride, Princess Eleanora, to England and had taken her to Windsor Castle.

Gloucester went immediately to greet Richard of Cornwall, his stepfather. The two men, so alike in build and coloring, gripped wrists in a familial salute.

"Richard, the king is enraged at the treasonous plot Simon de Montfort has hatched, but he is equally incensed that you and Edward would take sides against him and turn traitor."

"There is no plot!" Gloucester protested. "Henry signed the Provisions of Oxford and the first provision is to hold Parliament."

"Are you blind, Richard, or cleverly deceitful? Are you part of the conspiracy to put Edward on the throne?"

Gloucester's famous temper exploded. "These are fucking lies! I am England's leading peer and would never plot to depose her rightful king! Upholding the Provisions of Oxford is my duty."

"The Provisions of Oxford are moot. The Pope has issued Henry a Bull of Absolution. It is now imperative that we Plantagenets show the barons a united front."

"I am a de Clare," Gloucester pointed out.

Richard of Cornwall looked at him with affection, and slowly shook his head. "That is your name and rank, but you are a Plantagenet by blood. You are my real son, my firstborn, not my stepson. Why do you suppose your mother, my beloved Isabella, named you Richard?"

Gloucester was stunned, and yet it explained many things in his childhood. Royal Plantagenet blood gave him his towering pride and his temper. "Why did you keep this a secret?" he demanded, his voice hoarse with emotion.

"Your mother was wed to Gilbert de Clare; I could not bring shame down upon her, or you, Richard. They would have called you a royal bastard. When de Clare died in battle, you inherited his title and became the Earl of Gloucester." Richard poured wine for both of them and offered his son a silent toast.

"I have orders from the king to set up an inner council comprising you, myself, and Justiciar Bohun," Richard of Cornwall continued. "We will summon a select number of loyal barons. We must close the city of London to Simon de Montfort and his traitorous adherents to prevent Parliament being called. If de Montfort does not back down, it will mean war."

"What about Lord Edward?"

"It will be our job to wean him away from Simon de Montfort. I've already told him that Henry will name Edmund his heir, and the queen has brought his bride, Princess Eleanora, to tempt him back into the fold."

"Threats and bribes will have little effect on Edward, from what I've seen of him. He won't come to heel like an obedient hound."

"He has a shrewd head on his shoulders. He needs gold. I am having him followed. Today he will find himself locked out of the city, separated from his men who are billeted in the Tower. When he sees that many of the barons will remain loyal to the crown, and when Henry arrives with his three hundred French mercenaries, Edward will weigh the odds. I am counting on his insatiable Plantagenet ambition."

"You are forgetting de Montfort's magnetic personality and equally relentless ambition."

"Not for a moment, Richard. Sooner or later Edward will realize that they cannot both rule."

When Lord Edward and Sir Rodger rode from the lower ward of Windsor, they did not notice a horseman who waited in the shadow of the Curfew Tower. "We'll go straight to Durham House," Edward said decisively. "Then we'll get Harry, if he's still breathing. I'll leave Westminster until last. Undoubtedly that is where the queen has taken Eleanora, and I intend to take my wife back to Windsor, where she belongs."

As they traveled the now familiar road, Rodger became aware of hoofbeats behind them in the distance. As they approached the village of Westminster the sound grew closer. "I think we're being followed," he warned Edward. They deliberately changed direction and headed toward the river, concealing themselves behind the old palace wall to await their pursuer.

Edward grabbed the horse's bridle while de Leyburn

dragged its rider from the saddle and held his dagger to the wretch's throat. "Talk, while you still have breath."

The small, wiry man, dwarfed by his two assailants, wet himself from fear.

"Are you one of de Montfort's spies?" Edward demanded.

When he felt the blood trickle down his neck, the man nodded eagerly. The horse Edward held smelled the blood and suddenly reared up in a frenzy of fear, flailing its hooves above their heads. In a flash the man dove into the Thames and disappeared.

"I should have killed the son of a bitch while I had him," Rod cursed, sheathing his dagger and quieting his own and Edward's mounts while the prince soothed the terrified horse. "We should have had our squires at our backs."

"We'll take the nag to Durham House and see if it came from there. Bones of Christ, doesn't de Montfort trust me?"

"Simon de Montfort is too shrewd to trust you, my lord."

When they arrived at Durham House, a groom took charge of the three mounts, bowing low to Lord Edward. "Did this horse come from your stables?" Edward demanded.

"I am not sure, Lord Edward."

"You're a bloody groom here, don't you recognize your own horseflesh?"

"Forgive me, Lord Edward, there are so many new horses from Kenilworth, it is difficult for me to identify them all."

"Even the fucking grooms are trained to be noncommittal," Edward remarked.

When Earl Simon came out to greet his royal guest, Lord Edward made no mention of the disturbing incident. They followed their host to Durham's hall, where Lady Eleanor offered them food and drink. She kissed Edward and asked Rodger how Rosamond fared.

"I left her in high spirits, my lady."

Eleanor laughed at his carefully chosen words, likening his new bride to a filly. "Then I take it she is not broken to the bridle yet, and is still trying to take the bit between her teeth."

Rod bestowed a kiss upon the hand of the Demoiselle, who said, "Did you not bring Rosamond, Sir Rodger?"

"Darling," her mother said, "the men are here to discuss grave matters of politics. We will withdraw and let them get to their business."

Rod smiled at Demi. "I will carry a letter to Rosamond."

Demi dimpled at him. "Thank you, my lord."

When they were alone, Simon wasted no time. "What did Richard of Cornwall tell you?" he asked Edward.

"He said that there would be no Parliament, but I told him in no uncertain terms that you were adamant about it, that you were the undisputed leader of the barons, and that I had added my signature to the Provisions of Oxford."

"And his response?"

"He told me my father had asked the Pope for absolution, but I told him the Provisions would unite England, not divide her."

"Richard kept the whole truth from you. Henry has obtained his Bull of Absolution and is on his way home to resume royal power. He could be at Dover now."

Edward thought fleetingly of his brother Edmund, who was in charge of Dover Castle. "When the king arrives, I will talk with him. I am sure I can persuade him that the Provisions will unite the country. The last thing my father wants is civil war. He has always backed down when the barons have challenged him, and with my voice added to the barons', I'm sure he will listen to reason."

"And if he does not, Edward?"

The prince looked Simon de Montfort in the eye. "Then it will be time for England to be ruled by another. One who will never be weak. England is my inheritance."

Rodger de Leyburn held his breath, wishing Edward had not shown his hand, but the moment passed, as Earl Simon said, "I am a realist; the king's return will split the barons. I am making a list of those I can count on."

Edward and Rodger read the list. It was headed by Simon de Montfort, Earl of Leicester, followed by Marshal Bigod, Earl of Norfolk; John de Warenne, Earl of Surrey; John de Vescy, Earl of Northumberland; the two warlike Bishops of Ely and Worcester, and three Marcher barons, Clifford, Hay, and Montgomery.

"You've forgotten Richard of Gloucester and Harry," Edward said.

"Have I?" Simon asked cynically. "I have learned not to count on those related to royalty. They change their coats too often."

"Is that why you had me followed?" Edward flared, stung at the implication.

"I did no such thing! But mayhap I should have!"

Rodger intervened immediately, lest they come to blows. "It was my fault; I let the cur get away. No doubt he is in the pay of Richard of Cornwall."

Lady Eleanor stood poised on the threshold. "Richard? Is my brother Richard in London?"

"He is at Westminster; I spoke with him yesterday," Edward said.

Eleanor turned accusing eyes upon her husband. "You deliberately kept this from me, Simon?"

"Damn you, Edward, can you not control your tongue?" the earl said. He turned to face Eleanor. "If I had told you Richard was here, you would have gone running to Westminster Palace. I don't need you meddling in this matter!"

She drew herself up to her full height of just over five feet. "How dare you treat me like a nithing?" she demanded regally, her royal blood asserting itself. Eleanor was a princess, but spoke as if she were empress of the universe.

"Plantagenets think they rule the world; their blood pride borders on madness. I am always stunned at the convenient way you forget I am master in my own house, madam."

Eleanor, about to deliver a cutting retort, saw her husband's face harden, and changed her mind. She lowered her lashes to veil her anger. "Edward will think we are savages."

"I too am a Plantagenet," Edward said, "quite used to battles royal."

"Shall we get back to the list?" Rodger de Leyburn interjected. "The Marches, the West Country, and all about Kenilworth can be counted upon."

Earl Simon nodded. "Northampton also; my son Simon holds the castle. The Cinque Ports are an unknown quantity, but they are vital, and must be secured for command of the sea. When we hold Parliament, I shall call for a council of war!"

"Nay!" Edward protested. "I will talk to the king first, before you declare war. I will negotiate and mayhap he will concede."

Simon de Montfort was furious. "No appeasement! The time for concessions and compromise is over! There can be only one leader, one man who issues the orders. I am that man."

Edward's fury now matched Simon's. As the two men stared each other down, neither willing to bend to the other, Edward suddenly realized that de Montfort had no intention of putting him on the throne. He reined in his temper with difficulty. "Parliament will decide."

"Aye," Earl Simon conceded, "the barons are on their way here."

As prince and steward rode from Durham's courtyard, Edward said, "He has a deep-rooted hatred of the Plantagenets. I thought it was love for England that drove him, but it is hatred too."

"He does not hate *you*, my lord," Rodger protested.

"He does not *love* me either."

"Earl Simon recognizes your abilities in warfare, in leadership; he sees your energy, your shrewdness, your ambition, and knows you will soon be his equal. All you lack are his many years of experience. Mayhap he envies you your youth, and fears it too."

"If he makes an enemy of me, he needs to fear me!"

When they reached Ludgate, the western gate in London's wall, they found it closed. "Ho there! Open the gate!" Edward shouted to the guards.

"The gates are closed. Entrance into the city is forbidden."

"By whose orders?" Edward demanded, noticing the guards were heavily armed.

"By orders of the king!"

"I am Edward Plantagenet, open the gates!" he commanded.

"The gates into London are closed against the Earl of Leicester, Lord Edward, or any of their adherents," came the grim reply.

"They wear Bohun's device; they are the justiciar's men," Rodger observed. He glanced along London's wall and saw that armed guards were posted atop it to enforce the orders.

Edward's horse curvetted, sensing its master's anger. "Come, we'll try the next gate, where I will not announce who I am."

"All know you, Edward. There is only one six-foot-four giant with a golden head and beard."

They found Newgate, Aldersgate, and Cripple Gate heavily guarded and were bluntly refused admission. They skirted the wall to Moore Gate and watched in fury and frustration as every farm wagon seeking entry was searched. They spurred their mounts around the walled city toward the Tower, refusing to believe London was closed to them.

The Tower of London was sealed tighter than a tomb, its regular guards reinforced by Bohun's men, and it dawned on the two young men that they were effectively cut off from their men-at-arms, Harry of Almaine, and even their squires. Edward cursed everyone from the justiciar to the king, then for good measure cursed the saints in heaven.

"Durham House or Westminster?" Rodger asked.

"Westminster! De Montfort's spies will take him the news."

Their horses were lathered by the time the pair clattered into the old palace yard. They turned them over to a groom with orders to cool them down before they were watered.

Lord Edward, with his steward close upon his heels, went to seek out Richard of Cornwall. They could not locate him immediately, but curbed their impatience, knowing how vast Westminster Palace was. Edward decided to seek the queen in the royal apartments. His blood was up, and in this mood, he knew none would dare gainsay him access to his wife, Eleanora.

The royal apartments were deserted; not even a servant or a lady-in-waiting could be found within the chambers. Edward cursed to vent his frustration, he could have sworn he would find his mother and his wife at Westminster. He quit the apartments and strode to his own, asking a servant where everyone was. When he received a blank stare, he ordered him to fetch ale.

The two men heard the outer chamber door open, followed by soft footsteps and the rustle of feminine garments. Edward turned toward the door with an eager, expectant look on his face, which faded immediately.

"Chéri, 'ow did you find out so quickly that I was here? You are very impetuous, Edward; I only arrived this morning."

"Alyce, what the devil are you doing here?" he

demanded ungraciously, totally forgetting the plans they'd made for a rendezvous.

"Bringing your ale, my lord, to quench your raging thirst."

Rod wondered how she could make even ale sound erotic.

"Where is everyone? Where is Richard of Cornwall? And the queen, where is my mother?"

In a blood-red gown with her jet-black hair falling about her slim shoulders like black silk, Alyce looked bewitching. Slowly her mouth curved into a sensual smile. She had thought Edward was at Windsor with his child-like bride, but obviously not. "So many questions, so much information I 'ave that you would like. You will 'ave to pry it out of me, chéri. What inducements do you 'ave to loosen my tongue?" Alyce ran the tip of her tongue playfully about her bright red lips.

"Would a beating be inducement enough?" Edward threatened.

"Oooh, perhaps if your rod is stout enough," Alyce teased.

Edward looked at Rodger over her head, begging for help. Rodger shrugged, then inclined his head toward the prince's bedchamber, and Edward took his steward's meaning immediately. The prince curbed his anger with difficulty and led Alyce into the inner chamber.

SIXTEEN

Rosamond helped Nan unpack Sir Rodger's trunks and hang his clothes in the huge dressing room wardrobe. The scent of sandalwood stole to her as her hands caressed the rich materials of his garments.

"He's a fine figure of a man; his doublets need no shoulder pads," Nan mused as she stole a glance at her lady's face. She had overheard the newlyweds exchange sharp words late last night.

Rosamond ignored Nan's curiosity. "Since the queen is not in residence today, this is a golden opportunity for me to see the royal apartments. Would you like to come with me, Nan?"

"Nay, servants carry tales, and I have no business up there. As the steward's wife, you have a ready excuse. I shall unpack all your fine sheets and linen, my lady."

Rosamond spent the next two hours touring not only the king and queen's apartments, but also Lord Edward's and Princess Eleanora's. All were the last word in luxury. Lady Eleanor de Montfort had been right: Windsor Castle was a magnificent residence indeed. Rosamond put on a cloak and ventured from the new tower. She visited the chapel, then found a stillroom with bunches of herbs hanging from its rafters.

She crossed the Middle Ward and went through the Norman Gateway with its twin towers, toward the river where she had seen the royal barge yesterday. She hadn't gone far when she came face-to-face with Griffin and Owen. The squires, soaking wet and looking like river rats, bowed low. "Lady Rosamond," they said in unison.

She stared at them, more than puzzled. "Where have you been?"

"We came upriver by watercraft, my lady," Griffin offered.

"You look as if you had swum from London!"

"We did take a dip in the river, my lady," Griffin admitted.

"And did Sir Rodger and Lord Edward swim with you?" Rosamond's eyebrows arched with disbelief.

Griffin nodded, while Owen shook his head. From her question, the squires inferred that Rodger and Edward were not at Windsor as they had hoped.

"No doubt you swam to rid yourselves of the stink of wine and wenches!" Rosamond's words told them she was piqued, but also indicated that Lord Edward and Rodger had returned to Windsor last night.

Griffin had been trained to be closemouthed without seeming curt. There was no way he would divulge a whisper of the trouble Rodger and Lord Edward were in as a result of their alliance with Simon de Montfort. Early this morning, when the Welsh squires had awakened at the Tower and found themselves imprisoned because all gates were closed and guarded against de Montfort adherents, they had slipped into the Thames and swum across to the other side, and from there had taken a boat to Windsor.

Since there was nothing he could do to aid Sir Rodger's larger problem, Griffin decided to see what he could do about alleviating his master's domestic trouble. He lowered his voice to a confidential tone. "It was Sir Rodger's duty as steward to provide the men with food and drink to celebrate the Welsh victory and New Year's, but neither Lord Edward nor Sir Rodger stayed for the revels, Lady Rosamond. After a cup of wine, they left us to it and returned to Windsor. Our heads were a bit foggy this morning, but the river cleared them."

"I see," Rosamond said, mollified. "You'll catch your deaths; get out of those wet clothes immediately, you foolish young devils." She led them back to the new tower with a lighter heart. Why in the world hadn't Rodger explained things? She decided he had far too much pride to excuse himself to a woman, especially if that woman was his wife. The corners of her mouth rose in a smile. When Rodger returned tonight, she would make up for the tart tongue and cold shoulder she had given him the night before.

"Father!" Harry of Almaine levered himself to a sitting position in the rumpled bed. Unfortunately, his hands pressed down on the flesh of a naked female on either side of him. It roused Fanny, but Fancy merely rolled to the floor.

"Fancy that!" her sister muttered between yawns.

Harry scrambled to his feet, blushing to the roots of his hair as his father strode into the chamber. "Richard!" Harry said hoarsely as his half-brother Gloucester appeared. For a fleeting moment, Richard of Gloucester looked impressed, but then he quickly set his features in a grim mask of disapproval.

Richard of Cornwall, however, was plainly enraged. "Faugh! This chamber stinks. Get your clothes on and come below," he ordered, turning on his heel.

Caught at a complete disadvantage, Harry obeyed. He descended the stairs and said, "Father, let me explain—"

"I don't want an explanation for the whores, I want an explanation for why you have turned traitor against your Plantagenet blood!"

"I am no traitor!" Harry retorted hotly.

"You have taken sides against your king, your father, and your entire family to support Simon de Montfort."

"Earl Simon speaks for all the barons as he attempts to hold King Henry to the Provisions. Richard, you were at Kenilworth, tell him we are not traitors!"

"Circumstances have changed, Harry. The king is absolved by the Pope from the Provisions, and is on his way back to England. He has called for one hundred loyal barons to be ready for armed action. Justiciar Bohun is already in London and has closed the city gates against Simon de Montfort and his adherents."

Harry stared at his brother Richard with disbelief. "You are a turncoat!" he said.

"Richard is England's leading peer," his father pointed out. "And now he heads a new inner council. You are the turncoat, Harry. You seem to have totally forgotten that you are a royal Plantagenet!"

Harry almost choked on his choler. The drink he had consumed the night before threatened to spew up from his stomach. "What about Edward? He is heir to the throne, but stands solidly with Earl Simon!"

"Edward is far shrewder than you, Harry," his father said quietly. "He has already repudiated de Montfort." He watched his son closely to see how he took the lie.

In disbelief, Harry turned to his brother Gloucester for confirmation. Richard did not lie, but lent weight to their father's words. "Blood is thicker than water—especially Plantagenet blood."

Harry glared at Gloucester with disgust in his eyes. "Your own son, Gilbert, will never take sides against Simon de Montfort. He is made of sterner stuff!"

"It matters little whose side Gilbert takes," his brother replied, "since he has no men-at-arms to lead into battle."

"Speaking of men-at-arms, I have brought coin to pay your men," Richard of Cornwall told Harry.

The defiance seemed to go out of Harry at the mention of coin. Then he straightened his shoulders and declared, "I shall go and tell Earl Simon that I cannot play traitor to my family, but assure him that I shall never take up arms against him!"

His father clapped him on the shoulder. "You were ever honorable and idealistic. I'm very proud of you, Harry.

Now let's get these bawds out of the Tower. The Queen and Princess Eleanora are in residence up in the royal apartments."

Richard did not immediately follow his father. He needed to satisfy his curiosity. "Harry, about the whores—"

"They are sisters who work in tandem. I couldn't very well break up a matched set," he offered lamely.

"Women!" Lord Edward declared with disgust as he and Rodger de Leyburn cantered from Westminster's stables. "A two-hour joust garnered scant information. Her lips were sealed tight as a clam; only her nether lips opened wide!"

"She gave you no news whatsoever?"

"Only bad news," Edward said grimly. "Gloucester accompanied Alyce; Richard of Cornwall summoned him."

"Christ, Gloucester has defected!"

"Exactly! Simon de Montfort was right not to trust him. Gloucester weighed the odds and jumped to the Plantagenet side, as other barons will do," Edward concluded.

Rodger de Leyburn, a keen student of human nature, knew that Lord Edward himself was now carefully weighing the odds. "Had Alyce any notion where the queen had taken your wife?"

"Alyce swore she did not know, but we both know she can be a deceitful little bitch. Speculation is futile; we have so many royal residences, my mother could have hidden Eleanora anywhere in the country."

"Where to now, Windsor or back to Durham House?"

"Durham House," Edward said decisively.

Simon de Montfort was not at home. He had gone to the city gates to see for himself how well London was sealed. As they waited for his return Demoiselle de Montfort gave Sir Rodger a letter for Rosamond. "I would love it if she would visit and we could see London together."

Rodger knew instantly that Demi was ignorant of their situation, with no notion the gates of London were closed to her. Rod smiled gallantly as he tucked the note into his doublet. "Rosamond will be overjoyed to receive your letter."

Within the hour, Simon de Montfort returned to Durham House. He could not contain the fury he felt, and Rodger noted he had the wild look of a fanatic about him. De Montfort was wearing black riding leathers. His eyes burned like black coals in a face that looked both grim and gaunt.

"Gloucester was summoned to Westminster," Edward said tersely.

"Aye," Simon sneered, "I had a visit from Harry of Almaine, his sniveling brother, telling me his duty was to his father and King Henry, but that he would never bear arms against me." Simon laughed derisively. "I told him I feared his disloyalty far more than I feared his arms!"

"So, they got to Harry, damn them to hellfire!"

Simon de Montfort stared into Edward's eyes as if he were confronting the Devil. "At least your cousin had enough honor to tell me to my face that his loyalty lay with the Plantagenets; *you* would betray me behind my back!"

"That is a lie!" Edward roared.

"Today's lie is tomorrow's truth! Your father landed at Dover and his mercenaries are beating all the seaports along the Channel into submission. Since London is closed to me, I will hold my council of war in Oxford. You, Lord Edward, will not be welcome! I need no fucking Plantagenets to stab me in the back!"

Edward gave him a level stare. "You had my full backing, but suddenly you don't want me. You hope to win the war against my father so that *you* can rule through a weak king. You realize you could never do that with me on the throne."

De Leyburn closed his eyes in dismay. The two shrewdest and most powerful men in the country had just severed their relationship. Part of him wanted to cross over to Earl Simon's side, because de Montfort was a man of integrity who intended to right the wrongs done to England by a weak king. But his duty lay with Edward, and Rodger knew that de Montfort would have no respect for a man who did not honor his duty and remain loyal.

On the ride back to Windsor, Edward Plantagenet and Rodger de Leyburn remained silent, each submerged in his own private thoughts. The prince was making plans for his future, while his steward's thoughts were more immediate. He knew Rosamond would be devastated when she learned that they were no longer allied with the de Montforts, who had been her beloved guardians. After waging an inner battle, Rodger knew it would be in his best interests to keep his wife in ignorance for as long as possible.

Rosamond returned to the stillroom at Windsor Castle for some dragonwort to keep her from conceiving. She hid it from Nan, because her servant, like most women, thought that preventing conception was wicked. It was not that Rosamond didn't want a child, it was simply that she could not bear to have a baby, love it with all her heart, then lose it. Far better to avoid the risk completely.

Rosamond took an early bath, then donned a pale green underdress. It looked so feminine that she decided not to put the dark green tunic over it. When she opened her jewel coffer, her eyes fell upon the beautiful Celtic torque Rodger had given her the morning after they were wed. She had never worn it, because torques were reputed to be slave collars, but tonight the magnificent emerald tempted her, and she knew it would please her husband if she wore it.

From the long, arched windows, she saw Lord Edward and her husband canter up the Lower Ward. As grooms came forward for their horses, she watched their squires, Owen and Griffin, hurry out to meet them. All four were talking at once as they disappeared inside. Rosamond summoned a servant and asked him to fetch dinner upstairs for Sir Rodger and herself, then she lit the scented candles and waited.

It was an hour before she heard footsteps, but when

she eagerly opened the door, it was only the manservant with the food. She schooled herself to be patient and wondered if aught was amiss.

Finally, he came. For a moment he looked as if he had all the troubles in the world on his shoulders, but his expression changed the moment he saw her. Rosamond stood by the fire and waited until he came to her. He reached out to touch her hair, gilded by the firelight, then his fingers touched the green jewel at the base of her throat. "You are so lovely, you take my breath away."

"I'm sorry about last night. Griffin told me you did not stay for the celebration with your men." She looked up into his eyes. "Rodger, I will try to give you my trust."

He flinched inwardly. It was a day for breaking trusts. *Do not start thinking me a saint, Rosamond, for in truth I am a devil!*

"I ordered supper for us up here."

At last he smiled. "You are a good wife . . . you satisfy all my appetites." He brushed his lips against hers, then, when she did not pull away, he kissed her deeply.

They sat before the fire with the huge tray between them. He lifted the silver covers and took a hearty helping of pigeon pie, roast venison, and Yorkshire pudding. As he reached for the artichokes Rosamond laughed. "I thought something might be amiss, but I see by your healthy appetite, that cannot be."

You are far too perceptive, my love, he thought. *I only eat because I've had no food since yesterday.* "Artichokes are aphrodisiacs," he teased. "Won't you try some?"

She glanced at him from beneath her lashes. "What about wine?"

Already aroused, he hardened instantly, remembering the wine and what she'd done with it. "Wine is not an aphrodisiac; it simply steals your senses, heats your blood, and takes away inhibitions."

"I did not realize it was the wine that did that . . . I thought it was you."

"Flattery, be God! Are you trying to seduce me again?"

Rosamond shook her head and said softly, "Nay, I like it when you do the wooing."

He began the wooing with his eyes, allowing his smoldering gaze to fix upon her mouth, allowing her to see the desire, the hunger, the raw need, and the intent he had to taste her and possess her. Then his glance dipped to her breasts, and she saw the green fire blaze up in his eyes and saw his mouth harden.

When Rod licked his fingers, Rosamond felt her yearning begin. When he wiped his hands on a linen napkin and came around the table, she shivered, knowing that at any second he would touch her. He lifted her and slid beneath her so that she was sitting in his lap. She could feel his hard thighs beneath her soft bottom. She thought fleetingly of the scar, then the heat of his body began to seep into hers through the fine-spun material of her underdress.

His questing hand slipped up inside the diaphanous skirt and he feathered his fingertips along her satiny skin. "Who has the longest, prettiest legs in the world?" he whispered.

"I do," Rosamond said shyly.

"And who has a golden treasure between those pretty legs?"

"I do," she said breathlessly as he fondled it.

"And who will plunder that treasure?" he teased.

"'Tis buried deep," she teased back. "It will take a bold man indeed, methinks." She slipped eager hands inside his doublet to feel the hard muscles in his chest. She felt a paper and drew it out. "No wonder you found it so unerringly, you had a treasure map, you devil."

Rod cursed himself for a fool. He hadn't meant for Rosamond to read the letter from Demi. She unfolded the note and read it by the firelight, and he watched her face light up with pleasure.

"You were at Durham House!" Rosamond touched her lips to his. "Thank you, Rod, for being so thoughtful!"

His thoughts were full, all right, full of deceit, duplicity, and cunning; it was a good thing he was a master of guile.

He whisked the note from her fingers and dropped it on the tray. "Don't try to divert me from my wicked intent."

"I'll fight you," she whispered.

"Such promises only spur me on!" He laughed deep in his throat, ready to play the titillating game of love all night. Tomorrow would arrive all too soon. He set Rosamond on her feet, put the food tray on the floor, then removed his doublet and shirt with great deliberation. Then he lifted off her underdress, sat her upon the table, and moved between her silken thighs.

"Rod!"

He unfastened his codpiece, and his swollen sex rose up in rampant splendor. "Rod, indeed!" He fastened his fingers in her pale hair that excited him so much, and lifted her face for his kiss. "You smell so good."

"And you smell of sandalwood and . . . stallion, which is far more of an aphrodisiac than artichokes."

"I've been in the saddle most of the day."

"Poor Rod, can you manage one last ride?"

He flashed her a grin. "If I help you to mount, you can ride me, Rosamond . . . at least this first time."

"I once declared that unruly young stallions needed a horse whip. Do you not fear me, m'lord?"

"Aye, I fear losing my senses, fear losing my heart and soul to your witchery."

"It is your strength and power for which I lust, never your heart, m'lord."

Don't ever make the mistake of underestimating me, Rosamond.

Her fingertips stroked the blue-black shadow of his day-old beard, and Rosamond was surprised that even though he was unshaved and unbathed, she found Sir Rodger de Leyburn mightily attractive.

He slipped his hands beneath the soft curve of her bottom and lifted her onto his erection. "Hang on, beauty," he murmured, and felt her grip his shoulders as he slowly impaled her tight, scalding sheath, until he was seated to the hilt. Then he held himself still, as fire flamed through his groin, waiting for her to take her pleasure.

When Rosamond began to move, Rod could not help himself, but moved with her in the wild, savage ride. They were both so highly aroused, their kisses so fierce, their plunging thrusts so deep and hot with passion, they peaked long before they wanted it to end. She collapsed against him, her arms sliding about his neck, her cheek resting against his heart.

Rodger's arms closed about her possessively as he lifted her and carried her to their bed. He laid her back against the pillows and spread her beautiful golden hair all about her. He removed his chausses, then gazed at her for a long time, seeing her beauty, her passion, and her vulnerability. He knew that she was going to be deeply hurt by Edward's decision today to break with Simon de Montfort, and he also knew there was nothing he could do to prevent it. Tenderly he gathered her in his arms and began to make gentle, sweet love to her.

Later, after her husband had fallen asleep with his arm wrapped possessively around her, Rosamond lay still as her thoughts drifted back over the days since she had been married. On the whole, it was much better than she had expected. She was beginning to adjust to the separation from the secure de Montfort household at Kenilworth. She felt somewhat stronger and certainly more self-confident, and she wondered if she had Sir Rodger de Leyburn to thank for it. She smiled into the darkness, knowing Rod was definitely responsible for making her feel beautiful and making her aware of her female power. Perhaps power was more exciting than love!

She knew she had been terribly wary about giving him her trust, but now she felt he was doing his best to earn that trust. It was a new year, a new life, and for the first time, Rosamond was optimistic that their union held the promise of happiness.

SEVENTEEN

Rosamond slept late, and when she awakened and found herself alone, she assumed Rodger was long gone. Deciding that today she would ride out and explore Windsor Castle's great park and forests, she bathed quickly and opened up her wardrobe. The first thing to catch her eye were her brother's garments that she had brought from Deerhurst. She thought how practical men's clothes were for riding, and no sooner had she thought it than she found herself slipping into Giles's chausses and doublet.

"Griffin, where the devil is Sir Rodger?"

Rosamond, hearing Lord Edward's voice behind her, swung around to face him.

"Splendor of God, Rosamond, I thought you were your husband's squire! Your long legs make you Griffin's height, and I didn't expect to find a lady dressed in male garb."

"Forgive me, Lord Edward, these clothes belonged to Giles." When he gave her a tight-lipped look of disapproval, she blushed and quickly added, "Rodger isn't here, is there anything I can do?"

"Yes, my dear. I intend to bring my wife, Eleanora, back to Windsor where she belongs, and I hope you will befriend her."

"We are already friends, Lord Edward. Did you find out where the queen and your wife went?"

"Aye, Owen told me the royal barge was moored at

Tower Wharfe, so apparently they are in residence at London's Tower. An impregnable fortress, but my mother has reckoned without taking into account my determination." He suddenly gave Rosamond a look of speculation. "God's feet, I have an idea. Don't remove those clothes until I find your husband!"

Edward's powers of persuasion were put to the test when he explained his idea to Rodger de Leyburn. At first his steward refused point-blank to allow his wife to be part of what he thought was a ridiculous scheme, but when he saw with his own eyes that Rosamond might be able to pass herself off as Griffin, he hesitated. When Edward explained the daring scheme to Rosamond, she was eager to take part in the charade.

Skeptical about the plan, Rodger drew Edward into the adjoining chamber so that they could speak privately. "How do we get through the city's gates? How do we gain entrance to the Tower?"

"We'll stop at Westminster and get Richard of Cornwall. He issued the bloody order to keep me out, now he can issue another to let me in."

"I don't want Rosamond to know that we have withdrawn our support from Simon de Montfort."

"She'll find out sooner or later, my friend. You'll have to tell her sometime soon."

"Not yet! She assuredly won't help you if she knows you have defected. Eleanor and Simon were like parents to her!"

"Well, I certainly shan't tell her; we have always kept each other's secrets," Edward pledged.

In the end, Rosamond was dressed in Griffin's clothes, so that garbed identically, they might easily pass for one another. When the small cavalcade arrived at Westminster, Rodger headed to the stables with Rosamond and the two squires, while Lord Edward went into the palace in search of his uncle, Richard Plantagenet.

He was gone for the better part of an hour, but of course most of that time was taken up by Richard thanking his nephew for repudiating Simon de Montfort and returning to the Plantagenet fold where he belonged. Richard of Cornwall was more than happy to take Edward in his own barge to the Tower of London so that the prince could see his bride and assure the queen that he was a dutiful son.

Aboard the barge, Rosamond followed her husband's instructions and remained in the stern so that Richard of Cornwall could not see her face. In reality, Rodger did not want Rosamond to overhear any of Edward's conversation with his uncle. He remained with her and the other two squires, pointing out London's landmarks to his fascinated, wide-eyed bride.

"Which is Durham House?" Rosamond asked avidly.

With a sinking heart, Rodger pointed it out to her.

"They have waterstairs! When I visit Demi, perhaps I could come by watercraft and avoid the twenty-mile ride." She grinned at her husband and rubbed her bottom through the chausses she wore.

To change the subject, Rod gestured toward a cluster of buildings. "These constitute the New Temple, where all the banking is done. Goldsmiths make their loans here, but not without taking your worldly goods as security and locking them away in their vaults."

Rosamond wondered briefly if Sir Rodger had borrowed gold from these men, but stopped short of asking. What he had done in the past was really none of her business; only what he did now and in the future mattered to her.

Suddenly, there was the great city of London, its streets, lanes, and buildings so close and crowded, they seemed to be built one on top of another. She pinched her nostrils at the stench of the river, which was no longer clear, but dotted with small boats, floating rubbish, and a dead animal or two. Above their heads, seagulls screeched and swooped for dead fish or other offal.

"Oh, it's all so—"

"Disgusting?" Rod asked sympathetically.

"No! It's fascinating . . . enthralling!" Rosamond stood up to get a better view. "I've never seen anything to compare!"

"Sit down, hang on, we're about to shoot under London Bridge." Rodger pulled her down ungently, and Rosamond clamped her hands to her hat so it wouldn't go sailing off on the wind. The square barge suddenly picked up speed and bobbed about on the roiling tide as the oarsmen tried to control it. It shot beneath the bridge, nearly colliding with one of the stone arches, then almost immediately the massive, Norman-built Tower loomed before them.

When Richard Plantagenet took them through Traitor's Gate, Rodger watched Edward's face for any sign of guilt, but there wasn't even a flicker upon his handsome countenance, and Rod wondered if the prince was even capable of feeling guilty.

Owen walked directly behind Lord Edward, while Sir Rodger, flanked by his two squires, brought up the rear. When Rosamond almost tripped over her sword, making it clatter, as she climbed the stone steps, she sent Rodger a quick look of apology.

"Clumsy young devil!" he muttered, "watch your feet instead of gaping about like a Welsh bumpkin."

Rosamond lowered her head and kept her eyes on her boots as she and the men climbed all the way to the top floor. Richard entered the royal apartments alone, while the rest of them waited outside the door. When he returned, he said, "The queen has consented to see you, Edward; I advise an attitude of contrition." He led them into an anteroom, then led Edward through the door on the right.

Edward had described in detail the layout of the royal apartments to Rosamond, who knew she had no time to waste. Without hesitation, she slipped through the door on the left and strode through two more chambers, affecting a confidence she did not feel. Due to the small windows in the Tower, the chambers were dim, and the first sign Rosamond had that she was nearing the princess was Bebe,

Eleanora's Maltese terrier. He ran toward her, tail wagging, as Rosamond came upon three ladies who were doing embroidery.

Princess Eleanora followed the dog and apologized to the squire.

Rosamond swept off her hat and bowed low. "It is me, Eleanora, I have urgent messages from Edward."

The princess quickly dismissed her two ladies. When they were alone, the princess took Rosamond into her bedchamber and closed the door. "Oh, you are so brave to do this for me!"

"Nay, you are the one who must be brave. Edward has come to rescue you and take you to Windsor. You are to change clothes with me quickly and leave with your husband as one of his squires."

"I cannot put on male attire!" she said, aghast.

"If I can do it, so can you. Think of it as a game," Rosamond urged. "Do you wish me to go back and tell Edward you are too afraid?"

"Ah, no, no, but what will happen to you when they find you dressed in my clothes?"

"Nothing will happen to me. I am Lady de Leyburn, they will have to let me go. I shall bring your ladies and Bebe to Windsor." Rosamond hoped it would be as easy as she made it sound. She removed her tabard and began to help Princess Eleanora from her gown and petticoats. Then she removed her own boots, unfastened the chausses, and slipped them off. Eleanora gingerly stepped into the chausses and struggled to pull them over her round hips. Rosamond fastened them for her and pulled the wide, loose tabard over her head.

The boots, however, were too big for Eleanora's small feet, but she solved the problem by taking a pair of her own riding boots from the wardrobe. Rosamond then pulled the hat low on Eleanora's head and hoped no one would notice that the fair-headed squire now had dark brown hair. When Rosamond was satisfied she could do no more to disguise the princess, she donned Eleanora's gown and draped her lace mantilla over her golden hair.

"Keep your head down and your eyes on your feet so you don't trip over the sword," Rosamond advised. When she took Eleanora's hand, she found it trembling like a leaf. "It's an exciting game." The words were to reassure herself as much as the princess. She pulled Eleanora through what felt like endless chambers, then literally pushed her through the doorway where Rodger waited. The squires closed ranks about the princess, and Rodger gave her a reassuring smile and placed his finger to his lips.

Inside the royal apartments, Edward Plantagenet feigned contrition, but his mother's haughty manner soon set his teeth on edge, and he began to pace like a caged lion.

"I doubt your father will ever be able to forgive you for this betrayal, unless you go on your knees to him!"

"That will never happen," Edward promised. "'Tis not my knees, but my strong arm the king craves. I am taking my men and Eleanora to Windsor," he stated flatly.

The queen thrust out her chin aggressively. "When Henry arrives, he will decide if you get your men back."

Richard of Cornwall spoke up quickly. "I think we can release his men to him, Eleanor. Now that he has repudiated Simon de Montfort, he will need his men for his own safety."

"So be it, but I shall keep your bride here with me to guarantee your good behavior." Eleanor smirked slightly. "The bait worked."

Edward silently prayed that Rosamond's ploy had worked. If it had, he would give anything to see his mother's face when she found out he had spirited his wife from beneath her royal thumb!

Back in Princess Eleanora's bedchamber, Rosamond locked the door and stretched out on the bed to try to relax. It was almost impossible, because she found the Tower of London so oppressive. She had to determinedly push away thoughts of the ordeal that awaited her, but she consoled herself with the fact that she had Bebe for company, and gently stroked the small white dog nestled beside her.

It was at least an hour before one of Eleanora's ladies knocked on the bedchamber door. Rosamond jumped, and her heart began to thud, but she issued forth a couple of loud snores and went weak with relief when there were no more knocks.

Another hour went by before there was another tap on the door. This time, delaying tactics did not work, and reluctantly Rosamond had to open the door. The two Spanish ladies began to panic when they discovered that their mistress was nowhere to be found and that Rosamond had changed places with her. Both of them, reduced to tears, ran for Queen Eleanor, while Rosamond clutched Bebe and waited with trepidation.

The queen arrived with a gaggle of her own ladies. She stared hard at the tall, slim girl, then snatched the lace mantilla from her head. When she saw the pale golden hair, Eleanor's eyes narrowed with suspicion and envy. "Who are you, and where is Princess Eleanora?"

"I am Rosamond Marshal—that is, Rosamond de Leyburn, Your Highness." She sank into a respectful curtsy.

"Marshal? Marshal?" the queen hissed, knowing how much land that hated family had once owned in England, Ireland, and Wales. Suddenly her brows shot up with suspicion. "Not the Marshal girl who lived at Kenilworth with that she-bitch Eleanor de Montfort?"

Bebe began to bark, then he bared his teeth in a snarl.

"That dog is vicious; it needs to be destroyed! Where the devil is my daughter-in-law? Has she been kidnapped by the bloody de Montforts? Call the guard!"

Rosamond's heart began to hammer with alarm. "Your Highness, please, Princess Eleanora is perfectly safe. The de Montforts have nothing to do with this. Lord Edward has taken his wife to Windsor. I must confess I helped them."

The queen drew back her hand and slapped Rosamond full in the face. "De Leyburn, did you say? That rake whom Edward made his steward? His reputation stinks to high heaven; no woman is safe in his company. De Leyburn is a bad influence on my son, always has been, and now we have his Marshal slut of a wife added to the mix. Well, let me warn you, madam, in the war that is coming, we will destroy the de Montforts and you along with them!" She turned to the Tower guard, who had just arrived. "Remove her, and the damned dog too! Make certain she is secured."

It was the first time anyone had ever struck Rosamond, and she was mortified. The Queen of England had made it plain, not only by her words, but also by her actions, that they were enemies. The queen had actually ordered her *imprisoned* here in the Tower of London, and Rosamond tasted fear.

Rosamond was marched out by the armed guard and taken down two flights of Tower stairs, before they came to a halt. "My lady, are you Sir Rodger de Leyburn's wife?"

She clutched Bebe tightly. "Yes, I am."

"He appointed me a guard here, when he first became Lord Edward's steward; everyone likes Sir Rodger, my lady. I will carry out the queen's orders to the letter. She ordered me to remove you, which I have done. She also said to make certain you were secure, and I believe you will be most secure with your husband."

Rosamond looked at him with hope dawning in her eyes.

"Sir Rodger left the Tower only a short time ago with Lord Edward's Gascon men-at-arms. We will go down and see if there are any stragglers who can escort you back to Windsor."

Rosamond thanked him profusely. She was vastly relieved that he was purposely misinterpreting the queen's orders, because the Tower terrified her, making her feel trapped, and she did not dare to think what she would have felt if she had been placed in a cell.

When they arrived on the ground floor, there standing beneath an archway was Griffin. Tears of gratitude flooded her eyes. "Oh, Griffin, I thank you with all my heart."

"It is an honor to serve you, my lady." He took off his cloak and laid it across her shoulders. "It will be cold on the river."

"Did she get away?" Rosamond asked breathlessly.

"Lord Edward and Owen took the new squire into service, my lady. The uniform was so ill fitting, I warrant she will be most anxious to get her gown back."

Twilight had descended before the small boat reached Windsor. Rosamond saw that Rodger was waiting for her at the waterstairs, with Chirk at his feet. The minute her feet touched the first step, he swept her into his arms.

"Thank God you are safe; I should never have allowed it." He took Bebe and helped her up the steps. "Good work, Griffin."

Rosamond picked up her own dog, who immediately licked her face with joy. "I met the queen, but I wish I hadn't. Rodger, I have so many questions about the dreadful things she said."

"Not now, love, the princess is fretting about you, and she will be pleased you have brought her dog."

Rodger led the way up to Lord Edward's apartments in Windsor's new tower, and when they entered, Rosamond saw that Edward and Eleanora had just finished their evening meal in the privacy of Edward's chambers. "Your Highness, I managed to bring Bebe, but it was impossible to bring your ladies."

"Oh, Rosamond, thank you so much, but, please call me Eleanora." She took Bebe from Rodger and dropped a kiss on the dog's head, but he wriggled from her arms, showing far more interest in Chirk.

Rosamond set her own dog to the carpet, and the

two terriers ran off together. She eyed the princess, wondering whose gown she was wearing. "You have no clothes; I'll go and get you some of mine."

Lord Edward took hold of Rosamond's hands and drew them to his lips. "How can I ever thank you? You were so very brave, my dear, and it gave Eleanora the courage she needed."

"I wasn't brave at all, I was terrified."

"But that's what bravery is all about . . . overcoming fear enough to do the courageous thing. My sweet Nora had to put on one of the queen's gowns, but it is much too big for her. I deeply appreciate your lending her your gowns until she has a new wardrobe sewn."

"I'll get them now."

Eleanora blushed. "May I come with you, Rosamond?"

The two young women, one dark, the other fair, were already like old friends, because both had left behind everyone they had known and were starting a new life. Nan, who had no notion what Rosamond had been up to that day, curtsied to Princess Eleanora.

"Her ladies haven't arrived yet, Nan, but I know you will be pleased to serve her if there is aught she needs." They went into the dressing room and Rosamond opened her huge wardrobe.

The princess gasped with delight when she saw Rosamond's lovely clothes. "Ah, *muy bonita!* How very pretty your gowns are."

"Take whatever you like. I'm so tall, the gowns will be long on you. This peacock color will look wonderful with your dark hair."

"Ah, but the train will make it too long; I will tip."

Rosamond laughed. "You mean trip."

Eleanora touched the red velvet. "This is beautiful."

"Yes, and it will be even more beautiful when *you* wear it. Pick some others," Rosamond urged.

"One more . . . perhaps this lavender, embroidered with pearls?"

"Good choice! Now, what about tonight? You will need a night rail and a warm bedgown."

Eleanora blushed prettily. "Tonight . . . can I not stay here with you, Rosamond?"

"Oh, darling, Lord Edward wants you to be with him. Don't you want that too?"

"Ah, yes, I have waited for six years . . . but now I am afraid."

Sweet Jesu, Rosamond thought, *Edward is so big, no wonder she is afraid.* Rosamond touched Eleanora's hand. "I understand, I'm newly wed too." She chose a white lambswool bedgown and a white silk night rail for the princess. "You take these and I'll carry the gowns."

"Rosamond, I cannot undress upstairs . . . in front of Edward!"

"Well, let's see . . . why don't you put them on down here, and I'll help you? The bedgown is very modest and will cover you from chin to toes. I'll put mine on too, so you can have your dress back."

Eleanora nodded shyly. "I love him so much, Rosamond, my heart is chasing."

"Your heart is racing," Rosamond said gently, and warned, "Edward must do the chasing. Don't tell him you love him, not until he declares his love for you, Eleanora."

"Oh, I have not enough breath even to speak when Edward is near me."

They entered Lord Edward's apartments and carried the gowns into the adjoining chambers that had been especially designed for Princess Eleanora. They hung the garments in the wardrobe, then Rosamond called for Chirk, who came running to her with Bebe in hot pursuit. When they rejoined the men, Rod gave Rosamond a clear sign that he and she should leave so that Edward and his bride could be alone.

Rod and Rosamond bade them good night, then Edward closed the heavy oaken door and threw the bolt across it. When he turned to Eleanora, his breath caught in his throat. He had never in his life seen a maiden whose loveliness matched hers. She had an abundance of dark silky hair whose waves fell to her hips. Her huge almond-shaped eyes and dusky skin lent her a unique, exotic prettiness. But it was her air of sweetness and innocence that attracted him most. She was small, dainty, fragile almost, and Edward's heart turned over in his breast.

He held out his hands to her. "Eleanora, Nora . . . come to me." She hesitated for only a moment, but it told him she felt a measure of trepidation. As she came trustingly toward him and placed her hands in his, he was overcome with a wave of protectiveness. No female had ever provoked such a tender emotion in him before. "My little sweetheart, don't be afraid of me. I will never, ever hurt you. I shall cherish you always," he swore fervently, lifting her fingers to his lips.

Standing this close, he loomed over her, and he saw how tiny she was in contrast to him. Edward's overt maleness played counterpoint to Eleanora's delicate femininity, and he felt an urge to guard her with his strength, his power, his very life. He felt her small hands tremble. "Come and be warm, love." He led her to the fire and drew her down beside him on a couch.

He slipped his arm around her possessively and began to talk. He hoped it would soothe away her fears and help her to get to know him. He suddenly realized that his size and his rank could be most intimidating to a young lady who had likely never been alone with a man before. He dropped a kiss on her head and told her how lovely she was. She gazed up at him with adoration, and Edward realized that the gods had smiled upon him, to give him such a bride. Arranged marriages were seldom love matches, but for him it was love at first sight, or rather second; he had paid scant attention to the ten-year-old at their wedding.

He felt her soft body relax against his side, then her head slowly descended to his shoulder. He could see that her eyes were beginning to close as drowsiness overcame her. She was so trusting, his heart ached with tenderness as he watched her. She was completely in his keeping, and he vowed to do his utmost to make her happy. Very gently he lifted her against his heart, carried her to bed, and tucked her in.

One floor below, in the de Leyburns' bedchamber, Rosamond confided in her husband as he began to disrobe. "Facing the queen was a worse ordeal than I ever dreamed. When she demanded who I was, and I said Rosamond Marshal, she flew into a rage and said, 'Not the Marshal girl who lived at Kenilworth with that she-bitch Eleanor de Montfort?' Why does she hate Lady Eleanor so much?"

Rod took a deep breath. "When young King Henry wed Eleanor of Provence, her large family was penniless. When the new queen saw Princess Eleanor, the king's sister, bedecked in jewels and the latest fashions, reportedly she was very envious. Princess Eleanor was spoiled and apparently used to ruling the Plantagenet roost, so the two young women took an instant dislike to each other."

"The queen doesn't simply dislike Lady Eleanor," Rosamond said, "she hates her with a passion! When she discovered Eleanora gone, she accused the de Montforts of kidnapping her. I quickly tried to disabuse her of such a preposterous notion, explaining that Edward had taken his wife to Windsor, and I confessed I had helped them."

Rodger held his breath. Had the queen told her that Edward had repudiated Simon de Montfort?

"The queen slapped me full in the face!"

"The bitch struck you?" he asked angrily. "You should have told her your name was de Leyburn, not Marshal."

"Ha! She has little love for you, my lord. She called you a rake and said your reputation stunk to high heaven and that no woman was safe with you! She declared you a bad influence on her son, and lamented that now your slut of a wife was in the mix."

"I am profoundly sorry that the queen attacked you, Rosamond. She's a foreign witch who knows no better."

"Oh fie, that isn't what upset me; it was her terrible threat!" Rosamond came around the bed and took Rod's hand as if she were afraid. "She said there was a war coming, and they would destroy the de Montforts and us along with them!"

When Rodger enfolded her in his arms, she looked up at him with beseeching eyes. "Will there truly be a war?"

He tucked her head beneath his chin, his eyes clouded with dark thoughts of war. "Yes, I am afraid it has come to that, Rosamond."

"But we will win, won't we? With Lord Edward and my cousin Richard of Gloucester on Earl Simon's side, how can we lose?"

Rod knew he would have to tell her. But not tonight, he decided selfishly, softly stroking her back. "No more talk of war. Come to bed, Rosamond, and we'll talk of more pleasurable things."

EIGHTEEN

I need to recruit soldiers for this campaign," Edward told Rodger.

"Windsor will adequately house them, but your personal coffers are empty. We need wealth; we won't even be able to hold the Gascons unless they are paid for the Welsh campaign, Edward."

"You are right, nothing engenders loyalty like wealth, and I need it quickly. I learned warfare from Simon de Montfort himself, and he taught me that speed and fury win the day."

"There is only one place you can get coin, and that is the New Temple, but what will you give the goldsmiths for security?"

"They already have all of my mother's jewels and even some of the bloody crown jewels as collateral for loans she has taken over the last two years." Edward suddenly raised his golden head, and his blazing blue gaze pierced Rodger, who guessed his intent immediately.

"It will take nerves of steel and a couple of strong arms at your back." Rod flashed a grin, the sheer audacity of the scheme appealing to his darker side. "We'll get Harry; he has such an honest face."

Within the hour, Harry of Almaine arrived at Windsor with his Cornish men-at-arms. "Speak of the devil," Edward said to Rod, then decided to rub salt in his cousin's wounds. "Where the hell have you been since you turned your coat?"

Harry flushed to the roots of his hair. "I've been in such anguish. I was honor-bound to Simon, but my father, my brother Gloucester, and then you turned against him, and I realized it was my duty to stand with my family." Harry grimaced. "On top of that, I made the mistake of going to Westminster."

"Mistake?" Edward asked sharply.

Harry's blush deepened. "Alyce de Clare was there; she insisted on accompanying me here to Windsor."

"God's balls, Harry, you haven't the brains of a louse!" Rod admonished him as he saw the look of panic on Edward's face.

"I told her Rosamond was here with you, but she promised to be discreet," Harry said lamely.

"Discretion isn't her long suit," Rod said dryly. "I shall join the ladies and attempt to control the damage, Lord Edward, while you convince Harry that we need his strong arm and honest face."

Rodger found the ladies in the solar. Alyce was gowned in deep royal purple, while Eleanora was wearing a lavender gown embroidered with seed pearls. He thought they looked like the wicked witch and fairy princess from some mythic tale.

"Rod, it is too long," Alyce said, pausing suggestively as her eyes slid over his maleness, "since I have seen you, mon cher; I long to see more of you." She glanced at Rosamond to deliberately provoke her, then went on tiptoe to kiss de Leyburn.

"Alyce, is your visit prompted by curiosity, or have you more information to impart?" Rod asked smoothly.

"Ah, chéri, you know I was seduced into revealing all when you and Edward came to Westminster."

Realizing she was grass-green with jealousy at Eleanora's beauty and innocence, he warned, "Revealing all can be a dangerous game."

Alyce gave Rosamond a sly, sideways glance. "But I

adore dangerous games, Rod, and know you too love to play with me!"

Rosamond was ready to pull every hair from her head, but when Rodger looked into his wife's eyes, he communicated without words. Suddenly she realized that the byplay had nothing to do with Rod. Alyce de Clare was simply dying to let Eleanora know that she and Edward were lovers.

"Nan, would you take Lady Alyce to my chamber so she may repair her toilette? Her eyes are smudged with black."

Alyce's hand flew to her face and she threw Rosamond a look that was cold enough to freeze the marrow in her bones. Then she stormed out of the room, with Nan following meekly behind her.

Rosamond turned to the princess and said, "Alyce cannot help flirting with every male she meets; it is a game to her. She really came to Windsor to see what you look like, Eleanora."

"Lady Alyce is a most alluring female. The queen told me King Henry is much too fond of her," she innocently confided.

Rosamond exchanged a look with her husband. "No need for alarm, my lord, I will put out any wildfires Alyce starts."

He nodded his understanding and turned to leave, but Alyce came back into the chamber before he reached the door.

"What a clever wife you 'ave, my Rod. She uses dragonwort to prevent conception. Will you share your herbs with me, Rosamond?"

A deathly silence fell over the room, and Rosamond paled as she realized too late she had left the dragonwort on her dressing table. Only someone well versed in the properties of herbs would know the plant's secret; even Nan thought it was used for freckles. Rosamond felt everyone's eyes on her. Eleanora looked shocked, Nan looked outraged, but it was Sir Rodger she was most aware of. His green gaze bored into her with ice-cold fury. "I use it for my skin, Lady Alyce; what do you use to make yours look like porcelain?"

"I use crushed hellebore seeds, but hellebore, like dragonwort, has more deadly properties, *n'est-ce pas*?" Alyce asked silkily.

Rodger bowed stiffly. "I shall see you tonight, madam."

Rosamond knew he hadn't been fooled. Damn the man, he was far too wise in the ways of women. The moment Rodger departed, Alyce pretended she wanted to be friends, but Rosamond knew better.

"I would love to see the apartments King Henry had specially designed for you, Eleanora, and you must come to see mine at Westminster Palace," Alyce said. Turning toward Rosamond, she added, "We could all go about London together!"

"Thank you, but I am going into London with my friend Demoiselle de Montfort," Rosamond coolly informed her.

Alyce laughed in her face. "That would be impossible; London's gates are closed to the de Montforts and all their adherents. How fortunate that Edward has shrewdly repudiated the king's enemy."

Rosamond went cold all over. *Alyce is lying; it cannot possibly be true!* she thought. She felt as if icy fingers clutched her heart and were squeezing. If such a horrendous thing had happened, Rodger would have told her! Rosamond began to shiver. No, he would not have told her, because the main reason she had agreed to wed him was to strengthen the bond between Lord Edward and Earl Simon. If that bond was now broken, the pawn had been sacrificed for naught! "Richard of Gloucester, my cousin and your father-in-law . . . with whom does he stand?" Rosamond asked quietly.

"The Plantagenets, of course. He is England's leading peer; *naturellement* he stands with the king and the heir to the throne. When King Henry arrives, Simon de Montfort will be destroyed!"

The queen's vituperous words came back to her: *In the war that is coming, we will destroy the de Montforts and you along with them!* Well, at least the queen realized that she, Rosamond, would remain loyal to the de Montforts, even if Lord Edward and that devil de Leyburn turned traitor!

Rosamond was distraught. What made men so vile? She had begun to trust Rodger de Leyburn. She had done so against her better judgment, and now she realized why she had been so wary. Dear God, were all men created evil? Her eardrums were screaming inside her head, and she fought the faintness that threatened to overwhelm her. Then Rosamond saw Nan looking at her with pity, and her distress suddenly turned into flaming anger.

Princess Eleanora said politely, "Come, Lady Alyce, my apartments are most beautiful. When I was in the Tower, it was so dark, I could not see to embroider, but here the sunlight streams through my lovely, long windows."

"Embroider? Is that what you do for pleasure?" Alyce asked, amused. "Edward must find that most diverting."

"Men are diverted by the oddest things . . . war, whores . . ." Rosamond taunted, "there is no accounting for their strange tastes. Please excuse me, ladies. Nan, stay with Princess Eleanora, she has more need of you than I, at the moment."

Rosamond escaped to her own chambers and threw the bolt across the door. She was so angry she wanted to smash something, and if she had stayed in Alyce de Clare's company one more moment, she would have smashed the strumpet's insolent face. She went to the window and rubbed her temples to calm herself. A picture of de Leyburn flashed into her mind. *I shall see you tonight, madam.* He had been angry, but his anger would be as nothing compared to the fury she would unleash on him tonight!

Upstairs, in Princess Eleanora's chambers, Alyce de Clare was seething at the luxury that had been provided for Edward's bride. She gave Bebe a surreptitious kick and glanced through the beautiful windows. Across the ward, she could see Edward, Rodger, Harry, and their squires. They were mounting to leave and looked to be in a hurry. How dare Edward leave without seeing her? She'd be damned if she'd stay here with his dull Castilian wife. She turned to face her. "Edward is leaving! I must hurry, he is escorting me back to Westminster. Now, now, you must not be jealous, chérie . . . you are his virgin bride, I am just his mistress."

The three men decided their mission would be best accomplished with only their squires for escort. Six men would arouse less suspicion than an entire troop of men-at-arms. They had ridden less than a mile from Windsor when they heard galloping hoofbeats.

"The devil take her," Edward growled when he saw Alyce de Clare closing the distance between them.

"I'm sorry," Harry muttered in heartfelt apology.

"And where are you gentlemen off to in such a tearing hurry?" Alyce asked in a deceptively sweet voice.

"We are off to find a wife for Harry," Rod teased. "Bachelors will no longer be tolerated."

"Run for your life, Harry; marriage is a death sentence."

"Merely a life sentence, I believe," Rod bantered.

Alyce spurred her horse between Edward's and Rodger's, then, looking straight ahead so that Harry wouldn't know to whom she directed her words, said, "You 'ave been treating me like an inconvenience; can I expect to see more of you at Westminster?"

Rodger did not disabuse her of the idea they were going to the old palace. She would find out soon enough, when they left her at the gate. "Neither Westminster nor Windsor is convenient, my dear. With your husband's father at one and our wives at the other, you know the difficulties. Perhaps you could visit your castle of Tonbridge, a safe thirty miles from London."

Edward spoke for the first time. "Tonbridge . . . perhaps I will recruit there. The men of Kent are reputed to be stout fighters."

Alyce suspected it was a ruse to put distance between them. "I prefer London, but perhaps the men of Kent could prove amusing."

When they arrived at Westminster Palace, Rodger said, "We part company here, Alyce. Alas, we must attend to business this morning, not pleasure. Au revoir, chérie."

Her eyes narrowed, but she knew better than to make a scene, and rode off through the iron gates with a prideful toss of her head.

"Never did I see anyone dismiss a female so smoothly. Rod, you have a special touch with the ladies," Harry said with admiration. "I only wish I had half your charm."

"Alyce is no lady." Rod flashed his grin and the other two joined in the laughter. Then they sobered as they focused on the risky business that lay before them.

Once they passed Temple Church, Harry took Rodger's place beside Edward and Rod fell back with the squires. They turned their mounts toward the river and rode up to a great cluster of buildings known as the New Temple. They were met by one of the Jewish custodians, who recognized Prince Edward Plantagenet immediately.

"Your Highness, we are honored at this visit; how may we be of service to you?"

"Good morning. May I present my cousin Harry of Almaine, Richard of Cornwall's son."

Harry gave the man a sweet, beatific smile.

The custodian bowed again, highly pleased to have two royal visitors. Moreover, Cornwall had the wealth of Croesus.

Edward indicated the others. "These men are my bodyguards. I have come to be assured of the safety of the queen's property."

"Of course, Your Highness, it would be an honor to show you the vaults where Queen Eleanor's jewels are held for safekeeping." It was not an unusual request, and as the prince and his men dismounted, the custodian went inside to get his keys. He led them back to the center of the great cluster of buildings, until they came to the Temple vaults. When he located the one in which the queen's jewels were deposited, he fit the great key into the lock and turned it.

Rod had his dagger at the custodian's throat before the iron key even clicked. "I do beg your pardon for this inconvenience," he said, flashing his dark, Lucifer's smile.

Harry took possession of the keys while Edward proceeded to help himself to the vault's contents. Not only did he and his men take the queen's jewels, Edward also filched ten thousand pounds in gold which had been deposited by London merchants. When their saddlebags were full, Lord Edward and his men rode from the New Temple without haste. Only Rod remained, holding the custodian at knifepoint until the thieves were long gone.

The great dining hall at Windsor rang with laughter and song as Lord Edward's men-at-arms drained their goblets before they sat down to the evening meal. It was the first time in over a year they had coins in their pockets, and most of the Gascons planned an evening of dice. Both Lord Edward and Sir Rodger wanted their beauteous wives beside them in the hall this night, but both ladies were conspicuously absent.

Edward sent a pageboy with a message to Eleanora, but when the lad returned without a reply, the prince's golden brows drew together in a frown. "It seems the mountain must go to Mohammed."

"Eleanora is a princess, after all. I think it would be unchivalrous if we didn't escort our wives to the dining hall," Rod advised.

When the pair arrived at the royal apartments, they saw that Princess Eleanora's ladies had arrived from the Tower and the hallways were filled with trunks and baggage. "It looks as if my mother has conceded the game to me this time. Splendor of God, I shall take a lesson from this: There is nothing that can beat a fait accompli!"

Edward strode toward the door that led into Eleanora's private apartments, but when he turned the doorknob he realized that the door was locked. "Eleanora . . . Nora, where are you, sweetheart?" He rattled the knob. "Would someone open this door, please?" When he received no response, he rattled the door until it danced on its hinges. "Attend me!"

He heard a female clear her throat, and spun to face her. He saw that it was Rosamond's tiring-woman, Nan. "I've come to take Eleanora down to dinner; would you tell one of her damned women to open this door?"

Nan was loath to tell Lord Edward news he did not wish to hear, but knew she had little choice in the matter. She cleared her throat nervously. "Princess Eleanora ordered that the door be locked, Lord Edward."

"Well, I order that it be *unlocked*!" he commanded.

Nan's voice trembled, but she stood her ground. "That will avail you naught, Lord Edward. Your wife is indisposed and refuses to see you or talk with you."

"Splendor of God, if she is unwell, then I must go to her!"

Nan pressed her lips together and cast her eyes upon the floor.

"Nan, kindly explain what is going on here," Rodger requested.

"The princess is upset; her women have put her to bed."

"What have her women said to her?" Edward demanded. "Was it something the damned queen said?"

"Nay, Lord Edward, she was upset before her women arrived."

"Nan, for God's sake, spit it out!" Rodger ordered.

Nan turned beet red. "It was Alyce de Clare."

"Christ!" Edward groaned.

"Where's Rosamond?" Rod asked Nan.

"She's below, my lord . . . keeping to herself."

"Excuse me, Edward," he said quietly, then headed for his own rooms. That morning he had been angry when he had learned of Rosamond's use of dragonwort, but now he decided not to confront her about it. If she was afraid of bearing a child, it was far better to talk quietly about it and soothe her fears, than issue his demands.

The moment he saw her, he knew she was seething inside. It gave her a special beauty; she held her head high, her cheeks were flushed, and her violet eyes glittered like amethysts. Rod crushed down the urge to carry her to bed and turn her hot fury into scalding passion. At first he'd thought that she was angry about what Alyce de Clare had said to Eleanora, but her words, shot at him like arrows, told him her anger stemmed from what Alyce had said to her.

"Is it true? Can it possibly be true that Edward has defected from Simon de Montfort?"

"Lord Edward and Earl Simon have parted ways," he acknowledged.

"You kept this from me, purposely!" she said.

"I knew it would upset you, Rosamond."

"Upset? I am outraged, scandalized, devastated that Edward could do such a vile thing, and that you would condone it! How can you change sides and fight against Simon? Where is your honor?"

"Rosamond, there is little honor in war, none at all in civil war. Edward is a Plantagenet, the rightful heir to the throne of England. If Simon de Montfort wins the war, he will set himself up as the ruler of England. Edward could not tolerate such a thing; he is the wrong sort of man to be subordinate."

"*You* are not a Plantagenet, de Leyburn. Will you too dishonor your pledge to support Simon de Montfort?" she asked with contempt.

"My first allegiance is to Edward Plantagenet, no matter which side he chooses, Rosamond. I pledged to him years ago; we have a bond that cannot be broken."

"And what of *our* bond, my lord, our marriage bond? I only agreed to wed you to cement the bond between Lord Edward and Earl Simon. Now that that bond is broken, my sacrifice has been for naught!"

His green eyes narrowed at the cruelty of her words. "Your *sacrifice*? What cannot be cured, madam, must be endured. I have no time for female vapors. Edward and I must recruit men and fight a war. If you choose to be selfish and self-centered on our last night together, I shall find more amenable company in the hall." Rod paused on the threshold. "When Griffin comes for my war chest, I trust you will not savage him about his honor."

She wanted to hurl something at him, but finding nothing close at hand, she used words instead. "Go to the devil, de Leyburn!"

Below, Edward joined Rod as he watched the men-at-arms dice. "I could cheerfully throttle Alyce de Clare! Eleanora's in tears and has locked her doors against me. Do you think Rosamond could soothe the roiled waters for me?"

"Rosamond is in the middle of her own tantrum at the moment," Rod said dryly.

"Christ, look at the success we had at the Temple today. There isn't a problem we cannot solve, unless it involves a bloody woman! Can you explain to me why the fair sex chooses the damnedest times to be totally exasperating?" Edward lifted a goblet of ale and shrugged impatiently. "Well, I haven't time for female vapors. I have the daunting tasks before me of rebuilding royal strength and winning this war."

Rod glanced up at him, realizing with irony how very alike the two of them were.

NINETEEN

The lathered horse was ready to drop as it galloped into the courtyard of Windsor two hours past midnight. The messenger had ridden the thirty-five miles from Oxford nonstop with the momentous news that Simon de Montfort's baronial army was moving.

"Damn him, he's heading west to secure the Severn River and the Marcher barons who fought with us in Wales," Edward said. The prince, who needed little sleep, hadn't yet retired for the night.

"Not all the Marchers love de Montfort. Mortimer and Clifford, perhaps even Hay, will join our ranks if we recruit them," Rodger predicted. "You've committed our men to Richard of Cornwall, but I need only a small force to establish our communication with the Marcher barons. I'll get my own men of Tewkesbury, then ride on to Hay. I will leave now!"

De Leyburn, with Griffin and eight men-at-arms, set out within the hour for Tewkesbury and the border country that lay close to Wales. Edward longed to ride with them, but it was fortunate that he resisted his impulse, for later that morning he received word that the king and his men had arrived at the Tower of London.

What manner of man did I wed? Rosamond asked herself. She paced her chamber like a caged lion, tossing back her golden mane of hair, as she decided what she must do. *What cannot be cured, madam, must be endured.* His words ravaged her pride. Well, she could not, would not endure it. There could be no marriage if they were on opposite sides of a civil war; she would not live with a man who could not be trusted to honor his word.

Rosamond decided to go to the de Montforts at Durham House. Deciding against taking Nan, who seemed to be needed by Princess Eleanora at the moment, she did not wish to disrupt her serving-woman's life for her own principles. Nan could decide for herself later to which side she would pledge her allegiance. Rosamond also decided to leave Chirk at Windsor, as the poor dog had spent half its life in a traveling basket.

Rosamond packed only a few clothes; Lady Eleanor and Demi would lend her all the gowns she needed until she could have new ones sewn. She penned a note for Nan, then slipped through the Middle Ward to the stables just as dawn was breaking. Ignoring the curious glances of the groom who saddled Nimbus for her, she searched the rows of stalls for Rodger's black stallion. When she saw that Stygian was missing, she heaved a sigh of relief; the last thing she wanted was to encounter de Leyburn this morning!

As she rode alongside the river, the air was cold, and Rosamond wished she had gotten her fur-lined cloak back from Eleanora. She was glad when she saw Westminster Palace. She knew Durham House wasn't much farther, because she had seen it from the river.

The guard at the gate admitted her, but once she entered the courtyard, she saw it had a deserted air about it. A stableman in livery came forward immediately. "Are the de Montforts not in residence?" Rosamond asked, unable to hide the alarm she felt.

"Earl Simon left for Oxford days ago, my lady."

"But what of Lady Eleanor and Demi? I have come to Durham House to stay with them."

"They are on their way home to Kenilworth for safety reasons, my lady. They left yesterday at first light."

Rosamond literally felt her heart sink in her breast. She knew she had only two options: to return to Windsor or to try to catch up with Lady Eleanor's household. The first was intolerable, so she was able to make her decision immediately. "Would you kindly feed and water my horse, sir? I shall get something to eat at the kitchen, then try to overtake Lady de Montfort."

Rosamond knew the de Montfort cavalcade would travel by way of Berkhamsted, the great castle that they always used to break their journey north. She hoped to reach it before nightfall, but she had woefully underestimated the distance. When it was full dark and she was afraid to ride farther, she took refuge in a country church. She tethered Nimbus beneath the lych-gate and fed her oats, then stole inside the church and lay down upon a wooden pew. The stone building was freezing cold, but at least she was out of the wind. Soon, Rosamond grew fearful of the dead spirits that might be floating about. She chided herself for being fanciful; it was the living she needed to fear. Here, alone, in the middle of nowhere, how would she defend herself against an attack? She also knew that when she was beset by fear, she could not keep the trampling dream at bay.

Rosamond remembered how Rodger had banished the nightmare and filled her with his strength. Her warm bed at Windsor, complete with husband, suddenly seemed most inviting. She began a prayer to Saint Jude, patron saint of the hopeless. "O holy Saint Jude, apostle and martyr, near kinsman of Jesus Christ, the faithful intercessor of all who invoke your special patronage in times of need; to you I have recourse from the depths of my heart, and humbly beg you, to whom God has given such great power, to come to my assistance, and in return I promise to make your name known." Gradually she began to feel warmer, and safer, and her self-confidence returned. Tomorrow she would meet up with Lady Eleanor and Demi; she felt it in her heart.

Rosamond finally caught up with the de Montfort household, but not until she arrived at Brackley Castle, a good thirty miles farther than Berkhamsted. Eleanor was outraged that Rosamond had been so reckless as to travel alone.

"I gave you credit for more intelligence than to be riding about the countryside without escort. Have you no notion of the danger out there? Surely you know the country is at war, Rosamond?"

"I . . . yes, I do know we are at war, Lady Eleanor, and that is why I wish to return to Kenilworth with you. I cannot be disloyal to you and Earl Simon, who have been like parents to me."

"Does your husband know about this, Rosamond?"

"He knows how I feel, yes! I cannot live with a man who is without honor," she cried passionately.

"I have learned that women's ideas of honor differ greatly from men's. De Leyburn has honor, Rosamond, but it is his own honor, different from yours."

"When I agreed to wed Sir Rodger, you told me that I could come back to Kenilworth at any time," Rosamond reminded Eleanor.

"I love you, child; I want only what's best for you."

"Kenilworth is best for me," Rosamond assured her. "*You* are best for me."

On his way back from the Marcher country, Rod de Leyburn met up with Lord Edward at Wallingford. The prince and Richard of Cornwall were in charge of a large royal force and had ridden to Wallingford hoping to engage de Montfort's army near Oxford.

"I was fortunate to find Mortimer and Clifford at Hay, holding their own council of war. All three barons have pledged to the king, providing *you* stand with your father. The news isn't good; de Montfort has taken the Bishop of

Hereford prisoner, and his army is seizing livestock to feed itself. De Montfort's barons swarmed across the West Country, exacting tribute from any landowner with royalist sentiments. Those who objected had their fields burned."

"Would you believe that little cocksucker Gilbert de Clare opened the gates of Gloucester to de Montfort?" Edward was livid. "Richard de Clare has summoned the little redheaded prick. I'd not be in his shoes when Gloucester gets his hands on him."

"Gilbert hero-worships Earl Simon. We shouldn't have underestimated him. Where is de Montfort's army now?" Rod asked.

"Just west of Oxford," Richard of Cornwall informed him. "We will intercept them tomorrow!"

"Nay, my lord, we rode through Oxford, and the barons were long gone; de Montfort has eluded you."

"Splendor of Christ!" Edward cursed. "He moves with unbelievable speed. He will try to make London his headquarters; we must cut him off before he reaches the Thames Valley."

"We must move the army to Reading, and we must do it now!" Richard of Cornwall declared.

But when their steel-clad forces reached Reading, they were once again too late. All they found was the barons' dust upon the roads leading to London.

"I believe Simon will overthrow the royal forces who hold the seaports of Surrey and Kent before he tries for London," de Leyburn told Edward and Richard.

"The city of London must be his permanent base if he wishes to rule England," Richard of Cornwall insisted.

"But command of the sea is paramount. Any reinforcements from France can only come through the Cinque Ports of Dover, Hythe, Romney, Winchelsea, and Hastings."

"Simon would have to march his army through Kent to get to the ports, and Kent has always been loyal to the king," Edward argued.

But Edward was proven wrong. De Montfort marched to Romney and the men of Kent came out to support him, then the barons of all the Cinque Ports opened their gates to him.

Suddenly those who had been staunch supporters of the king, such as the Archbishop of Canterbury, fled to the Continent along with other royal advisers who had picked up the scent of danger. Londoners, who had ever been unpredictable, began rioting in the streets. King Henry and Queen Eleanor were now most thankful for the strong walls of the Tower of London when the mob turned upon the foreigners and the Jews because they had always financed the king in his opposition to the barons.

King Henry had no guts for adversity. He caved in immediately when Simon de Montfort rode in from Kent to take control. The king sent his brother, Richard of Cornwall, to acknowledge de Montfort's victory and accept the terms he proposed, promising to remain within the walls of the Tower of London.

It took Earl Simon only three days to set up his own government in London. He appointed a new Chief Justiciar to replace Humphrey de Bohun, who had guarded London's walls against him, and gave custody of the Great Seal of England to Nicholas, Bishop of Ely.

At Durham House, Simon de Montfort discussed with his sons the sweeping changes he planned. "I intend to select new castellans for all of the royal castles. Simon, I shall put you in charge of Northampton Castle, which lies near Kenilworth. That will demonstrate de Montfort strength throughout the Midlands." Earl Simon turned his authoritative gaze on his eldest son. "Henry, you are to take your men to Dover and guard the Channel. I have drawn up an official order for the king's younger son, Prince Edmund, to vacate the Castle of Dover."

"Am I to take him prisoner?" Henry asked.

"Nay, Richard of Cornwall negotiated freedom for himself and the king's sons. Only King Henry is to be held under guard. The Plantagenets are finished. I assure you there will be no more royal resistance," Simon de Montfort said with deep satisfaction.

Lord Edward Plantagenet, however, was furious that his father the king had given in. Edward's fighting spirit would not allow him to give up. Though the royal resistance had ended, it did not weaken Edward's resolve to go on with the struggle. He had a shrewd head on his shoulders and knew the weak links in the baronial chain. Edward returned to Windsor to begin secretly persuading and recruiting.

At Windsor, Chirk gave Sir Rodger an ecstatic welcome, and when he picked her up, he could feel that she was with pup. When he could not find Rosamond, he summoned Nan.

"She went where?" Sir Rodger demanded incredulously.

"To Durham House, my lord," Nan said, nervously fingering the note Rosamond had left her, then added hastily, "but I sent a message immediately, begging her to return."

"And?" Rod asked in an ominous tone.

"The messenger returned without a reply, my lord. They told him Lady Eleanor had returned to Kenilworth."

"Splendor of God, my wife is living with the enemy!" He went immediately to Lord Edward and asked leave to go and get his wife.

"Rosamond is at Kenilworth?" Edward asked in disbelief. "If you ride into the enemy camp, they will take you prisoner."

"I am resolved in this, Edward; no power on earth will stop me from returning my wayward wife to Windsor."

Edward shrugged. "So be it, my friend. When you have brought your own wayward wife to heel, perhaps you can do something with mine. Princess Eleanora treats me like a stranger."

Rodger de Leyburn took only his squire Griffin. They were well armed and wore breastplates and helmets as they rode north through enemy territory. Rod avoided both Berkhamsted and Brackley Castles, opting instead to sleep outdoors, since the weather had turned mild. They passed by the high-walled town of Northampton and saw that the castle, a gray-stone fortress of a place, was proudly flying the de Montfort flag. Rod made inquiries and learned that Northampton Castle was in the hands of Simon de Montfort's son Simon and his cousin Peter de Montfort.

Kenilworth Castle lay thirty miles west of Northampton, and de Leyburn arrived at its gates in the late afternoon, flying a white flag of truce. He gave his name to the guard on the barbican and waited while the man sought Eleanor de Montfort for permission to admit him. "Stick closer than my shadow," Rod cautioned Griffin.

Rosamond, on the ramparts with Sir Rickard de Burgh, saw her husband ride up the causeway to the gates, and rushed below to seek out Lady Eleanor. "Please, do not admit him, my lady; I have nothing to say to him!"

"Obviously he has something to say to you, Rosamond. I cannot deny him the right to speak with you. After all, he is your husband." Eleanor de Montfort could afford to be magnanimous with her husband in control of London.

Rosamond turned and fled up the stairs to her chamber, her emotions in total disarray. She could not deny that she was secretly flattered that he had come, yet she was afraid of what he would do to her for taking refuge with the so-called enemy.

Eleanor de Montfort, with Sir Rickard de Burgh at her side, listened as Sir Rodger de Leyburn demanded to speak with his wife. "You may speak with her, but that is all, my lord. Leave your swords here in the hall; Sir Rickard will escort you."

The muscle in de Leyburn's jaw clenched like a lump of iron at the sight of Rickard de Burgh. Yet he knew he should not have been surprised to find the knight in residence at Kenilworth. The Irish warrior was pledged to Eleanor, not Earl Simon, and would naturally be in charge of the fortification of Kenilworth Castle.

Sir Rickard extended his arm to indicate that the two men should climb the stairs before him. He was trained never to turn his back on any man save a loyal squire. But in spite of his precaution, de Leyburn had a knife at his throat before he could take a breath.

"If you have designs upon my wife, you will have to kill me for her." De Leyburn's green gaze pierced de Burgh's soul. The Irish warrior's green eyes stared back; they showed no alarm.

"I have told Rosamond her fate lies with you, but she refuses to listen. You and I both know this conflict is not over; her survival depends upon your strength, de Leyburn."

Rod stared at him fiercely. "I intend to take her with me now."

Sir Rickard de Burgh took the man's measure. "Excuse me, I am patrolling the ramparts." He took the stone stairs that led to the castle roof, and Rod sheathed his knife beneath his mail shirt.

De Leyburn threw open the chamber door, motioned for Griffin to enter, then closed it firmly behind them. His green gaze swept Rosamond from head to toe. "Explain yourself."

Rosamond took the offensive immediately. She lifted her chin and tossed her hair back over her shoulders. "My actions explain themselves. I refuse to live with a man who has no honor!"

"What of your own honor, Rosamond?" he asked silkily. "You vowed to love, honor, and obey me. You vowed it before God. I don't expect love, but I will have you honor and, above all, *obey* me, wife!"

"What an arrogant swine you are to come here and issue me orders. You changed sides and you *lost* because of it! Go, and leave me in peace, you cur!"

"Strip off your clothes and put on Griffin's," he said quietly.

"Are you mad?"

"Mad as a raging bull, madam; it would be wise to do as I say."

Rosamond watched wide-eyed as Griffin removed his helmet and breastplate. "If you don't leave immediately, I shall scream for the guard."

"For your knight in shining armor, Sir Rickard de Burgh?" Rodger taunted. "I have him gagged and trussed like a haunch of venison ready for the spit. If you have a tendresse for the man, you had best obey me, Rosamond, or I shall vent my spleen on him."

For the first time she faltered, and fell back on the defensive. "I cannot wear chain mail and a breastplate."

"You can and you will. Remove the dress!"

She saw that Griffin stood naked, stripped even of chausses. Slowly her hands began to lift off her gown.

Rodger's tone lightened. "Chirk will be happy to see you; she is with pup."

Rosamond gasped, and her hand almost flew to her belly, except she remembered in time. There was no way she would reveal her secret to Devil de Leyburn!

After she pulled on the squire's chausses, Rodger helped her into the mail shirt and the breastplate. Then he pulled Griffin's helmet over her long blond hair. He saw that she staggered from the weight of the armor, and crushed down the urge to aid her. He pulled Griffin's knife from its sheath and handed it to his squire. "If she makes any outcry when we leave this chamber, go immediately to where I have de Burgh trussed and cut off his balls."

Rodger de Leyburn descended to the Great Hall, retrieved his sword, nodded curtly to Kenilworth's steward, and without a backward glance, strode to the two horses tethered in the bailey. He was acutely aware of the tall, slim figure that followed on his heels, yet no one else paid the slightest attention to the armor-clad squire, not even when he had difficulty mounting his destrier. The two riders thundered through the gate, and out along the causeway that provided the only access to Kenilworth Castle.

Finally, Rodger allowed himself to turn in the saddle, and he was just in time to see Rosamond topple from the big bay in a dead faint. He dismounted in a flash and knelt beside her, his heart pounding. The noseguard covered a good deal of her face, but he could see that her eyes were closed. Rod lifted off the helmet and was shocked to see how deathly pale Rosamond looked.

He wanted to throttle her for forcing him to subject her to such harsh treatment, yet at the same time a fierce protectiveness rose up in him, bringing a lump to his throat. He unfastened the straps of the breastplate and eased it from her body, then he removed the mail chainse and shook her gently until her eyes opened. "Rosamond, you fainted . . . are you ill?"

"Nay," she said quickly, "the bloody armor was too heavy for me. Why did you play me such a devil's trick? If harm befalls Sir Rickard de Burgh, I will get even with you, so help me God!"

Rodger was so angry he wanted to strike her. It savaged his pride that she had obeyed him only because of the threats to the Irish knight. "I notice you have not the least concern for poor Griffin, who risked his life to help me rescue you."

"Rescue? It was an abduction, a kidnapping! Griffin deserves his fate."

Rodger smoothed her disheveled hair back from her brow. "I believe we all of us deserve our fate, Rosamond, even you." He fastened Griffin's armor to the bay's saddle, then tethered its reins to his own black stallion. He took his rolled-up cloak from his saddlebag and wrapped it around his shivering wife. Then he lifted her before him and set his spurs to Stygian's flanks.

It was now full dark, and Rodger de Leyburn knew Rosamond needed a bed. He headed to Daventry, where he knew Baron Bassingbourne had a manor house. Rodger had no idea if the baron was a king's man or a de Montfort man, but he was ready to ask Bassingbourne's hospitality.

Warren de Bassingbourne was at home and offered Sir Rodger and his wife shelter for the night. The young baron had inherited his land and title just before the Welsh campaign, and though the elder Bassingbourne had been a staunch supporter of Earl Simon, Warren had not committed himself in the civil dispute. Rodger sensed that here was an opportunity to plant some seeds for the future, and after escorting Rosamond to a small bedchamber where the servants lit her a fire and served her food, he descended and supped with the young baron.

"You are Lord Edward Plantagenet's royal steward, Sir Rodger. I was surprised that he broke his ties with Simon de Montfort."

"It is against Edward Plantagenet's nature to be subordinate to an earl, even Earl Simon. He will be *King* Edward, the next rightful King of England, when Henry's rule is done. Both Simon de Montfort and King Henry are well up in years. The future belongs to men our age, Warren. Lord Edward will have need of ambitious men and is prepared to reward them well."

Warren de Bassingbourne knew he was being wooed, and de Leyburn's words conjured pictures of lands and castles. "Do you believe that there will yet be civil war, Sir Rodger?"

"I do. I realize that Daventry lies in the shadow of both Kenilworth and Northampton and it may be easier to side with the de Montforts, but the rewards would not be as great. However, allow me to extend the hospitality of Windsor to you, Warren. Lord Edward will welcome you with open arms."

When Rodger retired for the night, he found Rosamond still wrapped in his cloak, sitting before the dying embers of the fire. "You should be abed; we have an exhausting journey tomorrow."

In reply, she turned away from him and stared into the last flickering flames.

Since she would have none of him, Rod, who was wise in the ways of women, left her to her ruminations. He undressed, climbed into bed, and blew out the candles. He knew that the chamber would become increasingly cold once the fire was dead, and anticipated that soon Rosamond would be glad to slip into the warm bed.

Though she was exceedingly tired and cold, Rosamond sat before the fireplace without moving. She stubbornly decided to freeze to death rather than share a bed with de Leyburn. She did not know how much time passed, but when she awoke, she found herself pressed against the warm length of her husband's body. She realized that Rodger must have undressed her and carried her to bed once she had fallen asleep. Rosamond almost jumped up in anger, then thought better of it. The bed was soft and warm, and if she left it from willful pride, she would be the only one to suffer. Far better to pretend that she had not awakened.

Rosamond lay still, wondering if what he had said was true. Did she deserve her fate? Although she had used dragonwort to prevent conception, she was nevertheless with child. They had been intimate only that one night when she had not taken the herb. Surely that was fate. She did not want a child for fear of loving it and losing it, as happened to so many women. Why, oh why had Rodger de Leyburn come into her comfortable, secure life to turn it upside down?

Her hand slid over her belly. Already she loved the babe

fiercely. She had sworn that she would never love anyone again, for to love something was to lose it. And slowly it dawned upon her that sometimes emotions could not be controlled, no matter how many vows and pledges were made. Rosamond sighed deeply and moved closer to the warm, powerful body of Rodger de Leyburn.

"I am so glad you are awake, chérie." Rod's voice, smooth and dark as black velvet, insinuated itself inside her. His fingers lifted her chin and he dipped his head to kiss her, thoroughly. "I once told you I'd never let you go. Mayhap now you believe me." He threaded his fingers into her heavy mass of curls. "Next time, I'll drag you back by your beautiful hair, you willful little bitch, and if you run to Rickard de Burgh, I shall kill him!"

Rosamond could hear the savage jealousy in his voice, and the thrill of it spiraled inside her in a delicious frisson of pleasure. She knew he was in a mood to possess her, knew he was about to put his brand of ownership on her. She wanted it, and yet she did not want it, and turned away from him to make his possession of her more difficult. Now all the most vulnerable, intimate places on her body were open to his wicked hands, and she knew instantly that she wanted him to touch her. His nearness made her conscious of every pulse of her heart.

From behind, his teasing hand came between her legs to stroke the satin of her inner thighs with feathery light strokes. He caressed her warm flesh from her knees to her cleft, over and over, before his fingers separated the curls upon her mons and slipped inside her. She knew she was hot and tight, and his playful fingers soon had her wet and slippery. His other hand captured one of her breasts, to toy with the nipple, and Rosamond found it unbelievably sensitive. She drew in a swift breath and his possessive touch turned gentle as he stroked her nipple with his fingertips. Now he stroked two buds, one above, the other below. She cried out his name, using the diminutive he liked best when they made love. "Rod . . . Rod!"

It was all the encouragement he needed. In a heartbeat, he curved his long body about hers and plunged into her from behind, holding her to him with hands that were clasped possessively about her breasts. When she cried out from the strange fullness, he whispered against her ear, "Sweetheart, open, take all of me."

Rosamond took a deep breath and yielded to him. When he began to thrust, it aroused her to a higher pitch than she had ever achieved before. He kept stroking her, plunging into her until she was ready to scream with pleasure. She grabbed fistfuls of the sheet beneath her, and arched her bottom high, wanting to draw out the incredible throbbing that was building inside her.

She heard Rod groan with pleasure, then both of them erupted like a volcano, and she screamed as the hot lava scalded her. Rosamond felt the intense shudder of pleasure reach the tips of her breasts and quiver down the entire length of her legs. She collapsed beneath him and loved the feel of his weight full upon her. She hadn't known it, but her need had been as great as his. Dreamily she realized that Rod had known how much she needed the loving, even if she hadn't.

TWENTY

At Westminster, Alyce de Clare paced the luxurious apartment that had been furnished for her father, the king's half-brother, before the barons had forced greedy Guy de Lusignan from England. She felt so caged, she was ready to scream and smash things. Edward had not visited her once; moreover, her father-in-law, Richard de Clare, had summoned her husband, Gilbert, from Gloucester. The young firebrand had opened the gates of Gloucester to Simon de Montfort, and his hot-tempered father was ready to give him a tongue-lashing.

Alyce hated her husband with a passion, and had managed to avoid him by coming to London. Now, however, Gilbert would share her chambers and the Earl of Gloucester would no doubt tell his son that it was time he produced an heir. Alyce, who longed to rid herself of the fiery-tempered Gilbert, knew she was shackled to him until death parted them, and as she paced the room a simple solution to her problem presented itself.

Alyce went to her dressing table and opened the drawer that held her cosmetics. She opened the box that contained her hellebore seeds, which she used crushed up in a paste with cowslips to remove spots and wrinkles from her porcelain skin. Alyce knew that when hellebore was ingested, it was deadly poisonous. She took out four long, black seeds and pulverized them with the heel of her shoe, then she sprinkled the powder into the flagon of red Gascon wine that sat on a table close by the fireplace in her sitting room.

When Gilbert the Red arrived, Alyce made a pretense of welcoming him. His father had gone with Richard of Cornwall to the Tower of London to deliberate with the king about the Parliament that Simon de Montfort had called for the following month. Alyce ordered a hot meal for her young husband and poured him a goblet of wine. Gilbert ate the food, but dispatched his squire for ale. When his squire returned, he informed Gilbert that his father had just arrived at Westminster and wished to see him immediately.

Gilbert ignored the summons, dismissed his squire, and proceeded to consume the entire gallon jug of ale that sat before him. He stretched his legs to the fire and inwardly fumed that his father still treated him as a child. When the door burst open, Gilbert was well primed for a fight. When Alyce saw her father-in-law's purple face, she hurriedly withdrew to the bedchamber.

"You ass-licking, brainless young dolt! When that cocksucking de Montfort marched on *my* city of Gloucester, you opened the fucking gates and welcomed the bastard inside. 'Tis a wonder you didn't open our coffers and let the son of a bitch help himself!"

"Simon de Montfort is the chosen leader of the barons. I rejoice that he won the war! He is on the side of justice, and so am I. King Henry is a spineless, craven weakling who has broken every promise he ever made!"

"*I, Richard of Gloucester, am the leading peer in this realm!* Have you the least notion of the humiliation I suffered when my own flesh and blood aided de Montfort to take over *my* city?" He cuffed Gilbert across the head. "Christ-all-fucking-mighty, I should hang you for treason!" Gloucester, sweating profusely with choler, snatched up the goblet of wine and drained it. "It's time you stopped playing soldier and got a son on your wife!"

"That faithless French slut you saddled me with isn't

fit to be the mother of my children!" Gilbert screamed, now more red in the face than his father.

Richard of Gloucester suddenly wrapped his arms about his belly and fell to the floor in a convulsion. He kicked his heels as his eyes rolled back in his head and agonized groans were torn from his throat.

"Father!" Gilbert dropped to his knees, his fury rapidly evaporating as it was replaced by concern. He grabbed his wrists to hold him still, but Richard of Gloucester suddenly went rigid, his arms and legs jerked one last time, and the last breath left his body. "Help! Help me!" Gilbert the Red cried in alarm.

Gilbert's squire rushed into the room, and Alyce came running from the bedchamber. Her eyes, black as obsidian, widened in horror. "What happened?"

"My father . . . drank the wine . . . then grabbed his belly. . . ."

Alyce retrieved the fallen goblet just as two more servants stepped across the threshold, followed by Richard of Cornwall.

"Splendor of God, what has happened here?" Richard of Cornwall said.

Alyce told him, "Gilbert and his father were having a terrible quarrel, when suddenly he grabbed his chest as if he were in great pain. I think his heart must have burst. Oh dear Lord in heaven, you know what violent tempers the de Clares have!" Alyce wrung her hands and began to cry. She was surprised to realize that her tears were genuine. Her dear father-in-law lay dead, while her flame-haired swine of a husband was still very much alive.

Richard of Cornwall tried desperately to revive his firstborn son, but his efforts were in vain. He knew the violent temper came from being a Plantagenet, not a de Clare! Within the hour, all Westminster was in mourning, then messages were dispatched to King Henry at the Tower of London and to Lord Edward at Windsor. Gilbert also sent a secret message to Simon de Montfort in residence at Durham House, telling him that he was still his ally. Gilbert was covered with guilt and grief over his sire's death and refused to be comforted by his wife.

"Get you out of my sight," he ground out between clenched teeth. "I don't want you under the same roof, madam. You may have been able to pull the wool over my poor father's eyes, but I have known what you were since I was fourteen!" Gilbert searched his mind for a place to send her; he certainly didn't want her back in Gloucester. "You may pack your things and remove yourself to my castle of Tonbridge."

Alyce did not give him an argument; she was quite happy to leave the scene of her crime. Gilbert was the new Earl of Gloucester, and the title made him the leading peer in the realm. Though her plan had gone alarmingly awry, at the same time there was consolation: She was now the Countess of Gloucester, which was the sole reason she had agreed to marry the boy Gilbert de Clare five long years ago. She decided that she would indeed move to Tonbridge, but not before she sailed up the River Thames to Windsor.

Nan was relieved when Rosamond returned with her husband to Windsor, but none was happier to see her than Princess Eleanora. "Oh, Rosamond, I have been so unhappy; you should have taken me with you. Edward doesn't love me, he loves that creature, Alyce."

"No, no, Eleanora, you are quite wrong! I told you that Alyce de Clare cannot help flirting with every man she meets."

"Rosamond, she told me that she is his mistress!" Eleanora's eyes glistened with tears just thinking about it. "I have locked my doors against Edward . . . and I have locked my heart against him too!"

"Alyce de Clare is a vicious woman who enjoys seeing others suffer. She would be delirious with joy if she knew that you had locked your doors against Edward."

"Oh, Rosamond, I cannot bear that they are lovers!"

"Eleanora, they are not!" Rosamond lied. "I will tell you a secret, if you promise never to tell anyone. It is my own husband, Rodger de Leyburn, who is her lover."

Eleanora's hand flew to her mouth. "Ah, Rosamond, you too? Is that why you ran away?"

"No . . . yes, that was one of the reasons, Your Highness."

"Not Highness . . . call me Eleanora, please?"

Rosamond nodded. "I want you to be happy, Eleanora. I think you and Edward make a perfect couple. Someday he will be the King of England and you will be his queen. I know how much you love him; why don't you let him show you how much he loves you?"

Eleanora shook her head sadly. "He married me because his family arranged it for political reasons. It was not for love. It was the same for you, no? Can you love your husband, Rosamond?"

She hesitated, searching for words. "Yes, I know I must learn to love him, if we are to have any happiness at all." Rosamond wondered wildly if there was a grain of truth in what she said. "You exchanged vows before God that you would love and honor each other," Rosamond reminded the princess.

"We were children," Eleanora whispered sadly.

Sir Rodger knocked on Princess Eleanora's door, which was opened by one of her women. "May I speak with Rosamond?" he asked softly.

Rosamond heard her husband's voice and was surprised he spoke in Spanish. She went to the door and saw by his face that something was amiss. "What is it?" she asked with apprehension.

"Sad news, I'm afraid, Rosamond. Edward just received a message from Westminster Palace that your cousin Richard of Gloucester has died suddenly."

"Richard?" Rosamond remembered the last time she had spoken with him at Kenilworth. He had been a man in his prime, his ruddy glow giving him an air of health and strength. "How did he die?" she asked in shocked disbelief.

"Apparently his son Gilbert had just arrived from Gloucester. The message suggests that it was his heart."

"I must go to the chapel. . . ."

"I will take you, Rosamond," Rodger offered gently.

"Nay, I want to be alone."

"I will escort you and wait for you at the door," he insisted.

Rosamond found that Rod was as good as his word, and as she knelt before the altar, she prayed for Richard's soul and prayed too for his mother, Isabella, who had been a very gentle lady. Rosamond had learned from Eleanor de Montfort that Isabella had not loved her first husband, Gilbert de Clare, but her second marriage, to Princess Eleanor's brother, Prince Richard of Cornwall, had been a passionate love match.

Rosamond reflected that her own marriage was a passionate one, but love was something else entirely. Richard of Gloucester had joined Edward in repudiating Simon de Montfort, but she realized with a little shock that his son Gilbert, the new Earl of Gloucester, would be firmly in Earl Simon's camp. Was this the hand of God, striking Richard down for his betrayal? Rosamond shuddered. Better to call it fate, yet how very strange fate was.

She heard a firm step behind her and turned accusing eyes, but it was not Rodger, it was Lord Edward who had come into the chapel to offer his own prayers for Richard of Gloucester. She watched as he prayed, the candles burnishing his bowed golden head and beard. She wondered if he feared the hand of God for his own betrayal. Then she realized that Edward Plantagenet feared nothing. He was the rightful heir to the throne of England. His was the power, and his would be the glory! Rosamond had to admit that he would make a magnificent king.

There was a commotion outside the chapel, and both

Rosamond and Edward recognized the voices. Rodger was having an altercation with Alyce de Clare. "I am the Countess of Gloucester, and I will go to him!"

Edward arose from his knees and strode to the door. Rosamond followed more slowly, but Alyce's voice carried to her clearly. "Edward, it was Gilbert's fault . . . he killed his father! It was terrible! They were having a vicious fight. Gilbert was drinking and screaming. . . . Richard's face turned purple with rage, and he grabbed his heart and fell to the floor. Then Gilbert turned his fury upon me—" Suddenly, Alyce burst into tears, and Edward put his powerful arms around her and drew her close.

"Hush, my dear, I know how upset you must be."

"Oh, Edward, he was always very kind to me, and I was so fond of him. It breaks my heart that he is gone! I cannot bear to stay at Westminster. I shall go to Tonbridge Castle tomorrow, but may I stay here tonight?"

"Of course you may stay here, my dear; you must not be alone tonight. Rodger will have chambers prepared for you."

Alyce threw both Rod and Rosamond a self-satisfied look.

When Rodger returned to their apartment, Rosamond was awaiting him. "If Eleanora learns that Alyce de Clare is here with Edward, she will run mad. Alyce told her that she was Edward's mistress, and Eleanora has closed her doors to him, and is ready to close her heart to him too. Rodger, I . . . I did my best to smooth things over—I told Eleanora that Alyce was *your* mistress, not Edward's. It was not too great a lie—most people think you are her lover."

"Is that what *you* think, Rosamond?"

Her eyes met his for a long moment, then a half-smile curved her lips. "No, my lord, I think you have better taste in women." She knew her response pleased him by the green flame that lit his eyes.

"I put Alyce on the top floor, in the queen's chambers."

"But that is directly above Edward's rooms, and you know what she is. Alyce will make sure Edward spends the night with her and then she will find a way to flaunt the fact to Eleanora!"

Rod cursed beneath his breath. "Surely you don't wish *me* to spend the night with Alyce to keep her from being with Edward?"

Rosamond raised a brow. "What an odd solution. Rather, you could spend the next few hours with Edward, to keep him from being alone with Alyce, but if you prefer otherwise—"

Rod had her in his arms in a flash. He brushed the honey-gold hair back from her brow with a tender hand. "You know with whom I wish to spend the night, Rosamond." He knew Richard of Gloucester's death had affected her deeply, and he didn't want her to have her trampling dream. "I'll join Edward for a while, but he may not be pleased. Princes like their privacy, especially this prince, and it's really none of our business with whom he sleeps, Rosamond."

As his wife had predicted, Rod found Alyce de Clare with Edward when he went upstairs. "You know you should not be here alone with Lord Edward," he chastised. "It is far better that you meet at Tonbridge Castle."

Alyce flashed Rodger a look of defiant outrage. "Do not let him speak to me like that, Edward; he is not my keeper!"

"If I were, Alyce, you wouldn't be able to sit down for a week."

"Oh, Edward, do you not hear him?" she cried.

"Yes, I hear him and I agree with him," Edward said shortly.

The arrival of Harry of Almaine prevented a shouting match. The young royal had a wild, distraught look about him, and both Edward and Rod stepped to his side. "Is it true?" Harry asked with disbelief, running a distracted hand through his brown curls.

Edward poured him a cup of brandywine. "Drink this, Harry."

"Tell me what happened to my brother!" He drained the cup.

Rodger spoke up. "He suffered some sort of attack, shortly after Gilbert arrived at Westminster. We have been led to believe it was his heart. But from all accounts he didn't suffer, Harry; it was over in moments."

"Oh my God, Gilbert saw his father die?" Harry was aghast.

"He was violently arguing with his father!" Alyce interrupted. This time she did not go as far as to say that Gilbert had caused Richard to die, because Harry was Gilbert's closest friend.

"I must go to Westminster," Harry said, looking greatly upset. "Edward, I shall leave my men in your command for the next few days."

Edward nodded. "Tell your father that we will come tomorrow to pay our respects."

Rosamond sat before the fire with Chirk upon her knee. "You foolish girl, why did you let Bebe get you with pup?" she murmured, gently stroking the little bitch's swollen belly. She could not think about Chirk's condition without contemplating her own. *Birth and death . . . life is naught more than a cycle of being born and dying!* It seemed that Richard's death was one more in a never-ending line. Everyone related to her, save her cousin Harry, was now dead and gone. Suddenly she felt apprehension for Harry, and she quickly crossed herself to banish the feeling. Rosamond knew she must stop dwelling on these dark thoughts. *I must separate birth from death, or the pups may be doomed . . . my baby will be doomed!*

She did not hear a soft tap on the door, but Nan did and opened it to find Princess Eleanora. Nan curtsied and invited her in.

"Rosamond, I am so very sorry about your cousin

Richard," she said, her soft brown eyes brimming with tears of compassion.

Rosamond was glad to see Eleanora; the princess would distract her from her morbid thoughts.

"It makes me realize how short life can be, and that we should not waste precious time being angry with those we love, over imagined hurts." Eleanora hesitated, then continued shyly. "I think I should go to Edward—we have been apart far too long."

"No!" Rosamond's thoughts darted about like mercury, searching for an answer. She could not let Eleanora find Edward consoling Alyce de Clare, or their relationship would be damaged beyond repair. "Edward should come to you, Eleanora! He should do the wooing. Because he is a prince, women throw themselves at him. You must be different; you are a princess and a lady. If you act a little aloof, he will lose his heart to you all the faster."

"Rosamond, you are so wise about men."

Dear Lord, if only that were true, Rosamond thought. *I know so little about my own husband, I cannot even tell him I carry his child!* "Go back to your own apartment and I will go up, pretending to seek out Rodger, who is with Edward at the moment. I will suggest to your husband that if he comes to you, you might be in a mood to forgive him." She saw that Eleanora's eyes lit up at her suggestion.

Owen stood guard outside the prince's chambers, but he admitted Rosamond into the anteroom. When she knocked on the inner door, it was opened by her own husband, who frowned at her intrusion. She gathered her courage and brushed past him to join Edward and Alyce de Clare, who were conversing intimately.

Rosamond took a deep breath and plunged in. "Forgive me, Lord Edward, but I must speak with you concerning your wife."

"Wives think they own their 'usbands, but they do not." Alyce gave Rosamond a pitying look.

"Is Eleanora all right?" Edward asked quickly.

"That is up to you, my lord."

"I will bid you good night, Alyce. Rodger, please escort the countess to the chambers you have prepared for her," Edward said in a firm tone that showed he would brook no refusal.

Alyce's fists clenched and her lips thinned, yet she had more sense than to argue with Edward, who was all-powerful. But she vowed to pay back the Marshal bitch for this untimely interruption. She moved across the room and tucked her arm into Rodger's in a most familiar fashion. "Darling Rod, you always manage to take care of all my needs, chéri, and I shall do the same for you, no?"

Rosamond turned her back upon her husband as he ushered Alyce from the royal apartment.

"He isn't her lover, Rosamond," Edward said quietly.

"No, my lord, *you* are. Rodger didn't tell me," she added quickly. "I heard you together one night at Kenilworth."

Edward's Plantagenet-blue eyes glittered. "Who else knows?"

"Eleanora knows, for Alyce took great delight in telling her!"

"Splendor of God, no wonder she shuts her door to me! Why would that black-haired bitch do such a thing?"

"Jealousy, of course. She is envious of Eleanora's beauty and innocence. Alyce flaunts you like a trophy because she fears her hold is slipping now that your virginal bride resides at Windsor."

"I knew that Eleanora had suspicions, but I had no idea she had been told outright!"

"I have assured Eleanora that it is a lie. I told her that Alyce is Rodger's mistress, not yours. Most people believe they are lovers."

"Does Eleanora believe it?"

"It is up to you to make her believe it. She knows that when you were married as children, it was for political reasons. She does not believe that you love her; you will have to convince her otherwise, Edward. Go to her now before it is too late!"

Once Rosamond left him, Edward paced the chamber thinking over what she had said. He was a decisive man who never dithered over the choices he made, and went immediately to the adjoining door that led to Eleanora's chambers. He knocked politely and waited to be admitted, though patience was not one of his virtues. He was extremely pleased that Eleanora opened the door herself. It was as if she had been waiting for him.

"Come in, Edward," she said, trying to hide her breathlessness.

"Eleanora . . . Nora, I won't ask why you closed your door to me, I will only tell you how happy I am that you have finally opened it." He took possession of her small hand and raised it gallantly to his lips. "I don't like us living separately. I don't want locked doors between us, sweetheart."

Eleanora blushed at the endearment, and Edward saw how lovely it made her look. "You are beautiful tonight, my Nora."

"Thank you, it is the peach-colored gown."

"It is not the gown, my sweet, it is your glorious hair and your exquisite face that are beautiful." Gently he tried to draw her into his arms, and felt her slight resistance.

"My women will see us," she said breathlessly.

Edward laughed. "They will have to get used to it."

"*I* will have to get used to it; we must get to know each other."

"Intimately," he agreed, drawing her into a possessive embrace in spite of her resistance. He bent his head to capture her lips and found her mouth so softly inviting, it made him reel. "Nora, I want you to spend the night with me . . . it is time our marriage was consummated."

"Edward, I . . . I don't feel married."

"My darling, that is because we haven't shared a bed."

"We were married for political reasons, not for love," she said wistfully.

"Nora, I *do* love you. When I came to Windsor and discovered you here, I fell in love the moment I laid eyes on you. You have my heart . . . all of my heart." More than anything in the world, Edward wanted to please his beloved and make her happy. "When you were ten, we *were* wed for political reasons, but now that you are sixteen I want you for very different reasons." Suddenly an idea occurred to him, and decisively Edward knew he would act on it. "Let's get married again . . . tonight . . . let me call the priest!"

"Oh, Edward, that is so romantic."

"You make me feel romantic; Nora, my love, will you marry me?"

"Yes, Edward, yes, yes!"

Lord Edward dispatched Owen for the priest, and since they were already legally married, he decided that witnesses were unnecessary. The royal couple exchanged vows in Edward's chambers with a myriad of lighted candles upon the mantel of the fireplace, as if it were an altar. When the words had been said, Edward unfastened the golden rose badge from his doublet, which was his emblem, and pinned it to Eleanora's gown. "This rose comes with my heart," he pledged solemnly.

"I will cherish it always, my husband," Eleanora whispered.

The priest, who had hastily donned his cassock over his nightrobe, departed along with Owen, who returned to the anteroom to stand guard against those who might intrude.

Edward took his bride's hand. "Make a wish, and we'll blow out the candles together." When the last one flickered out, he drew her into his bedchamber, which was lit by the fire and one large square candle on an iron stand. Still in possession of her hand, he sat down on the high bed, opened his long, muscled thighs, and gently drew her between them. He cupped her face with reverence and touched her lips with his. He kissed her a hundred times, sweet kisses, soft kisses, tender kisses, long, melting kisses, and short, quick, teasing kisses that made the corners of her mouth rise, then he kissed those too.

His knowing fingers reached behind her to unfasten her gown, then slowly he inched it down to bare her shoulders. His lips touched her throat, then caressed her collarbone and her soft shoulders. Edward smiled as he lowered her gown to reveal her extremely modest undergarments. With gentle hands, he removed the gown and then her shift and petticoats. Eleanora hid her face against his chest, but he placed his fingers beneath her chin and made her meet his eyes, so that she could see him worship her.

The soft, round globes of her breasts were perfection. They were full and lush with dark aureoles, and filled his huge palms. When he kissed them, her swift, indrawn breath told him that it thrilled her. Edward's fingertips traced her rib cage, then circled her navel, as he marveled at the femininity of her lovely curved body. He wondered how he had ever found Alyce de Clare's thinness attractive, and knew with a certainty he never would again.

Dozens of dark spiral curls covered her mons, and he could not keep his fingers from them. Her shyness delighted him, and he touched her over and over again in intimate places, just to watch the blushes come and go in her cheeks. Then he tasted her everywhere and watched her lashes sweep down onto her cheeks in shy disbelief. When he began to remove his own garments, however, he saw that she lifted her lashes and stared at him in fascination.

He had been six foot four when he was fourteen. Now, however, he was broad as well as tall, and Eleanora's eyes shone with admiration as she gazed at his wide shoulders and heavily muscled chest covered by golden hair. She was fascinated by the contrast in their coloring, as a naked Edward once again drew her body to touch his. He was fair-skinned and his torso was gilded by body hair. Eleanora's skin was dusky and shone like satin. She made no protest when he lifted her to the bed and lay down beside her.

She felt both bold and shy as she reached out to touch his golden beard, then trace the outline of his beautiful mouth with her fingertips. She laughed when he playfully pretended to bite her fingers, and happiness welled up inside her. Was this golden god, who would someday be king, really her husband? *Indeed he is*, she told herself, *for he has wed me twice over!*

Edward was completely enthralled by his adorable bride. Her innocence was the most precious gift he had ever received. Her beauty, her speech, her laughter, her daintiness, and her fragrance fascinated him. In fact, he was enchanted by everything about her. Edward made a silent vow to cherish her, to be faithful to her, and to protect her with his life. He could not wait to give her his child. She was everything a mother should be: sweet, gentle, kind, loving, and intelligent. *She must be a gift from the gods!* he thought.

When he began to arouse her, he touched her as if she were made of delicate porcelain. He had never felt so tenderhearted in all his life. Suddenly, Edward was all the things he had never been before: patient, gentle, tender, and above all, selfless. He was such a large man that he knew he would cause her pain when he tore her hymen, but he promised himself he would make up for it with the loving he would lavish upon her.

And love her he did. All night long.

Twenty-One

One by one, young men of influence in the country began to visit Edward at Windsor. The first to arrive was Warren de Bassingbourne, followed by the Marcher barons, Mortimer and Clifford. When, following the burial of his brother, Harry of Almaine returned to command his men, Rodger de Leyburn knew that if their ranks swelled further, it would be noticed by the opposition.

"More men are committing to our cause every day, Edward. You must choose a location farther afield than Windsor, where we can mobilize in secret."

"Aye, I've been thinking on it. Since it was the warlord who taught me all that I know of military strategy, I shall take a page from Simon's book and gather my army at Oxford, as he always does."

Rod nodded. "All roads lead from Oxford; it is a good choice in my opinion. We must not wait too long; at some point we must stop recruiting and take armed action."

"I know, my friend. Speed and fury win the day, but Mortimer says that Hay and Montgomery will be here shortly. Send a messenger to intercept them and have them wait at Oxford."

"I'll send Griffin; he rode in last night on Rosamond's palfrey, Nimbus. Poor devil, I half expected him to be wearing a gown, since I left him at Kenilworth naked!"

"Rod, you were there not long ago, do you think we

could take Kenilworth Castle?" Edward wanted to hear the honest truth.

"No, because it's surrounded by water and only accessible over the causeway. I doubt we could take it without a long siege, and we don't have time to waste in sieges, but if we are determined enough, I think we might be able to take Northampton."

Edward turned his attention upon his royal cousin, Harry of Almaine. "Do you think there is any chance of talking your friend Gilbert of Gloucester into changing sides?"

Harry shook his head. "Gilbert is Simon's man forever."

"Forever is a long time, Harry. Well, I am going to try my hand at persuading John de Warenne, the young Earl of Surrey, to defect from Simon de Montfort and join us. I believe he is an ambitious young man who won't be able to resist my fatal charm."

Rod nodded his agreement. "If you can get John to commit to us, his brother, Lincoln de Warenne, will no doubt follow."

Griffin stood before Rosamond with a worried expression on his face. "My lady, I hope you can find it in your heart to forgive my transgression against you."

"Was Sir Rickard de Burgh harmed in any way?"

"Nay, my lady, de Burgh is too formidable a warrior to fear aught from me."

"I will never understand why you follow de Leyburn's orders with such blind devotion, Griffin," she said dryly, "but I am learning to endure what cannot be cured. Thank you for bringing Nimbus safely home to me."

Griffin hesitated and looked even more worried.

"What is it? Is aught amiss with her?" Rosamond demanded.

"Not amiss exactly, my lady. But I took especial care with her because she is with foal."

Rosamond was stunned. "How on earth did that happen?"

Griffin flushed. "The usual way, I imagine, my lady."

Rosamond went immediately to Windsor's stables to check on her beloved palfrey. Every stall in the vast building housed a warhorse, and suddenly she felt afraid. When she found Nimbus and ran her hand lightly over her belly, Rosamond's heart sank. Indeed her beautiful little mare was in foal. She damned the male of every species for their impregnating proclivities. What made matters worse was the fact that as she looked around the stables, she saw that Lord Edward and her husband were preparing for war.

That evening she waited for Rodger to tell her about their imminent plans, but to her chagrin he said nothing. It was from Lord Edward himself that Rosamond learned they were leaving on the morrow. When she took Chirk to the garden, Edward approached her.

"Rosamond, I will be forever in your debt if you will watch over Eleanora for me while we are away on this campaign. She thinks me quite invincible, which is most flattering, but she has no idea of the very real danger we will be in, and the last thing I want to do is frighten her."

"She has become my dear friend; we will be good company for each other when you are gone, my lord."

"You are strong and have so much courage, Rosamond. Nora is far too gentle, sweet, and trusting for her own good, but I would not change her, in any way."

Rosamond's brows drew together anxiously. "Lord Edward, you must promise me that you will return, for I would never be able to console Eleanora if aught happened to you."

He squared his shoulders and told her what she wished to hear. "I promise I shall return."

No sooner did Rosamond arrive back at her own chambers than Rodger came in and began to pack his things. Still clutching Chirk, she turned accusing eyes upon her husband. "You are going tomorrow, perhaps into battle, yet you have not said one word about it to me!"

"I didn't want you running to the enemy again the moment my back was turned, so I kept silent."

"I suppose I deserve that." She searched his face anxiously. "My God, Rodger, what if you don't return?"

His brows went up in mock surprise. "Chérie, could it possibly be that you are beginning to love me a little?"

"Nay!" she said quickly—too quickly. "I need you. Whatever will I do when Chirk has her puppies?"

Rod began to laugh, then he stopped as he realized how afraid of birth Rosamond was. "Chirk will be all right, sweetheart." He patted the Welsh terrier and set her down on the rug. "Giving birth is part of nature's course. I cannot be here, but you will be with her, and if she gets into trouble, you will do the right thing."

"But Chirk isn't the only one who is pregnant!" She wanted to tell him about her baby, but found that she could not. "Nimbus is in foal, and it frightens me that she might die. . . . It frightens me that *you* might die."

Rod took her in his arms and kissed her brow. "Death is part of life, Rosamond, but you mustn't let the fear of it stop you from living. I know you have lost loved ones, but you must let go of yesterday, and you must accept that you cannot control tomorrow. All we have is today . . . tonight."

She gazed up at him, seeing his jet black hair and brilliant green eyes, whose intensity always startled her. His strong jaw was darkly shadowed by the day's growth of beard, yet he had never looked more handsome to her than he did tonight. "Take me to bed and make love to me, Rod."

His mouth curved with irony. "You really do expect me to die."

"No, Mother of God, don't say that!"

"Then you do love me?" he pressed.

"Nay!" she denied, "I could not bear the guilt if aught happened to you . . . everyone I love dies!"

"Stop it!" He swung her into his arms and carried her to their bed. "You'll love me, by God, every way a woman can love a man, and when I return you will love me all over again."

On the third day of April, the royal army that Edward had gathered moved north from Oxford, past the Chiltern hills, heading to Northampton. His men covered the thirty-five miles in just over one day, which was miraculous. He ordered his soldiers to attack the city of Northampton immediately, knowing surprise and speed were his greatest allies.

Edward had no experience of fatigue himself, but his dust-covered men-at-arms were dog-tired after their long trek, and the baronial forces easily repulsed them. The prince was sitting morosely in his war tent that night, when Rodger entered accompanied by a prior.

"Here is an ardent royalist, Edward. His monastery of St. Andrew was built at the corner of the wall by the north gate, and the monks have a tunnel leading under the wall into Northampton."

By dawn, Prince Edward and his forces were pouring into the streets. Young Simon de Montfort and his cousin Peter, who garrisoned Northampton, fought valiantly to hold them back, but were captured, and soon after, Northampton Castle surrendered. King Henry, still safely in the Tower of London, placed his mercenaries in the command of his brother, Richard of Cornwall, and they now pillaged the country from Northampton up to Simon de Montfort's city of Leicester, razing manor houses and burning villages.

Edward did not linger; he knew he must follow up his victory without delay. The young barons and Marcher lords who had joined Edward were in a triumphant mood and marched south, capturing the town of Winchelsea. The next town was Tonbridge, where Gilbert of

Gloucester's Tonbridge Castle was located. Alyce de Clare ordered the guards to throw open the gates to Edward, and for appearances' sake he had to take her prisoner. Naturally, the unpalatable job of guarding her fell to Rodger de Leyburn, for he was the only one who knew of Alyce and Edward's adulterous affair.

That night, Alyce used a douche of alum to tighten her woman's sheath. Since Edward had developed a taste for virgins, she used the trick her French mother had taught her. When she emerged from her bedchamber into the adjoining chamber, arrayed in a diaphanous robe, she announced dramatically, "I am ready."

"Ready for what?" Rod asked blankly, though he knew full well she was expecting him to take her to Edward's chamber.

"You bastard, how dare you try to keep me from him!"

"I am only obeying orders, Alyce."

Alyce laughed. "Then let me help you change your mind, my beautiful Rod." She drew close and put her arms around his neck; standing on tiptoe, she still could not reach his mouth with hers. She felt piqued that he did not dip his head to taste her mouth, and rubbed her slim body against his, urging him to intimacy.

Rod felt disgust rise up in him as he looked down at the woman who had betrayed her husband so blatantly. He could not keep the contempt from his voice. "You are most tempting, Alyce, but I do not need to eat the crumbs that fall from the royal table."

She drew back her hand and slapped him full in the face. "That bitch you married has you on a short leash. Let me warn you that it is most unwise to make an enemy of me . . . I know things about you, Rodger de Leyburn!"

"I happen to love my wife, Alyce, but that is a concept you wouldn't understand. You hate your husband enough to poison him—perhaps Gloucester drank wine that was meant for Gilbert? We could all tell terrible tales, Alyce, if we were fool enough."

Alyce de Clare, Countess of Gloucester, was sent to reside with the queen for safekeeping. Though she dwelled in luxury, she found the queen's household held as much excitement as a graveyard under snow. She blamed Rodger de Leyburn for keeping her from Lord Edward's side and swore to bring him down, along with Rosamond Marshal, his blond bitch of a wife.

Edward Plantagenet's strategy was sound. He knew that whoever was master of Sussex and Kent, ruled England. If the royalists controlled the country south of London, they could keep open the route for forces from France that King Henry and Queen Eleanor had recruited. Earl Simon's baronial party still controlled the Cinque Ports, so Edward's army held the country behind them and would attempt to take them over one by one.

Simon de Montfort's army was now out in full force. The main road from the coast to the capital went from Dover to Canterbury, then Rochester to London. The baronial soldiers had taken the town of Rochester and were now savagely attacking its castle. When King Henry learned the barons had taken Rochester, he fled London to join his son in the south. Edward's army took the road that went from Hastings to Lewes, then they would go north to London.

Simon de Montfort did not have enough men to guard both roads, so when his scouts told him the royal army was marching to London by the western route, he abandoned the siege of Rochester Castle and moved his men to Fletching, nine miles from Lewes. There he concealed his soldiers near the weald and waited like a wolf in its lair.

Edward Plantagenet took his army to Lewes, where he and his knights were housed in a castle belonging to John de Warenne. His own spies had told him that his royal army was larger than the baronial army, and his abundant energy, barely held in check, made him eager for battle. It was May 13, a month and ten days since his fighting force had left Oxford.

Under cover of darkness, Simon de Montfort moved his men beneath a four-hundred-foot ridge of the Downs, just north of Lewes. The great warlord wore a plain surcoat over his chain mail, and the barons wore the white cross of the Crusades on their backs as a symbol of the justice of their cause. There were two roads that led up the escarpment; one was a steep incline leading up between the peaks of Black Cap and Mount Harry. The other road was longer, but rose more gradually and wound around Mount Harry. Simon's foot soldiers and archers scrambled up the steeper incline, while the mounted knights and heavily armored troops took the latter.

Simon de Montfort was risking all to gain a foothold on the Downs and engage the royal army before they could be joined by their foreign mercenaries, who had scattered when he took control of London. When his army reached the top, dawn was streaking the gray sky red, and he and the knights in his vanguard saw they had a clear downward path to Lewes.

The royal army was only just awakening, and Simon de Montfort's arrival was a total surprise. Edward Plantagenet, Harry of Almaine, and Rodger de Leyburn were in the saddle in minutes, marshaling their knights and men-at-arms with furious energy. By some miracle, Edward had his troops in battle array before the baronial army was within striking distance.

Edward's father, King Henry, was adamant that he should command the center. Both Edward and Richard of Cornwall tried to dissuade him, but Henry insisted upon his kingly rights. Prince Edward, filled with explosive energy and a savage will to fight, knew in his bones it would be better if he took full command. Reluctantly bowing to his father's wishes, however, Edward led the right wing, and Richard led the left, leaving the center to Henry.

Simon de Montfort had given command of his center to none other than the new Earl of Gloucester, fiery Gilbert de Clare. His right flank was commanded by his two sons, Henry and Simon de Montfort, and on the left were knights commanding bands of soldiers from the city of London. Simon himself commanded a large troop of mounted reserves, waiting on the highest ground to attack any weak link that appeared in the royal army's chain.

Edward Plantagenet, filled with zeal and impatience, charged the enemy's London men-at-arms, who were streaming down the eastern ridge. Rodger de Leyburn, in the forefront with his mounted knights, gave a brief thought to the sixteen-year-olds on both sides, who would find themselves fighting a war for the first time. He well remembered that first shock of finding himself in the midst of a battle where he had committed himself to die or to kill those about him. Then there was no more time for thought, only for action, as the killing began.

They charged up the ridge in a deafening clatter of hooves, clash of weapons, and wild battle cries. The enemy's mounted knights and foot soldiers were no match for the onslaught of Edward's troops. They began to retreat back over the crest of the escarpment, and Edward's men followed in furious pursuit. They chased the enemy for four miles and systematically annihilated it.

Simon de Montfort could do nothing to aid his left flank, but when Edward's army disappeared over the crest, the earl saw a golden opportunity to ride down the slope and attack the king's center with all the strength he commanded. The battle swayed back and forth amid bloody swords, maces, and battle-axes. The dead fell under the hooves of the warhorses, while the wounded lay screaming and unheeded. Richard of Cornwall's line buckled beneath the hammer blows of the barons, and the king's brother was taken prisoner. Then the center broke, and King Henry retreated to the Priory of Lewes, where he took refuge.

When Edward had defeated the enemy's troops, he called a halt, but it took a considerable time to gather his men, who were spread out over four miles, and lead them back up the slopes to the battlefield. Edward's victorious cavalry intended to attack the baronial forces that had been held in reserve, but to Edward's disbelief he found that the battle had been lost in his absence. His bloodlust flaming, Edward wanted to fight on, even though he faced the full strength of Simon de Montfort's army, but Rodger de Leyburn told him flatly that he would be sacrificing every soldier in his command. Wiser to order the foot soldiers to disband and flee to the safety of Pevensey, so they would live to fight another day. Edward saw the wisdom of Rodger's words, issued the order, then he and his knights took refuge in John de Warenne's castle.

The streets of Lewes, piled with dead bodies and strewn with wounded men, looked like a slaughterhouse that night. Simon de Montfort surrounded both the priory and the castle, but instead of storming them, decided to arrange a surrender without more bloodshed. Intermediaries went back and forth all night long, between priory, castle, and de Montfort's headquarters, negotiating the terms of the royal surrender.

In the castle, Edward drew apart from his knights. It was the most humiliating night of his life. He had been so confident he could pit his strength against that of his godfather, from whom he had learned his military skills. He took the whole burden of the loss on his own broad shoulders, because he had thrown away the chance of victory in the excitement of pursuit of the enemy. In that moment, he hated himself, and he hated with a vengeance the undefeated warlord, Simon de Montfort.

Only one knight dared to approach Lord Edward. Rodger de Leyburn looked at the handsome young face above the bloodstained armor. "Do not blame yourself, Edward; you fought valiantly."

"I will blame no other!" he said grimly. "Excuses are for weak men. I made grievous mistakes today; I intend to let the lesson sink in deep. I will never make those mistakes again!" he vowed.

Rod had never admired Edward more than he did at this moment of adversity. "You must think of the future when you agree to terms," Rod said shrewdly.

"Aye, my father will promise anything, but I will not!" He looked over at his cousin Harry, sitting morosely in a corner, and motioned him over with a battered hand. "Harry, you will agree to be a royal hostage with me. I want my knights freed; Rodger here, John and Lincoln de Warenne, and most important is the freedom of the Marcher barons. The border lords must not be held captive. I'll tell de Montfort they are needed to keep the Welsh in check."

"We will pressure de Montfort to free you both," Rodger assured them, "but if all else fails, we will plot your escape." Rod flashed his devilish grin.

Prince Edward, Richard of Cornwall, and Harry of Almaine were taken to Dover Castle, but because the barons feared their escape across the English Channel, they were removed to Kenilworth Castle at the end of May for safer keeping. Simon de Montfort took King Henry back to London with him and lodged the king at St. Paul's, where Queen Eleanor had taken sanctuary. He set up a new government, with himself as Protector, but shrewdly, he made Henry put his royal signature on every official communication and issued them in the name of the king.

At Kenilworth, Countess Eleanor de Montfort presided over the household that now resembled a royal court in size and importance. Earl Simon had three couriers going back and forth between Durham House in London and Kenilworth Castle, but often he himself traveled there with an armed force of 150 lances at his back.

As Simon and his men thundered beneath Kenilworth's portcullis, his eyes scanned the walls, eager for a glimpse of his wife. As he strode inside the impregnable stronghold, his mood lifted the moment he saw her, and his heart rejoiced at the eager, warm welcome Eleanor gave him.

"I am so proud of you, Simon," she whispered.

"Nay, beloved, 'tis I who am proud of you. I could never have achieved victory without your love and support. Though you are a royal Plantagenet, you stand with me against your family, and it humbles me."

She laughed up into his eyes. "You? Humble? I don't believe either of us is capable of such a thing." Eleanor saw him for what he was, and ambition was no small part of him. To England, Simon de Montfort was a symbol, to the barons he was a leader, but to her he was love eternal.

"You have always given me such wise advice, Eleanor, and though I have never told you, I think of you as my equal. From now on, I would like your signature on all official documents."

She was flattered beyond belief at her husband's words, and quite willing to place her Plantagenet name next to that of Earl Simon de Montfort, Protector of England. Eleanor smiled proudly and touched his face. "I am your woman . . . forever."

De Montfort took charge of all royal castles and made his eldest son, Henry, governor of Hereford. He put his second son, Simon, in command of the forces of Surrey and Sussex. He also set up watchers along the entire eastern coast from north to south, to make sure that King Henry's brother-in-law, King Louis of France, did not invade England.

To ensure peace with Wales, Simon de Montfort invited self-styled king Llewelyn to Kenilworth, hoping he would sign a treaty promising no hostilities for a period of two years. The great warlord had become a statesman who was kept busy from dawn to dusk. But in the back of his mind were ever thoughts of Prince Edward Plantagenet. At the Battle of Lewes, he had experienced firsthand the prince's abilities regarding warfare. He had seen his fire and his sword, and knew Edward's vigor, strength, and determination. But what fueled his apprehension most was Edward's natural ability to lead men. Simon de Montfort wondered just how long the young lion could be kept caged.

TWENTY-TWO

Rosamond's emotions were in turmoil when she received the message from her husband. Her reasoning told her it was right and just that Simon de Montfort and the barons had been victorious at Lewes, yet she was sore at heart that Edward and Rodger had been defeated in battle and that all the royal males were now prisoners.

Rosamond expected Rod to return at any hour, and her hand slipped to her belly protectively. She was five full months with child, and though her flowing gowns hid her pregnancy well, her waist had expanded and her breasts were much fuller. She knew that once her husband saw her naked, he would know her secret.

At the beginning of May, when Chirk had given birth to three puppies, Rosamond had been racked with worry over her Welsh terrier's delivery. To her overwhelming relief, all had gone well, but then her fears had been transferred to the puppies' survival. Rosamond worried that bigger dogs would savage them, or horses would step on them, or they would fall down the well, but Chirk carried them in her mouth from harm's way and seemed to be actually happy in her new role as mother. Deep inside, Rosamond knew her fears for her animals were rooted in her own pregnancy and the child she would deliver in four months' time.

* * *

The lovely month of June had arrived, the afternoon sun was shining brilliantly, and a profusion of hawthorn petals was drifting from the trees on the gentle breeze, when Rodger de Leyburn rode into Windsor. Rosamond and Eleanora were playing with their dogs by the lake when they saw him. They hurried to greet him, and though the princess tried to be brave, she burst into tears when he gave her a private message from her husband.

"I cannot bear that Edward is a prisoner!"

"He offered himself as hostage so that his knights could go free," Rodger explained.

"He has so much courage!" Eleanora sobbed harder.

"You must take courage from him. He has been taken to Kenilworth along with Harry and Richard of Cornwall, and I know that Countess Eleanor de Montfort will treat them like honored guests, even though they will be closely guarded."

Rosamond knew Rodger's ability to always say the right thing, and was not surprised to see Eleanora dry her tears and smile at the news he gave her. She could not help staring at her husband; he was so much taller than she remembered and twice as handsome. Her gaze traveled the length of him, looking for signs of a wound or injury. "Are you well, my lord?"

"Your anxiety pleases me, though I hoped you would run to me and fling yourself in my arms." He grinned wickedly. "All my body parts are intact."

Her violet eyes sparkled. "You are still a devil, de Leyburn. I enjoy your occasional flashes of wit, though not as much as your occasional flashes of silence."

He looked at the pups, then addressed Bebe, Eleanora's white Maltese terrier. "So this is what your indiscriminate mating has produced; let it be a lesson to you!"

"They are beautiful pups!" Rosamond protested

quickly, then realized Rod was teasing her, and realized too how relieved she was that he had returned unharmed. She had missed him beyond reason.

When they were alone, Rod cocked an eyebrow at her. "If I didn't know better, Rosamond, I'd think you were happy to see me."

"Oh, I am! Nimbus and I will need you when she goes into foal. I managed with Chirk, but when my mare gives birth, it will be too daunting to face alone. You do realize that I suspect Stygian, your wretched black stallion?"

"You have a very suspicious nature when it comes to me and mine, but this time you are quite wrong, chérie."

"How do you know that?" she demanded, tossing back her hair.

"Have you any idea how long a mare carries its foal?"

"Well, cats take six weeks and dogs—"

His deep laugh rolled over her. "You haven't the faintest idea. A mare carries even longer than a woman—eleven and a half months, to be exact. The old stablemen call it nine months, nine weeks, and nine days, so it happened long before we came to Kenilworth after the Welsh campaign."

"Nine months," she repeated hopelessly, and suddenly her eyes became liquid with unshed tears.

Rod enfolded her in his arms, drawing her close, and suddenly he knew what prompted her tears. "Oh, love, you're having a baby! Rosamond, that's wonderful news; I couldn't be happier!"

She gripped his arms tightly. "I'm afraid," she blurted.

He kissed her brow. "I understand, sweetheart. Childbirth is painful; all ladies fear it the first time."

She looked up at him wide-eyed with disbelief that he didn't understand at all. "Rodger, it isn't childbirth I fear! I don't care about the pain, for God's sake. I'm frightened of losing my baby. There are so many infants who die!" Anger was the only thing that would stop her tears from falling. Her hands clenched into fists, which she beat furiously against his hard chest. "This is all your fault! I never wanted to marry . . . I never wanted a child!"

Biting back a curse, he sat down and gathered her into his lap. He knew Rosamond had a fear of death, and he had heard that females had unnatural fancies when they were with child, so he chose his words carefully as he tried to dispel her dread. "Rosamond, there is risk every day of our lives, in everything we do, but we cannot let it stop us from living. It is wrong to dwell on death. If I did that before a battle, I would be paralyzed with fear and I would not survive. I have learned that fear can become your *power* once you face it! You have the miracle of life within your body, and I want you to cast away all fear and rejoice!" His powerful hand slid over her belly possessively. "Our child will thrive!"

Rodger de Leyburn was so sure of everything, so strong, so positive, that she began to feel a little of his confidence seep into her. She twisted her wedding ring on her finger and prayed that her baby would indeed thrive.

Rod lifted her hand and slipped off her ring to show her the inscription inside: **Rosamond*Rodger**. "Don't think of life as having a beginning, a middle, and an end; think of it as a circle, never-ending, infinite, like our names within the ring." He slipped the gold band back on her finger and kissed her gently.

She looked up at him with a tremulous smile. "I will try."

"How would you like to go to Kenilworth and visit Lady Eleanor and Demi? You can talk to them about the baby; they will be so pleased. I don't believe they would object to my visiting Edward."

Rosamond began to laugh through her tears. "Two months ago you snatched me from Kenilworth and told me next time you would drag me back by the hair. Will you really take me?"

He kissed the tears from her cheeks. "For the mother

of my child, I would do anything." He did not tell her that it was imperative that he communicate with Lord Edward.

"Oh, I can't go," she wailed. "I cannot ride Nimbus and I refuse to leave her."

"Come, we'll go and take a look at her." He set her feet to the carpet and pulled her along by the hand. In the stables, Rod ran his hand over the mare's sides and saw that in the two months he'd been away she had grown heavy. He suspected twins, but kept the knowledge to himself. "We will take her with us; you can ride another mount. Nimbus won't deliver before the next full moon, and that's at least three weeks away."

"What about Eleanora? Can we take her with us?"

"Absolutely not! Edward would have my balls if I put his beloved wife in jeopardy. We are going into baronial territory; she could be taken hostage and used for ransom or other bargaining. I am to put her on the royal barge tomorrow for London. She will live in sanctuary at St. Paul's with the queen."

"But what if she refuses? She dislikes the queen."

"Eleanora will not refuse. She is a dutiful wife who would not dream of disobeying her husband's orders."

"Is that a deliberate taunt about my disobedience, de Leyburn?"

He flashed a grin at her. "Your pregnancy makes you especially perceptive. Have you chosen a name for the baby? I favor Edward, a strong and noble name," he said, adding quickly, "If we have a male child."

To taunt him back, Rosamond declared, "I favor Simon, another strong and noble name." When she saw his look of dismay, she added, "However, my favorite name is Jason, from Greek mythology."

He smiled into her eyes. "I am content to let you choose the name, chérie. Whatever pleases you will also please me."

* * *

Simon de Montfort had not yet arrived from London, and in his absence, Eleanor de Montfort and her royal brother Richard sat next to each other at the high table in Kenilworth's Great Hall, as befitted their royal status. Lord Edward, however, chose to dine at the far table, beside his steward, Rodger de Leyburn. Harry of Almaine longed to join his two friends, but at a discreet sign from Rod he remained on the dais beside his father, Richard. Rosamond sat at another table beside her dearest friend, Demoiselle de Montfort.

"Rosamond, I am very happy for you. You had so many misgivings about marriage, but it has made you bloom."

"It has made me bloom all right; I am having a baby!"

"How exciting, Rosamond! When will it be? Are you sure? You don't look as if you are with child." Demi's eyes roamed over her friend's slim figure beneath the flowing gown.

Rosamond knew her young friend was bursting with curiosity about pregnancy; all unwed girls were, because they were deliberately kept in ignorance. "I'm sure, Demi. I haven't had my monthly courses since I was married, and this is the middle of June, so I have about three and a half months to go yet. I have had some morning sickness and I fainted once. My breasts are larger, and quite sensitive to the touch." Rosamond blushed as she realized the intimate implication of her words. "I haven't told anyone yet except you and Rodger."

"I warrant Rodger has already told Edward. From listening to my brothers, I learned males have a towering pride in siring heirs."

At the far table, Rodger and Edward were deep in conversation, but it was not about sowing their seed. "All the Marcher lords have secretly pledged to you: Mortimer, Hay, Clifford, Montgomery, and Bassingbourne. Our base of operations will be at my castle of Tewkesbury, which is close to Hereford and Worcester."

"Humphrey de Bohun, Earl of Hereford, will never forgive Simon de Montfort for taking the justiciarship away from him, nor for arresting the Bishop of Hereford. Worcester *was* a royal town; now, however, that town stands with the barons." Edward shook his head regretfully. "The common man is on Simon de Montfort's side; the earl has the acclaim of the people."

"Edward, the common man has no property and little money; it is the great landholding barons we must sway to our side. There is already a sharp division among the nobility; the northern barons are standing aloof from Earl Simon and may refuse to attend the Parliament he has called."

Edward's deep blue eyes studied his friend for a moment. "You are the expert on human nature; why do you say they might refuse?"

"Granted, most are against bad government, and a weak, wasteful king, but I warrant it will go against the grain to see one of their own rank elevated to a position where he dictates to them." Rod spread his hands expressively. "Human nature is human nature."

Edward nodded shrewdly. "De Montfort made a tactical mistake when he took charge of all of the royal castles. That won't sit well with the barons. Even Gilbert of Gloucester's pride will rear its fiery head soon, unless I miss my guess."

"Gilbert is now the leading peer in the land, but because of his youth, Earl Simon will give him little say in ruling England. I shall make it my business to talk with Gilbert and increase his dissatisfaction."

"I believe the Marcher barons stand with me because we are all about the same age. They look to the future."

Rod grinned. "Human nature again. Both King Henry and Earl Simon are aging. The Marchers know you will be their king one day, and they don't want to anger you."

"They are greedy for land and castles, as is any man worthy of his salt," Edward said shrewdly.

"Aye, Mortimer of Wigmore is on our side because he wed Maud de Braose. Her mother and Eleanor de Montfort are mortal enemies because of land. She was heiress to vast lands in Breconshire, Wales, but it was a Marshal inheritance. When Eleanor's first husband died, she disputed the de Braose right to Breconshire."

"You seem to know every detail of Marshal landholdings," Edward said with admiration.

Rod grinned. "Before I wed Rosamond, I made it my business to do so; I hope I am worthy of *my* salt."

When Rosamond saw Edward give Rodger a congratulatory slap on the back, she assumed her husband had boasted of his virility. "I must tell your mother," she said to Demi, "before all at Kenilworth know my secret."

"You will need a whole new wardrobe! Mother has ordered new gowns for me because all the important men of the realm will be coming to Kenilworth to confer with my father. I will probably be betrothed before the year is out," Demi predicted humorously.

"The gown you are wearing is beautiful; I've never seen material where the silk is interwoven with gold thread to create flowers."

"It's called samite, imported from Syria. Wait until you see the transparent silks called sarcenet. They look as if the rays of the sun have been imprisoned in the threads!"

"I cannot wear anything transparent!" Rosamond declared.

"Silly, it is lined with sendal, and you must have a new girdle encrusted with precious stones."

"Alas, my gowns will have to flow freely, not be gathered at the waist with girdles, Demi."

"Well, the very latest fashion is a jeweled headband called a fillet worn over the forehead. That will divert attention from your waistline."

As soon as the servers removed the plates, Eleanor de Montfort came to greet Rosamond with an affectionate kiss. The countess appeared to be even more beautiful and vivacious now that her husband had gained so much power. To Rosamond it seemed that Lady Eleanor laughed more often, her eyes sparkled brighter, and she looked younger than ever before.

"I have something to tell you, Lady Eleanor."

"You are *enceinte*! And if not, you ought to be after five months of marriage to that magnificent black stallion. Tell me, Rosamond, did he beat you when he abducted you from Kenilworth?"

Rosamond found that she could now laugh about it. "No, but he threatened to drag me back by the hair if I ever came here again."

"Yet here you are," Eleanor declared.

"Rodger brought me to you out of concern for my well-being. He hopes that you will reassure me about having a child. Sometimes I am overwhelmed by fear," Rosamond confessed.

"Then he brought you to the right place. I have four grown sons and a beautiful daughter, which makes every anxious moment of their upbringing worthwhile. I know you very well, Rosamond; you have far more courage than you realize. A child will teach you that life really is worth the living."

Rodger de Leyburn joined the group of ladies and bowed to the countess. "Thank you for permitting this visit, Lady Eleanor. I shall return for Rosamond in a fortnight. Tomorrow I am off to see to Tewkesbury and Deerhurst; I won't be burdening you with my presence." He hoped this would allay any suspicions she entertained about his visiting Lord Edward, for he was aware that Eleanor de Montfort was an extremely clever woman.

Rosamond looked at him in surprise, though she was wise enough to say nothing in front of the others. Once again she was reminded of his hidden depths, which lay beneath the polished surface.

"Allow me to congratulate you, Sir Rodger. There is nothing like procreating to make a man walk taller." Eleanor looked directly into his eyes and said pointedly, "You must refrain from reckless behavior now that you are to be a father."

Rosamond's anger began to simmer, but she did not allow it to explode until they were alone in their bedchamber. "You devil, you came here for some devious purpose! How very naive you must find me, *Sir Rodger*; but Lady Eleanor is far more astute. I heard that veiled warning she gave you."

"You are being fanciful, Rosamond."

"Fanciful indeed! Fanciful enough to believe the visit to Kenilworth was for *my* benefit, rather than Edward Plantagenet's!"

"Anything I do for Edward will ultimately benefit you, chérie."

"If you get killed, will that benefit me?"

Rodger's heart soared; she really did care about him. Did her feelings run deep? He would take her to bed and find out! With a triumphant whoop of laughter, he lifted her high against his heart and carried her to the bed. "Sweetheart, I intend to die on the upstroke or the downstroke, not in some reckless plot you imagine Edward and I are hatching."

He undressed her with haste, riven with the need to see her naked. Her lips, so temptingly close, compelled him to explore her mouth, its softness, its lushness, then he drew the pink tip of her tongue into his mouth, tasting all of her sweetness. He lifted his head and gazed down at her loveliness. "Have you any idea how beautiful you look tonight?"

Rosamond shook her head, not feeling beautiful. "I am no longer slim."

"Nay, your soft curves make you extremely desirable. Your body is so lush, it arouses me to madness. Let me show you!" He scooped her up and carried her before the polished mirror. Then he let her body slide down his until her feet touched the carpet and she stood in front of him facing the mirror.

Rosamond watched, breathless, as his powerful hand slipped around her and cupped her bare breast, the calloused pad of his thumb toying with her sensitive nipple. She drew in a swift breath as a thread of fire ran from the tip of her breast, down through her softly curved belly, then burned its way to her woman's core. Rod gently pulled her back against him so that she could feel the hard length of his arousal against her soft bottom. She watched, mesmerized, as his fingers slowly traced the curves of her body with reverence. She moaned softly as he parted her legs and touched her most sensitive place with his fingertips.

Slowly she became aware of how erotic it made her feel to watch him in the mirror as he pleasured her. She arched back against his hard body, relishing the tantalizing rhythm of his fingers. Deliberately she brushed the soft curve of her bottom across the sensitive head of his shaft and saw him shudder with desire. She suddenly realized that in Rod's eyes she *was* beautiful, and it changed all of her perceptions. The reflection of their naked bodies, his so dark and powerful, hers so fair and fecund, revealed a sensual, primal beauty she had not recognized before.

He palmed her lush breast, stroking and caressing the silken globe until she shivered uncontrollably with the fierce need he aroused in her. When his hot and hungry gaze met hers in the mirror, she felt the tremors begin inside her and she thrust herself against his burning fingers.

"You are beautiful in your passion," he whispered against her ear.

"You make me feel beautiful."

He picked her up and carried her back to the bed.

Then he laid her down and spread her hair about her so that she lay in golden splendor. Rodger worshipped her with his eyes while he quickly disrobed, then, unable to keep from touching her, tasting her any longer, his hands and his lips caressed all her body's silken pleasure points where his gaze had lingered.

Suddenly, Rosamond felt ravenous for him. Hungrily she lifted her mouth for his ravishing and pulled him down to her. She opened her thighs, then wrapped her legs around him, sliding them high about his back. She was in a fever of need as she molded her body to his and cried out her pleasure as she felt him bury himself hard in the scalding heat of her sheath.

As he unleashed the fierce desire that had been riding him for hours, she cried out, "Rod . . . Rod . . ." Hearing his name on her lips inflamed him as nothing else could, making him groan with a hunger of his own. He whispered love words, hot passionate words that made Rosamond respond wildly. Her senses reeled with the male scent of him, her blood pulsed, and her body throbbed at the feel of every deep thrust.

Rodger felt exultant. He had vowed to make her crave him, ache for him, and he had succeeded beyond his wildest dreams. This was the way he'd always wanted her, moaning and frenzied beneath him, as he brought her to her final rapture. They spent together, clinging to each other in a hot, shuddering release, then his arms tightened possessively, holding her against his heart.

Rosamond sighed with pleasure as she lay against him, her body relaxing after the loving. "Rod, I wish I could believe you were not plotting . . . I wish I could trust you."

His arms tightened protectively. "You can believe this: If you give me your trust, I will never betray it." He stroked her silken hair possessively. "You know how I cherish precious things . . . you are precious to me, and this child is the greatest treasure you could ever give me. I kiss your heart, Rosamond."

In the morning when Rodger left, Rosamond watched him from her chamber window. He mounted his black stallion, then paused and looked up at the high tower. He touched two fingers to his lips, then pressed them against his heart, before he galloped out along Kenilworth's causeway.

He had ridden only a mile when he encountered Simon de Montfort at the head of a huge armed force. Rodger drew rein and Earl Simon did the same. The two men still respected each other despite the political choices they had made, and Rod felt it was necessary to offer Simon an explanation for his presence at Kenilworth. "My lord earl, I brought Rosamond to visit with Lady Eleanor. My wife is carrying our child and craves your wife's advice and reassurance."

The stern expression on de Montfort's face softened somewhat. "Congratulations, Sir Rodger. Rosamond has been like a daughter to us. She has always held a special place in my heart. Be sure you take good care of her."

Rodger nodded solemnly as he gazed into the war-lord's dark eyes. "Rosamond is a prize beyond compare. I pledge to you that I will guard her with my life."

Griffin and Nan had already arrived at Tewkesbury Castle by the time Rodger de Leyburn rode in. He had sworn them to secrecy because he did not want Rosamond to have knowledge of his plans while she was at Kenilworth. He intended to use both Tewkesbury and Deerhurst, which were only two miles apart, as gathering places for forces loyal to Edward Plantagenet.

During the next fortnight, the Marcher lords, Mortimer, Hay, Clifford, and Montgomery met with Rodger de Leyburn, pledging their men-at-arms, Welsh archers, and cavalry mounted on surefooted ponies. They were joined by the western barons, Bohun and Bassingbourne, and finally by Lincoln de Warenne, whose brother, the Earl of Surrey, was busy recruiting men in France. Foremost in their minds was a plan to free Prince Edward.

"It is virtually impossible to storm Kenilworth Castle and effect a rescue," Sir Rodger informed them. "Simon de Montfort is presently in residence because he has invited Llewelyn of Wales. Kenilworth not only bristles with men-at-arms, the only entrance is over its narrow causeway."

"If we cannot rescue him, then Lord Edward must escape," swarthy Lord Mortimer declared. "We will be ready with horses, and I offer my castle of Wigmore as a refuge for him."

Rodger nodded his thanks. "Escape from Kenilworth would be more than difficult. It would be far better if Edward were moved to a less formidable fortress." He flashed his dark grin. "I will see if I can precipitate his removal from Kenilworth."

TWENTY-THREE

At the end of June, Rodger returned to Kenilworth, and came face-to-face with Simon de Montfort, who was entertaining Llewelyn of Wales. "My lord earl, thank you for allowing me to visit Rosamond. I promised I would return in time for her mare to foal."

"Since it is full moon, I accept your explanation, even though my instincts tell me I should keep you and Lord Edward apart."

Rodger allowed a look of relief to transform his face. "He is still here then?"

"Still here?" Simon said sharply.

"You have no plans to move him from Kenilworth?" Rod asked anxiously.

Simon de Montfort was immediately suspicious that a plot was afoot to rescue the heir to the throne. "Why are you anxious that Edward remain at Kenilworth?" he demanded bluntly.

Rod tried to recover what he had said. "I . . . I only think that Edward would be happier here with Harry and his uncle Richard for company."

It was such a lame explanation that Simon de Montfort's suspicion immediately doubled. "Llewelyn of Wales is here to sign a treaty. Diplomacy works if given a chance; both countries will prosper from peace."

"If you trust the Black Wolf of Snowdon," Rodger said smoothly.

"I trust no one," Simon said pointedly.

When Rodger took his horse into Kenilworth's stables to rub him down, he found Rosamond in Nimbus's stall. She had placed a blanket in the straw and, from the look of things, planned to sleep in the stables.

"Oh, Rodger, thank you for returning today. . . . I thought you had forgotten about Nimbus." Her face shone with relief and trust in his ability.

"O ye of little faith," he teased. He was not surprised that she had made plans to face the mare's foaling alone, for Rosamond always found the courage to do what she thought was her duty. "I would much rather you left Nimbus to me, sweetheart."

"Oh, Rod, I cannot! It is not that I don't trust you, I do. But I must be here to soothe her. I have attended many births and given the women bayberry to ease the pain of long, hard labor."

"Rosamond, a mare foaling is different from a woman giving birth to a child. A foal is encased in a sack of fluid when it is born; the mare cannot have a long labor or the foal would die. It usually comes quickly, once a mare's labor starts."

"Really?" Some of her worry melted away, but not all. "Please let me stay with you?"

Rodger cursed silently. He knew Nimbus was carrying twins, and almost always the second foal was born dead. He could not bring himself to tell her. "When it starts, you must stand back and promise not to interfere."

Rosamond nodded her understanding and stroked Nimbus's soft muzzle as she murmured endearments to her. After a while, she sat down on the blanket next to Rodger and waited patiently. At dusk the mare started to get restless, and Rodger knew that as the moon climbed the sky, Nimbus would foal.

Suddenly the animal was taken with a great shudder,

and she began to whinny. Rodger was on his feet instantly, his powerful hand stroking down the mare's belly. "Stand back, Rosamond."

In fascinated horror, she watched her beloved palfrey go down to her knees, then get back up again, heaving and shuddering. All of a sudden there was a great swooshing sound, and an enormous quivering sack was deposited into the straw. She watched Rodger fall to his knees and tear open the thick membrane. All at once the air was filled with a sweet scent she had never smelled before. Then Rod was helping a cream-colored foal from the sack and pushing it toward its mother.

"Oooh, it's so very beautiful!" Rosamond exclaimed with joy, laughing nervously as it wobbled on its spindly legs. "Oh no! There's another one?" she cried, all the joy leaving her voice as she saw the small, limp foal in Rodger's hands.

Rodger knew the smaller twin colt was dead as he tried in vain to revive it. He made sure its mouth and nostrils were clear, then tried to revive it by pressing on its fragile rib cage in hopes it would take in air, but it was hopeless.

Tears of grief streamed down Rosamond's ashen face as she mourned the dead baby horse. Rod cleansed his hands with straw and took her in his arms. "Rosamond, can you not rejoice for the foal that thrives?"

She stared up at him through her tears, and the wisdom of his words slowly dawned on her. "Yes," she whispered, "I can . . . I must." She went to Nimbus and stroked her muzzle. "Good girl, sweet girl." She watched Rod rub straw over the foal, though in truth there was no blood as in a human birth. She smiled at him. "What is it, a male or a female?"

He smiled back. "It's a colt, a male, and he's hungry."

As they stood back watching Nimbus suckle her colt, Rodger's arm slipped about her and pulled her close to his side. "Thank heaven you were here," Rosamond said.

"I would have been lost without you." He felt his own child move in her belly and offered up a silent prayer.

"Be prepared to be moved to another castle," Rodger warned Edward. "Escape is not possible from Kenilworth."

"If it were possible, I wouldn't still be here. Is my wife still safe in sanctuary, Rodger?"

"Yes, and she is head over heels in love with you, my lord."

"And I with her. She is different from all other women."

"Therein lies the attraction, I believe—you find her different." Rodger lowered his voice, even though they appeared to be alone. "Mortimer offers his castle of Wigmore on the Welsh border for your safe haven. If and when you are moved, we will arrange to have fresh horses awaiting your escape. As a precaution, all the loyal forces we have gathered have been moved to Ludlow Castle, about seven miles north of Wigmore."

Edward nodded his understanding, then he cursed. "Llewelyn is being treated like the Prince of Wales he thinks himself."

"Simon de Montfort knows he cannot fight us and Wales at the same time, so he is kissing Llewelyn's arse."

"It makes me want to spew! The old lion, King Henry, my great-grandfather, conquered Wales for England a century ago, and our Marcher barons have held it ever since, effectively putting down all uprisings. Now de Montfort is handing it back to Llewelyn on a silver platter!"

"When you are king, you will simply have to conquer it all over again," Rod said lightly.

Edward pierced Rodger with an ice-blue stare. "Make no mistake, my friend, I *will* unite England and Wales."

In that moment, Rodger de Leyburn had no doubts that Edward would do as he pledged.

Edward grinned. "But first I must win back England!"

At the midday meal in the Great Hall of Kenilworth, Rosamond saw that the swarthy Llewelyn's eyes followed Demoiselle de Montfort to the exclusion of all other ladies. Noticing that he had the hungry look of a wolf stalking its prey, Rosamond shuddered and decided to warn her young friend when the meal was over. But when the tables were cleared, Demi sought out Rosamond, breathless with suppressed excitement. "What do you think of him?"

"Who?" Rosamond asked, dreading Demi's answer.

"The Prince of Wales, silly. He is so dark and dangerous looking, he makes my knees feel weak as wet linen! How fortunate that I studied the Welsh language, as I am to sit up on the dais with him tonight at dinner!"

"You are infatuated with him because he is an older man, much as I was with Sir Rickard de Burgh." Rosamond said. "However, you mustn't forget that Llewelyn is England's enemy."

"I know, isn't it exciting?" Demi licked her lips, and Rosamond was thankful her friend was too young for a serious relationship with the older man.

That night, Rosamond watched Llewelyn and Demi as they sat together on the dais. They appeared to be engrossed in each other as if they were alone in the universe. She glanced up at her husband and saw that he too watched Llewelyn of Wales. "Demi is infatuated with him," she said. "When he leaves, she will be brokenhearted."

"Not if they betroth her to him."

"Betroth? Demi has only just turned fifteen. Surely they would not wed their young daughter to the enemy!"

"Would they not? You don't know Simon de Montfort very well. Llewelyn is the self-styled Prince of Wales, king in all but name, as is Simon himself. A bond of marriage would ensure peace between England and Wales."

Rosamond studied Simon de Montfort, then she watched Lady Eleanor, who was every inch a royal princess that night. She saw them through Rodger's eyes and saw clearly that both were ambitious for power. If they could wed their daughter to a prince, would they do so, even if he were an enemy? Demi would be sacrificed to power!

Rosamond put her hand on Rodger's arm. "I don't want to stay at Kenilworth. Can we not go back to Windsor?"

Rodger held her gaze with his. "Not yet, love." He placed his hand over hers. "I will take you to Tewkesbury, and you can spend time at your own castle of Deerhurst, which lies so close."

"Oh, yes please, that would be wonderful."

He raised her fingers to his lips. "Let's go upstairs."

As Rosamond began to undress she felt her husband's eyes upon her and suddenly felt self-conscious. Since they had last made love, her pregnancy had become far more pronounced.

"Let me undress you," he said softly.

"I . . . my body is no longer attractive, my lord."

In a flash, he was before her. "You are wrong, Rosamond. You have never looked more lovely than you do tonight." He took the gown she was holding over her belly and tossed it to the foot of the bed. Then he sat down and pulled her between his thighs. "Your breasts and belly are lush." His hand stroked over the thin material of her shift, and he felt her quiver. As he lifted off the garment, she tried to turn from him, but he would not let her.

His hands slid down her satin smooth back, drawing her close enough for his mouth to caress her luscious curves. "The way you look excites me, Rosamond. Come, kiss me."

She found her own arousal had begun and slid her arms about his neck to bring her lips close to his. After only one kiss, she felt insatiable and the tip of her tongue came out to lick and taste him. It was not enough for her; she felt ravenous for him and tore away his doublet.

Rodger finished disrobing swiftly and took her down to the bed with him. "Your naked skin feels like hot silk against mine; I love its scent and its taste," he murmured huskily.

"Rod, I want to taste you." At last she had dared to reveal her inner longing, and it gave her the courage to be daring and bold. She rose above him to gaze down at his hard, powerful body, allowing her eyes to feast where her lips ached to follow. Slowly she lowered her mouth to cover one of his nipples, and as her pale hair pooled upon his chest, Rod almost came out of his skin.

His dark magnetism was like black magic tonight, arousing in her a sensuality she had kept dammed up inside her. His body was so hard and strong and powerful, it evoked a wildness in Rosamond she had no intention of suppressing. Rodger was easily the handsomest man she had ever beheld, and his green eyes and jet hair attracted her like a lodestone. That he found her beautiful and wanted to make love to her was like an aphrodisiac to Rosamond, and all her inhibitions melted away as hot passion flamed up, threatening to consume her.

Her palms stroked his flat belly, then she bent to dip her tongue into his navel and heard his groan of pleasure. Her glance lingered on his thick manroot that jutted so arrogantly, and the corners of her mouth rose in pleasure as she teased him with her eyes. "There is something I've wanted to do for a long time," she whispered. Then, without warning, her mouth was on his thigh scar, tracing its outline with the tip of her tongue, licking the silvery line that marred his flesh from knee to groin.

"Rosamond, don't!" he cried.

Her laugh was sultry. "It is part of you, and I find all

your parts irresistible tonight . . . Rod." She cupped his balls gently and rolled them one against the other, then she took the head of his cock into her mouth and swirled her tongue about it. She sucked him softly, rhythmically, slowly taking not only the head, but also half of his thick shaft into her mouth.

Rod watched, mesmerized as she fellated him. Her golden hair whispered over his thighs, cloaking the intimate thing she did to him, and he thanked the gods for this woman with whom he had been gifted. If he could arouse this much passion in her, surely he could make her love him. He felt his seed start and tried to withdraw, but she stayed him with her hand, and he gave himself up to paradise.

When he came up over her, his lips touched her between her breasts. "I kiss your heart, Rosamond."

"I love it when you do that," she said breathlessly.

He took possession of her mouth and tasted himself on her lips. "I love you, Rosamond." It was the first time he had admitted it, and suddenly he didn't need to hear her say it back to him. He suspected that indeed she did love him, she was simply afraid to admit it, even to herself.

"Then show me!" She needed to feel him inside her, needed his strength and his driving passion. Tonight, his was the power, but hers was the glory!

When Rosamond bade farewell to Demi, her friend confided that her father and Llewelyn of Wales were indeed discussing the possibility of a betrothal. The Demoiselle, her eyes filled with stars, was so joyously excited that Rosamond could not bring herself to spoil the young girl's happiness. "I was betrothed to Sir Rodger for many years before we were actually married. Do not be in too big a hurry to leave Kenilworth for Wales."

Rodger insisted they break their journey at Pershore, where Rosamond found her property flourishing under the direction of her new steward, and she knew in her heart she had her husband to thank for its prosperity. When they arrived at Tewkesbury, Rosamond was overjoyed to find Nan and Chirk awaiting her.

"Oh, my lamb, you are having a babe! Sir Rodger never breathed a word about it. You must be exhausted after your long journey. You shouldn't have been riding. . . . You must go up to bed and rest."

"Nan, stop. You are as bad as Rodger. It was only a long journey because he insisted we travel at a snail's pace. I would, however, like a bath in that outrageous Viking bathing tub!"

Nan eyed Rosamond as she undressed. "When is the babe due to arrive?"

"I'm not sure," Rosamond temporized, realizing Nan would try to curtail her every activity if she knew she was into her seventh month. "I believe I'm about five months."

Rodger came into the bedchamber and tried to dismiss the tiring-woman. "I will tend Rosamond if there's anything she desires, Nan."

"I must unpack all her lovely gowns, my lord; we don't want them to be ruined."

Rod flashed a wicked grin at Rosamond. "A gown has no value unless it makes a man want to take it off. I suppose I'll settle for a kiss, if Nan refuses to grant us privacy."

"The two of you've had enough privacy, by the look of things," Nan jested.

When he had received his reward and departed, Nan said, "'Tis only natural he wants his son born at his own castle of Tewkesbury."

Rosamond lay back in the scented water, contemplating Nan's words. Someday this magnificent castle filled with treasures would belong to their child, as well as Pershore and Deerhurst, and for the first time she understood and approved of Rodger's acquisitive ambition.

Landholdings meant wealth, power, and security, and she too was suddenly ambitious for her child.

She could still feel the imprint of Rod's mouth upon hers and between her breasts, where he had kissed her heart. She was amazed at how their relationship had progressed and how her feelings had mellowed toward him. His teasing words came back to her: *Sweetheart, I intend to die on the upstroke or the downstroke, not in some reckless plot you imagine Edward and I are hatching.* Then she recalled her own words: *Rod, I wish I could believe you . . . I wish I could trust you.* That is when he had given her his pledge: *You can believe this: If you give me your trust, I will never betray it.* She sighed with happiness and admired the dragonhead mast on the bathing tub. Perhaps a dragon could be tamed after all.

The very next day, Rosamond was disabused of such a notion. One young noble after another rode in, and Rodger spent long hours secluded with them. She asked Master Burke, the castellan, who they were, and he began to identify them for her.

"The swarthy one is Lord Mortimer. He has castles along the Welsh border at Wigmore and Chirk. The stocky lord who frowns is Hay, and the handsome one is Montgomery—"

"You need go no further, Master Burke. They are all Marcher barons who have strategic castles along the border."

"That is correct, my lady, except for the young man who has the coloring of a lynx. He is Lincoln de Warenne, whose family has castles in Lewes and throughout Surrey. If you will excuse me, my lady, I must check on the meat for the evening meal. Sir Rodger ordered venison, rather than mutton."

When Rodger came to their chamber to change out of his leathers for the evening meal, Rosamond took the offensive immediately.

"What secret plots are you hatching?" she demanded angrily.

"I would tell you, chérie, if they were not secret," he teased.

"Do not patronize me, sir! You deliberately lied to me, telling me I was being fanciful about plots involving Prince Edward!" She flew at him and pummeled his chest. "You gave me your pledge!"

Rod covered her clenched fists with his large hands. "I pledged that if you gave me your trust, I would never betray it. Clearly, you have not given me your trust, Rosamond."

"Dear God, you fought the war and you lost! Can you not accept it? Can we not live in peace?"

"We did not lose the *war*, Rosamond, we lost a *battle.*"

"You must be mad! Is war all you can think of? Simon de Montfort is a man of high principle. He is enforcing the Provisions of Oxford, he has called a Parliament, he is negotiating for peace with Wales. Surely this is best for the country."

"Let me enlighten you, Rosamond. The country is a seething hotbed of rebellion. Simon de Montfort is using an aging, weak king as a puppet to cram his policies down the barons' throats. He is fast becoming a dictator and a fanatic. After the Battle of Lewes, he promised that prisoners would be exchanged, but now he demands ransom from every noble. The Marcher lords have Welsh informants who tell us he has agreed to ridiculous concessions to Llewelyn. He has agreed to the independence of Wales, and there is talk that he will allow Llewelyn to retain all he has conquered in the Marches. You saw for yourself that Simon wants Llewelyn for his son-in-law!

"Does Simon insist upon including the commoners in Parliament because he realizes he must depend on them for money and support in the struggles ahead? All the barons in the North are holding themselves aloof from him. Most of the nobles are now suspicious that a brewer will have the same vote as a belted earl. He is taking into his own hands the possessions of Prince Edward: Bristol, Chester, Newcastle, Nottingham. He has given one son Dover and the other Hereford Castle. He is excluding the proud nobles such as Gilbert of Gloucester who aided him in the struggle, while he consolidates his personal power."

"I don't believe you!" Rosamond cried. "You are taking the side of Edward because he is your friend!"

"I am taking the side of Edward because he is our future king. The throne of England is his divine right. *His* must be the power, *his* the glory, not an earl of the realm."

Rosamond stubbornly placed her hands over her ears and turned her back upon him. Rodger took her arm and swung her about to face him. His voice was deceptively low, but his eyes burned with green fire. "I shall allow you your own opinion in this matter, Rosamond, and we shall agree to disagree. However, you will put on your prettiest gown, your sweetest smile, and come down to the hall to entertain our guests this evening. You are Lady Rosamond de Leyburn, chatelaine of Tewkesbury, and you will behave accordingly."

She tossed back her hair and raised her chin defiantly. Her cheeks blazed with fury, but she did not dare to defy him.

TWENTY-FOUR

Alyce de Clare could no longer bear being confined in the queen's household. Before the beauteous Princess Eleanora arrived, Alyce had found a receptive listener in the queen when she voiced her complaints against Sir Rodger de Leyburn. The queen already hated Lord Edward's steward, whom she believed had been a terrible influence on her son, and she blamed de Leyburn for the theft of her jewels from the New Temple. When Alyce suggested that the royal steward had made himself wealthy by dipping into the royal coffers, the queen launched an inquiry of the accounts and vowed to confiscate de Leyburn's landholdings at Tewkesbury.

The queen also was outraged that Alyce's husband, Gilbert de Clare, had supported the traitorous Simon de Montfort, and she urged Alyce to return to Gloucester and lure Gilbert back into the royal fold. Alyce began to reason that since she was now the Countess of Gloucester, her rightful place was beside her wealthy, powerful husband. The youthful Gilbert would be like putty in her hands! Alyce gathered together her servants and departed London.

During the summer, Rodger de Leyburn was seldom at Tewkesbury. He was overjoyed when he learned that before Simon de Montfort had returned to London for Parliament, he had moved Prince Edward from Kenilworth to Hereford Castle, putting his son Henry in charge of the royal prisoner.

Edward's Gascons, who had fled to France after the battle at Lewes, sailed back, landing at Pembroke in Wales. Harry of Almaine's forces, who had escaped to Ireland, returned as well, and Rodger de Leyburn, in league with the rebel Marcher lords, gathered the fighting men at squat Ludlow Castle, seven miles from Mortimer's castle of Wigmore.

Rodger de Leyburn decided it was time to recruit Gilbert de Clare. As England's leading peer, the youthful Earl of Gloucester had more men under his command than any other noble, and Rodger knew his fiery pride was smoldering because he had been relegated to the background of the political struggle. Rodger spent a week at Gloucester, flattering, persuading, and urging Gilbert to change his allegiance, as his father had done. "Surely you will not place Gloucester Castle in Simon de Montfort's hands as he has directed?" Rod questioned.

"That I will not do! De Montfort is Earl of Leicester, a much lower rank than Gloucester! If he appoints new castellans for my landholdings, I shall hang them!"

Rodger suspected that Gilbert held back from joining them because of the rumors and gossip about his relationship with his wife, Alyce de Clare, but when Rod broached the subject, Gilbert waved a hand dismissively and declared, "We will not speak of the woman." Referring to her as "the woman" did not bode well for Alyce de Clare, Rodger decided.

Gilbert was incensed when he learned that Earl Simon had betrothed Demoiselle de Montfort to Llewelyn of Wales. Rod recalled the hunger he'd seen in Gilbert's eyes when he had looked at Demi during his visit to Kenilworth last year. He suspected that Gilbert fancied himself in love with Simon's daughter.

Before Rodger left Gloucester, he hinted to Gilbert that Edward Plantagenet might honor the Provisions of Oxford when he came to power, and that is what finally tipped the scales and made Gilbert agree to meet secretly with Edward, if and when the prince could be freed.

Rodger returned to Tewkesbury for one day only before he was off to London to attend Simon de Montfort's Parliament. Rosamond remained cool toward him, maintaining a polite distance, and though Rodger wished it were otherwise, he did not have the time to devote to win her over to a loving mood. He was thankful that Rosamond was no longer riven with fear about the baby she carried, and promised that he would be back at Tewkesbury before their child was born.

Rosamond divided her time between their castles of Tewkesbury and Deerhurst. As head steward of both households, Master Burke always accompanied her and consulted her about every improvement at Deerhurst. The property now rivaled Tewkesbury with its herds of cattle and its prosperous tenant farms. Rosamond was particularly proud of its stillroom, in which there now hung both kitchen herbs and medicinal herbs. As she looked around, she knew Rod had been right in suggesting the union of the two properties. In fact, she admitted he was right about most things, including their own union. She could not, however, approve of his plotting with the Marcher barons. Simon de Montfort had won the war and now ruled England. Why couldn't they live in peace? Why did Rodger have to oppose her guardian? Rosamond's loyalties were hopelessly divided.

Her days were busy, but in the evening, when she sat with Nan, sewing tiny garments for the baby, her thoughts were filled with her dark, compelling husband. She missed him sorely and longed for his return. She regretted the cool way she had treated him before he left for London and acknowledged that his loyalty to Lord Edward was admirable. She ran her hand over her belly, wishing she could caress the child growing beneath her heart, and knew it was the fear of war that had prompted her anger toward Rodger. Though she loved Simon and Eleanor, deep down in her heart she knew her first loyalty should be to her husband, the father of her child. Moreover, she could not deny that Edward was the rightful heir to the throne, and he would indeed make a magnificent king.

The August morning was lovely and warm, and the air smelled of new-mown hay. At noon, when Rosamond heard the clatter of hooves in the courtyard, she ran out eagerly, expecting to greet her husband. Instead, her heart dropped as she recognized Alyce de Clare and her servants, accompanied by half a dozen packhorses loaded with baggage. She swallowed her chagrin and greeted her guest graciously as grooms came hurrying from the stables to water the horses. "Good morrow, Lady de Clare."

Alyce stared at Rosamond's obvious pregnancy with covetous eyes. "I am on my way 'ome to Gloucester and dropped in to give my dear friend Rod a message from the queen."

"Sir Rodger is away from home, my lady, but allow me to offer you the hospitality of Tewkesbury."

Alyce threw back her head and laughed. "How very droll!"

"What do you mean?" Rosamond lifted her chin, expecting a cutting remark.

"I hate to be the bearer of bad news when you are breeding, but the queen has decided to confiscate Tewkesbury, and all the royal steward's goods are to be seized," Alyce said with satisfaction.

Rosamond wanted to pull Alyce de Clare down onto the flagstones of the courtyard and rip the hair from her head, but she stood rooted to the spot, unable to move or even speak.

"Since Rod is not here, I won't stay. Gloucester is only

a stone's throw away, and the comfort of my own castle beckons."

Rosamond stood in a trance watching the cavalcade depart. When she felt Master Burke touch her elbow, she turned to him, thinking she might faint. But anger saved her. Suddenly she was seized by a blazing anger unlike any she had ever experienced before.

"Master Burke, I want everything and everyone at Tewkesbury moved to Deerhurst. We must get started at once!" Fury fueled her energy, and she swept through the castle issuing orders. She put Nan in charge of the maids, instructing them to dismantle all the beds so that they could be moved and to gather all the house linen so that Tewkesbury's treasures could be safely packed up.

Burke dispatched a groom to Master Gore at Deerhurst, telling him what to expect, and sent messages to all the tenant farmers to bring their hay wagons. Then he helped the servants carry furniture from the chambers and roll up the priceless carpets. It took two days to strip the tapestries from the walls, the velvet drapes from the high windows, and to wrap the valuable artifacts gathered from around the world, for transportation to Deerhurst. Hour after hour, wagons went back and forth, until Tewkesbury Castle was almost empty. With Nan's help, Rosamond packed her gowns and Rodger's fashionable garments from the great wardrobe. When they were done, she gazed about the master bedchamber. The great carved bed was gone, as well as the ebony tables, covered with Spanish leather; the only thing remaining was a feather mattress that lay on the floor, and it would have to be left.

In the courtyard, Nan climbed into the wagon with Chirk, and Rosamond handed her the pups. "I'd feel much better if you came too," Nan insisted, her lips pressed together in disapproval.

"I shall be perfectly all right with Master Burke. You go and make sure our beds are set up. I promise to follow you shortly. While the last wagon is being loaded, I must walk through the chambers and make sure we have left nothing of value."

As Rosamond climbed the stairs she became aware of how much her back had begun to ache. Up until now, she had been too busy to think about the nagging pain. She told herself that tonight she would lie in a tub of hot water to relieve it. Suddenly she remembered the Viking bathing tub. She hurried down to the courtyard, where Master Burke and the cart driver were loading the last wagon. "We've forgotten the red bathing tub! Do you have room for it?"

"Plenty of room. It can go right up top and we'll tie it down," they assured her.

Rosamond held the horse's harness while the two men went back into Tewkesbury. They carried out the tub, and Master Burke held it on his shoulders while the driver climbed up on the wagon. She was amazed at how easily the driver hauled it atop the other furnishings and fastened it securely, but then all of a sudden he lost his footing and came crashing down onto the courtyard flag stones.

Rosamond and her steward knelt down to examine the man as he rolled about in agony. "He's broken his leg!" she cried. "This is my fault!"

"It needs splinting, which is best done at Deerhurst. I can drive the wagon," Burke assured her as he lifted the injured man onto the cart.

"Hurry! You can bring the wagon back for me when you have attended to his injury."

As Rosamond watched them leave, she felt badly that her bathing tub had been the cause of the accident. The upsetting incident made her feel dizzy, and she knew she must sit down and rest. Slowly she walked inside and sat down on the stairs. A knifelike pain stabbed into her back, going all the way through to the front, contracting the muscles of her abdomen. Rosamond knew her labor had begun, even as an inner voice cried out. *It's too soon, it's too soon!* Panic gripped her as the emptiness of the castle echoed about her and she realized she was completely alone.

When her pain subsided, she tried to calm herself. *I'm only two miles from Deerburst . . . I'll be able to walk.* She stood up and walked to the iron-studded castle door. Then the wrenching pain came again, so swiftly it almost cut her in half, and she knew she couldn't make it to the stables, let alone all the way to Deerhurst. She clung to the oaken door to prevent herself from falling, then, when the pain subsided once more, she crawled back to the stairs.

Rosamond loved this baby beyond reason. She wrapped her arms about her belly protectively, having no fear for herself but only for the survival of her child. How ironic it would be if she saved all her husband's treasures, but in doing so, lost the thing that was most precious of all! She knew the task of removing Tewkesbury's furnishings to the safety of Deerhurst had brought on early labor, and asked herself why she had done it. The answer was amazingly simple. These things were precious to Rodger, and Rodger was precious to her!

It was like a revelation to Rosamond. She had continually denied that she loved him because she was afraid to admit it. But now she realized that all the denials in the world could not stop love. It had insinuated itself inside her, filling her heart and her soul until her very being overflowed with love for Rodger de Leyburn and for his child that flourished within her. Fear clutched at her heart. To love someone was to lose them!

No! Rosamond vowed, *not this time! I will fight to my last breath to save this child!* She remembered the feather mattress upstairs, and managed to crawl up two more stone steps before the next pain slashed into her. When it eased, she rested, but she was panting and damp with exertion. Somehow she found the strength to climb to the bend in the stairs, where the stone slab was larger than the others, but the next agonizing pain exhausted her and she lay down.

She bit her lips to stop the tears from falling when she thought of Nan and of a castle filled with capable women, all proficient as midwives. Then she remembered the lovely bayberry she had gathered to ease the pain of childbirth, and an unbidden tear rolled down her face. She dashed it away with an impatient hand. *I need no bayberry!* But then a hard contraction turned her body rigid, and she cried out, "Oh God, I do need it, I do!"

Time seemed to stand still for Rosamond. It seemed as if hours had passed, yet no one came to look for her. She had aided enough women during childbirth to know that she was in hard labor and the head of the baby should be presenting itself. She pressed down on her distended belly and felt the child's head was not in the proper position. She knew she needed help, but she also knew she would not get it. Vivid pictures of tragic births she had attended at Kenilworth flooded her mind, then the more recent memory of the dead foal that Nimbus had delivered haunted her. She pushed the images away, determined that Death would not cheat her. Fervently she began to pray, remembering a few words of a psalm: "For He shall give His angels charge over thee, to keep thee in all thy ways." Her words turned into a scream as a crescendo of pain engulfed her and mercifully swept her beyond consciousness.

Anxious to return to Tewkesbury, Rodger de Leyburn outdistanced his knights as well as his squire Griffin, who had been put in charge of transporting a large wooden cradle carved with lions. De Leyburn was glad he had attended Parliament, for it had confirmed all his suspicions. It had been well attended by commoners, and he had counted over a hundred members of the clergy, but only a scant twenty barons had shown up to offer Simon de Montfort their support. King Henry had been there, propped up like a puppet, but he was so aged and frail, he was only a shell of his former self.

As Rod rode into Tewkesbury's bailey, he lifted his visor and looked around, shocked to find it empty. When no grooms rushed out to aid him, apprehension gripped him. Had Tewkesbury been attacked and raided? An eerie silence hung over the castle, clearly warning him that much was amiss. When an agonizing scream shattered the silence, Rod drew his sword and began to run.

The chambers were empty of people and furnishings, and he could not comprehend why this was so. He started up the stairs, and then he saw her. "Mother of Christ, Rosamond!" He dropped his sword and threw off his helm, then he gathered her into his arms and lifted her off the cold stone landing. She opened her eyes and moaned his name in agony. Only then did he realize she was in labor. "Hush, love . . . I'm here, I'm here."

Rodger de Leyburn was furious at the servants for leaving Rosamond alone, but he had no time for anger at the moment and resolutely set it aside. He carried her to their chamber, astonished to find it empty, and laid her gently on the feather mattress. Firmly pushing away the panic he felt closing in on him, he spoke to her calmly, softly. "I'll help you . . . we'll do this together."

She gripped his hands, digging her nails into his flesh, and he knew the torment she suffered. Then her hands went slack as she spun down into the vortex. "Rosebud, don't leave me!" The command was so sharp, her eyelids fluttered open, then closed again. Rod's mouth went dry as he saw his child's buttocks and knew it was coming arse-first. Some instinct guided him to make a swift decision. With two fingers of each hand, he pressed down and back on her belly as firmly as he could.

Rosamond screamed, no longer drifting in and out of consciousness, and his heart was sore that he added to her travail, but miraculously he had manipulated the baby into a more normal birth position. When he saw the head, he ordered, "Push, love, push!" She did as he bid her, but it was agonizingly slow. He talked her through the long, drawn-out ordeal, encouraging, praising, cajoling, and when she was ready to give up, Rod urged, "Show me your anger, Rosamond!"

Suddenly his child was in his hands, its cord wrapped about its neck. With shaking fingers he untwisted the cord, terrified that he would have to tell Rosamond that her baby was dead. *Be calm, be calm!* he told himself as he gently squeezed the cord attached to the child. All at once the baby took its first breath, and Rodger laughed with relief. He had a knife to cut the cord, and a ribbon from Rosamond's shift to tie it off, but he was in no hurry; his hands were shaking too much.

His knights arrived at Tewkesbury at almost the same time that Master Burke and Nan returned, looking for Rosamond. Nan was the first to discover him, kneeling beside his wife, with his son in his hands. Nan quickly tied off the cord and Rodger cut it with his knife, then he gently laid the baby in Rosamond's loving arms. Nan rushed off to get water to cleanse the new mother and child, and when she returned, Rodger joined his steward and his men, who waited below. "What the devil happened here, Burke?"

"Alyce de Clare, Countess of Gloucester, brought news that the queen had decided to confiscate Tewkesbury and all your goods were to be seized. Lady Rosamond immediately ordered that everything of value be taken to Deerhurst for safekeeping."

A foul oath dropped from Rodger's lips. "The queen has no authority to confiscate property! It is Simon de Montfort who rules England at the moment."

"Then shall we move everything back, Sir Rodger?"

"The people and the ordinary furnishings can be moved back, but perhaps Rosamond was wise to remove Tewkesbury's treasures, since Earl Simon has ordered that all royal castles be placed in his hands."

A baby's cry came from above and the men raised their heads in disbelief. Rod flashed them a grin. "I have a son! Griffin, you'd best bring up that cradle." The men cheered and a dozen eager hands hoisted the cradle and headed up the stairs, while others lit torches against the gathering darkness.

Nan met the men at the door of the bedchamber. "They will need a bed, and linen, and food, and—"

Rodger held up his hands. "Tonight, we need nothing, save each other." He stepped across the threshold and firmly closed the door. Secing Rosamond with his son at her breast brought a great lump to his throat.

She gave him a tremulous smile. "Rod, thank you for coming, I needed your strength," she whispered.

He shook his head. "You were far stronger than I." Rodger picked up his riding cloak and tucked it about her, then he undressed and lay down beside her. With one finger, he gently touched the baby's dark hair. "Thank you for giving me a son, Rosamond. I kiss your heart."

"I love you, Rodger de Leyburn."

He brushed his lips against her temple. "My sweetheart, I've known that for a long time." With their child nestled between them, de Leyburn knew that tonight, he was the luckiest man on earth.

TWENTY-FIVE

At Hereford Castle, Lord Edward was on the best of terms with the young men who guarded him. He was a model prisoner who gave his cousin, young Henry de Montfort, no cause for suspicion. In their childhood, they had been playmates, and their friendship had lasted all their lives. Henry had received his knighthood at the hands of Lord Edward, whom he greatly admired, and he totally trusted him to honor his agreement to be held hostage.

But, in truth, Edward Plantagenet was filled with such a consuming fire to take up arms and vanquish the man who now ruled England that he was determined to escape Hereford and join his friends who were gathering a force only a few miles away. Edward, Henry, and their attendants spent each afternoon in an open meadow outside the castle, riding their horses for exercise. The high-spirited young men often organized races to alleviate their boredom, and each day Edward watched the woods and waited for a signal.

When it came, Edward was ready. He spurred his horse forward, easily outdistancing both Henry de Montfort and the attendants who guarded him. Just inside the woods, Lincoln de Warenne and his men awaited him with fresh mounts, and it was impossible for Henry de Montfort to prevent the prince from escaping with his heavily armed escort. They rode directly to the castle of Wigmore, where Mortimer's wife, Maud, awaited the royal fugitive and de Warenne with food, clothes, and warm hospitality. Although Wigmore was only twenty miles from Hereford, it was in wild border country, which made it a safe haven. Under cover of darkness, they rode north to Ludlow Castle on the banks of the River Jug, where the royal army was being gathered.

At Tewkesbury, Rodger de Leyburn was content to fill his days with domestic affairs while he waited for Edward's inevitable escape from Hereford. Rod knew it would be only a matter of time, and he took advantage of the respite to enjoy his wife and new son.

Rosamond quickly recovered from her ordeal, and basked in the attention her husband lavished upon her. It was clear to everyone around them that they were in love, for the pair, seldom apart from each other, spent most of their time talking, touching, whispering, and laughing. Rod had fallen into the habit of carrying Rosamond down to the hall each night, after he watched her feed their son and rock him to sleep in the carved cradle.

When Nan arrived to watch over the sleeping baby, she rolled her eyes as Rodger picked up Rosamond to carry her down to dinner. "I can walk," Rosamond protested, but Rodger held her possessively. In the hall, he sat her down beside him on the dais, seemingly oblivious to the grins of his knights.

Rosamond blushed. "Rod, I have legs," she murmured, "perfectly good legs."

He nuzzled her ear. "Mmm, I know. Have you any notion how many times I pictured them while you were playing the ice maiden? When I actually saw them, I couldn't believe how long they were. They are what made me fall in love with you."

She gave him a provocative look. "I thought it was my hair." She tossed the golden mane back over her shoulder and watched the green fire spark in his eyes.

"That too." He reached out and caught a tress between his fingers. "After I take you upstairs and undress you, I'm going to brush it until it falls in waves about your naked body. Then I'm going to wrap myself in it while you wind those long silken legs about me."

The lovers shared the same wine goblet, aching for the moment when the meal was over and they could withdraw to the privacy of their chamber. The moment their door closed, Rosamond was in Rod's arms, pledging her love and her trust to her beloved husband.

The next evening, just as the sun set, a lone rider brought the message that Rodger de Leyburn had been awaiting. Rosamond graciously showed the man every hospitality, seating him in the place of honor next to her husband at the evening meal and asking Master Burke to plenish a guest chamber. When she and Rodger were at last alone, she questioned him. "Is it news about Lord Edward?"

Rod did not want to deceive her. "Yes," he said quietly.

"The messenger is Mortimer's man . . . Has Edward escaped?"

Rod was surprised at how much she perceived. "Yes," he acknowledged.

"So, it begins." She lifted his hand and rubbed her cheek against it. "Thank you for trusting me enough to tell me."

Rod cupped her cheek with the palm of his hand. "I have complete trust in you, Rosamond. I believe in your strength, your ability, and your love. I do not have a moment's hesitation in entrusting our child to you when I go off to battle, even knowing I might not return. I trust you to guard him and guide him for the rest of your life." Tenderly he brushed a tear from her cheek, with his thumb. "The question is, do you trust me?"

The only times Rosamond had trusted him were when Fate had given her no choice to do otherwise, and yet he had saved her life both times. "I do," she pledged. "You once told me that if I gave you my trust, you would never betray it, and you never have."

"Tomorrow, I ride to Gloucester. Gilbert has agreed to meet with Lord Edward; I'm confident he will join us."

Rosamond lay secure in his arms all night, knowing that dawn would part them. When Rodger arose, he did not awaken her, but when the bed turned cold and empty, Rosamond roused and flew to the window. He was already mounted and ready to depart, and she knew there was no time to go down to the courtyard. She watched him pause and look up at their high window, and the heaviness of her spirit dissipated as he placed two fingers against his lips, then pressed them to his heart.

At Gloucester, Alyce de Clare was chagrined that her young husband Gilbert treated her with cold indifference. She had arrived when he was away for a few days, and by the time he returned, she had made herself at home, issuing her demands to the kitchen staff and treating the castle servants like dirt beneath her feet. Gilbert confronted her immediately. "Madam, you will limit your orders to your own women; you have no authority here at Gloucester."

"But I am your wife. . . . I am the Countess of Gloucester!" she protested.

"Are you indeed? I don't recall the marriage being consummated. Remember, Alyce, you are here on my sufferance." He glared into her black eyes until she submitted and lowered her lashes.

After that, Alyce changed her tactics and became all-submissive. Most days, Gilbert was absent from the castle, but when he returned in the evening, she tried to engage his attention by dressing and acting in a seductive manner. She was determined to lure him to bed her and consummate the marriage. If she could give him an heir, her position would be secure. When Gilbert remained indifferent to her, Alyce doubled her efforts.

As Rodger de Leyburn traveled through the Forest of Dean on his way to Gloucester, he saw that Gilbert was gathering a great force of armed men. When he arrived at the castle, Gilbert welcomed the news that Lord Edward had escaped, and readily agreed to accompany Rodger and meet with the heir to the throne at Ludlow.

"News travels fast," Gilbert observed. "I soon learned how few barons attended Simon de Montfort's great Parliament!"

"I am sure he was shocked when you did not arrive, Gilbert."

"After the shabby way I have been treated, he should not be shocked! I expect him any day at Gloucester, demanding the reason why I wasn't in London to support him."

"And if he does come, he will see that Gloucester is an armed camp. It is a considerable show of power, Gilbert."

"It will show him that he does not hold the preponderance of power without me, and I predict the numbers will double when word spreads that Edward has escaped."

At supper, when Alyce joined them in the dining hall, she took the seat next to Rodger, as if they were still intimate friends. It occurred to her that perhaps she could make use of Rodger de Leyburn's visit to make Gilbert jealous.

"Countess," Rod murmured politely, though in actuality he wanted to choke the bitch for the havoc she had wreaked at Tewkesbury. He held his tongue, wanting no trouble with hot-tempered Gilbert.

"Has your wife made you a father yet?" She toyed with his wine goblet, provocatively running her finger around its rim.

"As a matter of fact, I have a son." Rod moved his goblet away.

"Congratulations, Rodger, that's wonderful news!" Gilbert raised his wine in a salute.

Alyce de Clare placed her hand on Rod's sleeve, caressing his arm beneath his doublet. "It takes a virile man to produce a son; are you not envious, Gilbert?"

"I am envious indeed of his lovely wife, Rosamond."

With a provocative finger, Alyce traced a pattern on Rod's velvet-covered chest while she gave Gilbert a teasing glance from beneath her lashes. "Perhaps you should ask Rod to give you a lesson in how to go about the business of making an heir."

Gilbert's face turned bright red. He withdrew his dagger and thrust it into the wood of the trestle table in front of Alyce. "Touch him again, and you lose your fingers!"

Alyce jumped up in alarm. "Oh! How dare you threaten me with violence? Rod, do you not see how he treats me? I will not sit here and suffer such abuse!" She swept from the hall, and her attendant ladies followed her.

For once, Rodger de Leyburn was at a loss for words to smooth over the explosive situation. "Gilbert, I apologize—"

"Nay, my friend, it is I who apologize for subjecting you to such an unseemly display. The French slut knows no better." Within minutes, Gilbert was discussing their journey to Ludlow in the morning, clearly demonstrating to Rodger that the woman meant absolutely nothing to him.

Before Gilbert retired for the night, he sought out Alyce in her chamber. "I am leaving just after dawn. When I return, I want you gone from Gloucester. I intend to put you aside as my wife; you are unfit to be the mother of my children."

She ran to him and placed her hands on his chest in

supplication. "Gilbert, I swear I was never unfaithful to you with Rodger de Leyburn—I hate the arrogant swine!"

"Woman, it matters not to me that you have slept with others; it gives me the legal right to put you aside."

"Divorce? You cannot divorce me, I am the Countess of Gloucester!" Alyce protested frantically.

"Divorce or death," Gilbert said grimly. "One way or another, I do intend to be rid of you."

The last person in the world Rosamond expected to see at Tewkesbury again was Alyce de Clare. When a stone-faced Master Burke announced the arrival of the Countess of Gloucester, Rosamond handed her son to Nan and asked her to take him upstairs. Then she swept out to the courtyard to confront the woman she detested. To Rosamond's great consternation, Alyce burst into tears the moment she saw her.

"Whatever is amiss?" Rosamond asked warily.

"Lady de Leyburn . . . Rosamond . . . I must beg your hospitality."

Rosamond's gaze traveled from Alyce to her forlorn female attendants and the packhorses laden with baggage.

"It will only be for one night . . . have pity!" Alyce cried.

Since the sun was already setting and Rosamond could see the women could travel no farther that night, she said, "You had better come inside." She signaled the grooms who had come forward to take the horses into the stables. "Master Burke, please have the servants plenish chambers for the ladies." She led them into the spacious hall and offered them wine.

Alyce drained her cup and, pacing the chamber dramatically, began her diatribe. "My husband has thrown me out and forbidden me to return! I have done *nothing*, absolutely *nothing*, to deserve such cruel treatment!

Rosamond, you know he has a temper of fire! He threatened to *kill* me, and you know Gilbert's temper helped cause his father's death! He has sworn to set me aside as his wife. . . . I will no longer be the Countess of Gloucester!"

"What started all the trouble?" Rosamond asked, not unkindly.

Alyce dashed away her tears and hissed, "It was that lecherous de Leyburn! Gilbert and I were very happy until your husband arrived and made advances to me—"

"Alyce, that is a lie!" Rosamond was furious at the accusation. "You make advances to every man you see. Rodger would not do such a thing—he knows too much about you! My husband loves me, and I trust him with my life!"

Alyce began to laugh hysterically. "Love? Trust? You poor deluded wretch. Every man breathing is a selfish, greedy, ruthless swine. Every man is created evil!"

"Not Rodger de Leyburn," Rosamond said firmly.

"Your innocence makes me spew! It was Rodger de Leyburn who killed your brother Giles!"

"You lying bitch!" Rosamond's cheeks burned with anger, and her eyes flashed their warning.

"Rod hated Giles—they were bitter rivals in the tournaments."

Rosamond drew back her hand and slapped Alyce full in the face, then Alyce lunged at Rosamond, digging her nails into Rosamond's cheek, leaving five bloody scratches. "Months before they jousted at Ware, your brother left the guard off his lance—it pierced Rod's thigh. The wound left him scarred for life!"

Rosamond doubled her fist and swung hard at Alyce, knocking her to her knees. "Shut your lying mouth! You are jealous and seek to destroy my happy marriage to Sir Rodger."

Alyce sneered. "The marriage that brought him Pershore and your brother's castle of Deerhurst? De

Leyburn plotted Giles's death because it doubled your property! The avaricious swine didn't wait one day to ask Edward to betroth him to the little heiress!"

Rosamond's hand, about to deliver another blow, fell to her side as Alyce's words sank in. "How do you know all this?"

"I was with Edward and his companions after they jousted at Ware. I heard them plot to cover it up as an accident!"

Rosamond drew herself up to her full height and lifted her chin proudly. "I do not believe one word of these vicious lies. You may remain here tonight, only because I take pity on the women who must serve you. Tomorrow, when I come downstairs, you had better be long gone from Tewkesbury, or I shall set the dogs on you."

When Rosamond entered her bedchamber, Nan was alarmed. "My lamb, your face is bleeding!"

"It is nothing, Nan." *My heart is bleeding.*

"Let me bathe it for you."

"No, Nan, give me the baby and leave me . . . I wish to be alone." She sat down in a carved rocking chair, holding her son to her heart. *Lies! Lies! Lies!* The word repeated itself in her brain.

But was it really true? She pushed the thought away, horrified at herself. She began to rock to soothe her agitated thoughts, and slowly, gradually, a measure of calm descended on her. She unbuttoned her tunic and offered her baby son her breast. She smiled down tenderly as he began to suckle, bringing them both comfort.

The baby fell asleep at her breast, but she rocked him for another hour. Then she gently laid him in his cradle and tucked his blanket securely about him. Finally, Rosamond undressed and climbed into the wide bed. She lay there for a long time, staring into the darkness, then, trustingly, she laid her hand on her husband's empty pillow. Rosamond knew that Alyce de Clare had to be lying, for if Rodger had killed Giles, her life would be shattered forever.

A wave of stark terror swept over Rosamond, snatching her breath away. She began to run the moment she saw the dark horse and rider, knowing instinctively they would pursue her. Relentlessly! The rider was faceless. All she knew was that he was dark; it was the horse she feared most. It was huge, black, and terrifying.

An icy shiver slithered down her spine. Her pale golden hair tumbled wildly about her shoulders as she pulled her skirts high, baring long, slim legs in a desperate attempt to escape being trampled by the cruel hooves. Her lungs felt as if they would burst as she gasped for just one more breath that would carry her to safety. Her pulse hammered inside her eardrums deafening her as she turned to look over her shoulder. Rosamond's eyes widened in horror and a scream was torn from her throat as she saw the black forelegs rise above her. Suddenly, she saw the face of the rider. He had the Devil's own dark beauty with jet black hair and green eyes! Then, helplessly, she tumbled beneath the murderous hooves.

Rosamond's eyes flew open. Slowly she became aware of her surroundings. She was lying in her bed, her hair a wild tangle, her night rail twisted about her body so that her long legs were bared. She let out a ragged sob and sat up. She knew she had had her trampling dream; its terror lingered all about her. But this time she had seen the face of Death, and it was Rodger de Leyburn's.

Two days later as Rodger arrived back at Tewkesbury with Gilbert de Clare at his side, his eyes rose to the castle parapets. When he saw the figure of Rosamond, his arm lifted in greeting, and he anticipated her running down to the courtyard to warmly welcome him home. When she did not come, he assumed that she had seen Gilbert and as a dutiful chatelaine was preparing for their guest.

When he entered the hall, he found her beside Master Burke waiting to greet their visitor. In a jubilant mood,

Rod picked her up, swung her about, and gave her a lingering kiss of greeting.

Rosamond stiffened. "My lord, please."

"No need to be all formal in front of Gilbert; he's come to see our beautiful son!"

Rosamond dipped a curtsy to the redheaded youth she had known since he was a child. "My lord earl, welcome to Tewkesbury." She gave him a formal kiss of greeting. "I'll go up and see if the baby is awake. Please make yourself comfortable."

When Rodger followed her upstairs, Rosamond's heart sank, for she did not want to be alone with him. For two days she had walked about in a trancelike state, totally preoccupied with the terrible accusations Alyce de Clare had made. One minute she totally rejected the charges as heinous lies, the next minute, a shadow of suspicion clouded her thoughts. She told herself that the instant she saw him, she would know the truth, and if not, she would confront him. But because he had Gilbert with him, she could not.

Rodger's arms enfolded her from behind. "Sweetheart, I missed you sorely, but the meeting between Edward and Gilbert was a complete success! He's agreed to join forces with us, and word is spreading like wildfire that Edward has escaped. I'll tell you later how cleverly it was done."

As he lifted his son from the cradle, the look of love and tenderness that suffused his dark face made Rosamond's heart turn over. His hands were so gentle as he held his child, she told herself that it was impossible for those same hands to have killed Giles. Once more Rosamond assured herself that Alyce de Clare had deliberately lied to her.

They descended together to show off their prized possession, and Gilbert de Clare was suitably impressed, declaring that he would be the child's godfather and suggesting that Gilbert should be one of the boy's names, even though the infant wasn't a redhead.

After the evening meal, when Rosamond took her son upstairs to feed him, Rodger remained below with his guest. She hoped that they would talk late into the night and that she would be asleep when Rodger came up. She felt numb and emotionally drained, knowing that the lies Alyce had told her were erecting a barrier between herself and her husband.

When he finally came into their chamber, Rosamond pretended to be asleep. Through veiled lashes, she watched him stand over the cradle for a long time, then he gently rocked his son. Listening to his murmured endearments, she might have fallen in love with him all over again if her heart had not been encased in icy dread.

She could tell that he was trying not to disturb her when he climbed into bed, and when she heard his even breathing, she let out a sigh of relief and finally succumbed to slumber.

Rosamond awoke, screaming. In an instant, Rodger was awake, holding her securely against his heart. As she fought him, he tried to calm her. "It's all right, love, I'm here, I'm here!"

A ragged sob escaped her lips. "I had the trampling dream."

Rodger brushed back the tangled hair from her face. "Tell me," he murmured tenderly.

"I saw his face clearly. . . . The rider was *you*!"

Rosamond saw the look of raw pain and regret in his eyes before he quickly masked it. It was a look that told her something he dreaded had come to pass.

Twenty-six

When she awoke in the morning, Rodger was already gone from their chamber. She reasoned that he and Gilbert would break their fast together, since they would have so many plans and decisions to make before Gilbert left for Gloucester. During the night, when she had awakened screaming from the trampling dream, she had avoided a confrontation and allowed her husband to comfort her, but now in the clear light of day, Rosamond realized she could not go on in uncertainty. She must prove to herself that Alyce de Clare had been lying.

She searched for Griffin and found him at the forge with many other men-at-arms, who were repairing armor and sharpening their weapons. She beckoned to him, and they walked away from the others.

"May I help you, my lady?"

"I hope so, Griffin; I know you have been with Sir Rodger for many years." She hesitated for only a second. "He is loath to speak of the wound on his thigh . . . Did he receive it in battle?"

"Nay, my lady, he was wounded in a tournament. Tilting is extremely dangerous; he was disabled for many weeks."

"So it was a lance wound?"

"Aye, my lady."

Rosamond dreaded the next question, and dreaded its

answer even more. "Was it my brother Giles who wielded the lance?"

Griffin flushed. "Aye, my lady."

"Thank you for telling me the truth," she murmured. Then, as if in a trance, she walked back to the castle. She was in time to bid Gilbert goodbye as he and his knights clattered from the bailey. Rosamond watched Rodger close the distance between them. She could feel his excitement and his pent-up energy for the challenge that lay ahead. She looked up at him as he stood beside her, and knew these were momentous times for him and for the prince whom he served. The coming events would likely change the history of England, yet to Rosamond, none of it mattered at that moment.

"I must speak with you, Rodger."

He flashed his dark grin. "Can it not wait, sweetheart?"

"No, my lord, it cannot. Please come with me to the solar, where we may be private."

Her tone warned him of her solemn mood. He hoped she would not beg him to abandon his plans. He was aware of the danger, welcomed it even, but he knew of Rosamond's deep-seated fears about death.

"Did you kill my brother?" The words came out on a whisper, hanging in the air.

The question stunned him. It was the last thing he was expecting, yet hadn't he been expecting her to ask him this very question ever since she was twelve? "Bones of Christ," he swore, a look of raw pain in his eyes. "Rosamond, it was an accident!"

He watched her recoil from him, watched the color drain from her face along with her hope, and it was like a knife twisting in his gut. "It was an accident . . . I swear it!"

He wished she would fly at him and try to scratch out his eyes, wished she would rain vitriolic curses upon his head, wished she would vent her fury by kicking, biting, and screaming. But she did none of these things. Rosamond stood silently, almost drowning as his horrific admission hit her like a tidal wave.

Rodger took a step toward her.

"Don't touch me. Don't even come close." She stared at him with accusing eyes, as if he had given her a death blow.

"Don't you believe me?" he demanded.

"I don't know what I believe." *God in Heaven,* she thought, *I want to believe you because I love you!*

"Jousting is a dangerous sport. Deadly accidents happen too often. That is why tournaments were outlawed. The king forbade Edward, but we wouldn't listen; we were mad for the lists. That day at Ware, a socket came off the end of a lance. . . . Giles died instantly. Rosamond, you must believe it was an accident."

"Why? So I won't suspect you killed him out of revenge for the injury he did you . . . or greed? If it was an accident, why didn't you tell me the truth?"

"Rosamond, I swear to you I was amazed that you did not know the truth. At the time of the jousting accident, it was no secret that Giles died by my hand. By the time I found out that you thought he had been trampled, I did not dare risk telling you the truth. I would have lost you."

"And lost the properties that you killed to obtain?"

"That is a bloody wicked and cruel thing to say, Rosamond."

"Was it not bloody wicked and cruel to make me fall in love with you and agree to marry you, knowing my brother died by your hand?"

"I would give anything in the world to bring him back, but I cannot. Either you believe me when I swear it was an accident, or you do not. Either you trust me, or you do not. *You* must decide, Rosamond."

She lifted her chin. "I would like to believe it was an accident, but I am torn. I need time to think about this . . . away from you."

"I shall have Master Burke take you to Deerhurst."

"Deerhurst is not nearly far enough away, and it

would be too painful to stay at the castle that was to have been Giles's home. I shall go to Pershore." She spoke with the hauteur of a queen.

He bowed curtly to her, not telling her there was no need for her to go anywhere, since he would be riding far and wide, marshaling men, weapons, and horses for the impending conflict. Instead, Rodger immediately arranged a safe escort to take Rosamond and their son to Pershore.

He was not a man who indulged in introspection, but when she was gone, he felt empty inside. He saw himself through her eyes as he examined his role in her brother's death, and he experienced her pain. Rod felt so wretchedly guilty, he almost rode after her to beg her forgiveness.

His unbending pride, however, prevented him from doing so. It would not allow him to beg. In hindsight, Rod admitted he should have told her that Giles Marshal had died from a lance thrust, rather than from being trampled by a destrier. But the accusations that Rosamond had hurled at him were foul indeed. How could she think him petty enough to kill Giles in retaliation for the wound he had taken in the thigh? Far worse, how could she accuse him of murdering her brother so that she would inherit his castle of Deerhurst?

Fury rose up within him, almost blinding him. How dare she leave him? How dare she take his son from him? He should go and drag her back by the hair, lay down the law to her, show her that her place was beside him, her lord and master, whom she had vowed to love, honor, and obey, *no matter what*!

Once again, his pride prevented him from going after her. He did not want her unless she gave him her trust. Rodger loved his wife with all his heart, deeply, abidingly. He must trust her to sort out her tangled emotions and listen to her own heart. If Rosamond loved him, she would trust his word that Giles's death had been an accident.

* * *

Simon de Montfort had hoped to bring peace to England when he called the Great Parliament. Suddenly, however, things began to go wrong, and he was beset by problems on all sides. A new pontiff by the name of Pope Clement had been elected, who was openly and actively hostile to Simon de Montfort. Clement issued a papal bull excommunicating Earl Simon and backing the rightful king of England. This of course greatly increased the threat of invasion.

Simon was shaken by the low number of barons who attended the Parliament he had called. Only those with landholdings in the East came, while the western barons stayed away in droves. The Marcher barons were in open rebellion, and he knew he must strike at their base of operations and put down their insurrection before the western barons joined the revolt. He cursed the day he had agreed to Edward's pledge that he would remain as hostage if the Marchers could go free. He had underestimated the shrewdness of the heir to the throne.

De Montfort was counting on the support of Gilbert de Clare, Earl of Gloucester, to help put down the revolt of the rebellious border barons, and once they crossed the River Severn into Wales, Simon would also establish contact with Llewelyn, who had promised him hundreds of Welsh archers.

Since Eleanor de Montfort and her household had traveled to London for the Great Parliament, Simon now decided to send her to Dover Castle with a force of eighty knights, commanded by Sir Rickard de Burgh. This would ensure peace in the eastern counties, keep the Cinque Ports loyal, and make sure no aid for the king was brought in from France. With his son Simon commanding the forces of Surrey and Sussex to keep peace in the South, de Montfort and his own men-at-arms headed west to bring the rebel Marcher barons to heel.

When Simon de Montfort arrived at the city of Gloucester, the castle looked like an armed camp; moreover, he found Gilbert de Clare in a truculent mood. The fiery-tempered youth was incensed that the de Montfort family held all the power in England. That night, the sky was lit up by the fires of armed horsemen who were camped on the wooded hills surrounding Gloucester, and Simon realized that if he did not appease Gilbert the Red, they would be at war. Simon immediately promised Gilbert a governing role, but the young earl remained uncommitted.

The next day, Henry de Montfort rode in with the mortifying news that Lord Edward had escaped from Hereford. Although Simon berated his son for his lax vigilance, he had feared in his bones that Prince Edward Plantagenet could not be kept caged. He immediately issued his soldiers marching orders for Hereford, for if he allowed Edward to remain free, men everywhere would flock to his cause and civil war would erupt again. Before they could depart, however, Simon's spies brought him the urgent news that John de Warenne, Earl of Surrey, had landed at Pembroke with a huge fighting force. Knowing the Cinque Ports of the east coast were closed to them, they had sailed around England to land on the west coast of Wales.

Now, Simon de Montfort was torn. Should he try to recapture Edward, or should he march into Wales and, with the military aid of his ally Llewelyn, wipe out the forces that had landed at Pembroke? He decided the latter was more pressing and urged Gilbert, Earl of Gloucester, to join him. Gilbert was unfriendly and evasive, and Simon de Montfort realized he could not depend on his support, so before he crossed the River Severn, de Montfort sent urgent instructions to his son Simon to gather the loyal forces of the South and East and bring them to join his own army.

At Ludlow, the royalist army grew larger and stronger each day. Edward Plantagenet, exhilarated with his freedom, was filled with zeal and determination, which was contagious to those who gathered about him. He was a far different man from the impetuous and reckless commander who had fought at the Battle of Lewes. He had learned some bitter lessons on the battlefield, and during his months of imprisonment, he had had little to do but plot revenge and study strategy.

Edward was like a golden god, bursting with energy and filled with a consuming fire to take up arms against his enemy and win back England for the crown. The warlord himself had taught him that battles were won with speed and fury, but Edward now realized that with shrewd strategy and meticulous planning, battles could be won before they were ever fought. First and foremost, your men-at-arms must be well trained and disciplined to take orders. To win, you also needed to choose the battlefield and place your troops in the best position. If you could add the element of surprise, the battle was won!

Rodger de Leyburn's job was to maintain communication between the various groups and factions that supported the crown. Basically, he rode back and forth between Edward at Ludlow and the towns of the western barons, tallying numbers. Amazingly, he found that he need do little recruiting, for the news of Lord Edward's escape had turned the tide so that the whole of the western region was ablaze with martial activity.

Rodger thundered into the bailey of squat Ludlow Castle on his great black destrier, with Griffin at his back. Inside he saw Edward's tall frame bent over a map table as the prince conferred with Lincoln de Warenne. "The Lion and the Lynx, just the two I hoped to find. I've ridden straight from Gilbert in Gloucester, and the news is all good!"

Lincoln poured Rod a tankard of ale to wash the dust of the road from his throat, as Edward clapped his friend on the back.

"Simon de Montfort took his army to Gloucester expecting Gilbert to join him in bringing the Marcher barons to heel. It was at Gloucester he learned of your escape, and he immediately gave the army its orders to march to Hereford." Rod held up his hand when he saw Edward's look of savage anticipation. "Before they could leave, his scouts brought him the news that John de Warenne had landed at Pembroke with a fighting force, and Simon has crossed the Severn into Wales to meet them."

Edward threw back his head and laughed with glee. "The fool! His brain must be addled with age! He has made a tactical mistake crossing into Wales. His first priority should have been *me*! His force is greater than mine at the moment. He should have marched directly north and turned our flank toward the army young Simon commands, trapping us between."

"Our force here in Ludlow may be smaller than his, but you haven't seen the men Gilbert has gathered at Gloucester. The Forest of Dean and every foot of the hills about the city are covered with armed camps. It must have been a terrible shock for Simon de Montfort when Gilbert refused to join him," Rod declared.

"I appreciate the importance of detaching Gilbert of Gloucester from him, and I have you to thank, Rod, for persuading him to switch his allegiance to me."

The swarthy Mortimer stepped into the map room. "Three days ago, your brother John landed at Pembroke with a huge fighting force," he informed Lincoln de Warenne.

"Aye, de Leyburn has just brought the same news. Simon de Montfort has crossed into Wales to move against them," Lincoln said with a worried frown.

Mortimer grinned. "I had scouts posted in Pembroke to lead them north. They are more than halfway to Wigmore and Ludlow. When Simon de Montfort takes his army up the Usk Valley, the hunter will find his quarry has flown."

Edward straightened up and hit his head on a low beam. "Splendor of God, we are going to need bigger headquarters. There is no longer any need for us to skulk in the borders. Since de Montfort has crossed into

Wales, I intend to make this side of the River Severn mine! We will patrol the entire length from Worcester to Gloucester," Edward said decisively.

"In that case, my lord, I had better see what I can do about securing Worcester as our new headquarters." Rod was only half jesting; none in the room doubted his powers of persuasion.

At Pershore, Rosamond saw the results of Rodger's wise decisions everywhere. The entire household was happy and industrious under the caring management of her steward, Hutton, and his wife, Lizzie. The sunshine spilling through the sparkling windows showed that even the corners of the chambers were spotless and the furniture gleamed with polish. The kitchens were immaculate and the stillroom rafters hung with savory herbs.

The young maids were delighted to have a baby in the castle, and begged Rosamond to allow them to bathe him, dress him, and carry him about. Nan supervised them with a watchful eye while she kept the other on Rosamond, who was quiet, pale, and introspective. Nan urged her to spend time outdoors. The gardens were a profusion of late summer blooms, and beyond the trees, the River Avon flowed gently, bringing an air of tranquility to all of Pershore.

Rosamond knew this was the haven she needed to sort out her tangled thoughts and emotions. As she lingered in the solitude of the gardens, her mind went back to the time when she was twelve and she received the terrible news. Rosamond had never dared to do this before; fear and self-protection had prevented her. Now she remembered Lady Eleanor telling her there had been a tragic jousting accident, and that her beloved brother Giles had lost his life. She recalled being too numb with shock to ask questions, but recollected that she had overheard the kitchen servants whispering about dangerous tournaments where challengers were ofttimes trampled by their opponents' destriers. That was when her trampling dreams had begun.

Her grief had been unbearable, and she had been convinced that she had lost her brother because she loved him.

As Rosamond looked back she remembered how kind and compassionate everyone had been to her, and she now understood their reluctance to discuss the bloody details with a twelve-year-old girl. What she did not understand was why she hadn't asked questions and learned the circumstances surrounding the tragedy when she was older. Rosamond realized the answer was lack of courage; it had been easier to blot it out and never speak of it.

Now, as she thought about that day, it came to her how devastating it must have been for Giles's companions to know their reckless disobedience in attending the tournament at Ware had resulted in the death of their friend. How much distress, sorrow, and self-loathing they must have suffered. How sobering it must have been for fifteen-year-old Lord Edward . . . how horrific for Rodger de Leyburn!

Like a revelation, it came to Rosamond that he had betrothed her because he felt responsible for her. Because Giles Marshal had died by his hand, Rodger de Leyburn had stepped forward like a knight-errant to shoulder the responsibility of his friend's young sister. He had felt honor-bound. Then, five years later, when he saw her grown to womanhood, he had become instantly attracted.

Rosamond finally admitted that she too had been instantly attracted to the bold young knight, whose dark beauty was so irresistibly potent. She had rebuffed him because she never again wanted to suffer the wrenching pain of loss. But Rodger de Leyburn would not be denied. He had vowed he would never let her go, and in the end, she had surrendered. Her mind conjured a vision of him that was as vivid as if he stood before her. His powerful body exuded strength, and that was what had first attracted her. She shivered as she thought of the strength of his hands and his wrists, as thick as oak branches from wielding sword and lance.

Giles Marshal had died from a lance thrust, yet those

same hands that had couched the lance had snatched her from the raging river and helped Nimbus to foal twins. She remembered how gentle his hands had been when he had delivered her baby and ended her torture. He had taken one life, but given her back another, and she knew in her heart that Rodger de Leyburn could never commit murder.

As Rosamond's doubt dropped away, her thinking became crystal clear. Though she had fled from Rodger de Leyburn, his presence was ever with her. He walked beside her in the gardens, his hand joined hers when she rocked her son's cradle, and his warmth enveloped her throughout the night. A part of him was with her, whether she was sleeping or awake, and Rosamond realized that what she carried with her was his love.

She was inextricably bound to him, just as love and trust were inextricably bound together. It was amazingly simple. To trust was to love, and to love was to trust. Rosamond acknowledged that she loved Rodger de Leyburn with all her heart and with all her soul; and it followed that if she loved him, she must trust him. He had sworn that Giles's death was accidental, and Rosamond knew she trusted him enough to believe him.

She remembered the raw pain in Rodger's eyes, and realized how difficult it must have been carrying such a secret burden. To have accidentally killed the brother of the woman you loved must have often been unendurable. How he must have longed for her forgiveness, yet dreaded hurting her with the truth.

Rosamond realized that without Rodger she was bereft; with him she was complete. *My life's story is up to me*, she told herself. *I choose happiness!* Miraculously, she was suddenly filled with joy, and she understood that love really was a miracle. She looked down at her baby son, who was sleeping at her feet. She picked him up and kissed him. "I have decided that your name will be Rodger!"

TWENTY-SEVEN

When the royal steward arrived at Worcester Castle, Sir Rodger received his usual warm welcome from the staff, most of whom he had hired himself when he and Lord Edward first returned from Gascony. The exception was the new castellan appointed by Simon de Montfort when he had ordered that all royal castles be surrendered to him. De Leyburn relished the confrontation, and the new castellan soon bowed to the commanding authority of the dark, powerful steward. That night, the man wisely departed, convinced his life would be forfeit if he remained at Worcester Castle one day longer.

Rodger de Leyburn had little time for reflection or even sleep these days, but when all was in readiness to receive Edward and his growing army, he stood alone on the battlements of Worcester Castle and looked longingly toward Pershore, only seven miles away. He tried not to let his thoughts dwell on Rosamond, but in quiet moments like this, it wasn't just his body that ached for her, it was his heart.

The desire to see her, hear her laugh and sing to their baby, enfold her in his arms, touch her golden hair, and brush his lips against her satin smooth skin became so intense, he clenched his fists and smote the stone parapet before him. He decided that Pershore was far too close for him to keep his distance; he would go to her now.

Before he reached the stables, however, doubts assailed him. Never again did he want to see Rosamond recoil from him; never again did he want to watch the color drain from her face along with her hope. What if her lovely violet eyes were filled with accusation when she looked at him? What if her lips trembled at the unbearable pain he had caused her? What if her heart was closed to him forever?

Rosamond had said she needed time alone to sort out her thoughts, so reluctantly Rod resolved to give her the privacy she needed. He knew their future together hinged on what Rosamond decided, and he was loath to jeopardize that. Crushing down his longing to ride to her, he summoned Griffin and sent him off to Pershore with a note inquiring after his son's health. He worded it succinctly, politely, so that it was not intrusive, but at the same time it let Rosamond know that their headquarters were now at Worcester, should she need him for aught.

When Rosamond saw Griffin ride into Pershore's bailey, her heart jumped into her throat with apprehension. If there had been any question about how deeply she loved her husband, the truth was brought home to her when she thought harm had befallen him. When Griffin smiled, she felt her knees wobble with relief.

"Sir Rodger sends you greetings, my lady." Griffin handed her the note and she slipped it into her bodice so that she could read it in private later. It was doubtless a love letter telling her how much he missed her, and that he could no longer live without her. Just the thought of his impassioned words on the folded paper warmed her heart and brought a delicate blush to her cheek.

When a groom came forward to take the squire's horse, Rosamond tucked her arm through Griffin's. "Let me show you the hospitality of Pershore; the place is much improved since you were here last. Both you and your horse must have a well-deserved rest before you undertake the long ride back to Ludlow."

"Nay, my lady, we are now headquartered at Worcester."

"Worcester?" she exclaimed with surprise. "Could my lord not ride the seven miles himself?"

"He is busy from morning till night, my lady. He is Lord Edward's right hand. Sir Rodger is indispensable!"

Rosamond suddenly felt dispensable. In the hall, while Nan was making a fuss over Griffin, Rosamond pulled out the note and read:

> *Kindly inform Griffin of my son's health.*
> *R. Worcester Castle.*

It was so brief, it was insulting. Its tone was so coolly polite, it might have come from a stranger. Rosamond was also offended that he had written "my" son, rather than "our" son. "Griffin has been sent to learn of the baby's welfare," she told Nan. "I shall go and pry him from the hands of the maids so you may inspect him," she said self-righteously to Rodger's squire.

Rosamond returned shortly carrying her son, with two young maids following close upon her heels. She handed the child to a startled Griffin, who had never held a baby in his life. The look of pure panic that suffused his face was so comical, the maids began to giggle. He threw Rosamond such a look of desperate supplication that she took pity on him and laughingly relieved him of his terrifying burden. Her anger at her husband melted away, but she decided to answer him in kind and word the reply to deliberately annoy him. She wrote:

> *Your son thrives! I am amazed that you could spare Griffin from the duties that overburden you, day and night. Worcester and Pershore are so close, that next time you want to know about your son's health, I suggest that you go to the window and look out and I shall hold him up for your inspection! You will be happy to know that I have chosen a name for your son.*

* * *

Rosamond folded the note with satisfaction. She didn't tell him the name she had chosen, of course. He was arrogant enough, and if he wanted to know the name, he would have to come and find out! But before Griffin departed, Rosamond needed to reassure herself that Rodger was in no immediate danger. "I know Lord Edward is gathering an army; do you think the fighting will start soon?"

"There is no danger of that, my lady. Simon de Montfort has taken his army to Glamorganshire in Wales."

Headquartered in Worcester, Edward Plantagenet's army swelled to a formidable size. He was both amazed and gratified at the speed and fury with which royal sentiment had swept the West, but he was determined that this time he would not make the mistake of overconfidence. He spread his forces all along the interior side of the River Severn from Worcester all the way to Gloucester. Then Gilbert de Clare's forces were used to patrol the river from Gloucester all the way down to Bristol, where the river emptied into the Bristol Channel.

The prince was wary and watchful, and he made liberal use of spies and scouts. He knew that Simon de Montfort had to cross the Severn at some point to get back into England, and when he did, Edward intended to be ready for him. He gave orders that all the boats used to cross the river be captured or destroyed. He also dispatched scouts to locate young Simon de Montfort and track the movement of the men-at-arms under his command.

Edward and his lieutenants were gathered around a map table in the war room at Worcester Castle when a courier arrived from Gilbert de Clare. The prince unsealed the dispatch and read it. "Gilbert says Simon de Montfort intended to cross where the Usk and the Wye rivers meet and flow into the Severn, but there were no boats, and when he saw the great force that awaited him on the opposite bank, he had no choice but to turn his army north."

"It is obvious that Bristol was his intended destination," Rod declared. "If he had reached Bristol, he would have dug in and waited for us to come to him."

"Exactly!" Edward agreed. "He would have chosen the battlefield and strategically deployed his men-at-arms to best advantage, as he did at Lewes. Then he would have waited for his son Simon to move against us from the east, and trapped us between the two armies."

"He would have waited in vain." Rodger flashed his dark grin. "Young Simon received orders to meet his father at Kenilworth, and he is moving his troops north at a leisurely pace."

"Splendor of God, I don't know how you do it, and I don't want to know. This gives us the advantage over both armies. The old warlord will head up to Hereford, on the wrong side of the Severn, of course, and with young Simon at Kenilworth, there's no chance in hell of them uniting the baronial forces."

"Not with us squarely between them," John de Warenne agreed. "Our position at Worcester gives us the military advantage."

"My men have been busy," Rodger de Leyburn informed Edward. "Not only have they tallied our own numbers, they have managed to tally the numbers of both baronial armies."

"And?" Edward demanded impatiently.

"With Gilbert de Clare's men, our numbers are greater than the whole of theirs. We will be victorious against either army!"

A great cheer echoed round the war room. Edward hastily wrote an answer to Gilbert de Clare's dispatch, ordering him to bring his men-at-arms to Worcester immediately. When the courier departed, Edward signaled to Rod, and the two men climbed to Worcester's ramparts.

Edward paced the wall, stretching his long legs, then he returned to stand before his friend. "It will be a fight to the death, you know. It is fight and win, or fight and die, and I intend to win, *at any cost.*"

"Are you prepared to kill Simon de Montfort?" Rod asked quietly.

"Oh yes . . . by any means open to me. I just wondered if you—"

"There is no need to ask. I am your man, *no matter what.*"

Edward ran his big hand through his golden hair and spoke reflectively. "Simon is in his fifties, and must be tired of the long struggle, though he is still filled with passion for the cause, and passionate hatred for me."

Rodger nodded. "He is the last of the old chivalrous order."

"He taught me all he knew of war, but I also have my own modern ideas, none of which is chivalrous! It is old-fashioned to rely solely upon cavalry in heavy body armor to fight the battle, while the foot soldiers are left miles behind to handle the baggage carts. Every man in my army is well armed and has been taught to fight. The rules that say that it is unfair to attack at night, and that common soldiers must keep their distance from the mounted knights, are stupid! In war there is only one rule that counts—kill more of your enemy than they kill!"

"Then take their weapons and horses," Rod added grimly.

"Exactly!" Edward said with relish. "When will young Simon arrive at Kenilworth?"

"He has the Earls of Oxford and Suffolk in his train, and at the rate they are lumbering along, it will take at least two more days. Then they will have to spend long hours setting up camp and tents; there is not room for an army of four thousand inside Kenilworth."

"A wager, my friend, that we will be there before them!"

"I have more good sense than to bet against you, my lord, once you have set your mind on a goal."

In the darkness, Rodger de Leyburn and his men waited patiently for Edward Plantagenet's order. Rod knew it would not come until the hour before dawn, when most of the enemy, encamped in the fields around the town of Kenilworth, would be sleeping. As he waited he reviewed the incredible events of the day.

The moment Edward's scouts had spotted Gilbert de Clare's men arriving from Gloucester, Edward had called in the mounted patrols from along the Severn and taken his whole army, numbering about six thousand, out of Worcester, marching them north to Kenilworth. They covered the thirty miles in twelve hours, a feat never before accomplished, and arrived at dusk, just before the unsuspecting enemy. They took cover to watch and wait, heaving a collective sigh of relief when the entire baronial army pitched their tents and made their camp outside the town, rather than behind the impregnable walls of Kenilworth Castle.

With great decisiveness, Edward gave his lieutenants the signal to attack one hour before dawn, and they in turn relayed the order to their men. Rodger de Leyburn donned his helmet, mounted his destrier, then drew his sword and raised it high. It was the signal for which his men had been watching. With Griffin at his back, he thundered down the hill alongside hundreds of other mounted men, and thousands of foot soldiers armed with bills, pikes, and axes, in a surprise attack that caught the enemy completely off-guard.

It was a raid in the dark, rather than a battle. The unexpected attack made it a one-sided slaughter. The sleeping enemy emerged from their tents and either scattered before the onslaught or died where they stood. In the mad foray, coals from the campfires set the tents ablaze, further terrorizing the baronial troops. Hundreds were butchered, while thousands ran, fleeing into the surrounding countryside, or tried to swim Kenilworth's mere in a desperate attempt to reach the sanctuary of the castle.

In an attack, Rodger de Leyburn never kept count of the men he killed. He simply focused on the enemy before him, knowing Griffin covered his back. His sword and his right arm became one bloody weapon, slashing, thrusting, smashing, slicing, piercing, cutting, and stabbing. His left arm held his shield with which he warded off the heavy blows of his enemy's weapons. Tonight, fortunately, few fought back. The mounted man before him was an exception. Their swords clashed and their stirrups touched as their vicious warhorses slid about on the blood-slicked ground. Suddenly, Rodger de Leyburn was close enough to see his enemy's eyes, and he recognized young Simon de Montfort!

Rod stared, and stayed his sword, but the minute he did so, his opponent saw the opening and lunged savagely. Rodger brought up the edge of his shield with a brutal thrust that knocked the sword from Simon's hand. Rodger lifted the noseguard of his helmet to make his identity plain. Young Simon stared in horror, first at the blazing green eyes, then at the dripping sword. "Get to the castle, man!" Rodger roared, then he set his spurs to Stygian and wheeled toward a knight carrying a baronial banner.

By the time the sun came up, it was all over; the baronial forces were completely vanquished. Edward forbade pursuit of those who had fled. He knew he had destroyed the fighting ability of this half of the baronial army, and ordered his lieutenants to gather their troops together. It was an unqualified victory; they had captured all the baronial horses and taken thirteen banners.

As Rodger de Leyburn rode slowly through the camp, assessing their losses and tallying their gains, he was surprised to see the Earl of Oxford sitting on the ground amid the tattered banners. "Whose prisoner are you?"

Oxford's hands trembled visibly as he answered de Leyburn. "I came face-to-face with Prince Edward. He raised his bloody great broadsword and almost decapitated me! Then he gave me a piercing look with those ice-blue eyes, and said, 'I need all my English barons.' He took me prisoner and turned me over to his squire."

"You are a lucky man; Edward intended to give no quarter."

Kenilworth was impregnable and could only be taken by siege, so the captured horses were given to the foot soldiers, and Edward gave the order to return to Worcester without pause or rest. He knew his greatest challenge lay ahead of him, and he intended to be ready for it. The royal troops, buoyed by their victory, raised the captured banners on high.

"How many barons were here?" Edward asked Rodger de Leyburn.

"Thirteen, my lord."

"Fools! Did they not know thirteen is an unlucky number?"

At Pershore, Rosamond waited impatiently for the expected visit from her husband. When he did not come immediately, she was piqued at his neglect. She told herself that even if the stubborn man did not wish to see her, surely he would come to see his son. He was simply taking his own sweet time to deliberately annoy her. Well, she would be damned if she would sit here and wait for him. It was time she rode out to inspect Pershore's tenant farms, and with any luck, she would be out and about her business when the annoying devil arrived!

The next morning, Rosamond fed her baby, tucked him into his cradle, and instructed Nan and the maids to watch over him with special care while she and her steward, Master Hutton, visited her outlying tenant farms. She chose a striking emerald green riding tunic and tucked her long, honey-gold tresses into a snood embroidered with emerald and pearl beads. She pulled on her riding boots and stood before the polished silver mirror. Pleased with the newly slim figure she saw reflected there, she picked up her riding gloves and went to the stables.

Nimbus was already saddled for her, and Rosamond and her steward trotted their horses through the bailey. She listened intently as he described some of the improvements she would find, then they lapsed into a comfortable silence. Nimbus tossed her mane and fought the bit a little, impatient for a gallop on such a glorious autumn morning. Rosamond glanced at her sober, sensible steward, plodding along on his gelding, and was delighted to hear him say, "Go on, my lady, give 'er a run."

"Thank you, Hutton, I'll just have a gallop along the river." Rosamond gave Nimbus her head, and the mare almost danced through the goldenrod and purple Michaelmas daisies that grew in the tall grass on the banks of the Avon. There wasn't a cloud in the sky, and the sunshine made the water shimmer. Rosamond breathed deeply and lowered her lashes against the brilliance. She could feel the sun on her skin, hear the birdsong, and smell the wildflowers. She knew she was happy to be alive, and especially happy to be a woman.

Suddenly, Nimbus slowed, and Rosamond felt the mare shudder with fear. She knew danger was present, so she stroked her horse's neck to calm her, and glanced about for a predator. Rosamond was just about to turn Nimbus and ride back to Hutton, when something in the distance caught her eye. Up ahead, something was moving. It was about two miles away, and she narrowed her eyes in an effort to identify what it was. The black line that continuously moved across the river was made up of horses . . . and men . . . and wagons. A finger of apprehension touched her as she realized they looked like soldiers. She urged Nimbus to the edge of the water so that she could get a clearer view upriver, and immediately noticed an object floating past her on the current. It was a wooden shield painted with the baronial cross!

In a flash of recognition, she knew it was Simon de Montfort and his baronial army. They were not in Wales at all; they were here, crossing the River Avon at Pershore! Suddenly her blood ran cold, and her mind was filled with one thought, one name: Rodger! She wheeled Nimbus about and struck her on the rump. She galloped past a startled Hutton, crying, "Back! Back!"

Rosamond rode into the stable in a flurry of hooves. "Saddle me a swift horse, quick, quickly!" Her order was so urgent, two young grooms obeyed her immediately. Without a moment's hesitation, she sprang onto the big black stallion they had saddled and dug her heels into its belly, knowing she was in a race against time. Her mind was paralyzed by fear, but her instinct compelled her to ride like the wind. Rosamond knew she must reach Worcester and warn her husband of the danger that threatened his life.

The entire countryside surrounding Worcester was covered by the camps of men-at-arms, and as she reached the town, she saw that the streets were packed with soldiers. Rosamond had had no idea Edward's army was so vast. She began to panic; how would she find Rodger in this multitude? Instinct drove her to seek out Edward, perhaps in the castle, for wherever the prince was, Rodger de Leyburn would likely be close by.

She got as far as the bailey, but it was so overcrowded by the mounted men who were streaming in through the north gate, that they overflowed onto the adjoining grounds of Worcester Cathedral. Their surcoats and weapons were bloodied and Rosamond realized they must be returning from warfare somewhere. Anxiety for Rodger almost overwhelmed her. What if he were already lost to her? She could not bear the thought that they had parted in anger and mistrust. Rodger was her love, her life!

As royal steward, Rod was trying to maintain order amid mayhem. They had brought back so many horses that once the castle and cathedral grounds were filled, he had no choice but to direct them into the graveyard. The dog-tired men could sleep on the gravestones, and there was plenty of grass for their horses to crop. When he saw the beautiful female in emerald green, with her golden hair tumbling about her shoulders, mounted on the huge black stallion, he was momentarily thunderstruck. "Rosamond? Rosamond!"

She heard her name over the pandemonium, and saw him immediately. He was off his horse in a flash, lifting her down in protective arms. "What the devil are you doing among these rough soldiers? Is it the baby?"

"No, no, he's fine. Oh, Rodger, thank God you are not dead . . . thank God you are not wounded!" She always forgot how compelling his physical presence was. The impact of it was stunning. She clung to him, seeking the strength he exuded. "Rodger, please forgive me for doubting you?" she beseeched. "My darling, I want you to know, you have all my trust, all my love!"

His powerful hand stroked her wildly disheveled hair, and he offered up a silent prayer of thanks that she loved him enough to forgive him. His arms enfolded her possessively. "Sweetheart, were you not terrified of this brute of a stallion?"

She shook her head impatiently. "I had to get here to warn you. Simon de Montfort and the baronial army are crossing the Avon at Pershore!"

"My love, that's impossible. First he has to cross the Severn."

"Rodger, I swear it on my life! I saw them with my own eyes!"

He held her at arm's length and looked down into those lovely violet eyes that were imploring him to believe her. Then he glanced up at the black stallion she had ridden, and his doubt vanished. Rosamond had not only risked her life, she had done more, she had overcome one of her deepest fears to bring him this message. Moreover, it proved that she had finally taken sides in the conflict that tore England apart, and the side she had chosen was his! He swept her up in powerful arms, mounted Stygian, and grabbed the reins of the horse she had ridden. "Come on, my brave beauty, we had better find Edward."

TWENTY-EIGHT

Worcester's Great Hall was packed shoulder to shoulder with men who were eating for the first time in almost three days. The trestle tables had been stacked against the walls to make more room for the hungry horde. Even Lord Edward and his lieutenants up on the dais, still clad in their leathers and hauberks, ate where they stood.

Edward, in a jubilant mood from his resounding victory, hailed Rod and his beautiful wife. One huge hand held a whole haunch of venison, and the other, a quart jug of ale. "I am ravenous! Forgive my manners, Rosamond, though I know you believe princes have none!" He grinned at Rod. "You lucky devil, how I wish my Eleanora were close enough to welcome me home from battle!"

"My lord, she has ridden hell-for-leather to warn us that Simon de Montfort's army is crossing the Avon at Pershore."

Edward waved the half-devoured hindquarter. "That's impossible, he hasn't yet crossed the Severn. Gilbert would have detected such a large movement of troops."

Rosamond was aghast. "Gilbert is a boy of sixteen!"

"When your husband here was sixteen, he was a full-grown man capable of command, make no mistake."

Rod frowned. "With four thousand Gloucester men-at-arms under his banner, Gilbert should have prevented the barons from crossing the River Severn into England."

"Bones of Christ! Owen, find me Gilbert de Clare on the double; if that miserable redheaded miscreant has been sleeping while we've been defeating the bloody barons, I'll have his balls!" Edward continued his tirade. "I've been gone only three days. *Three fucking days* to march to Kenilworth, defeat the barons, and march back to Worcester with their horses and banners! He has four thousand men at his command, yet it takes one female to bring me the news I need!"

Edward dispatched scouts immediately and ordered his lieutenants to the map room for a council of war. "Warn your soldiers to be ready to march again," he told them.

Rodger de Leyburn beckoned his squire, then turned to Rosamond. "Griffin will see you safely back to Pershore. I would sell my soul for an hour alone with you, chérie; I love you more than life!" Tenderly he brushed back the tangled tresses from her brow and touched his lips to hers. Then his mouth sought her ear and he whispered, "I kiss your heart, Rosamond."

She wanted to cling to him and beg him to take care of himself. Neither he nor his men had had any sleep in days, yet the battle of a lifetime awaited him. Rosamond knew she must be strong, knew she must convince her husband that she believed in his invincibility, though dread for him coiled inside her belly. She did not dare to say goodbye, for fear she would never see him again. Instead, she gave him a radiant smile and told him something she knew would bring him happiness. "I've decided our son's name will be Rodger!"

He looked jubilant. "You honor me, my love."

Lord Edward conferred with Mortimer, whose Welsh scouts had just given him the unwelcome news that the baronial army had crossed the River Severn at Kempsey, only four miles south of Worcester. It was obvious that

Simon's spies had informed him the moment Edward had taken his troops north. The prince strode to the map table and fixed Gilbert with a piercing stare.

"Three days ago, when I marched my men to Kenilworth, Mortimer's Welsh spies informed me that Simon de Montfort's army was winding its weary way toward Hereford. I withdrew my entire army, believing your force of four thousand was an adequate deterrent to the barons. Today I have irrefutable information that not only has de Montfort crossed the River Severn, but the Avon as well. Explain yourself, Gilbert!"

As Rodger de Leyburn listened to the cutting words, he recognized the deadly dangerous tone of Edward's voice. Young Gilbert might have a fiery temper, but Rod knew the sparks de Clare could generate would soon be smothered by the conflagration of the infamous Plantagenet fury, should the prince unleash it.

Gilbert, his face flushed as bright as his hair, complained, "Since I do not speak Welsh, Mortimer's informants would not deal with me! They showed nothing but contempt for my youth."

"They are paid to spy, not kiss the arse of our arrogant English earls. But do not despair, Gilbert, I will give you every chance to make amends for your shortcomings, and for your youth!"

John de Warenne and Rodger de Leyburn were studying the map on the table before them. "By crossing at Pershore, Simon de Montfort has revealed where the barons will make their stand," de Warenne said decisively.

"It is Evesham, my lord, nothing could be more certain," de Leyburn confirmed. As Edward bent his head over the map, Rod drew his finger in a straight line across the Severn and Avon rivers to Evesham.

Edward raised his eyes to Mortimer. "What numbers?"

"Four thousand, tired, hungry, and badly equipped.

No more than two hundred mounted barons and knights; the rest are foot soldiers, except a few hundred Welsh archers Llewelyn grudgingly supplied."

"Counting the men of Gloucester, we have more than twice their number; five hundred mounted knights, and enough horses to mount another three or four hundred armed men," Rodger confirmed.

"With such an overwhelming advantage, our men will be able to snatch a few hours' sleep," Bassingbourne concluded with relief.

Edward's fist smote the map table. "They can sleep when they're *dead*! Battles are won with fury and *speed*! If we delay until morning, it could give young Simon de Montfort time to gather the forces we scattered, and ride to his sire's aid."

Rodger de Leyburn looked down at his hands and wondered if his act of mercy in sparing young Simon would come back to haunt him.

"Sound the trumpets," Edward ordered. "Close your ears to their bitching and complaining. If you've trained them well, your men will fall into line. Before dusk falls, I want them on the road leading to the Vale of Evesham. I will now listen to your suggestions for strategy."

Most of his lieutenants voiced their ideas for achieving the maximum military impact, while Gilbert de Clare maintained a wise silence. When they were done, Edward grinned for the first time since entering the war room. "I said I'd listen; I didn't say I would use your suggestions." His jest broke the tension that had been steadily building to an unbearable pitch. "I want two flying wings to prevent our enemy's escape. Mortimer, you will take two thousand Marcher barons to the east and plant yourself astride the road to London. Gilbert the Red, you will take your wing of two thousand Gloucester men-at-arms to the west and make sure the enemy does not retreat back across the River Avon. I will lead the rest of my lieutenants, with their force of five thousand, and drive head-on into the baronial army."

"Simon de Montfort must know our numbers. He will be feeling downcast and desperate at the moment," Lincoln de Warenne surmised.

"Never think it for a moment," Edward said. "He is a veteran war-lord who has emerged victorious from every battle he ever fought. He knew we withdrew, and no doubt guessed it was to fight his son's army. He is moving with such expediency because he hopes to reach the other baronial force and unite them. He has no idea we vanquished them and returned so quickly; Simon de Montfort would never march into the jaws of a victorious enemy."

"I wholly agree with Edward," Rodger de Leyburn said. "Simon de Montfort is an inspired and daring general with a valiant heart; he is also shrewd, devious, and ruthless. He believes in his cause, and above all he believes in *himself*! He is never downcast or despairing before a battle; make no mistake, this will be the fight of our lives."

It took a monumental effort by Lord Edward and all of his lieutenants to organize the massive undertaking, but by the time dusk fell, the entire royal army was on its way to Evesham. In the middle of the night, they arrived at the juncture where the two winged divisions must separate from the main body of the army. Edward called a last, brief council of war, gathering his lieutenants about him to give them their final orders, then he turned to Rodger. "Did you bring the thirteen baronial banners we captured at Kenilworth?"

Rodger de Leyburn had known all night that the question would come; Edward was far too shrewd to forget about the banners. He would allow nothing to stand in his way. He was prepared to do anything or sacrifice anyone to achieve his goal. Rod set aside any repulsion he felt. "Aye, my lord, I brought the banners."

"Give them to the flag bearers to hoist before us in the vanguard. This allows us to add the element of surprise;

our enemy will think we are the baronial army come to aid them."

The day dawned darkly as black clouds obliterated the sunrise. Thunder rumbled overhead, awakening the baronial men-at-arms, who had barely had time to drop to the ground for a much-needed sleep. When Edward's army came over Green Hill on the northern side of the town, Simon de Montfort's scouts mistook it for the baronial army and gave the news to their leader that his son had at long last arrived. Hope and joy, however, turned to alarm and desperation as the deception was discovered.

As the barons scrambled to throw on their chain mail and accoutre themselves with weapons, a scout brought de Montfort the news that Mortimer's forces blocked any retreat to the east. Simon summoned his lieutenants, along with two of his sons, Henry and Guy. "It is possible that Edward has positioned himself between our two armies to keep us separated," he told the men. "Our best chance is to form a wedge and drive up the hill into their center, break through the enemy's line, and hope we find our allies awaiting us on the other side."

"Why don't we retreat back across the River Avon?" Henry cried with alarm, seeing the royalist army spread across an area fifteen hundred yards wide, with double their baronial fighting force.

"Just as he has deployed forces to the east, Edward will of a certainty be blocking the west. His strategy will be flawless; he learned it from me." Simon de Montfort mounted the destrier his squire brought forward, unsheathed his broadsword, and led his men into battle.

The very first attack drove into Edward's forces hard, in the center of the line of troops. The impact of the flying wedge shocked but did not break through the line. Instead, the line of Edward's troops bent and closed in on each side of the barons, surrounding them, trapping them.

Above the soldiers, lightning flashed and thunder roared, melding with the horrific sounds of battle, drowning out the cries of mortally wounded men and the screams of terrified, maddened horses. The most furious fighting was centered among the mounted knights of both armies. There was no time for any man to do aught but protect his body with his shield and, at the same time, slaughter his enemy with his weapon. The blow of battle-ax, the jab of pike, the swing of mace, the stab of spear, and the thrust of sword took their terrible toll on flesh, and muscle, and sinew.

Blood was everywhere, the crimson sight of it, the sticky feel of it, the metallic smell of it, and the salty taste of it. Blood splattered, sprayed, spilled, bubbled, oozed, gushed, and flowed. The ground, littered with fallen weapons, horses, and men, became drenched and soaked with blood, vomit, piss, and entrails, all churned into foul, slimy, dark-red mud by the frenzied, trampling hooves of the warhorses.

Edward swung his broadsword with the unflagging strength of a colossus. His reach was longer, his energy greater, his will to win stronger than any other warrior at the Battle of Evesham. Rodger de Leyburn, fighting at Edward's side, saw the prince's destrier sink to its knees and roll on its side. Edward was out of the saddle in a flash, and so was Rodger. He handed Edward Stygian's reins, but did not wait for him to mount. Instead, he turned and took Griffin's horse. That horse lasted an hour, then went down beneath him, mortally wounded. Again he turned, but this time his squire was nowhere in sight and Rodger was forced to fight on foot. The arm that held his shield became so numbed, he could no longer feel the blows it took. The ache in his sword arm spread up through his shoulder and down his back. He began to stagger on legs that now trembled with muscle fatigue.

A huge destrier caught Rodger's attention. He wiped

the sweat from his eyes and saw Simon de Montfort mounted on its back. The great warlord at the height of his powers was such an impressive sight that for one moment Rodger doubted that Edward would be able to prevail against such a formidable foe. Rod banished the thought immediately and gave all his attention to dispatching any of the enemy foolish enough to come directly into his path.

The battle went on for hours, but slowly, gradually, inevitably, the larger royal army gained on the smaller baronial force. Then, when Mortimer and Gloucester realized there was no chance for the enemy to flee, they brought in their forces to fight. Edward's mounted knights and foot soldiers decimated Simon's army, then they ravaged, and finally vanquished their enemy. As the dark clouds rolled away and the sun came out, Edward's men raised their heads and saw there were no combatants left to fight. The entire baronial forces were either dead, wounded, or begging for mercy and surrendering their weapons.

Edward, still astride Stygian, picked his way through the carnage and slowly realized the only men left standing were his own. He saw Rodger de Leyburn, who had been fighting on foot, and urged the horse toward him. Edward had a stunned look on his face as he slowly dismounted and looked dazedly at his friend.

"Do you know what this means?" Rodger cried.

"I won," Edward croaked.

Rodger raised his sword on high and roared, "Thine is the kingdom, the power, and the glory!"

"Splendor of God, I won!" Edward cried, throwing his arms about Rodger and lifting him into the air. All about them the cheering and the tumult were deafening as victorious men-at-arms suddenly realized the battle was over and they had won the day!

The battle fever soon subsided in the two men and was replaced by compassion for their foes whom they had so thoroughly defeated. They called for fresh horses and, with their squires, traversed the battlefield, searching for their own wounded men while at the same time doing a cursory tally of the losses from both sides. When they came across young Guy de Montfort, who was badly wounded, Edward ordered that he be carried from the field and his injuries tended without delay. When they discovered the body of Henry de Montfort, tears came to Edward's eyes for his boyhood companion.

John de Warenne's joy in victory soon turned to sorrow when he found that his brother Lincoln had been slain. They met him as he carried his brother's body from the field. "Blood of God, Lincoln has two young children—if one of us had to die, why wasn't it me?"

Rodger de Leyburn said the only thing he could. "*You* must be their father now, John."

There was a crowd of Mortimer's men gathered about the spot where the body of Simon de Montfort had fallen. Their bloodlust was still high for the earl whom they had long hated, and they were in the process of dismembering his corpse when Edward and Rodger came upon the vengeful, senseless savagery. Both men recoiled with horror when they saw Simon's severed head. "Hold!" Edward commanded. "Stand back on penalty of death!"

Mortimer realized he had aroused the wrath of the Plantagenet who would now rule England. "My lord, they thirst for vengeance," he explained.

"I will never condone barbarity! Rodger, see that the great warlord's body is collected and prepared for burial. We will take him ourselves to Evesham Abbey and see that his bones are decently laid to rest."

Bassingbourne rode up to Edward to make his report. "My lord, of the one hundred and sixty barons and knights who stood with Simon de Montfort, only twelve are alive."

Edward crossed himself. "May God's grace have mercy on their souls. There will be no more blood spilled over what happened today at Evesham; no prisoner will be executed—let it be known that I stand for moderation and leniency."

At Pershore, only seven miles away, they would have been able to hear the battle had it not been for the terrible thunderstorm that rattled the windows and sent the maids scurrying into cubbyholes. Pershore also got the pelting rain that missed Evesham, keeping everyone indoors. Rosamond, who knew Rodger would soon be riding into battle, immersed herself in bringing her herbal remedy book up to date. It was the only thing she could think of that would prevent her imagination from running wild. It suddenly occurred to her that she soon might have to put these remedies to use.

She called together all the women of the castle and set them tasks. She sent the laundry maids to tear up sheets for bandages, then took the dairymaids into the stillroom and showed them how to grind dried roots, bark, and seeds into powder with pestle and mortar. Certain plants were used to kill pain; others, when mixed into ointments, took the sting from wounds and allowed them to heal. In the kitchen, they boiled animal fat, beeswax, and yarrow, then poured it into pots to cool into a salve that eased pain, lessened bleeding, and cured inflammation. Then Rosamond called the sewing women together to thread all the needles they could find.

The following day, the guards who patrolled Pershore's battlements sent an urgent message below to their lady, that Sir Rodger and a horde of mounted men, including one who was large enough to be Lord Edward himself, were less than a mile away.

Rosamond had just changed her gown and washed the yellow yarrow stains from her hands. She took up a snood set with turquoise to match her gown, then thought better of it, remembering the one she had lost on her wild ride to Worcester. Instead, she tossed her hair back over her shoulders, hoisted her skirts, and began to run. She went through the bailey, ignored the road, and cut across a meadow dotted with stacks of new-mown hay. "Rodger! Rodger!" she cried, unmindful of anyone but her beloved husband.

With his right arm, Rodger hoisted her up before him in the saddle, his green eyes devouring her exquisite beauty. Already breathless from running, she now panted from the close proximity of her dark warrior. She searched his face. "Is it over?"

"Aye, the past is over and done. The future starts today."

As she turned to look at Edward, the sun shone down upon his golden head and upon the golden lions on the fluttering pennons. To Rosamond he looked every inch a royal prince. Rodger was right, it was Edward Plantagenet's birthright to become the King of England, and he had been determined that no one would ever take it from him. As she gazed at him she clearly saw his invincibility. He *would* be their king, and in her heart she believed he would achieve greatness, both for himself and for his people.

Edward grinned at them. "Rod de Leyburn, you are a lucky man!"

"Where are your wounded?" Rosamond asked. "Pershore is in readiness to tend injuries and offer what succor we can, Lord Edward."

"We are extremely fortunate to have the monks at Evesham Abbey tending those most grievously wounded, but our knights have plenty of broken bones and superficial wounds that you can minister to. Our greatest need is food, and in a weak moment your husband offered to provide it. Our destriers will make short work of yonder hay too."

"As royal steward, it is my responsibility. Fortunately, Pershore's farms are grazing abundant herds of cattle."

The moment they arrived at the bailey, Rod was out

of the saddle, organizing the men about him and issuing orders. The grooms were put in charge of taking the horses out to pasture, the men-at-arms who had not already bathed were sent to the river, and Master Hutton was at his elbow, advising him which farms had the largest herds. "As soon as I've seen my son, we'll ride to the farms," Rodger informed Pershore's steward.

Lord Edward dismounted and lifted Rosamond from Stygian. "At last, I get to see my godson. Let us hope he has his mother's golden beauty."

"Alas, my lord, he has his father's dark visage." Rosamond dimpled, revealing just how much that pleased her. She put Lizzie Hutton in charge of tending the wounded and directed her to set up an infirmary in the hall. Nan stood by proudly with the baby in her arms. Rosamond took him and was about to lay him in his father's arms, when Rodger shook his head in refusal. "I cannot."

For the first time, Rosamond noticed how stiffly Rodger was holding his left arm. She thrust the baby back to Nan. "Sit down," she ordered her husband. "Let's get rid of this bloody chain mail," she said to Edward, who immediately lifted off his friend's mesh tunic. She examined the arm, her heart in her mouth. She did not think it was broken, but either the elbow, shoulder, or collarbone was dislocated; perhaps all three. "Why the devil didn't you say something?" she scolded.

"It's been numb since the battle; I've not felt much pain."

"Well, you'll certainly feel pain now," she informed him.

Edward held him immobile while Rosamond manipulated his arm. The pain was so sharp and sudden, Rod howled like a hound that had been kicked by a stallion. Then she lifted his arm and rotated his shoulder. Again he cried out, but miraculously the arm was restored to its normal state, except for an ache deep in the bones.

"Where did you learn that gentle touch?" Rod asked with irony.

"I learned it from the nuns," she said, laughing.

"Notoriously cruel bitches!" Edward laughed irreverently.

"Rosamond will soon wipe the smile from your face when she stitches the ragged gash on your arm," Rod said with satisfaction.

"'Tis merely a scratch, it doesn't need stitching," he protested.

"Off with your bloody chain mail, my lord; you don't want to repulse Princess Eleanora with ugly battle scars, do you? I'll get my needles, and you can go and find yourself a comfortable seat outside where the light is better."

Rosamond emerged into the bailey carrying a goblet of brandywine she had laced with rue. She was in time to see Rodger and her steward leave for the farms. "Master Hutton, be sure you get a good price from Sir Rodger for our beef. The crown is paying for it, and I warrant now that Lord Edward is in charge of the realm, he will soon have the royal coffers overflowing."

Edward, who was sitting on a hay cart, threw back his head and laughed heartily. He took the goblet Rosamond handed him and drained it. "Ah, it feels so good to sit in the sunshine and laugh, and be tended by such a beautiful, capable chatelaine. You know, Rosamond, Rodger is—"

"I know, I know"—the corners of her mouth lifted—"Rodger is a lucky man!" She took a needle from the pocket of her smock.

Edward suddenly became serious. "No, Rosamond, I wasn't going to say that at all. My dear, *you* are the lucky one. Once Rodger de Leyburn gives you his pledge, nothing on earth will make him break it; he is pledged for life. He has been with me from the very beginning, since I was a wild, irresponsible boy. I know I sometimes do things that make his gorge rise, but his steadfast loyalty and his belief in me have never wavered. I truly could not have done it without him."

Rosamond gazed at him and listened with rapt attention as the prince revealed his innermost feelings, and she realized the rue was loosening his tongue.

"When we were youths, he was the only one who came close to matching my strength. But Rod had an inner strength too, and I thank God that I have at last acquired it. Our friendship is precious to me. There is no deception, no falsehood between us, only total honesty and truth . . . and now I must share a truth with you, Rosamond."

Their eyes met and held as he made his confession. "Your brother, Giles, died by *my* hand at Ware. It was an accident, of course, a bloody careless accident on my part!" His blue eyes darkened as he remembered that terrible time. "I was already in serious trouble—I had a violent argument with another youth which came to blows, and to my horror I realized I killed him with my bare hands. The boy was a commoner; I breached the laws of chivalry even to challenge him, and his death brought shame upon the royal name of Plantagenet."

Rosamond licked her suddenly dry lips as she realized Edward was telling her the absolute truth.

"At the joust, when I saw another had died by my hand within a month, I went to pieces. That Giles was my friend and companion made it all the more devastating. Rodger stepped in immediately to take the blame and shoulder the consequences, whatever they might be. No boy or man ever had a more faithful or devoted friend."

Tears flooded Rosamond's eyes, and she swallowed the lump in her throat as she slipped her hand into Edward's. "Thank you for telling me the truth, my lord, but I beg that you never let Rodger know you have told me." She saw his brows draw together in a question, and gave him her reason. "What Rodger did was so noble and self-sacrificing . . . we must never take that away from him!"

Edward squeezed her hand. "So be it. Can you forgive me?"

Rosamond nodded. "It was an accident; I have finally come to terms with it."

Edward raised her fingers to his lips. "Rodger *is* a lucky man."

With neat stitches, Rosamond closed the long, ragged gash that stretched from the prince's shoulder to his elbow. She knew he would heal without a lasting scar, and now, so would she.

"Promise me you will both come to Windsor? I cannot manage without Rodger, and I know my Eleanora will be much happier if she has your company and your friendship, Rosamond."

As Rod had pledged to Edward Plantagenet for life, so she had pledged to Rodger de Leyburn. "You honor us, my dearest lord."

A fortnight later, a small cavalcade arrived at the Abbey of Evesham. Eleanor de Montfort had asked Lord Edward for permission to visit her husband's grave to say her last goodbye, and her nephew had granted her request.

Rosamond stood at the back of the abbey with Rodger and Edward, keeping a silent vigil as the monks led Lady Eleanor, two of her sons, and her daughter to the place where the shattered bones of the great warlord had been laid to rest. Simon de Montfort had been buried beside his eldest son, Henry, and Rosamond knew that Eleanor's pain must be unendurable.

Rodger slipped his arm about his wife and bent his head to whisper, "Simon once told me that you held a special place in his heart, and he admonished me to take good care of you."

His words touched Rosamond so deeply, she could not reply for the lump in her throat. Instead, she slipped her hand into his.

Guy de Montfort, with his wounds bound up tightly, and his brother Simon stood beside their mother and sister with their heads bowed. Only Eleanor held her head erect, and the pride evidenced in her small figure was so poignant that Rosamond was moved to tears.

Young Simon, filled with grief and remorse for arriving too late to aid his father, fell to his knees, sobbing for forgiveness. His mother touched his shoulder. "Get up off your knees, my son. Never forget that your name is Simon de Montfort."

Twenty-Nine

Lady Rosamond de Leyburn, holding her baby son in her arms, stood beside Princess Eleanora in Windsor's beautifully arcaded chapel. The priest in his gilt robes stood beside the carved stone christening font, waiting respectfully for the gentlemen to take their places. Rosamond swept Prince Edward, Harry of Almaine, and her husband, Sir Rodger, with a disdainful look of disapproval for their late arrival. The men had arisen at dawn to indulge in their second favorite sport of hunting, with total disregard for the time that had been set for the baptism.

The priest began by admonishing the courtiers crowded into the chapel that they should attend services regularly, not just on the festive occasions of weddings and christenings. He then launched into a Latin prayer, but switched to the vulgar tongue of English when he heard the congregation shuffle its feet restlessly. When Edward Plantagenet pointedly cleared his throat, the priest skipped to the heart of the matter. "Sanctify this water to the mystical washing away of sin; and grant that this child may receive the fullness of Thy grace, and ever remain in the number of Thy faithful and elect children; through Jesus Christ our Lord. Amen."

Rosamond tenderly removed the white knitted shawl and held out her naked child. The priest took him from his mother and held him suspended over the font of holy water. "Name this child."

"Rodger de Leyburn." Rosamond's clear voice carried to the farthest recesses of the chapel, and all could hear the pride in it.

The priest dipped the male child into the water. "Rodger de Leyburn, I baptize thee—"

Sir Rodger stepped forward to amend the name of his son. "He shall be called Rodger *Jason* de Leyburn."

Rosamond gave her husband a radiant smile, and her violet eyes became liquid with unshed tears at the thought that her beloved had remembered her favorite name was Jason. Seeing the love on their faces, Princess Eleanora began to cry softly.

The priest dipped the child into the water a second time. "Rodger Jason de Leyburn, I baptize thee—"

This time it was the prince who stepped forward with great authority. "He shall be called Rodger Jason *Edward* de Leyburn."

With a forbidding scowl, the priest defied anyone else to step forward, then he dipped the child into the water a third time. "Rodger Jason Edward de Leyburn, I baptize thee—"

At this point, Rodger Jason Edward had had enough of dipping. Turning red, he protested at the top of his lungs and, at the same time, directed an arc of pee into the priest's eye. The holy man uttered a blasphemous oath and covered it with, "In the name of the Father, and of the Son, and of the Holy Ghost. Amen." He made a cross on the baby's forehead, raced through the prayer of Saint Chrysostom, exhorted the godparents on their duties, and thrust the offending child back into its mother's arms.

At the christening breakfast that followed, Rodger laid his son in the middle of the table, where he became the center of attention. Eleanora looked at the baby longingly and wiped away a tear. "There wasn't a dry eye in the chapel," she said innocently, which sent the entire court into convulsions of laughter.

"Splendor of God," Edward said, raising his goblet, "your son has coined a new toast: Here's *piss* in your eye!"

* * *

The next evening, a great banquet had been planned at Windsor Castle. Its objective was twofold—it would establish that Edward Plantagenet now ruled the country, King of England in all but name; and introduce beauteous Princess Eleanora to the royal court of Windsor. King Henry and Queen Eleanor had been persuaded to retire to their castle of Winchester, almost seventy miles from London. Henry was already being referred to as the "Old King" by the people of the court. All the nobles and barons who had supported Edward in the civil conflict were invited to the celebration along with their ladies. All knew that rewards for loyal service were in the offing, and ambitious lords were busy taking note of the lands and castles that had been confiscated from the barons and nobles who had set themselves against the royal House of Plantagenet.

The de Leyburns again occupied the spacious suite of rooms in the tower that had been especially built for Prince Edward and Princess Eleanora. It now comprised three luxurious chambers, smaller rooms for their servants, as well as a nursery for the baby, for Rosamond had refused to leave him behind. She had brought one of the young maids from Pershore to be his full-time nurse, so that Nan could resume her duties as Rosamond's tiring-woman in charge of her fashionable new wardrobe, for clothes were of paramount importance at the court of Windsor.

Nan brought the new ruby velvet gown from the wardrobe and held it while Rosamond slipped her arms into the fashionable wide sleeves, which ended in points decorated by golden silk tassels. The neckline was cut extremely low to show off jewels, and Rosamond stepped before her dressing table mirror, trying to decide on a necklace, while Nan fastened the back of her gown.

Rodger emerged from the dressing room with a towel slung about his narrow hips. Nan, quite used to seeing him in various stages of undress, paid no heed until she saw his signal for her to leave. He picked up a small, flat case from his bedside table and approached his wife. She saw him in the mirror and knew he would not be able to resist touching her. The corners of her mouth rose in a secret smile. His touch made her feel extremely beautiful, and his love made her feel special.

Rosamond caught her breath as her husband's hands slipped about her throat, then moved to her nape to fasten the necklace he had had made for her. Her eyes widened with pleasure at the magnificent jewels that sparkled against her throat and fell in a glittering cascade over the curve of her breasts. The precious gems had been fashioned into roses, with ruby petals and diamond centers; the leaves were wrought from jade. "Rodger, it's exquisite, but it must have cost the earth!"

"I thought it a fitting bauble for a countess."

"A countess?"

"I have reason to believe Edward will make me Earl of Tewkesbury." He flashed her a wicked grin and unfastened the back of her gown.

"Rodger! What the devil are you doing?"

"Exactly what you think I'm doing . . . what you hope I'm doing. I warrant a female with your passionate nature cannot wait for her first sexual encounter with an earl of the realm, chérie."

She cast him a provocative glance from beneath her lashes. "Whatever makes you think it will be my first?"

His arms tightened possessively; his green eyes glittered dangerously. "By God, madam, it had better be!"

Her laugh was sultry. "You'll ruin my gown."

"I'll buy you another!"

"Indeed you will, my insatiable devil, and another, and another! You will find a countess far more expensive than a mere lady."

"And you will find an earl far more demanding than a mere royal steward. Remove your gown and your shift . . . it has been a long time since I've seen a naked countess."

Rosamond knew he was teasing her, but she also had

no doubts that he had seen more than his fair share of naked noblewomen. But how could she blame them? His devastating charm, his dark, dangerous looks, and his virile, warrior's body made him utterly irresistible. The amazing thing was that she didn't care about the others he had known before her. His love had given her supreme confidence in herself, and her self-confidence in turn attracted him like a lodestone.

Rosamond stood before him stark naked, save for the magnificent jewels. She tossed her long hair back, felt it brush against her buttocks, and lifted her chin proudly. "If you will dispense with your towel, my lord earl, we can begin our mating dance."

Rod reached out a finger to trace her delicate collarbone adorned with the ruby roses, then his hands roamed over her curves until Rosamond thought she would go up in smoke. Only when he had caressed every inch of her naked skin, and her hands had explored his magnificent muscles, did he take possession of her mouth. He threaded his fingers into her hair and held her captive while his lips and his tongue commanded her to open for him. His other hand pressed her bottom cheeks, so that his arousal slid between her legs. With a matching rhythm of tongue and cock, he thrust slowly, sensually, teasing her in the male-female game of domination and submission.

Rosamond decided she could tease too. "If you want something, Rod, all you have to do is *ask*!"

"Permission to enter," he whispered, and Rosamond lifted herself so that he could slide up inside her sleek heat. When he remained motionless, she bit his shoulder. "You devil, will you make me ask for what I want?"

His green eyes dared her to put it into words.

"Rod, I think I'll scream if you don't take me!"

"You'll scream if I do," he promised wickedly. He thrust into her hard, his lovemaking suddenly savage and demanding, but Rosamond made demands of her own, and with ferocity Rod satisfied those demands. She cried out her release and collapsed against him, clinging to his powerful body, her legs suddenly too weak to support her.

Rod swept her up in his arms and carried her to their bed. He had not spent and was still rampant with sexual energy. Rosamond knew his needs, knew the extent of his lusty passion, and gloried in that knowledge. Rod watched, mesmerized, as she stretched out before him, arms above her head, arching her back enticingly. Savage desire rose up in him, hot and wild, and he knew she would match his passionate mood and yield herself completely. This coupling would be dark, primitive, rapacious, slaking their sexual hunger for each other. The next would be slow, sensual, and filled with tenderness, allowing them to express their deep, abiding love.

Between matings, they rolled together until Rosamond was above him. She sat straddling his hips, her hair wildly disheveled from their uninhibited sex play. The corners of her mouth lifted in a smile. "Countess," she said tasting the word on her tongue. "You know, I rather like this new elevated position."

He knew her words were deliberately provocative. "I'll show you a position," he threatened, setting possessive hands to her waist.

"Let me stay up here a little while longer, it makes me feel splendidly erotic." She felt him harden and lengthen, and raised herself up high enough to plunge down and hold him captive within her. "Gallop as hard as you like, I'll hold on tightly." She bent forward to grip his shoulders and allow her golden tresses to trail temptingly, teasingly across his chest.

"It seems you've acquired a taste for stallion riding. You will allow me on top once in a while, won't you, chérie?"

"That depends upon whether you measure up to your name or not."

"Tewkesbury?"

"The name I have in mind isn't Tewkesbury, it's *Rod*!"

With a ferocious growl, Rod rolled with her until he was in the male-dominant position. Then the night exploded as he mastered her with a rough, elemental mating. When Rosamond surrendered, and yielded in sweet submission, his lovemaking gentled, and she melted against him with a soft moan. Rod covered her mouth, tasting his name on her lips, knowing he would never have enough of her.

After the loving, when they were both replete, Rosamond lay enfolded in her lover's arms, with her cheek against his heart. Dreamily she thought back over the long, eventful year that had brought her to this safe, happy haven. She smiled secretly as she thought of her girlish infatuation with Rickard de Burgh. A pale emotion indeed, when compared with the consuming love she now felt for Rodger de Leyburn. The Irish warrior, with his amazing gift of second sight, had been right after all. His prophetic words floated to her from the past.

Rodger de Leyburn is best for you, Rosamond. His strength and position will give you the protection you need in the great conflict that lies ahead. It will be a rough road for all, but in the end you will not just survive, you will flourish.

At the time, she had paid little heed to his words. In the end, she had only agreed to marry Rodger to bond him to the de Montforts, and for his strength. It had been his physical strength for which she had lusted, never dreaming that he possessed an inner strength that was worth far more than any other quality. Like his love, it was priceless. She touched her beloved's face with awe. "My darling." Her voice was as soft as velvet. His love, unconditional and absolute, surrounded and protected her with its precious magic. Like a circle, it was never-ending, infinite, like their names within her wedding ring.

The couple's late arrival at the banquet was not without its advantages. All eyes were on Rosamond as she made a grand entrance wearing the ruby gown and magnificent jewels. She joined Eleanora, who wore white and gold as befitted a princess.

"Oh, I am so glad you are here, Rosamond . . . all these people make me mix up my words."

Rosamond squeezed her hand. "You look so lovely tonight, all you need do is smile."

Rodger bowed gallantly, kissed Eleanora's hand, and took himself off to join Edward and the noblemen who surrounded him. Edward acknowledged his arrival with an amused glance that told Rod the prince knew exactly why he was late. There was much to discuss, however, and their thoughts quickly moved from pleasure to business. A date for calling Parliament had to be set, and punishment decided upon, not only for the forty prisoners taken at Evesham, who were being held at Windsor, but for the Lord Mayor of London and the city's wealthy merchants, who had staunchly supported the enemy.

Any noble who was thought to have influence with Edward Plantagenet was being deluged with petitions for land or places at court, but ambition for themselves was uppermost in his nobles' minds.

Edward was determined to restore order to the entire country. He and his lieutenants still had the responsibility for all military operations, but one by one the castles were surrendering, from Dover and the Cinque Ports to Kenilworth.

Edward himself would restore and keep order in the southern shires, while his royal cousin, Harry of Almaine, was given command of the northern provinces. It would be his responsibility to subdue any uprisings and keep the peace. Mortimer was put in charge of all the Welsh Marches, and Gilbert of Gloucester was reconfirmed in his father's earldom and vast landholdings.

Edward Plantagenet wanted no more bloodshed, but he intended to bleed dry the coffers of those who had opposed him. He set a fine of twenty thousand marks for the City of London, and each of his prisoners would forfeit his property and pay a hefty ransom in return for his freedom. The wealthy bishops and heads of religious houses would be summoned and allowed to buy the crown's pardon.

When the food was ready to be served, Edward took his place on the dais beside his future queen. When he indicated that Rosamond was to sit next to her, Eleanora whispered her thanks to him, then blushed when he whispered something back to her. Soon, however, he and Rodger became engrossed in conversation.

Eleanora's eyes shone with joy as they lingered on the golden head of her husband. "I am so happy to be back at Windsor with Edward; his mother the queen is not a very nice lady."

"I shall have to teach you to swear," Rosamond declared. "The queen is a bitch, and I am delighted that she and the king are to live out their days in far-off Winchester. Edward will never allow her to interfere in your marriage again."

Eleanora leaned close and whispered, "Speaking of bitches, the scandal about Alyce de Clare is on everyone's tongue. Is it true, Rosamond, that Gilbert has petitioned the church and the courts for a . . . divorce?" Eleanora hesitated over the dreaded word.

"Yes, it is perfectly true. Gilbert says the marriage was never consummated, though Alyce swears otherwise."

"I heard whispers that her ladies were worried she might . . . harm herself because of the terrible shame."

Rosamond laughed. "Don't you believe it. Alyce is so in love with herself, she would choose dishonor over death any day. Gilbert once threatened to kill her, but I think he has decided that covering her with shame is a much sweeter revenge. Poor Alyce, I wonder which hurts most, losing her title of Countess of Gloucester, or losing the vast wealth and castles her marriage brought her?"

"Where will she live?" asked tenderhearted Eleanora.

"Well, certainly not in England. After she's been completely humiliated, Gilbert will send her back to her father, Guy de Lusignan. He, by the way, already asked your husband to restore his estates, but Edward refused him." Rosamond had too much delicacy to tell Eleanora that Edward firmly believed England was for the English.

"I persuaded Edward to let us have dancing tonight. I want our court of Windsor to be filled with music and laughter. Do you like to dance, Rosamond?"

"I love to dance! What is the point of our wearing gorgeous gowns and dazzling jewels if we cannot lure the two handsomest males in the room to whirl us about the floor and make the other females green with envy?"

"We are so fortunate, Rosamond."

"Fortune favors the bold," Rosamond declared, then she leaned forward to catch her husband's eye and said, "Would you partner me in the next dance, my lord?"

An hour later, Rosamond was overjoyed to see her dearest friend, Demoiselle de Montfort, arrive quietly in the hall. She hugged her lovingly. Rosamond's heart overflowed with compassion for the lovely dark-haired girl who had so recently lost her father in battle. "Demi, what in the world are you doing here? I thought you were in France!"

They found an alcove where they could talk in private. "My mother and two brothers *are* in France. Lord Edward came to Dover himself to arrange their safe passage. He was most tender and considerate of my mother, allowing her to take all her furniture and personal belongings. They have gone to live on the de Montfort estates in Normandy. My father came from a wealthy and influential family, and my brothers will have the family's potent influence behind them."

"How is your mother, Demi? Simon was her life, the center of her existence. She loved him beyond reason; my heart goes out to Lady Eleanor."

"She is very strong, Rosamond. She made Lord Edward promise to restore the members of our household to their homes, and she demanded an annual pension of five hundred pounds for her dower lands, and

Edward has granted it to her. Her spirit is not broken, but I fear her heart is. And nothing can mend it."

"Did Sir Rickard de Burgh accompany her to France?" Rosamond asked softly. When Demi nodded, she said, "Then Lady Eleanor's heart will heal, given time. Sir Rickard gave his pledge to her when they were very young, and he has loved her all these years. His devotion is absolute. She will always have his strength to lean upon; Sir Rickard will never fail her."

"You were in love with him, Rosamond."

"Nay, that was a young girl's fancy. I hadn't the faintest idea what love was until I wed Rodger de Leyburn. He was my destiny, and I thank all the saints in heaven."

"I too am married, Rosamond. I was wed by proxy to Llewelyn, Prince of Wales, though I feared we would never see each other again. That is why I am here. Edward has told Llewelyn that if he comes to Windsor and signs a peace treaty with England, he may take his bride back to Wales with him."

"And will he come?"

"Oh yes," Demi said with complete conviction. "We love each other; he will come for me, Rosamond."

She squeezed her hands and kissed the Demoiselle's forehead. "I am so happy for you. Tomorrow you must come and see my son. It is so wonderful to have you here, if only for a little while."

"I must go; I only came to the hall to see if I could find you."

"Tomorrow we will spend the entire day together. You must meet Princess Eleanora; she is as sweet and lovely as you are, Demi."

After Rosamond bade her friend good night, she turned to find her husband waiting to claim her. "Are you angry that Edward is using Demoiselle de Montfort to force Llewelyn to his bidding?"

She searched his face. "They are in love. She is a willing pawn, just as I was."

"You? Willing? You were an ice maiden who set your heart against me from the very beginning," he teased. "I swear it took the longest wooing on record to thaw you to a giving mood."

Rosamond brushed against him. "The wooing isn't over, not by a long chalk!" She licked her lips provocatively in anticipation of what was to come.

"Now look what you've done to me! How the devil do you expect me to dance in this condition?"

"I think you can manage the mating dance."

He slipped a powerful arm about her, and was moving purposefully toward the door when Edward's voice stopped him.

"A moment, de Leyburn. From now on you must observe protocol when we hold formal occasions at Windsor."

Rodger led Rosamond before Edward and Eleanora's carved gilt chairs, and bowed his head graciously. "My lord, will you excuse Lady de Leyburn and myself?"

Edward's blue eyes narrowed, but he could not hide his amusement. "I know where you are going . . . all at Windsor know where you are going. Bed, if you make it that far. You are an inconsiderate devil; I have to stay here another two hours before I can take my wife up to bed."

Eleanora hid her blushes against her husband's shoulder.

"If I were you, my lord," Rodger advised, "I wouldn't stay longer than two minutes. We bid you good night."

"Hold!" Edward leaned toward his friend and lowered his voice so none but Rod could hear. "I forbid you to get Rosamond with child again until I've had a chance to catch up!"

Once the lovers were free of the banqueting hall, Rosamond picked up her skirts and began to run. "I'll race you!"

He was after her in a flash, picking her up and swinging her high, then took the steps two at a time.

"What did Edward say to you?" she asked, breathless with laughter.

"That's a secret, chérie! Suffice it to say he issued me a challenge, one that is impossible to resist."

"You are a devil, de Leyburn!" Rosamond yielded her mouth up to him, and knew she wouldn't want him any other way.

VIRGINIA HENLEY is the author of sixteen romantic novels, including the *New York Times* bestsellers *Seduced* and *Desired* and the national bestseller *A Woman of Passion*. Her work has been translated into fourteen languages. A recipient of the *Romantic Times* Lifetime Achievement Award, she lives in St. Petersburg, Florida.